BITE
at First
SIGHT

BROOKLYN ANN

sourcebooks
casablanca

Published by Sourcebooks Casablanca, an imprint of Sourcebooks, Inc.
P.O. Box 4410, Naperville, Illinois 60567-4410
(630) 961-3900
Fax: (630) 961-2168
www.sourcebooks.com

Printed and bound in Canada.
MBP 10 9 8 7 6 5 4 3 2 1

Dedicated to Karen Ann
06-11-62–02-14-09
Thank you for always believing in me. You were the best mom in the world.
And to Kent
Thank you for always being there for me.

One

"IF ONE DESIRES A TASK ACCOMPLISHED CORRECTLY, one must do it herself." Cassandra Burton, Dowager Countess of Rosslyn, repeated the litany as she pulled the rickety little wagon through the moonlit aisle of tombstones.

She shivered under her velvet cloak. Her fingers had long since gone numb with the effort of navigating the dratted conveyance over uneven ground and across slippery, damp grass. Shovels and pry bars clanked across the wagon's worn pine boards. The winch rattled on its frame.

Something flickered across the corner of her vision.

Cassandra jumped. She stopped and rubbed her gloved hands together for warmth, surveying the graveyard. The area was still and silent as…well, a tomb. Yet the chill in her spine refused to abate. A scornful frown turned her lips at such irrational behavior. Ghosts were an illogical figment of uneducated imaginations, and no one could possibly have business out here at this hour...except herself.

"Worthless curs," Cassandra whispered in as haughty a tone as she could manage.

If only the men to whom she'd offered a more-than-generous sum to perform this troublesome task had done their duty, rather than disappearing. She shook her head. If not for their unreasonable negligence, she would now be comfortably ensconced in her laboratory unraveling the secrets of the human body...not out in this cold, dreary place, jumping at shadows.

Surveying the newest graves, she read the dates to decide which would be the best specimen. The mysterious disappearance of her hired hands nagged at her. Could a murderer be on the loose? She shook her head and pulled the folds of her cloak tighter. No, by now the authorities would have found their bodies and the news would be sensationalized in *The Times*.

They were cowards, but she was not. To prove her lack of fear, Cassandra halted her wagon and fetched out a shovel. Her hands trembled nervously as she grasped the wooden handle.

Removing the dead from their graves was illegal. If a constable caught her, she'd be sent directly to Fleet Prison. A fresh surge of trepidation curled in her belly.

Exhuming a corpse was quite a different matter from having one ready on her operating table. As objective as she tried to be, the prospect of removing the body from its carefully arranged resting place by winching it out of the ground and loading it onto her cart was undeniably gruesome. However, gruesome or not, Cassandra needed a specimen to continue her work. And she *would* acquire it, no matter how much her nerves protested.

Despite being barred from official education as a physician because of her sex, Cassandra was determined to learn the skills required to become a doctor. That included studying human anatomy, and for that, she required cadavers.

Returning to the graves, she made her selection. Alfred Lumley, born September first, 1801; died September twenty-sixth, 1823. Two days ago Alfred had been a living twenty-two-year-old man, three years younger than herself. Whether or not he'd been healthy, she would soon determine. A pang of sorrow struck her heart. *His soul is in heaven,* she reminded herself. *A mere shell remains. A shell that will help me to aid the living.*

She raised the shovel, ready to plunge it into the soft soil. "I am not afraid. I am *not.*"

"You should be." A sinister, accented voice pierced her consciousness.

The shovel fell from her nerveless fingers, thudding onto the cold ground.

Cassandra knew that voice; it had the rich, dark cadence that had haunted her dreams since the night she'd first met *him.* She spun around, the hood of her cloak falling to her shoulders.

Rafael Villar stepped out from behind a mausoleum. The shadows embraced his bronze skin, obscuring the scars on the left side of his face while moonlight highlighted his exotic features on the right.

Known as "the Spaniard," Villar had been an infamous pugilist in Cheapside despite having only one functioning arm. The eccentric and wealthy

Duke of Burnrath was his sponsor. Cassandra had often encountered Villar at Burnrath House when attending the duchess's literary circles. Right away she'd suspected that there was more to the relationship between Rafael and Their Graces. And she'd been utterly and completely fascinated by him.

When the duke and duchess departed for the Continent to travel, Villar had leased Burnrath House. By all accounts he was rich as a nabob. For the remainder of the Season, *Don* Villar was all the *ton* could gossip about. But when months passed without the Spaniard making the slightest attempt to join Society, he was forgotten. Cassandra would have forgotten him as well, if it weren't for those damned dreams. Now he stood before her in the most unexpected place and at the most inconvenient time.

Good Lord, will he turn me in to the authorities?

She opened her mouth to ask the reason for his presence, but the words caught in her throat when she saw that his amber eyes were glowing like a funeral pyre. His sensuous lips—lips she'd unreasonably dreamed of kissing—drew back to reveal white, even teeth…with two gleaming fangs for incisors.

Before she could scream or flee, *Don* Villar's fiery gaze widened, then narrowed in recognition. "You! *You've* been the one disturbing my people?"

"Y-your people?" Cassandra stammered, staring raptly at those sharp fangs. She'd certainly never seen *those* during their previous encounters. Her heart leaped into her throat in dawning horror. This man was not human.

His lips curled back in a sneer, puckering the scars

on the left side of his face. "Don't play coy with me, *Countess*." The word was filled with disdain. "Some of my subordinates reported hunters disturbing their lairs." He gestured at the mausoleum behind him. "It is hard to fathom that you're behind this, though I should have guessed. Is that why you befriended the Duchess of Burnrath?"

"I haven't the slightest idea what you are going on about. I came here to… Well, it is no concern of yours." A wave of indignation bolstered her courage. How dare he speak of her most treasured friendship in such a manner? How dare he accuse her of duplicity when he stood before her sporting unnatural teeth and luminescent eyes? And of what exactly was he accusing her? "What does Her Grace have to do with this?" Cassandra took a shaky step back. "And, in the name of heaven, what *are* you?"

In a blink of an eye, Rafael stood inches from her. With the same impossible speed, he grasped her shoulder, pulling her close against him. Dizziness swarmed her mind at the feel of his firm heat and his intoxicating scent of forbidden spices. His crippled left arm moved lightly around her waist, his fingers delicately brushing across her lower back. The heady combination of rough and gentle made her tremble.

His eyes locked on hers. "I will show you, Countess."

Then his mouth was on her neck, firm lips caressing the sensitive flesh, somehow more intimate than anything she'd experienced during her ill-fated marriage. Cassandra melted against him, tangling her fingers in his silken hair.

Sharp pain exploded in her throat as his fangs broke

her skin. Cassandra cried out and tried to push him away, but his iron-like right arm mercilessly held her immobile. The pain took flight, and drugging pleasure fluttered within her belly. A low moan escaped her throat as she pulled him closer. Liquid desire pulsed between her thighs. Whatever this was, she needed more, craved it with mindless longing.

Rafael pulled away, muttering a foreign curse. "You're a *grave robber*?" Lifting his finger to his mouth, he pierced his flesh with one pearly fang and then gently touched the wound on her throat. The soft touch was juxtaposed by his blazing eyes and furious snarl.

She barely heard his words as her eyes locked on those deadly fangs. Cassandra froze as realization shook her to the core. He wiped her neck with a handkerchief. In confirmation of her suspicions, blood spotted the snowy cloth like an accusation.

"Vampire," she gasped, struggling to breathe. The foundations of her scientific beliefs quaked within her consciousness. Fairy tales were not true, and magic was not real. Yet here he stood, ready to devour her blood and perhaps her soul. Terror gripped her heart like ice.

The creature that should not exist outside of myth nodded. "Yes, but you will not remember the fact."

His eyes glowed brighter, capturing her gaze. The intensity caused a fresh wave of dizziness, but Cassandra fought it off. The vampire stood like a statue, continuing to stare at her in a most unnerving manner.

After an endless moment, she shook her head and took another wary step back. "Why are you looking at me like that?"

Villar blinked and the fire dimmed from his gaze.

An explosion of Spanish expletives came out in a growl as he seized her arm. "I apologize, Countess. You'll have to come with me."

"C-come with you where?" Cassandra stammered in confusion, trying to pull away. He'd already bitten her and drunk her blood. What more could he want? "Why? And f-for how long?"

"I am taking you to Burnrath House," Rafael snarled through clenched teeth. "I have no choice but to place you under arrest until I can determine what to do with you."

&c&

Rafe bit back another growl. *Madre de Dios*, why did the mysterious intruder have to be *her*? The Countess of Rosslyn was the only mortal in over three centuries to have gotten under his skin, and he still did not know why. And why did she have to be one of the rare individuals immune to mesmerism?

He'd wanted a brief moment to punish her for being a nuisance to him yet again. He'd wanted to punish her, to show her the folly in seeking out a monster, before banishing her memory. It was the worst of luck that the first mortal he'd deliberately revealed himself to was impervious to his power.

"Arrest?" Lady Rosslyn struggled in his grip, her warm flesh slipping beneath his grasp on the sleeve of her cloak, drawing his attention back to the vexing situation at hand. "Are you a constable?"

"Constable? Hardly. I am Lord of this city." He held her fast.

"*Lord?* Of all of London? Whatever do you mean?"

The countess tried once more to pull away. "And what of my wagon?"

Rafe tugged her closer before she could trip over a gravestone. "Damn it, woman. Devil take your wagon! You fail to grasp the severity of this situation."

Truly, it would have been a simple matter had he succeeded in clearing the woman's mind of the memory. Hell, it still would have been simple if the woman hadn't been *her*. Not when her sweet, rich taste lay thick on his tongue. Not when her intoxicating scent of rose petals and woman engulfed his senses.

"Well, of course I do not grasp the situation!" Lady Rosslyn exclaimed, maddeningly oblivious to the tentative hold he had on his temper. "You have failed to explain it! First, I had no idea that vampires existed outside fiction. Furthermore, I have no notion why one would arrest me for exhuming a corpse for my studies. I am fully aware that my actions are illegal, but the logic eludes me as to how that should mean anything to you."

Rafe sucked in a hissing breath through his teeth, biting back a stream of curses. Conversing with humans had never been his strong suit, but talking with Lady Rosslyn was always especially trying. "Your morbid hobby is of no concern to me. I had mistakenly believed you were hunting my people. You're fortunate that my people didn't take action themselves. That you weren't beaten bloody by a mob, your house set aflame!"

Rafe closed his eyes, remembering how Ian's third-in-command and a gang of other vengeful vampires had done exactly that to a prominent surgeon only three years ago. Ian had been apoplectic with rage. If the man's wife hadn't been in the country, she would surely have perished. Ian had punished the mob and issued a law that all suspicious mortals were to be handled only by the Lord of London from then on.

"*Morbid?*" Cassandra repeated, oblivious to the rest of his words. "You drank my blood only moments ago and you call *me* morbid?" Her sea-green eyes glared up at him from beneath impossibly long lashes. The captivating contact was broken too soon when she shook her head. "Well, if it is a mistake, then *why* are you arresting me?"

Ah and what a sweet drink it was. Yet somehow her life and memories had been more potent. Rafe usually closed his mind to his victims' lives when he fed, but in the case of Lady Rosslyn, he had needed to discover what she was up to.

Lady Rosslyn seemed to have been a very busy woman during the last year. She'd had the daring to apply to Oxford, Cambridge, and Saint Bartholomew's to master the healing arts. All those establishments had turned her away because of her sex. But she did not give up. Instead, she'd set forth with her studies alone, even robbing graves to learn the secrets of the human body.

Rafe sighed. This evening's events had all been a misunderstanding. Unfortunately, one that could not be rectified. The Elders would not permit her to leave his presence alive.

"It is forbidden for mortals to know of our kind. I attempted to banish your memory of the encounter, but it appears you are immune to my powers. So now you must come with me until…" He trailed off, strangely reluctant to voice the rest aloud.

"Until when?" Her voice emerged in a frightened whimper.

Rafe closed his eyes, took a deep breath, and let it out slowly. Unexpected sorrow churned in his gut at the consequence this encounter would bear.

"Until it is decided whether I kill you or Change you into a vampire."

Two

"Change me?" Cassandra squeaked, struggling to reason as her heart pounded in her ears. "Make me undead like you? Would that not, in fact, be k-killing me?"

"I am perfectly alive." Rafael resumed walking, tugging her along. "Now be quiet and come along, or I can kill you now."

She blinked and clamped her mouth shut. Though his words seemed to be motivated more by irritation than true intent to do her in, she thought it best to err on the side of caution, lest she vex this monster into fulfilling his promise. Ceasing her struggles, she walked mutely beside him, vowing to flee the moment his grip eased. But he did not loosen his grasp on her arm. As if reading her intentions, he tightened his hold once they left the cemetery gates. A sudden breeze lifted his heathenish long hair, brushing silken locks across her cheek. Cassandra shivered.

What a catastrophic night this has been. She'd ventured out into the cemetery to rob a grave, only to be abducted by the very man who'd captured her fascination and held it long after their brief acquaintance…a man who happened to be a mythological monster. Even if she'd been a fanciful type of person, Cassandra never would have guessed that the surly, scarred Spaniard was a nocturnal predator with a taste for blood. Her scientific mind simply could not contemplate the possibility of the existence of fairy-tale monsters. *Why was he friends with the Duke and Duchess of Burnrath?*

Rafael released her momentarily to flag down an approaching hackney. Cassandra attempted to bolt, but his arm snaked around her waist the moment the carriage slowed. Cassandra's fists clenched with silent recrimination. *Drat, I should have fled the moment I glimpsed his fangs.* Then again, with the impossible speed he'd displayed earlier, such an attempt certainly would have been futile. As if to concur, a tremor ran through her belly at the heat of his grip. Did he steal his warmth from her, or did his body produce his own?

With unyielding strength, he lifted her into the conveyance and settled next to her on the rickety bench seat. Again, her stomach pitched in the most alarming manner.

"To Burnrath House, number six, Rosemead Street," he clipped out to the driver.

The driver, worn and weathered for such a young age, eyed the vampire nervously, his gaze unwittingly darting back to Rafael's facial scars. "Aye, guv'nor."

As the carriage bobbed and rumbled down the cobblestone street, Cassandra trembled with intense awareness at the feel of the hard, warm body pressed next to hers. One of the wheels struck a pothole, nearly tossing her to the floor, but Rafael held her securely with gentle strength. How often she had dreamed of being this close to him…closer, if she were to acknowledge the truth of those wicked visions. *No wonder my mother-in-law called me unnatural. I've been smitten with a vampire the entire time.*

Quickly and as intensely as lightning, the memory of his mouth on her neck sent a shiver down her spine.

This could not be happening. Clearly she was dreaming. She pinched the sensitive skin on the back of her left hand…and bit her lip at the sharp pain.

"What the hell are you doing?" Rafael asked.

She eyed him warily. "I am trying to wake up from this fantastical dream."

He raised a brow and grumbled something in Spanish.

The hackney stopped outside the wrought-iron gates of Burnrath House. The enormous Elizabethan manor loomed over them like a menacing sentinel. Meager candlelight illuminated the windows, making them look like hungry eyes.

As Rafael led her down the drive, Cassandra observed that the once-manicured lawn was now wild and overgrown. The butler who greeted them at the door was not Burke, who served the Duke and Duchess of Burnrath. In fact, not only did he look too young to be a butler, with his bright yellow hair and boyish blue eyes, but he wasn't wearing livery. The young man's eyes narrowed with suspicion and malice as they raked across her with decidedly un-servile insolence.

"William, this is Lady Rosslyn, my prisoner," Rafael began without preamble. "She is not to leave this house unsupervised."

William's eyes widened momentarily and his fangs glowed in the candlelight. "Yes, my lord."

More vampires? Cassandra froze, all of her instincts crying to flee from this den of monsters. So that was why Rafael had dispensed with the former servants. And the lack of good staff was apparent the moment Rafael led her inside. Even in the dim candlelight, she could see that the house lacked upkeep. Cobwebs hung from the rafters and covered the unlit gas lamps in the drawing room.

Disgruntled with the vampire's rudeness, she swiped a finger across a mahogany side table, grimaced at the dust, and gave William a pointed stare. *Have I gone mad?* an inner voice gasped. *I should be planning my escape, not taunting vampires about their poor housekeeping!*

William bared his fangs further. Rafael pulled her away, though she swore she heard him chuckle under his breath.

Footsteps sounded on the stairs and another male emerged, peering at her curiously with glittering sherry eyes. "What is this I hear about a prisoner?"

Rafael squeezed her arm before addressing the man. "Anthony, this is Lady Rosslyn. She's the one who's been skulking about the cemetery."

"*This* is our fierce vampire hunter?" Anthony laughed and ran a hand through tousled chestnut hair.

Rafael's lips curled in a scowl. "Not a hunter at all. Merely a grave robber."

Cassandra bristled at the term. She was a scientist, not a common thief. "I was going to put it back!"

"*Grave robber?*" Anthony gaped, revealing his fangs. "She looks too fancy for such a dirty crime. Well, if she's no threat to us, why is she a prisoner?"

Other than a deepening scowl, Rafael continued to ignore her. "Because she is one of those rare mortals who possess an unyielding mind, I was unable to extinguish her memory of our encounter."

"I see. So we will be keeping her then?" The other vampire smiled playfully for a moment. Then his mirth dimmed. "Until…"

Rafael cut him short. "I shall write the report to the Elders now. In the meantime, would you please go to the nearest inn and procure Lady Rosslyn something to eat?"

Anthony's shoulders slumped in obvious reluctance, but he bowed in assent. "Very well, my lord."

"Lady Rosslyn." Rafael fixed her with such a piercing gaze that she regretted once more gaining his attention. "You will accompany me to the study."

Without acknowledging her brusque nod, he guided her up the stairs. Her mind raced with panic at the talk of keeping her as if she were some sort of exotic pet. Until…*until Rafael kills me or transforms me into a bloodsucking monster.*

The study at least was clean and organized, with a cheery fire blazing from the hearth. Rafael bade her to sit in one of the green baize overstuffed chairs before opening a cabinet and pouring her a glass of sherry. Cassandra sipped the heady vintage, watching with fascination how well the vampire managed to perform such a task with only one fully functioning arm. With fluid grace, he rifled through the desk drawers to fetch parchment and a quill. Dipping the quill in the ink blotter, he proceeded to write with such intensity that it was a wonder to behold.

But his injured arm had moved earlier…when she'd

been in his grasp with his mouth on her neck. The movement had been weak, but it had been there all the same. How had he damaged the limb? Could it be repaired? Her physician's mind raced with a thousand questions. Unfortunately, if the ever-deepening scowl on his face was any indicator, now was not the time to voice them.

Rafael folded the missive and summoned William with a bell. "I want you to find me a runner to dispatch this right away."

William eyed her with a truculent frown before seizing the letter. "Yes, my lord."

Anthony returned soon after with a small crock of stew and a crusty roll. The stew was the greasiest, most unpalatable concoction she'd ever seen, but Cassandra willed herself to choke it down. Who knew when she would again have the opportunity to eat? Her stomach pitched in dread. She forced the thought away. The roll, at least, was quite delicious, though it could have done with some butter.

As much as she tried to hide it, Rafael sensed her dissatisfaction. "Tomorrow evening I shall arrange for you to have more worthy sustenance, Countess. Now, I think it best you retire."

"So you are not going to lock me in a dungeon?" she ventured, finding courage from his polite words and promise of better victuals. Except for his threat of impending death, he was not treating her as a prisoner.

A slight smile twitched his sculpted lips. "Of course not, tempting as that may be. For one thing, I don't have one. All we have are the cellars below...and I do not want to contend with William or Anthony taking a bite out of you. For another, I am unwilling to let you out of my sight for long."

"That is indeed reassuring, *Don* Villar." She struggled to match his casual aplomb and finished the last sip of sherry. "Although I must say, I am not the slightest bit tired."

His scowl returned. "That is too bad, I'm afraid, for I have business to attend to and cannot risk you attempting escape. So you will have to remain in my chamber."

The world seemed to tilt as the breath left her body. "I-I beg your pardon? *Your* chamber?" *Surely he did not mean...* Her traitorous body warmed at the thought.

"Yes, *my* chamber." His eyes blazed with irritation. "You needn't look at me as if you fear I'll ravish you. I may be a repulsive monster, but I am not a reprehensible one. It is the only way I can ensure you cannot escape."

For some reason, his utter dismissal of the notion stung. Truly, she shouldn't be surprised. Her own husband had never found her desirable either.

Her face flamed but she managed to raise a brow. "Why should you worry about my safety when you may very well decide to kill me soon?"

Rafael sighed and extended his arm. "Stop being foolish. Now will you come along, or will I have to haul you down the corridor myself? I assure you I am quite capable of doing so, despite my disability."

Cassandra took a shaky breath and placed her hand on his muscular forearm, marveling once more at his strength as she allowed him to escort her. *My parents would be reeling in their graves. Not only have I allowed myself to have been abducted by a male, but I am now consigned to sharing a room with him.*

When they reached an ornately carved oak door, Rafael released her to pull an iron key from his pocket and fit it into the forbidding lock. Cassandra remained frozen in shock as the reality of her situation gripped her with icy fingers.

The door swung open and the vampire guided her into the massive chamber. This room was also thankfully clean, though the bed was unmade. Heat crept to her cheeks once more at the implied intimacy.

"When I return, I will either sleep in the chair or on the floor," Rafael said stiffly behind her. "A few books are in the drawer by the bed, as well as a deck of cards, should you care to practice your hand. I will leave one lantern"—his voice suddenly turned savage—"but if you attempt to use it against me, I swear you will regret it until your last breath."

Cassandra studied the slightly rippled scars on the left side of his face. "You were caught in a fire?" Further questions died in her throat as she witnessed the fury in his eyes.

"Of a sort, only worse than that…*much* worse." He stalked away from her to light a small oil lamp, striking the match with his one good hand.

Unbidden, her gaze strayed to his bad arm and she burst out, "It moved earlier."

Rafael stiffened and whipped around to meet her stare.

"Yes," he said softly. "It has its good moments here and there." He handed her the lantern and headed back to the door, suddenly turning back. "Although such a platitude is useless, and you will not believe me, I truly am sorry things happened this way."

Cassandra was rendered speechless once more by the sincerity in his tone.

He swept his gaze over her for an endless moment before inclining his head in a slight bow. "Good night, Countess."

The door closed behind him. The sound of the lock clicking back into place grated her nerves with terrifying finality and left her trapped in a vampire's lair.

⌘

William awaited Rafe below with the messenger. He glared with disapproval as the report to the Elders was sent on, along with a letter to Clayton Edmondson, Rafe's second-in-command, informing him of the situation.

When the runner departed, William shook his head. "I do not see why you are subjecting yourself and us to all this trouble. Why did you not kill her then and there?"

"Killing mortals is illegal now," Rafe reminded him curtly. "These days the risk of discovery is too high."

William scoffed. "You could break her neck and toss her into the Thames without anyone being the wiser."

"The Elders will likely order me to do just that, so there is little for you to be concerned with," Rafe snapped. "In the meantime I will do my duty and I recommend you do yours. This house needs to be cleaned up. We have a lady in residence." Before William could protest, Rafe raised his good hand. "Or should I audition another candidate to be my fourth?"

William sighed and shook his head. "No, my lord."

"I do not like this any more than you do." Quelling his irritation, Rafe softened his tone. "Just do some light dusting for now and then you may go hunt."

"Yes, my lord."

Anthony emerged, carrying a tray holding a decanter of ruby liquid and a glass. "No need to dust the kitchens, William. I've already taken care of that area. The lady will need to eat, after all. I've also poured you a glass of Madeira, my lord. Where shall you take it?"

"Thank you, Anthony. The library will do. Pour yourself one as well. I have a few things to ask you."

William glared at Anthony and muttered under his breath, "Arse-kisser."

Anthony shook his head, smiling as they headed up the stairs. Rafe nodded in approval. At least his third-in-command was handling this disaster with competence and dignity.

In the library, Rafe settled in a wingback chair and lit a cigar, taking his Madeira with gratitude. "Tell me, Anthony, can you cook?"

His third frowned. "I doubt I could even boil water. And William likely cannot discern the difference between sugar and salt."

Rafe blew out a cloud of smoke with a sigh. "Yet another complication. I cannot very well allow the countess to starve, and we cannot rely on fare from inns every night."

Anthony regarded him strangely, leaning forward. "You behave as if you know her."

"She is a friend of the Duchess of Burnrath. Naturally we have had a few brief encounters."

And potent encounters they were. Rafe closed his eyes at the memory. While all other members of the *haut ton* regarded him with suspicion and disgust, Lady Rosslyn had sought him out with bold curiosity. The rapt fascination in her glittering green eyes had been nearly enough to undo him. So he had been rude to her to drive her away, to protect her from himself. Little good it had done.

"So now you'll have to either kill her or make her one of us," Anthony mused aloud. "I do not envy you for that responsibility, though I must say that she is very beautiful and seems to possess courage as well as a strong spirit. She may make a fine vampire indeed. And you could do with a bit of companionship."

Rafe shook his head and took another drink. "I am afraid it is not as simple as that. I couldn't Change her even if I wanted to."

Anthony's brows drew together in confusion before his eyes widened as understanding dawned. "Do you mean you've Changed someone recently? Without sanction from the Elders?"

"I owed the duchess a favor." Rafe nodded with impatience and more than a touch of shame for breaking the law. The Elders required a vampire to notify them any time they intended to Change a mortal, not only to keep track of the vampire population, but also to ensure that no one was Changed who could pose a risk to their kind, such as criminals, prominent figures, or children.

Anthony leaned forward with avid curiosity. "Who did you Change?"

"It is none of your concern, and do not tell anyone,

especially the countess." Rafe ground his teeth. Yet again, the duchess had caused trouble for him. It took years to gain the power to Change a mortal. If he tried it again so soon, Cassandra would likely not survive.

"I could Change her," Anthony said quietly. "I'm one hundred thirty years of age. Surely that is sufficient power."

Rafe's fingers stiffened on the arm of the chair as he struggled to conceal his shock. Gratitude at the vampire's loyal offer warred with rage at the thought of Anthony's fangs penetrating Cassandra's lovely neck.

"Let us wait and see what the Elders say before making any drastic decisions. Besides, you do not want to squander such power lightly." Rafe stood and crushed out his cigar before Anthony could say anything further. "Now I am going to Mark her."

Cursing under his breath, he left the library and stalked to his chamber, pausing at the door. Marking her would make things worse for him, but it had to be done. He couldn't risk her escaping or falling into the clutches of another vampire.

Fitting the key into the lock, he opened the door as quietly as possible. Relief filled him at the sight of her still form on the bed and the sound of her even breathing. He hadn't the patience to hear more questions for which he did not have answers.

A pang of guilt struck him as he approached the bed, noting that she'd only managed to unfasten a few of the tiny buttons on the back of her gown. Doubtless she was uncomfortable sleeping in such a garment. She would need a lady's maid to help her with such things…and more clothing, for that matter.

Tomorrow they would have to go to her home and fetch her things before someone noted her disappearance. Yet another complication.

Rafe clenched his teeth as he stood over Lady Rosslyn, taking in her tumble of fiery auburn curls, her fine-boned features, the sweep of her lashes, the curve of her lips. Reaching out a shaky hand, he brushed his fingers across that silken mass of hair with a whisper of a touch.

He snatched back his hand with an inner curse. She was too fine to be handled by the likes of him. However, this business had to be done. Raising his index finger to his mouth, he pierced the digit with a fang, watching his blood bead up from the wound. Never in centuries had he imagined performing such an act.

Carefully, Rafe held his finger above Lady Rosslyn's parted lips, allowing his magical blood to drip into her mouth.

In as low a voice as possible, he recited the words that would bind her to him for the rest of her life. "I, Rafael Villar, interim Lord of London, Mark this mortal, Cassandra Burton, as mine and mine alone. With this Mark I give Cassandra my undying protection. Let all others, immortal and mortal alike, who cross her path sense my Mark and know that to act against her is to act against myself and thus set forth my wrath, as I will avenge what is mine."

The Mark sang between them with such dark harmony that Rafe stumbled back. Cassandra moaned and her eyes fluttered open.

"What…?" she moaned sleepily.

His breath caught with desire. With her tousled hair and slumberous gaze, she looked like a well-bedded woman. Rafe shook his head. Such thoughts were dangerous.

"Nothing." He struggled to sound gentle. "Go back to sleep, Countess."

She murmured something unintelligible and rolled over, groaning in discomfort at her constricting gown. How he wished he could relieve her of it. Instead he headed back to the door and sprawled next to the heavy oak barrier to await the dawn. There would be no sleep for him this day.

Three

29 September 1823

WILLIAM GLANCED ABOUT FURTIVELY AS HE KNOCKED on Clayton Edmondson's town-house door. Clayton, Rafael Villar's second-in-command, answered the door himself. The older vampire seized William by the shoulders and yanked him inside.

"Is it true?" Clayton demanded, eyes glowing with fury.

William nodded, fists clenched in outrage. "You do not know the half of it. She's a goddamned *countess*…and Villar seems intent on treating her as such. He made me dust the main floor as if I were a common parlor maid!"

Clayton rubbed his jaw. "That does not sound as if he is keen on killing her."

"Well, he can't Change her. I overheard him telling Anthony."

"*What?*" the other vampire growled. "Then he should have killed her right away."

William leaned back and crossed his arms. "He claims he will wait until the Elders answer his report, but I think he is stalling for time to find an excuse to keep her. She is quite the fancy piece, after all."

"So he is as big a fool as his predecessor," Clayton mused. "Well, I think it is time to embark on the plan we'd discussed. Find those who you believe would be receptive and tell them to meet at the abandoned warehouse on the wharf Thursday at midnight."

William arched a brow. "What of my payment?"

Clayton sighed and strode to a cabinet, pulling out a small wooden box. The cloying odor of opium filled the room as he handed William a small cloth-wrapped parcel.

"This is less than last time."

Fangs bared, Clayton's snarl made the younger vampire cringe. "If you expect to become my second, you will have to wean yourself off this vile substance by the time I become Lord of this city."

❧

Cassandra thrashed in the bed, biting back a cry as memories haunted her dreams with such vivid clarity that it was like reliving them all over again.

Her mother's face, contorted in pain as she struggled to sing a lullaby...the doctor's helpless shrug...solemn footmen carrying Mother's shrouded corpse out of the house...

Papa staring out the window, cold and silent as the statues in the garden...a bottle of port slipping from limp fingers to shatter on the floor...ruby droplets gleaming like blood... There had been no blood when he died a year later. He had simply clutched his chest, muttered a curse, and collapsed... quickly, with no warning. If only Cassandra had known. Perhaps she could have fixed him.

Trembling, Cassandra's hand is placed in the grip of the Earl of Rosslyn as the parson drones on. No! I don't love him! I don't want to be a countess. I want to be a doctor!

Clammy lips pressed against hers in the darkened bed-chamber. John awkwardly fumbling beneath her nightgown. Pain…only a few moments… It seemed to last forever.

Whispers and laughter at Cassandra's eccentricity echo behind fans at the Devonshire ball. She escapes into the garden and sees John in the arms of her former chaperone. Relief, blessed relief. With her husband occupied, there will be more time to pursue her studies.

John gapes in shock as Cassandra encourages him to continue with his lover. When returning home from Sarah's embrace, he often brings her a new scientific text.

Sarah crying in Cassandra's arms. John's heart gave out with no warning, just as Papa's had. But why? He was so young. Rifling through her medical books. There must be an answer. Widowhood at least gave her time to study.

Cruel faces looking down on her at Cambridge, Oxford, and Saint Bartholomew's. All said the same thing: "I am sorry, Lady Rosslyn, but women are not permitted to attend." Her fists clenched in fury. She would show them. She would become the best physician in Britain on her own.

Trudging through the cemetery, shivering in the cold, raising her shovel to plunge it into the frosty soil.

Rafael Villar emerges from the shadows. Her heart races as he pulls her into his arms. Desire pulses between her legs. Only this man, this dark, dangerous man, had affected her in such an alarming manner. Moonlight glistens on deadly sharp fangs as they pierce her soft flesh—

Cassandra jolted from the dream, a cry dying on

her lips as her eyes snapped open. Fresh panic gripped her throat as she took in the almost completely dark bedchamber. Unfamiliar shadows and a foreign, yet compelling scent of spices overcame her senses. This was not her room. *Where am I?*

Scrambling from the unfamiliar bed, she adjusted the meager oil lamp with trembling fingers. As her surroundings were further illuminated, memories of the previous night crashed down upon her. She was at Burnrath House, a prisoner of Rafael Villar…and he was a *vampire*.

Choking back a gasp, she glanced at the doorway. He was gone, but he could return any moment.

Cassandra struggled with the buttons on the back of her gown, shoulders throbbing with the effort. Managing to fasten all but the top one, she sighed and shook her hair down her back to cover it, setting the pins on the nightstand. She was far from presentable, but there was nothing to be done. Besides, why should she care? It was not as if she'd chosen to be abducted by a vampire and locked in his bedchamber without any food or so much as a change of clothing.

A vampire… All her thoughts and questions from the previous evening returned. Never before had she encountered such a fascinating being. Rafael possessed unfathomable strength. His speed defied the laws of nature…and his bite, *good God*, his bite. How could something so macabre feel so pleasurable?

She placed a hand on her neck where his mouth had been, awed at the smooth and unblemished skin. Somehow, he had healed the wound. *Magic.* Cassandra shook her head. Impossible. She'd never believed in magic and she wasn't about to start. A scientific explanation must exist.

Pacing the room, she observed the lack of windows. Cassandra froze as memories assaulted her consciousness. The Duchess of Burnrath had been responsible for the renovation, removing all windows on the upper floors, claiming to mitigate the recent window tax.

Her breath fled as Rafe's words to her the previous night came back. *"Is that why you befriended the Duchess of Burnrath?"*

"My God," she whispered as it all came clear.

Gossip *had* circulated about the duke being a vampire after the publication of John Polidori's story, "The Vampyre." Cassandra had been in mourning at the time and dismissed the tidbits she'd heard as pure folderol. The talk silenced when the duke married, but the rumors seemed to have been true all along.

The duke and duchess were vampires. That was why Rafael had thought she was a vampire hunter. Her dearest, eccentric friend, Angelica, with whom Cassandra had enjoyed dozens of literary salons, musicales, and phantasmagorias, had been an immortal, blood-drinking creature all along. Now that she thought of it, Her Grace had never once paid her a call during the day.

Now the couple's eccentricity made sense—they had only entertained at night. Rafael had said he'd been burned by worse than fire. Could he have been referring to the sun? She couldn't begin to imagine such an unnatural vulnerability.

As she awaited his return, and hopefully a meal,

Cassandra pondered her dilemma. What would her servants think when she didn't return? Granted, they were accustomed to her autonomy and late hours, but even they would take notice if she didn't return by the morning, or the next…

She shook her head. It was best to focus on things she could possibly control.

She needed to learn more about Villar and his kind. Therein lay the key to her survival. Perhaps if she discovered a way to heal Rafael's arm, he would allow her to live. Closing her eyes, she devised a tentative plan.

The sound of the key in the lock had her bolting to her feet. It was time to face her captor.

"Good evening, my lady," Anthony said cheerfully, carrying a cloth-wrapped object.

Cassandra didn't know whether to be relieved or disappointed to see the other vampire. Then the aroma of seasoned meat and freshly baked bread emanating from the basket he carried teased her nostrils. She'd never passed an entire day without eating.

"I've brought you some breakfast. Tea is brewing below stairs. However, I thought you might want this hot and fresh." Anthony unwrapped the cloth to reveal a flaky meat pasty.

"Thank you very much." Salivating, she needed all her effort to take the food gracefully and not snatch it from his grasp like a wild beast. Past the capacity for manners, she took a bite of the steaming pie without further preamble. It was much better than the previous evening's greasy stew. "Is *Don* Villar about?"

Anthony shook his head. "No, my lady. He is out seeking his own sustenance."

"Ah yes, blood." Cassandra wiped her mouth with the cloth. "I wonder what makes your kind require it."

The vampire's eyes widened at her candor. "I'm sure I do not know, my lady."

"No matter." She shrugged. "Who are these Elders to whom Villar is sending a report?" she asked before she lost her nerve.

Anthony shivered and looked down at his boots. "They are a council of twelve of the most ancient and powerful members of our kind. They make the rules and we obey."

"Ah, so they have decreed that I must be imprisoned to face a potential death sentence?" Despite Anthony's fearful reaction at the mention of such formidable vampires, Cassandra felt a measure of relief that Rafael hadn't been directly responsible for her current circumstances.

The vampire nodded. "Yes, and he was obligated by law to report your situation, lest he be punished. For the safety of our race, they need to be notified any time a mortal is apprised of our existence. It may be small comfort, but I believe Rafe doesn't want to kill you."

A light laugh escaped her lips. "Actually, that is a *substantial* comfort." Though the prospect of becoming a nocturnal blood-drinker alarmed her, it was far preferable to being slain by one. Taking a deep breath, she leaned forward and whispered, "Do you think he will Change me then?"

Again the vampire looked down. "It is not really my place to say, my lady." He shifted uncomfortably on his feet. "Truly, we shouldn't be having this conversation. The master will not be pleased."

She sighed in defeat. "Very well. I shall have my meal as well as my tea in the parlor. Please inform *the master* that I should like to speak to him there."

Anthony gaped, but he was no match for her long-held authority as a countess. He seemed to know it, because a small smile of admiration crossed his lips. "Very well, Lady Rosslyn. I shall escort you there and bring your tea shortly."

Tamping down her trepidation, Cassandra squared her shoulders and followed the vampire down to the parlor. Her tea was delivered soon after, much weaker than she preferred, but she was grateful all the same. Hopefully it would help calm her nerves.

"Ordering my people about already, I see." Rafael's richly accented voice poured over her like dark honey as he strode into the room with the grace of a panther.

She rose from her seat quickly. "I, ah, wished to speak with you."

His amber eyes glittered. "I gathered as much. You may carry on."

Folding her hands behind her back so he couldn't see them shaking, Cassandra began. "I have put some thought into this situation and I have come to a few conclusions."

"Oh, have you now?" His deceptively mild tone belied his raised brow.

She forced herself to meet his burning gaze. "Well, first off, the Duke and Duchess of Burnrath are vampires as well, are they not?"

He scowled and did not answer.

Cassandra chuckled. "I shall take that as confirmation. However, that is not among my main concerns."

"And those would be?" he inquired, eyeing her as if *she* were the newly discovered species.

She refused to let him unnerve her further. "I shall need food. It would be silly indeed if I were to starve to death before you decide to kill me properly."

He inclined his head, that silken black hair falling forward to frame his face. "Your logic has merit. What else?"

"I need more clothing." Before he could mock her, she held up a hand. "This is not an issue of vanity, only mere practicality. You cannot mean to keep me here when I only have one gown to wear."

Leaning against the door frame, he regarded her with what appeared to be amusement. "What makes you presume so?"

She swallowed. "You can't possibly be so cruel."

He stalked closer to her like a feral predator. "Oh, I can be cruel, Countess. I can be *very* cruel indeed."

Cassandra willed her knees to cease trembling and lifted her chin. "Well, if you can be cruel, sir, then *I* can be difficult, though I would prefer to not be so."

Rafael's eyes narrowed and he bared a hint of fangs. "What do you mean?"

She held her ground, fighting the instinct to step back. "I mean, I-I've been quite cooperative with your abducting me and facing a possible death sentence and, well…"

"Well?" he prompted in a dangerous, velvety voice.

She sucked in a breath. "Well, most people would be having hysterics and doing their utmost to fight you and escape. And I've been thinking perhaps I should do so as well. Although I daresay I would be more reasonable with a few accommodations."

"Fighting me would be an exercise in futility, *Countess*." As if to assert his point, he reached out to grasp her jaw, tilting her chin up to meet his gaze. "As would trying to escape."

Narrowing her eyes, she held her voice firm. "Yet I am certain my attempts could be *very* vexing."

For an eternity, they stared at each other, locked in a silent battle of wills. Rafael's scowl deepened before he released her. "What is it exactly that you want?"

"I would like my clothes to start with. This gown was not meant for sleeping in. And I should like to bring my servants, especially my cook—"

"No servants."

"But—"

"Do you want to endanger any more people?"

"The Duke and Duchess of Burnrath had human servants," she argued, then faltered. "At least, I'm fairly certain they were human. How else could the cook get supplies from the market during the day?"

"The duke and duchess did not eat food." His brows drew together. "At least not after Her Grace was Changed."

"Exactly. She needed to eat, and so do I." She put her hands on her hips and leaned forward. "And I need my clothes."

Rafael sighed. "Fine. We'll fetch your cook and wardrobe tonight as long as you promise never to reveal the truth behind you being here. Your safety, as well as hers, depends on it."

"What of my other servants?" she ventured, gaining

courage at his indulgence thus far. "This house is in vital need of upkeep."

He sighed again and ran a hand through that magnificent hair. "I'll hire some of my own people to take care of that. You must also inform your friends and family that you are to be my guest here. We don't want to put any more humans in danger."

"Agreed." She managed a prim curtsy and took a deep breath. "There is one more thing." *The thing that was most important to her.*

A low growl tore from his throat. "Damn it, *señora*. You are trying my patience."

"I–I w–would like my books and laboratory equipment," she pressed on. "Without my studies and my work to occupy my time, I fear I shall go mad and cause quite the uproar during my stay."

He slammed his fist on the table next to her, making her teacup clatter in its saucer. "You presume to threaten *me*?"

"It is not a threat at all." She forced an airy tone, refusing to balk. "It is merely the inevitable result of being confined with no intellectual stimulation. And if you are to kill me, I would appreciate the chance to make one last discovery before I die." Lowering her head, she peered through her lashes, attempting to play the coquette. "Perhaps I could learn how to repair your arm."

A brittle, ugly laugh escaped him. "That would be impossible. The limb has been this way for fifteen years."

"Did you have a doctor look at it?" she challenged.

"Of course not," he growled. "It is forbidden for

mortals to know of my kind, which is why you are here in the first place."

Cassandra ignored the taunt. "Then how can you be certain your injury cannot be treated? It has not even been properly diagnosed."

Rafael's exotic features contorted into a mask of pain and rage. It took every ounce of her will not to cringe.

"Enough!" he growled. "You may move your laboratory here. But you will *not* experiment on me. Also, no corpses. My sense of smell is heightened and I cannot abide the odor."

Biting back a protest, she nodded. It was the best she could expect for now.

"And you *will* give me your solemn oath that you will not tell any mortals my secret or attempt to escape." His adamant tone forbade argument. "It would mean not only your death, but also the demise of any whom you confide in."

Cassandra extended her hand, hiding a smile. "I promise." Anthony's theory seemed to be correct. If Villar wanted to kill her, he wouldn't keep *threatening* to do so, he would merely do the deed.

Rafael blinked in surprise before taking her hand in his warm, firm grip. She shivered at the contact.

"Very well, it appears we have a bargain." He shook her hand briskly. "I will summon the carriage and we will be on our way."

She bit back a cheer at her victory. Regaining access to her medical texts and equipment would be the first step in her quest to study the vampire and prove herself to be an invaluable asset to him.

Four

DAMN HER. RAFE GNAWED THE END OF HIS CIGAR AS he watched Lady Rosslyn's cook, who had also served as her housekeeper, begin another spat with William on the state of the kitchen. Ten subordinate vampires dashed around the place, sweeping and dusting and polishing as they eyed the cook with hunger. Cassandra herself was upstairs with Anthony in one of the larger guest suites, supervising the unpacking of her laboratory, cheerfully oblivious to the further havoc she'd caused.

Did she truly not comprehend the fact that he could kill her at any moment—and might have to, whether he liked it or not? Or was she flouting his threat, determined to vex him until her last breath? He could admire the latter. The former…he could not bear to contemplate it.

At least he only had one more human to contend with. The remainder of Lady Rosslyn's staff did not question or protest their abrupt dismissal. They'd taken one look at Rafe and accepted their severance pay and references with unconcealed relief. He absently rubbed the ridge of scars on his cheek. His monstrous appearance could be beneficial at times.

And with no lady's maid, Rafe would have to be the one to assist her in dressing. He sure as hell wouldn't allow anyone else to touch that silken flesh. A tremor of anticipation filled him at the thought of the pleasure…and torment of that chore.

"May I have a word with you about tonight's menu?" the cook interrupted his fantasy.

Rafe waved her off. "That matter should be addressed to the countess…" He paused, seeing merit in an excuse to speak with her. "I will fetch her."

Yes, he asserted, it would be good to make certain she was not causing any mischief. Not because he wanted to gaze upon her regal features and sea-green eyes. After all, the menu *did* need to be seen to.

Quietly he opened the door, taking a moment to covertly admire the curve of her backside as she removed a stack of books from a crate. At the sight, Rafe's body quickened in lust. *If only…* He shook his head. To want the impossible was foolish.

Clearing his throat, he took small pleasure in her wide gaze and pink cheeks as she whirled around to face him. "Your cook would like to discuss tonight's menu. As I and my people can eat very little, I feel the task should go to you."

"Very well, *Don* Villar." She nodded briskly before holding up a ghastly sharp device. "But first might I have a sample of your blood?"

Rafe scowled. "Persistent wench, aren't you?"

An unreasonable wave of anger washed over him. Couldn't she see him as more than a specimen? He didn't expect her to view him with as much admiration as he did her. But at the very least, couldn't she see some semblance of the man before her?

"You said there's a possibility you may make me into what you are. If that is the case, I need to understand more of what I would become." Cassandra continued to argue, heedless of his darkening mood. "I want to know why you need to drink blood to survive. I want to know how you are stronger than ten men and can move as fast as a hummingbird. I want to know how you healed the puncture wounds on my neck and why the scars on your face and arm are not healed." Her eyes darkened to deep pools of compassion. "The sun burned you, didn't it?"

Rafe nodded stiffly, not wanting to think again of that terrible day. Some nights he could still feel the scorching celestial flame.

"I need to learn these things, Rafael," she pleaded. Her lower lip trembled. "Is there anything I can do to change your mind? Anything I can bargain?"

The sound of his name on her lips made his pulse skip. The utter passion and desperation in her voice struck a chord deep within him. *Anything…* The word held tempting possibilities.

"Perhaps," he said gruffly. "Allow me to think a little longer on the matter. For now, go speak with the cook. I need to hunt."

As Rafe stalked the London streets, he did indeed think about her offer to bargain. He also thought of her lush lips, silken hair, and tempting figure. He lingered in the chill night air, hoping to cool the heat Cassandra had ignited within him.

When he returned shortly before dawn and escorted her to his bedchamber, the heat refused to abate. As his fingers unfastened the delicate buttons on her gown, revealing creamy, tempting flesh visible through her thin chemise, his desire became an inferno.

"Are you certain you wouldn't rather that I summon Mrs. Smythe for this?" she asked, peering shyly at him over her shoulder.

Rafe shook his head, loathe to give up this enticing duty. "Your housekeeper cook is not a lady's maid, and I want her in here as little as possible for her own safety."

Too soon he finished, and Cassandra fetched a voluminous nightgown and ducked behind the privacy screen to remove her stays, stockings, and garters. He ran his tongue across his fangs, tantalized by her delectable silhouette behind the thin barrier. When she emerged, she hurriedly climbed into his bed and yanked the covers to her chin.

Despite such maidenly modesty, she eyed him fearlessly. "Have you given any thought to bargaining with me?"

"I have, but as I have not determined what exactly I will ask for, we may discuss it tomorrow." Extinguishing the lantern, Rafe stretched out once more on the floor, wishing he could join Cassandra in the bed, if only to feel her warmth next to him.

❦

1 October 1823

Cassandra leaned over the microscope, cursing under her breath. She needed more light. If only this dratted room had windows and she was allowed to work during the day. Squinting into the eyepiece, she frowned. Higher magnification would also aid her in analyzing her own blood and comparing it to the vampire's... That is, if Rafael would consent to allow her to study him. Thus far he had refused, but she was determined to change his mind.

A knock on the door pulled her from her reverie. Anthony poked his head in the room. He'd been perfectly willing to volunteer as a test subject, but Rafael had forbidden it. "You have a visitor, my lady. Mrs. Smythe says she came earlier as well. The woman refused to give her identity, though she insisted you should be expecting her."

Cassandra frowned as she deciphered the cryptic statement. The frown deepened as she realized only one woman would dare. "Drat, you are right. I may as well get this over with."

The woman awaiting her in the drawing room was completely unrecognizable due to her heavy cloak and the mask disguising her face. However, Cassandra's dreaded suspicion was confirmed the moment the lady opened her mouth.

"So it is true, then!" her former mother-in-law exclaimed in outrage. "You have become the Spaniard's mistress! Have you any idea how this will reflect upon our family? That you have chosen to live in sin is bad enough, but for it to be with a foreign, disfigured—"

"That's enough, Agnatha!" Cassandra cut her off, outraged at the hypocrisy. "What I choose to do with my life is no one's business but my own. I am a widow now. My days as an over-scrutinized debutante are long behind me, and I thank God for that every day."

Agnatha gasped and yanked off her mask, revealing her beady, black eyes and almost nonexistent chin. "You do not understand. As long as you are a part of Society, what you do is everyone's business. I beg you, come home now and perhaps we may be able to dissuade the gossips." Her voice softened and grew more wheedling. "Thank heaven the Season is over. You can join me in the country and perhaps this dreadful scandal will blow over by the time everyone returns to Town in the spring."

Cassandra could do nothing but stare in fascination. She'd never seen Agnatha beg before. Her mother-in-law had always commanded.

"Please." Agnatha reached for Cassandra's hand. "Do not dishonor my son's memory."

"I am sorry, but I must stay here." She couldn't hold back her jubilation at the statement.

Ever since Cassandra had married the late John Burton, Agnatha had been her constant tormentor, always ordering her about and scorning her for not living up to the family's expectations. To be rid of the vexing woman once and for all was a great relief, despite the circumstances.

Squaring her thin shoulders as if to do battle,

Agnatha surveyed Cassandra with piercing contempt. "So this is how it is to be? After I risk my own reputation coming to this den of iniquity to save your ungrateful hide? And at night, no less?" Her narrow face flushed as her beady eyes spat daggers. "I always knew you were unworthy of my Johnny. You couldn't even provide him with an heir!"

Before Cassandra could reply, a shadow fell over them both.

"You should leave now, madam, before I throw you out," Rafael Villar told her in a low voice. He leaned indolently in the doorway, apparently having witnessed the entire confrontation.

Agnatha's miniscule chin quivered with outrage as she spluttered, but her venom was no match for the vampire's fearsome scowl. Cassandra almost wished he'd bare his fangs at her ex-mother-in-law as well. Swallowing her vitriol, Agnatha donned her mask and departed without a by-your-leave.

Once Agnatha was gone, Rafael's arched lips curved in a slight smile. "I gather your relationship with your late husband's mother was less than amicable?"

She grinned. "Your assumption is correct. I'd thought that once John passed away, she'd leave me alone. Instead she's determined to ensure that I'm an even more respectable widow than I was a wife. I am glad she thinks I am your mistress." Her face heated at the implication of intimacy between them. "Perhaps now I shall at last be free of her."

His smile faded as his brows drew together. "She thinks you are my mistress?"

"Oh yes, I'm perfectly ruined now," she said

cheerfully. "Perfectly ruined and perfectly free…well, except for my situation with you, of course." Her smile wavered.

Rafael continued to frown as if he hadn't heard her. "Perhaps I should marry you to put a better light on things, as the Duke of Burnrath did with his bride. Lord knows I don't need any further attention from the human world."

Men had only proposed to her to better their positions in life in one way or another. Coming from him, this sort of offer was all the more repugnant. She'd thought him nobler than that. Still, the suggestion made her heart flutter irrationally. She shook her head, avoiding his gaze. "That is hardly necessary. For one thing, it is too late. My reputation was blackened the moment my trunks were carried into this house. I never intended to remarry anyway. For another, it seems a silly inconvenience for you in the light of my as-yet-undecided fate."

For a moment he appeared upset by her refusal, but it must have been a trick of light, for he began to laugh. "After all you have put me through, now you are concerned with inconveniencing me?"

His laughter stung.

Cassandra fixed him with an icy glare. "You inconvenienced *yourself* when you brought me here against my will."

"Indeed, I did." His expression sobered and he once more stepped closer, leaning in until his breath brushed across her lips. "Though perhaps you should take care not to exacerbate matters. Or else I may be tempted to wed you just for the legal right to take you over my knee."

With that, he turned and headed out the door for his nightly hunt, leaving Cassandra trembling from his momentary closeness and outraged by his words.

Anthony's form filled the doorway. "I see you've survived another encounter with His Surliness."

Cassandra's face flamed. "Good Lord, did you hear us?"

He shrugged. "I could lie, but somehow I do not think you would appreciate even the most well-intentioned deception."

"So you were hovering by the door?" Her eyes narrowed.

The vampire shook his head emphatically. "Not at all. Our kind has superior hearing." He held out an embossed envelope. "This arrived for you during your blessedly brief visit with that masked termagant. She was your mother-in-law?"

She took the envelope and nodded.

"You have my sympathy." He offered her a warm smile. "You should know that Rafael is not the beast he would have you believe he is. He may be harsh, but he is fair. However, I highly recommend that you endeavor to be on his good side."

She raised a brow. "Does he have one?"

Anthony chuckled. "I am certain you will soon discern that for yourself. I'll leave you to your letter now, my lady."

She glanced at the embossed envelope. It appeared to be an invitation. Apparently someone must not have heard she was now a fallen woman. She frowned. No, they had to know or else they would not have sent the invitation here.

Shaking her head in bemusement, she broke the seal. Either way, it didn't matter. Rafael was unlikely to allow her to go anywhere and she'd never much enjoyed social gatherings anyway.

But as Cassandra scanned the invitation to a dinner party hosted by one of her dearest friends, her eyes widened. This was different. She *had* to go…which meant that she had best try to follow Anthony's advice. She needed to get on Rafael's good side.

∾

When Rafe returned from his hunt, he found Cassandra pacing through the drawing room. Her eyes lit up when she saw him. He felt a strange pull in his chest.

"*Don* Villar, I've just received an invitation from Sir Patrick Blythe for a dinner party Wednesday evening." Her cheeks were flushed with excitement… excitement that was apparently not for him.

He scowled. "No."

The animated joy fled from her face to be replaced by despairing panic. "You do not understand! Thomas Wakley shall be there. He's the creator of the new medical journal, *The Lancet*, and I've been desperate to meet him."

Remorse at killing her happiness warred with irritation at her excited mention of another man. "I thought you were now ostracized by Society for becoming my mistress." Rafe tried to ignore an uncomfortable twinge of guilt at that fact. He knew all too well what it was to be a pariah.

Cassandra dismissed his reply with a wave of her hand. "Sir Patrick does not give a fig for such trifling nonsense. He only cares about our shared interest in science and medicine." Her voice turned soft and pleading as she looked up at Rafe with large, imploring eyes. "Please, sir, allow me to attend." She placed a hand on his bad shoulder.

"You seem to forget that you are a prisoner here." His voice came out rough and labored, as if her light touch held immeasurable weight. He pulled away.

Her lush lips pouted as a thin line of vexation appeared between her brows. "I have always attended Sir Patrick's dinners, even when I was in full mourning. If I do not make an appearance, I wouldn't be surprised if he grew so worried he sent a constable here to investigate."

"You exaggerate." He eyed her warily. Was this another threat?

She lifted her chin stubbornly. "I wouldn't be so certain. I cannot fathom why you are being so unreasonable. It's only a dinner party. I promise to return here as soon as it's over."

Rafe shook his head. "You do not understand, Countess. Even if I could believe such a ridiculous promise, I cannot allow you to leave this house without me."

She shrugged. "Then come with me."

The words stunned him. For a moment all he could do was stare at her in shock. Was this woman mad? "You would arrive at a social gathering with a grotesque cripple on your arm?"

"You are *not* at all grotesque." Cassandra threw up her hands in frustration. "Honestly, there is no need to be so melodramatic. Besides, I would allow the devil himself to escort me to this party."

Rafe let out a bitter chuckle. "Now who is being melodramatic?" When she remained silent with a mutinous frown, he sighed and ran his good hand through his hair. Perhaps it *would* be a good idea for them to make an appearance in public, solidifying the fact that she belonged with him. "All right, I'll take you to that blasted party. But if you do anything that risks endangerment to me or my kind, you *will* suffer the consequences. Is that understood?"

"Yes!" She clasped her hand in glee. "Thank you, *Don* Villar."

She moved forward as if to embrace him. Rafe stepped back.

"And one more thing." He gave her a stern glare, fighting the urge to respond to her infectious smile. "You must keep your pestering to a minimum. I have much more pressing responsibilities than tending to your whims."

Cassandra flinched and a measure of happiness drained from her face. "Yes, of course."

She curtsied stiffly and walked away, leaving Rafe feeling like a lousy curmudgeon.

That nagging emotion intensified when she avoided him for the next three days. Reluctantly, he had to admit that Cassandra hadn't done anything wrong. That he'd been unable to erase her memory and had to imprison her wasn't her fault. She was an innocent, suffering under the harsh laws of his kind.

However, that did not change the fact that her presence under his roof was disrupting. Aside from having to guard and care for her, he had to contend with her servant squabbling with his, her frequent bustling back and forth from her laboratory to the library, her questions about his arm, and the ever-increasing temptation of her beauty. Hell, even her scent tormented him.

She was driving him mad. Completely mad. Why else would he have proposed marriage, even in jest? And why else was he willing to escort her to this dinner party, which would force him to endure looks of disgust and mean-spirited whispers from the host and guests? He'd put up with his limit of such loathsome ordeals when Ian had been Lord of London.

And yet there he was, pacing the drawing room as he waited for Mrs. Smythe to help the countess dress. Rafe himself was immaculate in a black dinner jacket, pressed trousers, and a meticulously knotted cravat. He carried a jeweled walking stick to disguise the uselessness of his arm.

"I am ready, *Don* Villar." Cassandra walked down the stairs, breathtaking in a shimmering gown of turquoise watered silk. Rafe's mouth went dry. The male guests of the party would really despise him now, not because of his disfigurement, but because he would have this beautiful woman on his arm. A woman he was completely unworthy of.

"I appreciate your punctuality, Countess," he said gruffly. "The carriage is ready."

She beamed as she took his arm and immediately began to prattle on with unabashed enthusiasm about medical journals and scientific innovations.

Rafe fought back a surge of lust at her proximity. Perhaps he agreed to this ordeal out of a perverse desire for self-torture. Perhaps it was impossible to resist her infectious smile. Or maybe it was because she'd said he wasn't grotesque with such sincerity in her sparkling eyes that he could almost believe it.

Five

As Sir Patrick's butler led Cassandra and Rafael into the drawing room, everyone fell silent, staring at Villar as if he were a new breed of insect. Cassandra's lip curled in irritation at their rude scrutiny. Lifting her chin, she moved closer to him, declaring her allegiance.

"Lady Rosslyn!" Sir Patrick Blythe called out jovially as he rose from his seat. "I am delighted you were able to attend!" He gave Rafael a warm smile and extended his hand. "And this must be *Don* Villar, the infamous pugilist. I've heard impressive tales of you. Welcome to my home."

The vampire blinked in surprise at Patrick's friendly tone and slowly shook his hand. "I am honored, sir."

Cassandra's heart warmed. In publicly welcoming Villar, Sir Patrick had made it clear to his guests that they were to treat Rafael with courtesy. She gave Sir Patrick a grateful smile.

As the other guests were introduced, a few cast censorious glances her way. Oddly, she felt a measure of satisfaction. At least Rafael was not singled out to be a figure of disapproval.

Thankfully, the guests were few. Cassandra detested large gatherings, and she guessed that Rafael shared the sentiment. However, when introduced to Thomas Wakley, it was all she could do not to squeal in excitement and prattle on about his wonderful journal. Sir Patrick then presented the physician Philip Brewer, a sullen fellow who appeared to have a foul taste in his mouth. Hamilton Crowley, a prominent apothecary, looked to be already deep in his cups, though he was a cheerful enough fellow, and as usual, the Earl of Densmore was there.

Aside from herself and Sir Patrick, Lord Densmore was the only other member of the peerage in attendance. Cassandra was the sole female. Patrick had never cared for inane customs such as balancing the guest list according to rank or sex. His only concern was having guests who could provide new knowledge and stimulating conversation. It was one of the many reasons why Cassandra placed him among her dearest friends. Patrick never cared a whit about her sex. He had treated her with as much scholarly respect as he did his other friends.

Suddenly, Thomas Wakley, who'd been most blatant in staring at Rafael, charged toward the vampire. His face broke into a wide grin. "It's you! You're the man who saved my life!"

Rafael winced as if displeased at being recognized. However, he did not pull away as Wakley clasped his good hand and pumped it vigorously.

"We have a hero in our midst?" Sir Patrick's eyes were wide with curiosity. "Do tell."

Wakley turned to address his host and the other guests. "Three years ago a gang of ruffians broke into my home in the middle of the night. They beat me to a pulp and set my house aflame. This man pulled me out just before the roof collapsed."

Cassandra gasped as she remembered something Rafael had said the night he'd taken her prisoner. "*I had mistakenly believed you were hunting my people. You're fortunate that they didn't take action themselves. That you weren't beaten bloody by a mob, your house set aflame...*"

"I recall reading about that incident in the papers." Mr. Crowley leaned forward. "Wasn't it the Thistlewood gang?"

Wakley nodded. "The authorities were never able to prove anything, but who else could it have been?"

His attackers hadn't been the Thistlewood gang. They were vampires who'd believed Wakley was a hunter. He must have been exhuming corpses in St. Pancras. Cassandra shut her gaping mouth as Villar gave her a warning look. *But Rafael had saved him.*

"Why would you suspect them?" Lord Densmore inquired. "Weren't they only targeting members of Parliament?"

"Some believe that I was the hangman when Arthur Thistlewood and his fellow conspirators were executed. Utter nonsense, of course," Wakley answered absently before turning back to Rafael. "I owe you a debt, Villar."

The vampire shrugged his good shoulder. "It was nothing."

Nothing? Cassandra longed to shout. *After what happened to you, you had to have been very brave to run into a burning house to save a stranger!* A small, secret smile curved her lips. The Lord Vampire of London wasn't the terrifying monster he wanted her to believe he was.

Sir Patrick clapped Rafael on the shoulder. "It is an honor to have such a valiant hero here all the same. Well, shall we adjourn to the dining room?"

The vampire nodded in relief.

"I wish the Duchess of Burnrath could be here," Patrick told Cassandra as he walked beside them. "Her Grace always facilitates lively discussions. I do so miss her literary salons."

Lord Densmore cut in with a sneer. "Yes, you do have an affinity for scandalous women, Patrick." As always, he gave Cassandra a scornful glare.

Rafael's scowl deepened and Cassandra fought back her usual grimace of disgust. She'd never liked the pompous earl. He'd been friends with Patrick since their days at Oxford, so she'd been forced to become accustomed to his odious presence.

Patrick coughed awkwardly. "Shall we be seated?"

Everyone complied with tangible relief. As the only female, Cassandra was placed at the host's left. Rafe sat across from her, between Thomas Wakley and Lord Densmore. He looked displeased with the arrangement.

"Lady Rosslyn," Lord Densmore said in an artificial sugary tone, "I haven't seen you since you applied to attend Oxford last year after you'd shed your widow's weeds. It is a relief to see that you've recovered from such a fanciful delusion and have now taken a position more suited to your femininity." He looked over at Rafael, eyes narrowed in scrutiny.

"However, I must say your choice of protector is quite…unconventional."

Rafael stiffened and slowly turned his head to face the earl. His amber eyes took on a fiery glow.

Before she could make a warning sound, Thomas Wakley interjected, "Oxford, eh? What did you aim to study there?"

"Medicine." She fought not to stammer.

Densmore, Dr. Brewer, and Mr. Crowley guffawed. Cassandra tamped down a wave of humiliation. She had long since become accustomed to such ridicule. Yet it was difficult to feign composure in front of Rafael, the man who'd turned her life upside down, and Thomas Wakley, a man she idolized.

"A female doctor!" The apothecary wiped tears of mirth from his cheeks.

Rafael's lip curled up, revealing a glimpse of his fangs. Cassandra met his blazing gaze and shook her head in warning.

Wakley did not laugh. "Good for you, Lady Rosslyn. I have learned the most practical and effective medicinal treatments from nurses and midwives. In fact, if our dearly departed Princess Charlotte had had a midwife in attendance, rather than that bumbling fool Sir Richard Croft, she might have lived. I think it completely daft of academic institutions to exclude women from attaining a university degree."

The anger in Rafael's eyes dimmed as he raised his glass in Wakley's direction, still glowering at Lord Densmore. "An apt observation, Mr. Wakley."

Cassandra met his gaze and her heart turned over at his support.

"Didn't you also apply to the Royal College of Surgeons?" Densmore continued in his mocking voice. "I heard that Sir William Blizard laughed until he fell out of his chair."

Before Cassandra could respond, Wakley interjected, "The Council of the College of Surgeons remains an irresponsible, unreformed monstrosity in the midst of English institutions—an antediluvian relic of all that is most despotic and revolting, iniquitous and insulting on the face of the earth."

Brewer, Crowley, and Densmore gasped as if he'd spoken blasphemy. Rafael and Sir Patrick laughed and raised their glasses.

Densmore opened his mouth, doubtless to deliver a blistering retort, but Cassandra quickly spoke. "I've studied the first issues of *The Lancet*, sir, and I must say it is the most edifying medical publication I've read. I completely agree that only proven treatments should be published."

"Why, thank you, Lady Rosslyn." Wakley smiled. "Your praise is most humbling. Tell me, how long have you studied medicine?"

"Ten years. I've studied the texts of Galen, Vesalius, and de Luzzi, and have kept up with all current medical publications. I've also successfully stitched wounds without infection setting in, as well as having treated a variety of minor ailments for my servants."

Wakley stroked his chin. "If that is true, you'd be more than prepared for the Oxford examinations." Suddenly, he turned to Dr. Brewer. "Tell me, Doctor, if a man falls and cracks his skull open, how would you treat him?"

Dr. Brewer straightened his cravat. "First I would give the poor fellow laudanum to ease his suffering. Then I would bandage his head tightly, bleed him, and advise him to stay abed for a month."

"And what would you do, Lady Rosslyn?" Wakley queried, eyes intent, though with no trace of mockery.

Cassandra swallowed. "I would not allow the patient to sleep for several hours. I have read from many sources that victims of head injuries can die if they fall asleep. I would then carefully clean the wound of all debris and bone shards and stitch the wound shut. Afterward, the patient would be kept under continual observation for signs of fever or swelling of the brain. If swelling did occur, I would trepan the skull."

Brewer laughed. "You would close his skull and open it back up again?"

"If necessary." She nodded. "No two head injuries are alike. Surely you've learned that over the span of your practice."

The physician opened his mouth to protest, then closed it, shoulders slumping in defeat. "Yes, that is true, my lady. However, I cannot say I'd condone such a dangerous procedure."

"I regret interrupting such an edifying conversation"—Crowley's face had taken on a green-ish cast—"but I am being put off my meal. Pray could you leave off until we are finished?"

"Of course, Mr. Crowley," Wakley answered politely. "I apologize." He lifted his fork and tipped Cassandra a subtle wink.

Rafael remained silent throughout, nibbling halfheartedly on his meal. Cassandra realized she'd never seen him eat before. His house had not been stocked with food when she'd first arrived. Was he even able to digest solid food? Or were vampires limited to blood for their diets? She would have to ask him later.

The conversation shifted to the weather and continued through the remainder of the meal. Rafael resisted all attempts to engage in the dialogue, claiming that he was content to listen. However, he continued to stare at her with an intensity that was most unnerving.

When the table was cleared, Sir Patrick declared that as she was the only female, Cassandra did not have to retire to the drawing room while they enjoyed their port and cigars.

Boldly, she asked Rafael for one of his. She'd always enjoyed the smell of his cigars. *Hell, if I'm a fallen woman, I may as well act like it.*

The vampire gave her an odd look but held out his case for her to select one. He even lit it for her, using his good hand to strike a match with practiced efficiency. Everyone stared. Cassandra ignored them, pretending she was accustomed to having a dangerous Spaniard lighting her cigars. Despite her feigned indifference, she didn't know which held more heat: the flame or his gaze as he held the match.

Their fingers nearly touched. Cassandra drew deeper than she intended and exhaled carefully, trying not to cough. It had been months since she'd last smoked. Rafael's lips twitched with what looked like amusement.

"*Don* Villar, I have heard you are an infamous pugilist," Sir Patrick ventured.

"Not anymore," Rafael answered brusquely.

Dr. Brewer eyed his scars. "Is it because of your, ah, injury?"

"No." He did not elaborate.

Cassandra wondered if his duties as new Lord Vampire of London prevented him from boxing anymore.

Lord Densmore's voice was laced with skepticism. "How were you able to box with only one arm?"

"I am very fast."

Densmore leaned forward. "I am quite a proficient pugilist myself. Although *I* was trained at Gentleman Jack's, rather than Scallywag John's." His smug tone implied whose training he considered superior. "I don't suppose I could challenge you in the ring?"

"I said I've retired." The vampire's voice held a dangerous note.

Wakley looked at Densmore. "If you're looking to spar, I'd be happy to accept a challenge."

Densmore paled before lifting his chin. "I only spar with peers, though Villar's foreign title hardly counts, now that I think of it."

Dr. Brewer laughed. "More likely you've heard of Wakley's reputation."

Rafe eyed Wakley with speculative appreciation while Densmore's knuckles whitened with anger as he gripped the edges of the table.

Sir Patrick steered the discourse to more amicable territory. "Will you attend the auction tomorrow night, Lady Rosslyn? I heard that a genuine Van Leeuwenhoek is up for sale."

Cassandra gasped. "You're joking!"

"I am not." Sir Patrick grinned. "I swear it on my mother's honor."

Rafael raised a brow. "What is a Van Leeuwenhoek?"

She turned to him with a grin. "Van Leeuwenhoek invented a microscope that can magnify up to five hundred times. Even after more than a century, no one has been able to duplicate his miraculous lenses. If I had one, my research could rapidly progress."

"Not if I win it," Densmore drawled.

Cassandra ground her teeth. Before she could deliver a cutting retort, Sir Patrick announced that it was time to adjourn to the conservatory.

"*Hobbyist*," she grumbled loud enough for Densmore to hear as they filed from the room.

Rafael leaned down to whisper in her ear. "I could pummel him for you."

She laughed, unsure whether he was jesting or serious. "As much as I would love to see that, I do not think it will help his disposition."

Sir Patrick's conservatory was the most unconventional in London. Instead of housing orchids and roses, the room was a trove of fantastical curiosities. Skulls of various beasts adorned the walls alongside stuffed birds from around the globe and trophies of antlers, horns, and tusks. Shelves lined the chamber, displaying collections of rocks, shells, and fossils.

The men settled into various chairs and sofas cast off from the main house. Rafael remained standing in a corner near a mounted lion's head, cloaked in shadows.

"Ugly fellow, isn't he?" Lord Densmore muttered to Mr. Crowley.

Rafael's glare deepened as the apothecary nodded in agreement.

My God, he can hear them, Cassandra realized with

shock. Anthony had said vampires have exceptional hearing.

A lump formed in her throat as she remembered all the parties and gatherings the Duchess of Burnrath hosted at which Rafael had been a guest, likely against his will. He'd always been unobtrusively tucked in a dark alcove, wearing his hair down to hide his scars. Yet no matter how inconspicuous he'd tried to be, people noticed him. Cruel speculation and malicious whispers always abounded when the Spaniard was in attendance...and he'd heard them all. Cassandra's heart clenched in sympathy. No wonder he despised being out among people.

"I understand Lady Rosslyn is, ah, living in sin with him?" The apothecary flushed.

Cassandra flashed him a glare at his rudeness. It didn't require preternatural auditory function for her to hear his gossip. But he was too far in his cups to notice.

Densmore did, and gave her a leer before returning to his conversation. "I wonder what she sees in him. Not only is his face a veritable ruin, but with only one arm—"

"It's not his *arm* that interests me," Cassandra cut in coolly.

Rafael's gaze whipped in her direction. He looked like he didn't know whether to be outraged or pleased at her brazen remark. In truth, she surprised herself. Rafael was her jailer. Why did she feel the urge to defend him?

Mr. Crowley guffawed while Densmore fumbled for a response.

Wakley broke the uncomfortable silence. "How was he injured, my lady?"

"He will not say," she said pointedly. "And do not presume to ask him. He finds the subject most vexing."

Rafael gave her a grateful nod from the shadows across the room.

Cassandra found herself wishing she wasn't here. After all of her excitement and pleading to attend this party, all she wanted to do was whisk Rafael away from these nosy people and their rude questions.

I can't believe I want to rescue a vampire. Perhaps I am as mad as people say. She shook her head. She'd never given a damn what people said. Why should she start now?

Densmore grew more malevolent in his whispered remarks about Rafael as Thomas Wakley continued to speculate on his injury. Rafael's growing anger and discomfort became more apparent. They needed to leave before he punched someone—or bit them.

Cassandra crossed the room to stand at his side, leaving no doubt as to where her loyalties lay. Rafael's eyes widened as if he didn't expect her support. Now, standing with him, she once more questioned her feelings. *Why am I being loyal to my captor?* She lifted her chin. *Because nobody deserves to be treated the way he is.* The vampire could have drained them all. Instead, he bore their cruel remarks with stoic dignity. And it was not as if he had imprisoned her by choice.

She placed a hand on the vampire's sleeve, fighting back a wicked tremor at the minute touch. "I'm afraid I am coming down with a most dreadful headache. May we please go home, Rafael?"

He gave her a surprised look at her intimate use of his name, but nodded curtly.

Sir Patrick clucked sympathetically. "I'll order your carriage brought around."

Once they were ensconced in the carriage, Rafael said, "I did not need you to rescue me, Countess." He regarded her sternly. "And as for your earlier defense of my value to you, are you aware that those men thought you were referring to my—"

"Your cock?" Cassandra supplied helpfully, praying she wasn't blushing. "Yes, that was my intention."

He blinked in surprise and she felt a thrill of satisfaction that she was able to shock him.

Before he could scold her, she spoke again. "Wakley was attacked by vampires, wasn't he?"

Rafael nodded. "The previous Lord's third-in-command had seen Wakley repeatedly visiting St. Pancras cemetery at night and suspected him of being a hunter. He and the vampires who rest there knocked Wakley unconscious and set his house on fire, planning to kill him."

"Why didn't they just drain his blood?"

He sighed impatiently. "Because it is forbidden to kill mortals that way. It must look like an accident."

She frowned. "But what they did was no accident."

"Precisely."

"Is that why you saved Wakley?"

Rafael shrugged. "That and it didn't take too much investigation to learn that the man was innocent of any crimes against our kind. I only wish I could have arrived in time to stop them."

"What happened to the vampires responsible?"

"Ian jailed them for six months and made a decree that only the Lord of the city would handle matters with suspicious mortals from thenceforth." A dry laugh escaped his lips. "Which is how the damn fool ended up with a wife."

Cassandra blinked, curious as to what her friend really did to become the Duchess of Burnrath. "How—"

"It's a blasted long story." He looked out the window, pointedly not wanting to elaborate.

She settled back against the carriage squabs, sighing in disappointment. It had been such a fascinating conversation, and so…companionable.

The cold silence became unbearable. Cassandra broke it once more. "*Don* Villar, thank you so much for bringing me to the party. I know it was not an enjoyable experience for you."

"It was more tolerable than others." The scars on his face were tight.

"Yes, I can imagine. I myself do not care much for balls and musicales, though dinner parties with my colleagues are events I much enjoy. The intellectually stimulating conversations, the sharing of new discoveries…" She sighed in bliss. "About that auction…"

His brows drew together. "Don't push your luck, Countess." Rafael leaned forward until his knees nearly touched hers. "However, I have decided to bargain with you in regard to your other request."

"Oh?" Her traitorous body quivered at his proximity.

Rafael's voice was low and provocative as he answered slowly. "I will let you study me…in exchange for one thing."

Her breath caught. "And that would be?"

His burning gaze swept her with tangible intensity. "I want a kiss. One for each study."

Her heart lodged in her throat and her knees turned to water. Surely she could not have heard him correctly. "You want me to kiss you?"

"It is a human need I never quite outgrew." His black hair fell in a heavy sheaf, hiding the scarred half of his face. "Even the hardiest prostitutes are reluctant to provide me with that service, so I shall ask you."

Cassandra's mind and emotions roiled. How could he sound so cold, mentioning prostitutes even as he was speaking of the need for her kiss? And how could any woman be reluctant to do so? Were they frightened of his scars? The ones on his face were not even that prominent. Only a slight furrow of roughness along his temple and left cheek. She didn't find them frightening. They made him appear powerful, a survivor.

With predatory grace, Rafael leaned forward, placing a hand on each side of her hips. He moved closer until his face was inches from hers. "You did say you'd be willing to bargain *anything*, Countess."

She studied his lips, her mouth going dry at the sight of the wicked arches and sensuous curves. For over a year, she'd dreamed of being in his arms, tracing the faint ridged scars on his cheek as his mouth claimed hers.

"Yes," she said breathlessly, frightened at the deep well of desire within her soul. Had he read her mind? Was that why he was asking this? Was he toying with her?

Something fiery and primitive flickered in his eyes. "We have a bargain, then?"

Cassandra nodded and reached up to touch his face. He drew back and seized her hand and shook it as if she had sold him a piece of property, not her... She couldn't finish the thought.

He inclined his head respectfully and released her, leaning back against his seat. "We may begin tomorrow night if that is acceptable to you."

"That will be"—she struggled to breathe—"most adequate."

Thankfully, the carriage stopped, temporarily halting the perplexing situation.

Rafael gave her a long, penetrating look that made her shiver as he led her back into the house. "Now I must see about procuring my own supper. Until later, Countess."

As the door closed behind him, Cassandra released a long sigh that did little to quell the rapid thudding of her heart.

Six

5 October 1823

TENSION CHARGED THE AIR THE MOMENT RAFAEL entered Lady Rosslyn's laboratory for her first experiment. The fingers of his bad hand twitched as if aware of her presence. His stomach felt as if a leaden weight rolled around within. This had been a terrible idea. When she looked up from whatever gadget she was tinkering with, he opened his mouth to call the whole thing off.

"Brilliant. You're precisely on time," she said with a businesslike smile, picking up a horrifically sharp instrument. "I would like to start by collecting a specimen of your blood."

Rafe clenched his teeth. Damn her irrepressible courage. How could she face him so coolly, wielding what was surely a torture device? He couldn't allow her to have the upper hand.

He strained to return her smile. "Very well. How shall we proceed?"

Lady Rosslyn gestured to a chair at her right. "If

you would sit over there and, ah, roll up your shirt-sleeves, I w-would be most obliged."

Had that been a tremor in her voice? Rafe sat and studied her closer. Her hands shook as she placed the needle, a cloth, and two small squares of glass on a tray. The objects rattled on the tray as she carried it toward him. So she was nervous after all.

He frowned. Suddenly her trepidation didn't please him as much. She planned to stick him with that instrument, so it would be more comforting if she was confident about it.

Forcing a smile, he attempted to joke. "I say, Countess, I am unaccustomed to having *my* blood drawn."

Her eyes narrowed and her lip curled in anger. "Please do not call me that. It's only a courtesy title, a silly one at that…and I get the feeling you mock me with it."

Rafe blinked in surprise at her sudden shift in demeanor. A twinge of guilt gnawed in his gut. Perhaps he had mocked her a little. "What shall I call you then?"

"Well, as I cannot legally be addressed as 'Doctor,' Cassandra will have to do." Bitterness laced her voice.

"Cassandra…" For the first time since he'd performed the Marking ritual, Rafe tasted her name on his tongue and found it to be as rich as ever.

She shivered once more, so he decided to put her at ease before she came near him with that needle. "What made you want to become a doctor anyway?"

With the impressive amount of knowledge she'd displayed at the dinner party the previous evening, she must have harbored her ambition for some time.

Cassandra blinked at his inquiry, wide green eyes full of suspicion.

When Rafe continued to look on with polite interest, she sighed. "I've always been fascinated with how things work. I had a cuckoo clock when I was a little girl. One day it quit working and I opened it up to see what was inside."

Rafe chuckled and shook his head in admiration. "You disassembled an entire clock when you were but a child?"

Cassandra nodded, a nostalgic smile playing across her lush lips...lips he would soon claim. "As you can imagine, the mass of gears and cogs was quite over-whelming. I asked my father for a book on clocks. He was skeptical at first. I studied for months until I was able to understand how the devices function." Bending down in front of him, she took his hand and continued her story. "My clock had a worn gear. Papa took the gear to the clockmaker and had a new one made. I installed it myself and repaired the clock."

"Amazing," Rafe couldn't help saying aloud. He'd spent his childhood climbing trees and frolicking in the fields with his cousins. Had she had no one to play with? The thought prompted him to ask, "Were you an only child?"

She nodded indifferently, and before he was aware of it, she'd pricked the ring finger of his bad hand with the needle.

He chuckled, watching her place a drop of blood on one of the tiny glass panes and cover it with the other. "Sly wench."

How lonely she must have been without even

knowing it. Fighting back sympathy, Rafe leaned back in the chair. "What made you go from clocks to medicine?"

Her delicate face and form seemed to reverberate with a deep chord of pain. "My mother died a year later from dropsy. My father perished soon after from a heart ailment, just as my late husband did. Since then, I've been studying the human body and how it functions." She lifted her chin in determination and took a deep breath. "I may not have been able to save my parents, but perhaps I can save another little girl from becoming an orphan."

Rafe stared at her in wonder. Unlike most mortals who crumbled in the face of such misery, she had found inspiration and built her dream from loneliness and tragedy.

Cassandra blotted his finger with a clean cloth. Rafe could have told her to spare the effort yet he refrained, enjoying her touch. Slowly, she trailed her fingers along his forearm. He knew she was probing, examining, but it felt so good.

"How did this happen?" she asked suddenly.

He attempted a stern glare. "You will never give up until you hear the story, will you?"

"Of course not." She fixed him with an equally level gaze. "If I do not know the cause of an injury, it will be much more difficult to discern its treatment."

Rafe took a deep breath and let it out slowly. Very few knew the tale. But after hearing Cassandra's heartrending story, he felt that confiding in her would be a fair trade.

His good fist clenched at his side at the infuriating, humiliating memory. "It was my temper that did it. I was traveling to London. I'd just begun the journey and had taken up residence in a cave outside of San Sebastian for the day before I could catch a ship. Exhausted from traveling, I didn't wake up soon enough. A vampire hunter nearly staked me in the heart. I killed the man, but there was another one." Rafe closed his eyes as regret washed over him. "Blind with rage, I chased the other hunter out of the cave and into the sun. I had hold of him and didn't let go until my face and arm caught flame. I was such a fool."

"We all make mistakes." The compassion in her eyes was enough to undo him. She opened her mouth to say something else, then gasped, suddenly examining the finger she'd recently pricked more closely. "Your finger is healed!"

He nodded impatiently. "Yes, we heal very quickly most of the time."

"How?" she prodded, undaunted.

"I haven't the slightest notion." With her sitting so close that he could feel the heat of her body and smell her intoxicating female scent, he did not care. "I think you've done enough tests and observations this evening. It is time for my payment."

Her breath hitched and her cheeks flushed crimson, but she did not cringe in revulsion. Instead she moved her stool closer and gave his own words back to him. "Very well. How shall we proceed?"

Nearly drugged from her beauty and the warmth of her presence, Rafe reminded himself to tread with caution. He did not want to frighten her.

"Close your eyes," he whispered roughly.

Cassandra gave him a suspicious glance before she

obeyed. Reverently, he reached forward to caress her hair, wishing he could use both hands. The heady scent of rose petals perfumed the air between them, charging the narrowing chasm with promise. Savoring the softness of her skin, he trailed his fingers across her cheek before moving lower to grasp her chin. His cock hardened immediately.

Giving her ample time to pull away, Rafe leaned forward and pressed his mouth to hers. At first her lips were stiff and tense, but then they yielded in exquisite supplication. *Warm, so warm.* Hunger blazed within him, though not for her blood. What he wanted was more of this. He wanted to pull her closer, devour her mouth, and claim her heat as his own.

A soft moan escaped Cassandra's lips, making his cock harden further. Rafe pulled away before he lost control, biting back a growl of savage need.

Long lashes lifted to reveal sea-green eyes blinking up at him. "Fascinating…" she whispered.

Rafe stepped back farther, straightening his spine and willing himself to regain composure. "I believe that is satisfactory payment for now. I will leave you to your experiments."

Before she could respond, he left the laboratory, not daring to look at her lest desire overcame him and he hauled her into his arms.

"*Cristo,*" he muttered under his breath as he strode down the corridor to his study.

He'd never imagined that such a chaste kiss would have such a profound effect. Just one touch of Cassandra's luscious lips, and he was straining against his trousers like an untried lad.

Rafe sighed and lit a cigar, willing the tobacco and peace and quiet to calm the raging fires of his lust.

"My lord." Anthony entered the study, holding an envelope in shaking hands. "You've received a missive from the Elders."

The harsh chill of winter seemed to enter the room, stealing the breath from Rafe's lungs despite the merry glow of the fireplace.

"Give it to me and leave," he snapped, hating the way his voice cracked.

Anthony handed him the letter with a bow, as if hiding his reaction to Rafe's ire.

Eyeing the Elders' crest with dread, Rafe sliced open the envelope with a fang. He winced as the sharp edge of the paper cut his lip.

Lord Villar,

We commend you for your promptness in informing us of your prisoner and your summary of the circumstances and reasoning behind your decision to take this mortal into your custody. After our deliberation, we have decided that you shall have thirty nights to decide whether to dispense with this female or to submit a petition to bring her into our fold as one of your people.

We trust you will use your wisdom on this inconvenient matter and anticipate your response as soon as you've determined your course of action.

The letter was signed by all twelve Elders.

"*Cristo.*" With his good hand, Rafe crumbled the

letter as if the action could destroy its dire edict. Blood trickled into his mouth like an ominous portent.

⤙⤚

Clayton Edmondson paced the dusty floor of the abandoned warehouse, eyeing the gathering of vampires before him. Only thirty had deigned to arrive. For now that would have to be enough for his cause. If all went to plan, he would no longer be second-in-command. No, he would be Lord of London and that disfigured, pathetic excuse for a vampire, Rafael Villar, would be knocked from his throne and vanquished.

Bile rose in his throat at the thought of the Spanish cur. After decades of kowtowing to the Duke of Burnrath, London's true Lord, Clayton had only wrangled the position of third-in-command. Despite having only one fully functioning arm, Villar had been named second. The insult had never ceased to rankle, but soon it would be avenged.

Clayton surveyed his audience, allowing them to build up anticipation. He'd been a skilled orator since his mortal days on the stage. Proper delivery of his lines had never been more crucial.

Clearing his throat, he gave the assembly one more piercing stare before he began. "Blood drinkers of London, I have gathered you here today to bring attention to a grievous error made by our absent Lord. An error that, as members of this prestigious city, we must rectify if we hope to maintain not only our dignity, but perhaps even our safety."

His announcement was greeted with wide eyes and

curious murmurs. Clayton hid a smile of triumph. He had them in his palm.

He cleared his throat. "Though Ian surely meant well, I can no longer ignore the fact that he may well have brought ruin down upon us all when he put the Spaniard, Rafael Villar, in charge during his absence."

Most of the vampires nodded in agreement. However, a few exchanged skeptical glances. Clayton paused and straightened his spine. This would be the tricky part.

"I truly wanted to believe that Villar was a wise choice to lead us. Despite his foreign title, he lived as humbly as the rest of us. I believed he would do a better job looking after the interests of those of our unprivileged standing, which at times the Duke of Burnrath, being a blue blood, could not help but overlook." Heaving a mournful sigh, he met their gazes. "Tragically, I was wrong. From the moment Villar was declared interim Lord, received his wealth, and moved into the duke's palace, he has taken his place among the Quality and thus seems to think he's above the lot of us!"

Another vampire stepped forward. "I wouldn't say he's all bad. He's provided many of us with gainful employment and generous wages."

Clayton hid a grimace with a stiff nod of acknowledgment. There were bound to be naysayers. He anticipated such, and now he finally had the means to subdue them.

"That is true, but now I must tell you what the Spaniard has done." Pausing until he was certain he had their undivided attention, Clayton formed his features into a mask of regret for his next line. "Do you recall the several instances in which intruders were rambling about the St. Pancras cemetery? Intruders that may very well have been vampire hunters?"

Again, the majority nodded. A tentative voice inquired softly, "Wasn't Lord Villar supposed to have looked into the matter?"

Clayton infused his tone with sympathy. "Of course you all remember this frightening time. After all, a number of you take your day rest within the cemetery's crypt. Well, Rafael Villar has caught the culprit."

A cacophony of voices shook the rafters. Most sounded jubilant, though concerned about why they had not yet heard. Others sensed the ominous tone.

"Was it a hunter?" many voices echoed. "Did he kill the intruder?"

"No, he did not kill *her*." Clayton gestured, ignoring the first question. "William, come forward and tell them what the Spaniard has done."

William stepped out from the assembly as the audience processed the information that the culprit had been female. Clayton warned him with a glare and slight shake of his head to wipe the smirk from his face. Now was not the time for jubilance at this treason.

William complied, clenching his fists in mute rage. "He ain't treating her like a prisoner a'tall! Then he's treating Anthony and me like mortal footmen, ordering us to dust and fetch things for her. *And* he's allowed her to bring a servant to cook and wait on her, as well as all her gowns and frippery. Not only that, he's placed her in his own chamber! I think he means to have her as his fancy piece."

The vampire's testimony accomplished more than Clayton had hoped for. The assembly snarled and cursed in outrage, their affronted roars rattling the dusty windows.

Clayton held up a hand for silence and faced them with a sneer of his own. "Do you see the utter and complete negligence in Villar's actions? In failing to kill this woman when he caught her, as he was well within his rights to do, he has failed to protect you. It was his *duty* to destroy anything that threatens the blood drinkers of this city, but he has disregarded that duty."

He paced before them like a general, looking each vampire in the eye as he passed by. "The Spaniard has put us all in grave danger. Such callous behavior must be stopped. Alas, there is only one thing we can do, although it makes my heart ache with regret to say it."

"What can we do?" the vampires chorused, dangling on his line like caught trout.

Spine straight and stature firm as the times he played Julius Caesar, Clayton lifted his chin and said one word, projecting his voice to reverberate across the chamber like thunder: "Revolution."

Seven

7 October 1823

"My lord?" Anthony poked his head into Rafe's study. "A man is here to call on Lady Rosslyn. What should I tell him?"

Rafe set down Cassandra's copy of *Frankenstein* and fought back a grimace. He despised being interrupted when reading a good book. "*I'll* talk to him and decide what to tell him. Did you take his card?"

Anthony shrugged. "No, I hadn't thought of it."

"Some butler you're shaping up to be," Rafe muttered, drawing deeply on his cigar.

"I am a vampire, not a butler," his third retorted. "Perhaps you should hire Clayton instead. He is far more educated on the mores and rituals of the upper classes than I am."

Rafe raised a brow. "Would you *truly* wish to have him under our roof?"

Anthony shook his head vigorously. "Good God, no! I was only jesting. I can scarce abide that pompous ass for the duration of our meetings. And I know you can't either. *Why* didn't you replace him when you took over?"

"I couldn't risk inciting further malcontent. You know very well that my designation as interim Lord of London was not well received by many." He rubbed his temples, blowing out a cloud of smoke. *However, now I am reconsidering that decision.*

Clayton was doing a poor job as second-in-command. Not only was he neglecting to deliver reports on time and communicating only when pressed, but Rafe couldn't tamp down a wave of revulsion whenever he was near the vampire.

Anthony folded his arms and leaned against the door. "You shouldn't have to please them at the cost of ruling efficiently."

"Yes, but I must maintain peace in my city." Rafe ground out his cigar and stood. "I'll deal with Clayton when the matter with Lady Rosslyn is resolved. That way I can better attend to the upheaval that will result from sacking him. I had better see to Lady Rosslyn's caller. You may go hunt now."

Anthony smiled and gave him an exaggerated formal bow. "Very good, my lord."

As Rafe made his way down the stairs, he worked to conceal his irritation. When the Duke and Duchess of Burnrath departed for their honeymoon trip, he'd anticipated a few decades of peace and quiet with limited interaction with mortals. That peace had been destroyed since Lady Rosslyn came under his roof. And it seemed her captivity would cause further disruption. How many callers would he have to deter?

He wasn't surprised to find Thomas Wakley

waiting in the drawing room. The surgeon had been captivated with Cassandra at that blasted dinner party. Any fool could have observed that.

"Mr. Wakley, to what do I owe the pleasure of your visit?" Envy roiled in his gut at the sight of the man's handsome, unblemished face and strong arms.

The surgeon bowed. "I hope to speak with Lady Rosslyn."

"She is occupied at the moment. What is the nature of your interest in her?" The question ended more harshly than he intended.

Wakley chuckled. "I am not here to court her, if that is your concern. I am *very* happily married."

The tightness in Rafe's chest eased. "I am pleased to hear that. Would you join me for a cigar?"

"I do not smoke." The surgeon withdrew a parcel from his greatcoat. "The first reason for my visit is that I managed to outbid the odious Lord Densmore for the Van Leeuwenhoek microscope Lady Rosslyn coveted and thought she might like to purchase it from me."

"I'll buy it for her." Rafe reached in his pocket for his banknotes. "How much?"

Wakley grinned as they made the exchange. "That was simple enough."

"And your other purpose?" This time Rafe made his impatience clear.

The surgeon flushed. "Well, I, ah, could not help but be impressed with her ladyship's medical knowledge and I can hardly quell my outrage at the injustice of such a brilliant mind being barred from serving the community."

"Yes, it is an injustice indeed. A fact I am certain she is well aware of. Have you a point in reminding her?" Rafe drummed the fingers of his good hand on the side table.

Ignoring his warning tone, Wakley nodded. "Though it is not in my power to make her a real doctor, I can give her the same examination that is received at Oxford and perhaps offer her some training, so that she may at least gain some sense of vindication."

Rafe opened his mouth to refuse, yet the words caught in his throat at the man's logic and consideration. However, he couldn't risk further involvement with mortals, for him or Cassandra. Not until her fate was decided. And he still had no notion how he would resolve his predicament. Hell, he hadn't even told her about the letter from the Elders yet.

He coughed. "I—"

"Oh, Mr. Wakley!" Cassandra gasped in unabashed delight as she rushed down the stairs. "Would you?"

The surgeon nodded. "As long as you understand that it is only a ceremonial gesture."

"I understand." Cassandra's voice quavered with hope and gratitude.

Rafe hid the wrapped parcel by holding the microscope behind his back before she met his gaze.

Slowly, she approached him, her eyes deep pools of abject longing. "Rafael…?" The question hung in the air, tangible as an embrace.

He closed his eyes as his mind warred with his heart. She stood so close that her hair brushed his sleeve and he could smell her intoxicating scent.

Taking a deep breath, he uttered an impractical reply. "I am certain you shall pass with alacrity."

She could be dead within the month. The least he could do was allow her to touch her dream.

Cassandra rose on her toes and kissed him on the cheek. Her lips felt like a healing balm on his scars.

"Thank you." Her breath caressed his ear before she turned to Wakley. "Would you like to see my laboratory?"

"I would be honored." The surgeon ran a hand through his golden hair and smiled.

As Cassandra led Wakley up the stairs, Rafe hid her gift in his waistcoat pocket before he followed.

The moment they entered the laboratory, Wakley exclaimed in awe over every book and item. Rafe should have found it tedious. Instead he felt a warm surge of pride for his…prisoner. He frowned. She was his prisoner, nothing more.

"When will you give me the examination?" Cassandra asked suddenly.

Wakley smiled. "Right now if you like."

"Now?" She looked around her laboratory in confusion. "Won't we require a cadaver?"

The surgeon laughed. "No, though ideally you should have witnessed at least a few operations. I shall find out how knowledgeable you are during the examination. Shall we begin?"

"Yes." Cassandra bit her lip, looking so nervous that Rafe had the urge to pull her into his arms.

"Do you speak Latin?" Wakley asked.

"Yes, my father hired me a tutor."

"Greek?"

Cassandra nodded, a hint of pride gleaming in her eyes.

Wakley took one of her medical books from her shelf, opened it seemingly at random, and instructed her to read the page.

As her melodious voice poured out in flawless Greek, Rafe felt another wave of amazement. Along with his native tongue, he only knew Latin, French, and English, the last of which took him nearly a century to master. That was four languages in three centuries. Cassandra had learned as many in a fraction of the time.

"Now explain the treatment," Wakley said when she finished.

Though the response was in English, Rafe could barely grasp the meaning of her words. The reply satisfied Wakley. He gave her another book and pressed her to do the same in Latin.

"Very good, Lady Rosslyn." He proceeded to pose to her the same sort of questions as the one he'd first presented at Sir Patrick's dinner party.

Her answers were so brilliant, knowledgeable, and practical that Rafe could believe she'd been a practicing physician for years. His fist clenched at his side as anger roiled through him. She should have been able to take this examination officially.

After Cassandra answered the final question, there was a long moment of silence before Wakley began to clap.

"Very good, *Doctor* Burton."

She raised a brow and frowned in disbelief. "That was all?"

"For an Oxford-trained physician." Wakley's lips twisted in a bitter smile. "Gentlemen aren't supposed to dirty their hands. Now if you wanted to become a surgeon, you would need to undergo an apprenticeship, which I'm afraid would be impossible. No surgeon would take you on, and no one would allow a woman to operate upon their person."

Her chin lifted, eyes glittering with determination. "Could I learn on a cadaver? I've dissected them to learn anatomy as well as a few basic operations already."

Wakley chuckled. "Why, Lady Rosslyn, don't you know that it is illegal to harvest cadavers?"

"And dangerous," Rafe added, clenching his fists. If she hadn't been robbing graves, she wouldn't be in this situation. And Wakley never would have been attacked.

The mirth bled from Cassandra's sparkling green eyes, making him regret his words. Would she tell the surgeon who had been responsible for his attack?

A tense silence hung in the air before Cassandra uttered a strained laugh. "Come now, Mr. Wakley, do not attempt to deny that you do it as well."

The surgeon darted a nervous glance toward Rafe. "I suppose I could give you a few lessons, though not many, for I am busy with *The Lancet*. What would you like to focus on?"

Rafe shook his head and opened his mouth to protest. Cassandra ignored him.

"The musculature of the arms," she said firmly.

Wakley eyed Rafe's disfigured limb with a knowing smile. "A wise choice."

Cassandra also studied Rafe's arm, and for the first time since he'd become crippled, he wasn't discomfited by the scrutiny. This time he felt a gossamer thread of hope. What if he *could* be healed?

However, there was the matter of Cassandra remaining under his supervision. Rafe thought quickly. There was only one option, though he did not like it.

"You will have to teach her here," he told Wakley. "The cadaver can be stored in the icehouse." Another thought sprang to mind. "And do not harvest it from St. Pancras or Whitechapel. They are, ah, being patrolled, from what I understand." The last thing he needed was more grave robbers bothering his people. Or for Wakley to come under scrutiny once more.

Cassandra fetched her reticule from the desk in the corner. "Allow me to pay for procuring the specimen."

Rafe raised a brow. "*I'll* pay for it."

She blushed and turned back to Wakley. "When may we begin?"

"If only all students had your enthusiasm." The surgeon chuckled. "If my arrangements go as planned, I can be here tomorrow evening with a wagon. If not, I'll send a note. Now I had best depart before my beleaguered wife worries."

After Wakley left, Cassandra rushed to Rafe in a flurry of skirts. "Thank you so much for this. What can I do to repay your kindness?"

"I do not know if it was precisely kind." At the conclusion of her imprisonment, she might even call him cruel. Yet when he looked down at her flushed cheeks, glittering eyes, and parted lips, his lust took control of his mouth. "Kiss me, *Querida*. That is all I ask."

She sucked in a breath, whether from revulsion or anticipation, he could not tell. Then she stepped forward until her breasts pressed against his chest, warm even through the barriers of fabric between them. Slowly, she reached up with both hands and caressed his face before rising on her toes until her lips were inches from his.

"Like this?" she whispered and pressed her lips against his.

Rafe closed his eyes and savored the taste and feel of molten satin. Feather-light, her lips caressed him as if exploring the curves and angles of his mouth. He'd never before felt anything so subtly erotic. Immediately, his cock grew stiff.

Reaching out with his good arm, he pulled her tighter against him as he returned her kiss, feeding at her mouth like a man starved. He felt Cassandra's pulse accelerate, and a shiver ran down his spine when the tip of her tongue slid between his lips. Hot lust roared through his being, along with savage hunger.

With painful reluctance, he drew back before he lost his senses. "I need to go hunting now," he rasped. *Before I tear off your clothes and plunge my cock and my fangs inside you.*

Her white teeth nibbled her plump lower lip as she nodded.

He hurried down the stairs and out into the cold October night air. It wasn't cold enough.

❧

Cassandra slumped against the wall, shivering long after Rafael departed, though her body remained flooded with heat. What was it about his kisses that affected her so?

They had been nothing like her late husband's grand-motherly pecks by day and slobbery assaults by night.

Rafe's lips had been so warm, so gentle, yet firm with restrained, compelling danger. Perhaps he used some manner of vampire magic. Placing her hand on the wall, she steadied herself. *No.* There was no such thing as magic. And his mesmerism didn't work on her. There had to be a logical explanation for how he made her feel.

Her mind raced in circles, unable to formulate the slightest hint of a hypothesis. On shaking legs, she left the laboratory and went downstairs. Perhaps some tea would settle her fluttering stomach and slow her racing heart so she could think.

Mrs. Smythe failed to hide a yawn when Cassandra rang for her. "I apologize, my lady. These late hours your protector insists upon take getting used to. And I do wish he would hire more staff…and more efficient people as well. That Anthony means well, but he is simply not up to snuff. And that William…" Her eyes narrowed in disgust as she broke off. "I'll get your tea."

Protector? "Jailer" was more apt. However, she couldn't agree more about William. Aside from his insolence, there was something decidedly shifty about that vampire. She considered talking to Rafael about him but immediately dismissed the idea. She was a human prisoner. What say could she have on vampire affairs?

Mrs. Smythe brought her tea, hiding another yawn. "Thank you. You may retire now."

"Are you certain, my lady? What if you need something later?"

"I shall have Anthony or *Don* Villar see to it." Cassandra felt a pang of sympathy at the dark circles under the poor woman's eyes. "And please do not be up too early."

The housekeeper smiled gratefully. "Very good, my lady. If you don't mind me saying so, you should get some rest as well. You look flushed."

The observation made her blush further. Cassandra hid the reaction with a sip of tea, relieved when she was left alone. Dwelling on Rafael's effect on her was clearly dangerous to her constitution. Instead, she forced her thoughts to Wakley's visit.

"I passed the Oxford examination," she whispered aloud.

The words gave her a sense of pride, despite how anticlimactic the test had turned out to be.

"What was that, now?" William inquired from the doorway.

Her teacup slipped in her hands. "Nothing. I was only woolgathering." She winced as the hot liquid splashed on her fingers.

The vampire smirked. "Are you all right, Lady Rosslyn? You look feverish."

His eyes had a strange, glazed look to them, as if he had taken laudanum. Could vampires take laudanum? Or was he merely hungry for blood? Either way, his stare was most unsettling.

"I am well." Cassandra drank the rest of her tea, eyes watering as the hot liquid burned her throat. Trying not to shake, she set the cup on its saucer and stood.

His foggy eyes raked down her body. "You needn't leave on my account. I won't bite."

I wager you would if Rafael didn't forbid it. She wished he were here now.

"I am only tired." She curtsied stiffly and left the room without a backward glance.

Not wanting him to follow, Cassandra rushed up to the bedchamber she shared with Rafael and locked the door. Pacing the length of the room, she felt more like a prisoner than ever. Muttering under her breath, she cursed William's odious presence. Why couldn't it have been Anthony? He had such kind eyes and such a merry smile that his presence was never discomfiting.

The mantel clock ticked in time with her pacing. When would Rafael return from hunting? Hunting... He was out there somewhere biting someone and drinking their blood. *And I kissed him.* Shivering, she took some wood from the bin and fed the fire.

Sitting before the hearth, she watched the flames. They looked so much like his eyes when they glowed with preternatural heat. Mesmerized, she moved closer. A stray spark singed the back of her hand. Cassandra winced and rubbed the tender spot. How had Rafael borne his entire arm being burned? She shuddered at the thought of such pain even as her physician's mind wondered how deeply the damage went.

By the time Rafael returned and unlocked the door, her legs had gone numb beneath her. Heart pounding, she scrambled awkwardly off the floor as he entered the bedchamber.

He frowned at the sparking fire and took the poker, carefully adjusting the blaze. "Dawn approaches. Shall I help you with your gown now?"

Blushing, she nodded and turned around, trying

not to quiver at the feel of his fingers moving down her spine as he worked the buttons loose. When she stepped from behind the privacy screen, having changed into her nightgown, he'd already laid out a pallet in front of the door.

"Ah, did you have a successful hunt?" she ventured shyly.

He raised a brow and his lips twitched in a half smile. "Yes. Sleep well, Cassandra." With that, he lay down and rolled over to face the door.

Cassandra sighed and climbed into the large bed, wondering how long it would take to fall asleep despite the acute effect of the vampire's presence in the room.

Eight

8 October 1823

WHEN CASSANDRA AWOKE, HER PULSE RACED WITH anticipation. Thomas Wakley would be here this evening for her lesson. Shoving the bedcovers aside, she sat up and looked at the mantel clock, its face dim in the light of the fireplace's dying embers. It was a quarter after four. The sun would set sometime after five.

Her gaze strayed to Rafael. He was still asleep on his meager pallet on the floor. His dark brows creased in discomfort. Her heart gave a sympathetic twinge. With his damaged arm, sleeping on such a hard surface was surely painful. Could Wakley help her find the key to healing him? Or did the answer lie within the vampire's unique biology?

Lighting the oil lamp on the bedside table, she removed her journal and quill from the drawer. For the next hour, she scribbled notes on everything she knew about musculature and burn injuries, along with what she'd learned about vampires and their physiology, searching for something that would cross-reference.

Unbidden, she glanced at Rafael again, entranced by the sharp angles and curves of his lips. Heat flowed through her body at the memory of those lips against hers. As if sensing her stare, Rafael opened his eyes, his amber gaze trapping her breath.

"Good evening, Cassandra," he said softly. Stretching like a jungle cat, he rose to his feet with predatory grace.

Her nipples hardened under the thin fabric of her bedgown. "Good evening."

Folding her arms across her breasts, she carefully climbed out of bed and headed to the wardrobe before he could see the effect he wrought.

After he assisted with buttoning her gown, Rafael reached into the pocket of his greatcoat and withdrew a prettily wrapped package. "Wakley intended to sell you this thing. I purchased it instead," he said gruffly. "I presume it will be useful in your studies."

Cassandra opened the box and gasped. It was the Van Leeuwenhoek microscope. She nearly dropped the priceless instrument in her surprise. Joy, awe, and confusion warred within her mind as she stared at his gift.

"*Don* Villar…" she said softly. "Thank you. This will be invaluable to my work."

His sensuous lips—lips that had pressed against hers only last night—curved down into a scowl. "I think we are familiar enough with one another that you should call me Rafe."

She swallowed, thighs trembling at the potent memory. "As you wish, ah, Rafe." Her cheeks burned at addressing him in such an intimate manner.

His eyes flared intently. "I will join you in your laboratory after your lesson later this evening so you may resume poking and prodding me."

On weak knees, Cassandra sat back down on the bed after he departed. What were his motives in giving her such a priceless gift? Was the action akin to giving a mistress a bauble? After all, not only did all of London Society already believe she was Rafe's mistress, but her bargain with him was indeed similar to prostitution.

But he only wants me to trade him kisses, her mind protested. The hot pulse between her thighs while she was pondering those kisses argued otherwise.

Cassandra shook her head, fighting off the confusing emotions. Likely his gift was motivated by guilt at imprisoning her. She lifted her chin. He *should* feel guilty.

She had not asked to be hauled from her comfortable life and busy studies. And she most certainly did not ask to be imprisoned in his bedchamber every day, facing either death or transformation into a legendary creature that should not logically exist.

Unbidden, her speculative mind pondered such a transformation. Being forced to drink blood and suffer such vulnerability from the sun were distasteful prospects to be certain, but what of the advantages? Rapid healing, lack of aging, superhuman strength, speed to rival a hornet…those were quite tempting compensations. One would think that Rafe would be happier with such abilities and not act so surly.

Yet Cassandra couldn't help feeling a pang of sympathy for him. From the moment he'd removed his fangs from her throat, Rafe had made it clear that he did not want this situation any more than she did. In fact, she could almost believe that he detested the predicament more than she did.

Her brow furrowed. Was she destined to be a burden on everyone? From the time her parents died and she was taken into her aunt's home with obvious reluctance to the moment she was foisted off in marriage to a man who loved another, this had been the pattern.

Yes, Rafe's present was likely motivated by guilt. But what a glorious gift it was! Once more she caressed the finely made brass edges of the microscope. Either way, what was done was done. They could do no more than make the best of the situation. She with her fascinating new study, and Rafe with his kisses.

And there would be more this night. Cassandra's belly fluttered and a tender ache pulsed between her thighs. She frowned. Was she anticipating *that* more than her studies? No, that certainly wouldn't do. She was a *doctor*, not a mindless wanton.

What should be foremost in her mind were the questions she should ask Wakley tonight. Already, a multitude resided in the forefront of her mind, but first she must eat. That would be impossible later, with her stomach's irrational manner of pitching about whenever the enigmatic Spaniard was in her presence.

Her course of action decided, Cassandra took her microscope and made her way downstairs to the monstrous dining room, made even more cavernous by the shadows cast about in meager candlelight.

Anthony immediately emerged from the kitchens,

a soup tureen in one hand and a bottle of claret in the other. "Good evening, my lady," he said with exaggerated, albeit warm formality as he ladled the soup into her bowl.

Cassandra couldn't help but smile. "A vampire footman," she mused aloud. "How very original."

The vampire grinned, displaying a curious dichotomy of deadly fangs and charming dimples. "Only as you require the next course." As if to prove the point, he plopped down in the seat to her left, pulled the tureen in front of him, and sipped the soup directly from the ladle. "Mmmm. Salmon chowder."

Hiding a smile at his outrageousness, Cassandra tasted her own soup. The chowder was indeed delicious. Remembering the greasy fare she'd been served her first night here, she reminded herself to thank Rafe once more for allowing her to bring her cook.

"I say, what the bloody hell is that thing?" Anthony interrupted her thoughts, frowning at her microscope. "It looks like something devised by the Marquis de Sade!"

Cassandra raised a brow. "Who?"

"Never mind. I forget I am in the presence of a lady." Unbelievably, the vampire appeared to be blushing.

Shaking her head at his incongruous reaction, she explained, "It is a Van Leeuwenhoek microscope."

"A what?" Anthony's brows creased.

Cassandra sighed. Did nobody read these days? "It is a device that allows me to see the fine details of the smallest things. This one is said to magnify five hundredfold. I hope to observe Rafe's blood cells and see how they compare to mine."

"What are cells?"

By the time Cassandra finished explaining, her soup had gone cold and Cook was making tsking sounds at Anthony from around the corner. With a murmured apology, he swept away the tureen and her bowl and returned with a platter of roast beef.

"So you mean to learn more about what makes Rafe and me what we are," he said as if the delay hadn't occurred. "Fascinating. This whole time I thought it was magic. I never entertained the notion that science could explain us."

Cassandra fixed him with a level stare. "Science can explain everything."

"I don't know about that. I'd rather believe in miracles. By the by, I couldn't help but notice your preoccupation with Rafe's injured arm. Do you intend to heal it?"

She nodded and replied with a confidence she didn't feel. "I mean to try."

The vampire's eyes widened. "You cannot fathom what it would mean for you to succeed."

"I always welcome a challenge." Cassandra toyed with the food on her plate and attempted to keep her tone light, but Anthony's severity resonated within her mind. For a man...vampire...like Rafe, what *would* regaining at least some use of his arm mean for him? Her heart thrummed. No, she could not fathom. However...she could imagine.

"Do you have any idea how you'll go about it?" the vampire interrupted her thoughts.

Cassandra touched the smooth, unblemished skin on the side of her neck where Rafe had bitten her.

"I do, but I am afraid I will need the assistance of another vampire."

Anthony leaned forward, all the playfulness gone from his features. "I'm your man."

This time, Cassandra couldn't hold back an answering grin. "I had hoped you'd say that."

True to his word, Anthony followed her up to the lab and complied with her requests and, most importantly, endured her syringe with no complaint.

With just as much aplomb, the vampire bowed. "I hope this will work, my lady."

"I do as well," Cassandra agreed emphatically. "I have reason to believe—" Her words broke off as she looked around the laboratory and noticed a change. Four gas lamps had been placed in the corners of the room. Lamps that could illuminate the chamber like daylight.

Her lips parted in awe. "Did *Don* Villar do this?"

Anthony nodded, a strange smile curving his lips. "He seemed to think you need more light for your work, but isn't this a trifle excessive?"

Cassandra shook her head. Again, that strange warmth curled through her at Rafe's thoughtfulness. "No, this is perfect! Please, light them all."

Before Anthony could reply, she dashed past him down the stairs and out to the icehouse. Teeth chattering from the frigid air, she seized the chilled vials containing samples of her blood as well as Rafe's. Her heart pounded with exhilaration at the prospect of a new discovery.

Once back in her laboratory, Cassandra prepared slides of hers and Rafe's blood with utmost care. The gas lamps were so bright that they nearly made her eyes water. Sucking in a breath, she positioned the microscope close to one of the lamps, angling it for the best possible illumination. Willing her hands to cease shaking, she carefully positioned the specimen of her blood below the lens. Would the Van Leeuwenhoek truly be able to show her blood cells?

It did. Cassandra gasped at the tiny specimens. Not only was she able to see the red cells, but the often-doubted presence of white corpuscles was apparent. Quivering with excitement, she replaced the slide with one containing Rafe's blood. Just as she'd suspected, there were obvious differences. His red blood cells appeared to be denser and were more oval in shape. Also, there were nearly twice as many white corpuscles than her sample contained.

Checking for consistency, she made a slide of Anthony's blood. His specimen displayed the same anomalies as Rafe's. There were also some oval-shaped cells in both vampires' blood samples that differed from hers. Unfortunately, she couldn't magnify the slides well enough for a sufficient view.

"Fascinating," she said softly as she grabbed her notebook to make sketches and record her observations.

Anthony interrupted shortly afterward. "Thomas Wakley has arrived, my lady. He has brought a corpse." His mouth twisted in disgust. "I'm going to have to heft the thing up here, aren't I?"

"Most likely."

Wakley grinned when she greeted him in the drawing room. "Lady Rosslyn, I have the perfect specimen. Male, aged twenty-eight, and he died only two days ago. Nice and fresh."

"Splendid."

Anthony grimaced. However, he assisted Wakley in hauling the linen-shrouded corpse up to the laboratory without complaint, although he was looking quite green about the gills when he left them alone.

Cassandra and Wakley each donned aprons, took up a scalpel, and began making incisions in the arm. Wakley explained the function and connection of each muscle, showing her which tendons were most susceptible to damage. They worked quickly, before the scent of decay became unbearable.

When they finished, Wakley covered the specimen with the shroud and removed his apron. "You intend to operate on *Don* Villar's arm, don't you?"

"Perhaps."

His blue eyes narrowed. "I should help."

"I am not certain he would permit it." She avoided Wakley's gaze. It wouldn't do for a human to witness the methods with which she intended to experiment. She changed the subject. "What would you recommend to treat pain during and after a surgery?"

Wakley ran a hand through his golden curls. "Unfortunately, very little can be done during the actual cutting. I suppose you could give him laudanum or perhaps coat your scalpel in a tincture of morphine. Some fellows are experimenting with ether and nitrous oxide, though the latter may be more difficult to procure. As for afterward, I would recommend cannabis. I have found the herb to be effective on muscle spasms and other ailments."

Cassandra smiled gratefully as she put away her scalpel and jotted down a list. "I cannot thank you enough. When will you be able to give me another lesson?"

"I cannot come tomorrow. I have a lecture scheduled as well as more work on *The Lancet*. Perhaps the night after?"

"That is agreeable." She rang for Anthony.

Wakley stroked his chin, suddenly looking speculative. "Lady Rosslyn?"

"Yes?"

"The enterprise that you are about to undertake is admirable and ambitious. I would very much like to publish a portion of your results in *The Lancet*."

Her breath caught as one of her most secret dreams was voiced. "You want me to write for *The Lancet*?"

He nodded. "Anonymously, I'm afraid. If word got around that the articles were penned by a female, my journal would be discredited."

"You wish me to write about the surgery?" The implications of his request chased away her elation. Rafe was a vampire and the operation she planned was unlikely to work on humans. And that would surely be more damaging to *The Lancet* than studies published by a dowager countess.

He shook his head. "Alas, no. Though it could very well prove to be a monumental medical breakthrough, I'm afraid that the mere mention of such an unprecedented operation would raise far too many questions among our peers. Instead, I would like you to reveal your observations on the various anesthetic treatments you'll be trying."

"I would be honored." She couldn't keep the palpable relief from her voice. Joy suffused her being. Writing for *The Lancet*! *Her*! Making a contribution to the best medical journal in Christendom!

Anthony arrived before she abandoned propriety and dissolved into girlish vapors.

Once the cadaver was stored in the icehouse and Wakley had departed, Cassandra gave Anthony the list of supplies she'd require from the apothecary and returned to the laboratory to examine Rafe's blood.

As she was placing the slide under the microscope, a shadow fell over her.

"Is my gift pleasing to you?" Rafe's voice slid over her flesh like warm silk.

The slide fell from her numb fingers to shatter on the floor. "Yes, *Don* Villar."

His eyes narrowed on the shards of glass at her feet. His scowl deepened as he met her gaze. "I thought I told you to call me Rafe."

Cassandra's knees trembled as she avoided his gaze and fetched a broom. "I–I'm sorry. I am unaccustomed to informality. That is not how I was raised."

Her explanation seemed to vex him further. "Give me the broom," he growled, snatching it from her grasp. "It is my fault you dropped...whatever that is, and only fair that I clean it up."

With amazing dexterity, he swept up the broken glass with his one good arm, fetched a dustpan, and removed the mess, only experiencing momentary awkwardness with the last. "Does it have to be so goddamned bright in here?"

Cassandra stiffened. "You could ask me nicely to turn them down."

"I apologize, Cassandra." Something flashed across his features before his countenance softened. "I was dwelling on some unpleasant news." He strode over and extinguished one of the lamps before she could reach it. "I'll leave the others on for whatever you intend to do with me tonight."

Not knowing how to respond to his odd shift in demeanor, Cassandra moved a chair into the light and got straight to business the moment he sat. "W-well, Rafe, I would like to try something, but I'm afraid I will need to cut you."

One black brow rose. "*Cut* me?"

Biting her lip, she nodded. "Not too much, only a tiny incision on your left *extensor carpi ulnaris*."

Now both brows lifted. "My *what*?"

"Roll up your sleeve and I will show you."

Rafe complied and Cassandra choked back a gasp at the still formidable muscles displayed under his scarred flesh. Tentatively, she reached out and caressed a section of his forearm. "This, right here."

"Very well." Rafe sighed. "And do not worry about hurting me, I have little sensation there." After a long pause, he frowned. "Won't you require a blade?"

Cassandra glanced down. Her finger was still trailing lightly up and down the muscle.

Cheeks burning at the inappropriate contact, she snatched her hand away and crossed the room to fetch a small table and a clean scalpel. "Now, rest your arm on the table and keep it still. I do not want to cut anything vital."

Taking a deep breath and whispering a silent prayer for steady hands, she made the incision on his forearm. Not daring to meet his gaze, she retrieved the fresh vial of Anthony's blood along with a dropper.

"That appears to be blood," Rafe commented, though he sounded more perplexed than disturbed.

"It is," she said agreeably and began dripping the ruby liquid into the incision. Immediately the cut began to knit back together.

Rafe placed his good hand on her shoulder, squeezing it with almost enough pressure to hurt. "*Whose* blood is it?"

"Anthony's," she whispered, worry curling in her stomach at his intent gaze. Had she caused him harm?

Her alarm deepened when he froze for what seemed to be an eternity.

"*Cristo,*" he breathed at last. "I should have considered something so simple." Suddenly, he went rigid, eyes widening. "*Dios mío!*"

Cassandra placed her hand on his. "Did I hurt you? I swear, I did not intend—"

"*Hurt* me?" A harsh burst of laughter escaped his lips. It was a rusty sound, as if long disused. "I can feel it! Hell, I can *move* it. Look!"

Sure enough, the tip of his ring finger was bending back and forth. This time, it didn't twitch. This time, it moved with *purpose*. Not only that, but the scarring had diminished slightly where she'd cut him.

"*Saint Jude.*" Triumph swelled in her breast. "It worked!"

Gleefully, she fetched her notebook and jotted down the success of her procedure.

"You have my eternal gratitude, my lady." Rafe's voice was laden with wonder. "For this, I will rescind my demand for payment."

Cassandra's gaze whipped back to him, taking in

his silken mass of obsidian hair, cinnamon-tinted skin, amber eyes, and wickedly sensual lips. What woman in her right mind would not want to kiss such a striking man?

"Nonsense," she replied, surprised at the low, throaty cadence of her voice. "We had a bargain."

Those exotic eyes flickered with heat. "Are you certain you still wish to honor it?"

Ignoring her quaking legs, she managed a level nod. "I do."

Before she had time to gather her breath, Rafe rose from the chair and snaked his good arm around her shoulders, pulling her tightly against his firm body. His bad arm draped about her waist, fingers lightly caressing her hip. Hot and cold tremors wracked her entire being, and he hadn't even begun. Cassandra stared up at his feral, glowing eyes as he bent to claim her lips.

Unlike last night's gentle teasing, this was an assault. A low growl trickled from his throat, sending shivers up her spine as his mouth crushed against hers. Cassandra melted into his embrace, lips parting in welcome hunger for his kiss. Like quicksilver, his tongue darted in, tangling with hers in a forbidden dance. Electric frissons coursed through her form as liquid heat pulsed below. Desperate whimpers escaped her lips as she pulled him closer, deepening the kiss.

Rafe broke away with a hiss. "I must go before I lose control and…"

"And?" her treacherous mouth prodded.

His eyes smoldered and his fangs glistened in the gaslight like the predatory devices they were.

"It would be best not to continue this conversation."

Before she could respond, he left the room like a flickering shadow.

Legs weak, Cassandra stumbled to the chair he'd been sitting in only moments earlier and collapsed. Her heart pounded, her nerves tingled, and her legs felt like custard. All thoughts of her successful experiment had fled from her mind like birds from an open cage.

What was happening to her? What was it about Rafe that evoked such irrational reactions from her body and dissipated her reasoning?

Cassandra heaved a sigh. As far as she knew, no tests or documented information could explain her predicament.

Nine

RAFE AWOKE THE NEXT EVENING TO A STRANGE, YET not unpleasant tingling in his left arm. The sensation flowed all the way down to his fingertips, gaining in intensity. Holding his breath, he concentrated, willing the digits to move. Two fingers complied, creaking like rusted hinges.

"*Dios mío*," he said softly, rising up from where he reclined on the floor of his bedchamber. It hadn't been a dream.

Cassandra had worked a miracle.

Rafe shook his head. Vampire blood. It was so simple. All this time he'd been using his own blood to heal the puncture wounds of the humans he fed on, but he'd never thought that the same principle could apply to himself. Hell, aside from his maker, he'd never even fed on another vampire, not caring for the idea of such intimacy. And after he was burned, he never considered it because of his ugliness.

A derisive laugh escaped his lips as he leaned against the door. Neither had anyone else of his kind.

At the sound of his laughter, his prisoner stirred. A hot jolt of lust speared him at the sound of rustling sheets. If only he were up there on that bed with her.

"Rafe?" Cassandra's voice, velvety from sleep, further inflamed his desire.

Avoiding the delectable sight of her tousled hair and slumberous eyes, Rafe concentrated on getting to his feet. "It is me, *Querida*. I'm going to hunt. I'll send a servant up with your breakfast and return in time to help you dress. You must attend a meeting with me later tonight."

"I propose an alternative course of action," she replied, all drowsiness fleeing from her face. Her russet brows drew together in willful determination.

Disappointment crept through him at her all-too-familiar analytical tone. He was now speaking with the scientist, not the woman. Somehow that did nothing to quell his lust.

Fixing her with a stern gaze that would make anyone else cringe, Rafe replied in a low and silken tone, "And what would that alternative be?"

"Help me dress now and take me with you." Rising from the bed like a queen, Cassandra looked so cool and undaunted that he nearly missed the blush in her cheeks and the faint tremor in her voice. "I want to watch you, ah…take sustenance."

"No." Revulsion curdled in his gut at the thought of Cassandra watching him prey upon a human like the monster he was.

Her lush lower lip pouted. "Why not?"

His fist clenched at his side as he fabricated an excuse. "It would be dangerous…and unseemly to bring a mortal woman to my usual hunting grounds."

"That is entirely illogical." Her auburn curls danced in the lamplight as she shook her head. "For one thing, you are capable of protecting me. For another, if the possibility still remains that I am to be transformed into a vampire, should I not learn how to feed myself?"

He bit off a curse. Again, her reasoning trounced his. Her scent filled his awareness, beckoning his blood thirst with intoxicating temptation.

Rafe ran his tongue along his fangs. "Because, *damn it*, if I do not leave now, I'm going to lose control of my hunger and make *you* my sustenance, Countess."

Cassandra's eyes widened, yet still she did not flinch. "The need is *that* intense, then?"

He nodded and bared his fangs further to reinforce his point.

"Perhaps you could drink from me." Her blush intensified, crimson on alabaster. "At least enough to, ah, tide you over."

Rafe couldn't stop his ravenous gaze from caressing her ripe form, maddeningly shrouded beneath the folds of her voluminous nightgown. The smooth column of her neck was bare, flooding him with memories of its satin heat against his lips. His cock hardened.

Her offer was too enticing to resist. Of their own volition, his feet carried him closer. "Just a taste."

Cassandra shivered, inciting his predatory instincts. He seized her arms, reveling in the warmth of her skin. For a long moment, Rafe was content to merely stare at her, drowning in the deep, sea-green pools of her eyes, admiring the sculpted perfection of her features and the decadent curve of her mouth.

Though he should feel guilt for holding such a treasure in his monstrous grasp, he couldn't manage more than a wisp of contrition. She felt too damned good.

And she tasted even better. As Rafe slowly plunged his fangs into her flesh, he couldn't hold back a groan of pleasure at her sweetness. A soft, provocative sound escaped Cassandra's lips as her body melted against his. The feel of her firm, round breasts pressed to his chest brought forth another dangerous wave of desire.

With painful reluctance, Rafe withdrew his fangs, not yet willing to relinquish her. Prolonging this moment as long as possible, he licked her puncture wounds, savoring every last flowing drop of her blood and Cassandra's hot, panting breath against his ear. Her hand tangled in his hair, sending delicious shivers down his spine. Unable to resist, Rafe ground his hardness against her as his tongue strayed from her wound to explore the delectable curve of her neck.

"Rafe..." Cassandra moaned. "Please..."

Her soft, imploring voice slammed into his awareness like a hammer on an anvil. Was she begging for him to continue or to stop? Either was proof that the moment had become dangerous. If he didn't stop now, he would ravage her, despite his promise to the contrary.

Rafe broke away before her seductive fire could burn him any further. "Procure a gown," he said through clenched teeth. "And a scarf as well, to cover your wound."

She blinked up at him in confusion and put a

shaking hand to her neck. "Why will you not heal it this time?"

"Tonight I must present you to my people and explain this…situation. It would be best if they saw visible evidence of my claim on you."

Is that your only reason? his sardonic inner voice taunted. As he took in the vision of her flushed cheeks, rosy lips, and still heaving breasts, Rafe closed his eyes to blot out temptation. What sane man wouldn't want to claim this woman in every way?

Cassandra stiffened, eyes narrowed in outrage. "Do you mean like a brand?"

"In a manner of speaking." Rafe sighed. Only moments ago he'd had his fangs in her neck and been on the verge of ravaging her senseless, and she was concerned about *this*? The woman was unbelievable. "Now hurry and find a dress. I am still hungry."

Still huffing, Cassandra did as bidden. As he laced up the back of the forest-green velvet gown, Rafe gritted his teeth with the effort to not lick her creamy back and shoulders. Already, he was addicted to the taste of her.

"Unbelievable," he muttered under his breath.

"What did you say?"

He shook his head. "Nothing. Put on your cloak. I'll fetch you a pasty from the kitchen."

She inclined her head in acquiescence, threw on the heavy, black wool garment, and followed him down the stairs.

"Unbelievable," Rafe muttered once more as they walked the gaslit streets.

Cassandra paid him no heed. She was far too

occupied with juggling her massive journal and quill, with a meat pasty held in her teeth in a most un-countess-like manner. He constantly had to steer her shoulders to prevent her from colliding with lampposts.

As they passed his favorite tobacconist, Rafe couldn't resist the urge to pop in and view the new wares. The proprietor was the only one in Town who kept his doors open after nightfall, and Rafe paid him a hefty sum to keep doing so.

"You're taking sustenance here?" Cassandra glanced up from her scribbling.

"No. I want to look at the cigars."

"Why?"

"I like to smoke."

There were no new varieties to sample, so Rafe purchased a box of his favorite Cuban cigars and a pouch of a good Turkish blend for his pipe. He bit back a smile at Cassandra's moue of distaste when Sampson offered her a sample of snuff.

Once they left, she returned to her note-taking. Rafe shook his head. Did she presume that vampires lacked hobbies?

Shortly after they reached Covent Garden, snide whispers caught his ears.

"Look, Victoria. It's *Lady Rosslyn*!"

"Good heavens, it is! So the rumor is true, then. She's taken up with *him*!"

Two ladies leaving the opera peered at them insolently above their fans, tittering maliciously. Rafe favored them with a glare, while putting a protec-tive arm around his countess. Cassandra glanced up distractedly and nodded politely as she saw the other

women. The pair of bitches lifted their noses and
crossed to the opposite side of the street with such
pointed haste that their foppish escorts had to dash
after them.

"Stupid *coños*," Rafe growled, pulling Cassandra
closer to shield her from such spite.

"Hmmm?" she murmured, chewing on the last bit
of the pasty.

"They are snubbing you because they believe you
are a fallen woman." He spat in their direction. "As if
their morality is lily white."

Cassandra blinked at him. "Why should I care
what they think? I am no longer obligated to be part
of their world, and to be truthful, I am quite relieved
by that fact."

Rafe shook his head in bemusement. This woman
would never cease to surprise him. In his mortal days,
if his stepsisters had been snubbed in such a manner,
they would have been devastated and taken to their
beds. As daughters of the wealthiest *don* in Navarra,
they thought nothing was more important than pre-
serving their social status.

"How do you select a person to be your, ah, meal?"
Cassandra interrupted his nostalgic reverie. "Do you
seek out the weak ones, like a wolf?"

He raised a brow at her cool inquisitiveness. "All
humans are weak compared to me."

She cocked her head to the side. "How do you
choose?"

"Discretion is the main priority. Our kind cannot
allow mortals to retain knowledge of our existence."
Rafe's sensitive hearing picked up a light cough from

a nearby alley. "Which is why we shall be going this way. Now be quiet."

Cassandra complied, tucking her journal under her arm as she pulled an ink blotter from the pocket of her cloak to replenish her quill. Rafe paused at the alley's entrance, lifting his gaze to the heavens. Why had he agreed to this?

Unfortunately it was too late to turn back and take her home. Already the scent of prey teased his nostrils, inflaming his blood thirst to a fevered pitch. He needed to feed now. Giving Cassandra one last look, he stalked his victim, praying she wouldn't muddle up this hunt.

As Rafe's shadow passed over the vagrant hunched against the wall, the man looked up and gave him a toothless grin. "I say, guv'nor, could ye spare a shilling or two?"

"Of course." Rafe immediately captured the man's gaze, pulling his waking mind under a sea of unconsciousness. With a gesture and mental command, Rafe made the man stand.

Just as he bared his fangs and prepared to strike, Cassandra whispered, "What is wrong with him?"

Rafe turned to face her. She was far more preferable to the filthy unfortunate before him. Like comparing claret to rotgut. Forcing his attention back to the matter at hand, he explained, "I have taken his mind under my power so that he will neither feel nor remember this moment."

"How?"

Grinding his teeth in impatience, he fought off a growl. "How am I to know? It is just the way it is done." Before she could interrupt again, Rafe seized the man by the collar and sank his fangs into his meal.

As anticipated, the blood was tepid and bland compared to Cassandra's heady vintage. Rafe continued to drink until his hunger was sated. Then he released his victim and turned back to Cassandra. She did not recoil in terror or even flinch. Instead, she continued to jot down her observations in that infernal journal.

Now she peered at him over her quill as if he were a specimen in her laboratory. "How much blood did you take?"

Rafe sighed at her clinical tone. "A trifle more than a pint. Now I shall release him."

The scratching noise of the quill returned as the man's eyes regained awareness. Rafe handed him a guinea.

"Bless ye, guv'!"

Rafe stepped back before the man could grasp his lapels and grovel.

"Fascinating," Cassandra said as he led her out of the alley. "You do this every night?"

He nodded curtly, exasperated with her tenacity. "Usually twice. Do you think you could handle doing this every night for the rest of eternity?"

Her eyes widened before she quickly looked away. At last he'd cracked her composure. "I am…uncertain. I suppose I would have to do whatever is necessary… and…it doesn't seem as if it causes lasting harm." She fidgeted with her journal and quill. "In fact, it's much like bleeding a patient, which doctors have prescribed for centuries."

Irritating though it was, Rafe admired her rationality in the face of such dire prospects.

She looked up at him with intensity that stole his breath. "Do you mean you've decided my fate?"

Something raw and harsh knotted in his stomach. "I have not."

God help him, but he was already resigned to the fact that he didn't want to kill her.

❧

Cassandra's curiosity rose with every new detail Rafe revealed about his world. "How did you become a vampire?" she whispered after making certain the streets were empty.

For a moment he looked as if he wouldn't reply, but then he answered. "My *tío*, my uncle, Changed me… or rather, my great-great-uncle, three centuries ago. He wanted a wise Villar to always be around to watch over the family while he had to be away from the country."

"You still have family?" She gasped, feeling a twinge of envy at his nod. When he didn't elaborate, she asked, "How were you Changed?"

"He drank my blood until I was nearly drained, then he cut his wrist and I drank it back."

She stoked the feather of her quill against her chin. "So the catalyst is in the blood. Is that what you will do to me then?"

A dark, chilling expression crossed his features before he spoke. "We will discuss that later. It is time for me to present you to my people. Remove your scarf. I must blindfold you."

Cassandra froze with her journal half stuffed into her reticule. "How am I supposed to make my way through these dark streets? I can hardly see as it is."

Rafe gave her a long, considering look. "I will carry you."

"But your arm—" She broke off as pained anger slashed across his harsh features.

"Remove the scarf." His voice promised dire consequences if she didn't comply.

With shaking hands, she closed her reticule and obeyed. Rafe snatched the length of wool from her grasp and looped it around her head with inhuman speed. His fingers curled in her hair as he deftly knotted the fabric with one hand, making her shiver. Before Cassandra could process her sudden blindness, Rafe's arm snaked around her waist, lifting her to rest against his hip.

"Wrap your legs around me and hold tight," he whispered into her ear.

Surely he cannot be serious! The protest died in her throat as he hitched her up higher. The world tilted, and before she realized what she was doing, her thighs grasped his waist as if she belonged there. Immediately, Rafe burst forward with the speed of a pistol shot. Cassandra shrieked and flung her arms around his shoulders, burying her face against the side of his neck as if she could retreat from the biting wind. Surely no human was made to travel at such unnatural speed. She squeezed her eyes shut, praying he wouldn't drop her.

Awareness of their intimacy flooded her senses. *His skin is like rough satin*, an inner demon mused. Rafe's spicy scent and his heat seeped into her body like forbidden confections. His hair brushed across her fingers, impossibly soft. The myriad of new sensations made Cassandra's heart pound.

Rafe stopped so abruptly that her stomach lodged in her throat. "We're here. It is best if you do not speak."

He set her down, bracing his good hand on her shoulder while she regained her balance. Once her dizziness fled, Cassandra reached for the blindfold.

"Not yet," he commanded. "Take my hand and I will lead you."

She took a deep breath and reached for him. *I will not be afraid.* As his strong fingers laced with hers, she could almost believe that declaration—until the ominous creak of a heavy door sent her pulse to her throat.

"There will be a lot of steps. Just walk slowly." Rafe squeezed her hand and gently led her forward. "I will not let you fall."

Carefully, Cassandra proceeded. *I will not be afraid.*

For an eternity, the only sound was her boots echoing on the cold stone stairs. Then, whispers and mutters crept into her ears like the voices of sinister specters. The noise gradually escalated, picking and pulling at her nerves until thin tremors shook her.

"One more step," Rafe said softly.

She felt his fingers gently untying the knot of the scarf. The fabric loosened, and for a moment his touch seemed to linger in her hair. Then the blindfold fell and candlelight blurred in her vision like captive stars.

"Blood drinkers of London…" Rafe's voice echoed through the chamber in stark command. "As most of you have heard, circumstances have forced me to take a prisoner. This is Lady Cassandra Burton, Dowager Countess of Rosslyn. As Lord of this city, I have brought her here so you may all look upon her, feel my Mark, and know that to touch her is to risk my wrath."

Cassandra choked back a gasp as the vampires came into view. More than a hundred of them loomed before her, and they did not appear pleased to see her. Glowing eyes and sharp fangs gleamed unnervingly from faces that otherwise appeared human.

Her only consolation was that she and Rafe stood upon a raised dais several feet from the masses.

One of the vampires bared his fangs, making her rethink her safety. The wound on her neck from Rafe's bite burned. "I'd heard this woman is a vampire hunter. Is it true?"

"It is not." Rafe's brows drew together in consternation. "She is a doctor. The reason she was in the cemetery was to collect a corpse for her medical studies."

Another scoffed. "A *female* doctor? Surely you didn't believe that Banbury tale."

Cassandra couldn't hold back a snort of indignation. Before she could open her mouth to deliver a scathing retort, Rafe placed a warning hand on her arm.

"Clayton." Rafe's voice was calm, yet laden with undercurrents of danger. "Surely you cannot believe that a Lord Vampire would lack the power to discern falsehoods from a mere mortal." He then addressed the rest of the throng. "Since even my second-in-command has failed to grasp the obvious, I suppose I must inform you that the reason I was forced to imprison her is because she is one of those rare humans whose mind is impervious to our powers."

Clayton looked away with a petulant frown while the rest dissolved into a cacophony of arguments and rebuttals.

Yet another vampire stood to face Rafe. He had

a stump where a hand should be. Had the injury occurred before or after he became a vampire? "Do you mean it does not work on everyone? Why not?"

"Some, like the countess, have such strong and willful minds that they seem to have a natural resistance to hypnosis. Especially if they also possess a massive degree of intelligence," Rafe explained impatiently. "Others possess supernatural mental powers similar to ours and thus are able to shield their minds from invasion."

"Do ye mean witches?" a female vampire inquired in a thick Cockney accent.

Rafe shrugged. "I would not venture to refer to them as such. Most of them, anyway."

Cassandra's lips parted in awe at this intriguing information. As discreetly as possible, she unfastened her reticule and withdrew her journal to jot down a few notes. The vampires' gazes swiveled her way, brows raised in surprise and confusion.

Without looking at her, Rafe commanded, "Put that away, Countess."

Cassandra flushed and stuffed the journal back into its compartment. Many vampires glared and bared their fangs at her. Clayton's mouth twisted with palpable scorn.

Without missing a beat, Rafe continued. "In the old days, we either killed such persons on sight or made them one of us. Under the new laws, I had to take Lady Rosslyn as my prisoner and report the incident to the Elders. They have given me a month to weigh the same options. In the meantime, you are all to treat her with the same respect you do each other, because she may be joining our ranks."

A tendril of warmth curled through her belly at Rafe's defense, quite at odds with the offhand manner in which he spoke of killing her. His words appeared to have varying effects on the vampires. Many countenances softened. Others remained suspicious, yet nodded in solemn compliance. A few increased their hostility.

"And how is he supposed to keep hold of such a delicious piece with only one arm?" one whispered loudly.

Cassandra's blood boiled as Rafe flinched almost imperceptibly.

"Would you care to find out just what I can do with this arm?" he snarled at the offender. Turning back to the rest, he continued. "In the unlikely event that she does escape me, I will inform you all. If you catch her, you are to detain her and return her to me." His eyes glowed like the fires of hell. "She is not to be harmed in any way, or so help you God, you will regret it until your last breath."

❧

Rafe stared at Cassandra as he led her back home. *Dios*, she was brave. Despite facing more than a hundred vampires who would have gleefully drained her dry, she refused to cringe. She'd even had the nerve to pull out her blasted notebook as if they were all her specimens.

Now she walked beside him, spine straight and chin held high, despite the fine tremors that shook her body. As if sensing his scrutiny, she looked up. "Well, that was certainly an interesting experience."

"You shouldn't have brought out your journal. Do you not understand how dangerous that was?"

Meeting her wide gaze, he sighed. "Never mind. We'll discuss it later. Right now I want to forget about tonight's events for at least a while." He hid a smile at her bravado. "You look pale, Countess."

Her eyes narrowed in irritation at the name as she stomped up the walk. "That is likely because I did not have a decent meal."

"That is your own fault. If you hadn't insisted on following me on my hunt, you would have had one." Rafe nodded at William as he opened the door. "Please inform Cook that her ladyship is ready for luncheon."

William bowed, but not before Rafe glimpsed another petulant frown. "Yes, my lord."

As he removed his coat, he heard William and Anthony sniping at each other, only to be reprimanded by Cassandra's housekeeper. Rafe gnashed his teeth. The whelp's insolence was becoming insufferable. He would have to do something about William soon. Unfortunately, there were more pressing matters to deal with.

They entered the dining room and Cassandra settled into her seat with an appreciative sigh, grinning at Anthony as he entered with two steaming trays of food.

Rafe frowned. Her presentation to the London vampires had not gone well. He hadn't expected anyone to be pleased with the situation, but the level of hostility had been quite unexpected...especially from Clayton.

His scowl deepened. He had a bad feeling about Clayton. Was his second-in-command up to something? If so, he needed to be prepared.

"When can you perform another operation on my arm?" Rafe demanded. The sniping about his malady had been too much to bear. If he were whole again, he could show them.

Cassandra glanced up from buttering her roll. "Well, as long as I have a supply of the…ah"—she looked at Anthony and lowered her voice—"proper medicine, any time shall suffice."

"Then we will proceed." Rafe turned to his third-in-command. "Anthony, I will require your services once more."

Anthony nodded. "Of course, my lord. I am pleased that I am able to help." He turned to Cassandra with a grin. "Especially since I have the privilege of aiding so lovely a genius in performing her miracles. Tell me, what part of my master will you be hacking up next?"

Cassandra returned his smile and took a sip of wine. "I would like to proceed further this time and make incisions in the medial and lateral portions of the elbow, and then I'd like to try an incision in the carpal area before attempting an inversion in the ulnar side of the wrist." She picked up her knife and began to slice her steak. "And if I can devise a way to dull your lord's pain, then I will examine the common flexor tendon."

Rafe couldn't help but gape as she popped a chunk of pink meat in her mouth. How could she discuss such gruesome topics at the dining table with such enthusiasm?

To his amusement, Anthony paled visibly, saying, "I'll leave you to your meal."

Lady Rosslyn smiled and continued to devour her meal with unladylike haste. Had the evening's adventure, coupled with his drinking from her, caused her to be overtaxed and starved?

Then she tossed her napkin on the table and stood. "I had best go up to the laboratory and ready my supplies."

Before anyone could respond, she rang for Mrs. Smythe and ordered a pot of boiling water to be sent up to her laboratory and a bath to the bed-chamber afterward.

Rafe shook his head and followed her. No, she wasn't taxed at all. If anything, she was energized by her work. As he entered the laboratory and watched Cassandra gather up a hazardous bouquet of sharp and cruel instruments, he was reminded that her work was on *him*.

"If you will oblige me and remove your shirt, I can proceed in examining you," she said briskly as she donned a snowy white apron.

Rafe eyed her as he unbuttoned the shirt. He could think of far more enjoyable reasons to disrobe. Reasons that would also have her out of her garments and in his arms. He bit back a groan of arousal as her soft hands slid up his forearm and across his bicep, gently probing.

"Amazing." Her breath teased his cheek. "The atrophy and scarring here are greatly reduced. At this rate, we may have functionality returned to the limb in a matter of weeks!"

Rafe couldn't help wishing that passion was for him as a man, rather than an experiment. If only he weren't so ugly. His gaze dropped to his bad arm, studying the diminished scars where Cassandra had cut him. Could she do something about his face? Would she then find him appealing?

His mouth twisted into a scowl of self-loathing at the ridiculous thought. He should be grateful that she had the power to heal his arm. He didn't need affection. He needed power to protect his people and defeat his enemies. He needed his arm back.

Yet when he looked at her flushed cheeks and lush lips, Rafe couldn't help but want more. Her beauty must be driving him mad. That was the only logical explanation.

The sound of Anthony's tread on the stairs made Cassandra jump and snatch her hand away. Had she been thinking of things other than cutting him open?

Anthony entered with a pot of boiling water. "I hope you are not intending to scald him."

"Certainly not." Cassandra removed a bottle from her shelf of potions, uncapped it, and poured a measure of pungent liquid onto a cloth. The stench intensified as she brought it to Rafe. "Take this and breathe in deeply."

Rafe frowned. "What is it? It smells foul."

"It's ether. I have reason to believe that it will have a numbing effect on your pain." She grabbed her syringe and gave him a stern look over her shoulder. "Now please do as I say."

"Yes, Doctor." He snatched the offending cloth and inhaled the acrid fumes with reluctance as Cassandra washed her hands and surgical instruments in the steaming water.

"Why are you doing that?" Anthony asked. "Those blades look much cleaner than those of the usual sawbones."

Her cheeks pinkened. "I believe that dirt causes

infection. I did an experiment on myself when I was young, where I cut my finger on each hand. For the next week I only washed my right hand to see if it would heal faster if kept clean. My assumption proved correct."

For some reason, Rafe chuckled at her words. She could be so amusing at times without intending to be. "Did you also inhale this dreadful potion?"

Cassandra nodded and drew Anthony's blood with her syringe. "I did. As Wakley said, ether did indeed bring me to a state of euphoria. Are you feeling such a sensation?"

Now that she mentioned it, Rafe realized that the room had taken on a shimmering quality, and a ring of light had formed about her head like an angel's halo. Also, every muscle in his body felt like warm custard. "I believe I am, *Querida*."

"Then we may proceed." Cassandra took her scalpel. "You will have to remain still."

To his disbelief, Rafe could barely feel the blade cutting into his arm. He looked down at his own bleeding flesh with detached fascination. This was a much larger cut than last time...and Cassandra was carefully prying his flesh apart to look at the mess of muscle and tendons beneath, all the while muttering in her physician's Greek.

"You're making me feel as if I am Frankenstein's monster," he said.

Cassandra paused. "You shouldn't take that as an insult. That is my favorite novel. Besides, you're not a monster. You are a fascinating and powerful being, with natural gifts any human would envy." She glanced up at him, eyes full of wonder. "You heal so fast that I have to keep cutting you. And your blood coagulates at such an astonishing rate. You're…amazing."

Stunned by her poignant speech, Rafe could only watch silently as she administered Anthony's blood to the wounds. Immediately, his arm began to burn and tingle, and he couldn't help but shift in his seat.

She placed a hand on his shoulder, holding him firm. "I told you… You must remain still."

"I think the ether is wearing off." Then again, she still resembled an angel…and her touch definitely intensified his euphoria.

Cassandra commanded Anthony to bring some more ether. "Only inhale a little this time. I have no idea if too much will make you ill. When I tried ether, the effects lasted over an hour and I had a devil of a headache afterward."

Rafe inhaled from the cloth Anthony proffered while Cassandra continued to operate.

"You didn't tell me I would suffer a headache," he accused.

"Well, I am almost finished. Perhaps if you find something upon which to focus your attention, the pain will remain at bay a while longer."

As she leaned forward, Rafe could see the tantalizing display of her breasts above the fabric of her apron. "I think I've found just the thing."

Anthony chuckled beside them, but Cassandra was too occupied with her surgery to notice Rafe's gaze. He *wanted* her to notice. He wanted her to see him as more than the subject of her experiments. He wanted her to see him as a man. He wanted to see if her beautiful breasts felt and tasted as delicious as they looked. He stared, transfixed, until she finished. The moment the last incision knitted back together, Rafe gave Anthony a pointed look.

His third-in-command needed no further urging. "I shall take my leave now."

Cassandra cleaned the blood from Rafe's arm with a damp cloth. "How do you feel now?"

Slowly, Rafe lifted his arm higher than it had moved in more than fifteen years. He flexed his fingers, extending them. *Madre de Dios*, his little countess was a miracle worker.

"I feel very well indeed, *Querida*. Well enough, in fact, to do this…" With strength he hadn't possessed in years, he deftly caught her by the waist and hauled her onto his lap.

A startled squeak escaped her lips just before Rafe claimed her mouth with his, reveling in her taste. Cassandra moaned and tangled her hands in his hair, crushing her breasts against his bare chest. His hardness ground against her soft heat. He longed to yank up her skirts and thrust deep inside her sweetness. As he reached to do just that, a knock sounded on the door.

"*Cristo!*" he hissed as Cassandra scrambled off his lap.

"My lord, her ladyship's bath is ready," William intoned.

"Thank you, William," Cassandra stammered, and she fled the room as if chased by demons.

Rafe slumped in the chair and buried his face in his hands. And perhaps she was. Just one, anyway.

❧

Clayton squinted at the trio of vampires who stood nearly thirty meters away beneath a copse of trees at the edge of Rafael's territory. "Come closer so I can get a better look at you."

The one in the center shook his head. "Not until I hear your terms and you can guarantee our safety."

"Don't be foolish." Clayton sneered. "You are rogues. You forfeited safety the moment your lord exiled you. The only thing I can offer is shelter, hunting grounds, and my silence as to your presence in this city. And I will only do so if you agree to my terms."

The male on the right scratched his shaggy beard. "Quit toying with us then and tell us what you want."

Clayton tamped down his ire at the rogue's insolence. Thankfully his need for such a cur would only be temporary. "Very little. Only a few abductions and perhaps a killing or two if necessary." He shrugged. "It's not as if you haven't done worse."

The three rogues regarded him with mutinous glares before huddling together to silently confer.

Finally, the one in the center cleared his throat and stepped forward. "Very well, what do you want us to do?"

Clayton forced his features into a solemn visage. "The current Lord of this city is corrupt and placing the vampires of London in danger. He must be overthrown to preserve our safety. To do so, I need to prove his incompetence. That is where you gentlemen come in." Smiling, he folded his hands behind his back. "I need you to kidnap a London vampire, but do not harm her unless it is absolutely necessary."

"I see…" The lead rogue smirked and laced his fingers together under his chin. "And what happens afterward?"

"You do not need to be privy to the exact details. But I will say this: if you three do your jobs well, you will rise to the top ranks of my hierarchy when I become Lord of the city." Clayton surveyed them all. "What say you?"

The three rogues conferred a moment longer before intoning in unison: "We agree."

Clayton grinned and beckoned the new members of his rebellion forward. Now it was time to execute the next step of his plan.

Ten

12 October 1823

CASSANDRA AWOKE TO HEAR A SHARP HISS OF PAIN. Seconds later, Rafe struck a match and lit an oil lamp, illuminating his agonized grimace.

"My God, Rafe, what is the matter?" Then she saw. His hand, along with the muscles in his arm and shoulder, were overtaken with pulsing spasms.

He followed her gaze. "Ironic, isn't it? For years I've wanted sensation in this godforsaken limb. It seems I've gotten my wish."

Cassandra threw off the covers and climbed out of bed. "I must examine you at once."

"There isn't time right now. I need to hunt. Besides, I am quite certain everything is fine. Look." He moved his fingers and rotated his arm, smiling despite tight lines of pain around his eyes. "I can move this arm threefold as much as yesterday. My discomfort is likely part of the adjustment process."

Her eyes widened as she grasped the obvious. "Of course! Why didn't I foresee this? The muscles have been atrophied for so long that naturally there would be pain from them 'waking up,' for lack of a better term." She crossed the room to the wardrobe, threw open the mahogany doors, and grabbed a gown. "We must go to the laboratory at once. I have some cannabis."

Rafe took the gown. "You are not doing anything until you eat, *Querida*. You've grown thinner since you came here." He threw the cranberry velvet garment over her head, working through the buttons twice as fast as before. "We will talk further when I return."

Just when he'd finished helping her dress, there was a knock on the door.

"Yes?" Rafe growled with apparent irritation and impatience.

William's voice echoed through the wood, timid and trembling. "Clayton is here, my lord. He says the matter is urgent."

"*Cristo*." Rafe jerked the door open and followed the vampire down the stairs.

Rife with curiosity, Cassandra saw no reason not to accompany them. After all, no one had forbidden her to follow. But once they arrived downstairs and Clayton's gaze met hers, filled with burning scorn, she was tempted to flee.

No, I won't let him frighten me. Cassandra lifted her chin and met his gaze with all the aristocratic hauteur she could manage. Her dreaded mother-in-law would have been proud.

"What is it, Clayton?" Rafe interrupted the silent exchange.

Clayton glared at Cassandra once more before

turning to the Lord of London. "Lenore has gone missing, my lord."

"Lenore?" Rafe frowned in confusion.

An air of nearly imperceptible chiding laced the other vampire's reply. "Yes, she is one of the vampires who take refuge at St. Pancras. Don't you remember?"

"Ah yes, the frail one with the dark hair." Rafe nodded. "We must begin a search, though I shall have to hunt on the way." He turned to William, reluctance lacing his tone. "Fetch Anthony. He'd better come along. You will stay behind and guard Lady Rosslyn."

If William was vexed with being relegated to such a lowly task, he concealed it well under a bland countenance. "Yes, my lord."

Clayton regarded him with a strange look before returning his attention to Rafe. "Let us be off then. I have a bad feeling about Lenore. It is not like her to be absent without notifying anyone."

Rafe followed his second-in-command, glancing over his shoulder at Cassandra. "Behave yourself, Countess."

Cassandra frowned as Anthony joined them and the three vampires departed. Something strange was afoot, and she couldn't help feeling that there was more to the situation than a missing vampire.

William coughed behind her. "Your breakfast is ready, my lady."

"Thank you." She fought to keep the bewilderment from her tone. Even he was behaving oddly.

She sighed and settled down at the vast dining-room table as the food was brought in. Breakfast at five o'clock in the evening, vampire secrets, and the phenomenal medical breakthroughs with Rafe's surgery...her world had certainly taken a strange turn. Was she caught in a dream?

"May I join you, my lady?" William interrupted her musings, still behaving with unusual shyness.

Though she preferred to remain alone, she saw no reason to refuse him in the face of his politeness. "Of course."

William inclined his head and sat across from her. "I do not think it right for you to be held captive like this." He lifted his head, gazing upon her with eyes as tragic as those of a starved puppy. "You have done nothing to deserve it."

Cassandra raised a brow at his unexpected display of sympathy. "That is true." *Yet when I came here, you wanted Rafe to kill me.*

"And that is why I've decided I shall help you escape." He folded his arms and regarded her with determination.

She nearly choked on her bread. "I beg your pardon?"

William nodded. "It is unfair for you to be trapped here any longer. And it should be fairly simple for you to get away."

"How so?" she asked doubtfully. "Rafe Marked me, which as far as I know means that he can use his unique...abilities to locate me anywhere."

"That power has limits." William favored her with a conspiratorial smile. "If you get far enough away, he'll have difficulty sensing you. And if you leave the city, it is doubtful that he will bother to seek you out. He has far more substantial concerns."

For some inexplicable reason, Cassandra felt slighted that Rafe would consider her an "insubstantial concern."

Feigning indifference, she took a delicate sip of tea. "What is to stop him from sensing his Mark on me on my way out of London?"

"Sometimes, strong emotions blur the Mark, which would make it difficult for him to trace you. However, you're not an overly emotional sort of female, are you, Lady Rosslyn?"

She shook her head. "Of course not." *Though lately…*

"Then that method will likely not work. However, there is a better way." He leaned forward and said softly, "He cannot trace you if you are unconscious."

That did not sound agreeable. She couldn't hide her suspicion. "What do you mean?"

William held out his hands in the age-old gesture of innocence. "Nothing nefarious, I swear. I am sure you have many a sleeping draught in your pharmacopeia. All you have to do is take one, and I will transport you out of Villar's clutches and away from the city before you awaken."

"No." The adamant conviction in her refusal surprised even her. "Although I dislike the idea of being a prisoner, I have been given the chance to study mysteries that other scientists and physicians could only dream of. I cannot turn my back on such an opportunity."

But is that the only reason you wish to remain here? her inner voice taunted. *No. I want to stay with Rafe.* The realization struck her like a bolt through the chest, intensifying the ache in her heart at the thought of leaving him.

Cassandra scrambled up from her seat. "Excuse me. I must return to my studies. Mr. Wakley should be here soon for my lesson."

William eyed her warily. "You won't tell Rafe of my offer, will you? He might kill me if you do."

"Certainly not. You were only trying to do me a kindness after all, and I would hate to see you punished for that." Before he could continue this discomfiting conversation, she fled the dining room.

Was William really trying to do her a kindness? Considering all of his hostility toward her when she'd first arrived, it was hard not to suspect his motives. He may have even intended to kill her himself once he smuggled her out of the city. However, Cassandra decided it would be best to try to sort out the matter on her own before speaking to Rafe.

Rafe... The memory of his burning amber gaze and the delirious heat of his kiss weakened her knees so suddenly that she had to cling to the banister for support, lest she tumble down the stairs. Cassandra dug her fingers into the fine-grained wood until her knuckles turned white. What was happening to her? Where had her reasoning fled?

The moment she recovered her balance, she charged up the stairs and into her laboratory. Slumping against the door, she focused on the meticulous organization of beakers, medical texts, and surgical instruments, willing the comforting sight to calm her tumultuous thoughts.

Staring at the tools of her trade, she evaluated the facts. *I've been taken prisoner by Rafael Villar. He is a vampire. Because I know this, he will eventually kill me or make me like him. His arm is crippled but he is allowing me to examine and operate on him...in exchange for kisses.* Taking a deep breath, she continued her inner recitation. *William has offered to help me escape and I refused. I refused because I want to heal Rafe's arm. I am healing his arm. I want to learn more about vampires. I want to know more about him. I want him to kiss me more. I want to remain with him because I lo*— Her mind cut off the illogical word with a mute cry of alarm. No, she mustn't even think it!

But her traitorous emotions refused to be quelled, forcing Cassandra to acknowledge defeat. If not the fanciful, likely imaginary manifestation of love, she felt *something* for Rafael Villar. She could not claim indifference, or even casual fondness. He'd captured her fascination from the moment she'd laid eyes on him a year ago. His touch made her weak and left her longing for more. His kisses made her reasoning flee, only to be replaced by a passion she'd never felt. Even his company affected her.

What if he only kissed her because she was there and he had no more preferable alternative? What if he felt nothing for her?

A strange emptiness filled her when he was gone. And when she saw or read something interesting, she felt the urge to share it with him. It was so very odd.

Shaking her head, Cassandra crossed the laboratory to her library of medical texts. It did no good to ponder what she couldn't control. What she *could* do was find the best way to progress on Rafe's treatment. The best way to ease his pain. Anthony had brought her some cannabis—apparently Rafe was supposed to smoke it like tobacco—though she had no guarantee of how effective it would prove to be.

Cassandra scanned the books and selected the

volumes she thought would contain the most useful information on atrophy and muscle spasms. Once she was settled in an overstuffed chair by the fire, her nerves calmed as she absorbed herself in the soothing routine of studying.

She came upon a remedy for Rafe's pain and spasms. It was unorthodox, yet completely logical. The thought of performing such a treatment made her pulse race and her entire being kindle with desire. Cassandra now understood what Hippocrates meant when he'd stated: *"The physician must be experienced in many things, but assuredly in rubbing."*

Another tendril of heat curled through her belly. Oh yes, she would love to "rub" Rafe. Cassandra shook her head at the unreasonable craving. Never before had she wished to touch another person so intimately. Her experience in the marriage bed had been a chore she'd endured with dread. But with Rafe…

Torrid mental images played across her mind. *Her fingers buried in his silken hair…her breasts pressed against his hot, muscled chest…his amber eyes glowing with savage hunger as he thrust inside her, deep and hard…*

Cassandra gasped as moisture pulsed between her thighs. She knew it would be different with him than with her late husband. Just how different, she had no notion…but she was now resolved to find out.

After all, she could be dead in mere weeks. Why not experience physical pleasure for the first time in her life? And what better prospect than Rafe, whose kisses warmed her in places that had long since been cold?

She glanced back down at the book, memorizing the instructions and techniques. Yes, this would be the perfect method to begin her seduction. And if that failed, at least she would still be aiding the treatment of his arm.

Thomas Wakley arrived and Cassandra had to hide a smile over William's discomfort at helping him bring the cadaver back up to the laboratory. For monsters who were supposed to terrorize the night, vampires were decidedly squeamish.

Once they were alone, she handed Wakley the article she'd written about the effects of ether, though she'd omitted the fact that her patient had required a second dose.

"Splendid!" Wakley declared after skimming the piece. "And how fares his arm?"

"It is too soon to tell," she said evasively. "I must wait for the incisions to heal."

He nodded. "Well, we had better get on with the next lesson if there's any hope for the operations to be successful."

She learned even more this time. As they made further incisions and delved deeper into the tissues, her mind synchronized the new knowledge with the old and mapped out the course of Rafe's next surgery.

Once were finished, she asked more questions about burn wounds and muscle injuries, jotting down notes in her journal.

Praying she wasn't blushing, she dared ask another question. "What do you know of massage?"

Wakley regarded her with a knowing smile. "The Eastern physicians have prescribed it for millennia and documented its effectiveness. Alas, our *proper* Western society is far too prudish to acknowledge such a treatment." He winked. "It is quite effective on my wife, and I daresay you should have little trouble experimenting with it on a *certain* patient. I may even want to publish a portion of the results."

Her blush deepened. "I shall have to keep that in mind."

After Wakley departed, Cassandra rang for a bath, feeling a decadent thrill as she added scented oils. Afterward, Mrs. Smythe helped her dress in a sapphire tulle confection adorned with frothed lace and brushed her hair until it shined like burnished copper.

She glanced at the clock, eagerly awaiting Rafe's return so she could begin.

The sound of the front door opening and slamming shut made her heart jolt with excitement. Rafe had returned.

It was time to start her seduction.

Eleven

CLAYTON BARED HIS FANGS AT WILLIAM, WHO HAD been cowering against the sideboard ever since he entered Clayton's town house. "What do you mean, she refused to escape? How could you have possibly bungled matters so much that the chit would want to remain a willing prisoner?"

Damn it all, Lady Rosslyn's escape would have further discredited Villar, as well as providing a handy place to set blame for Lenore's disappearance. Of course, Clayton would not have allowed the countess to leave the city alive, but no one needed to know that.

William flinched. "I played my role exactly as you instructed me, word for word, I swear! But she insisted on remaining with Villar so she could study him."

"What do you mean, study him?" Clayton narrowed his gaze on his incompetent lackey.

The other vampire shrugged helplessly. "I don't know precisely. Most of what she says is in physician's gibberish and somehow involves desecrating human remains. She even has a surgeon coming round to give her lessons in cutting up corpses."

Physician's gibberish…human remains… Clayton's eyes widened as comprehension dawned. Rafe had told them all that the woman fancied herself a doctor. The memory of her pulling out a journal and quill played in his mind. It all made sense now.

Rounding on William, he snarled, "Why didn't you tell me this sooner? Isn't it obvious what she's doing?"

The fool shook his head in confusion.

Clayton threw up his hands in frustration with such idiocy. "She's trying to learn all of our secrets! She's writing them down in a book, for Christ's sake! And what does one do with a book? They share it! Blast it all, she'll expose us to the world and have mobs pursuing us with stakes and torches, bent on exterminating our race!"

"Good God." William gasped, eyes wide as saucers.

Clayton stroked his chin thoughtfully. "However, this is a good thing for us."

"How so?" The lack-witted sod looked even more perplexed.

"We now have the perfect means to fully discredit Villar." Clayton's mind raced, savoring the possible outcomes…all in his favor. "Hell, if I notified the Elders now, they would execute them both."

William grinned. "Well, that solves everything. Would you like me to fetch you parchment and quill so you may begin the missive?"

Clayton shook his head emphatically. "No, not yet. If the Elders arrive before I prove myself a competent leader, they may very well install a replacement of their own choosing."

"So what do we do then?"

"Villar has less than a month before he must decide whether to kill or Change the countess, correct?"

"Yes." William appeared pleased to have an answer for something at least.

"And a message can take up to a fortnight to reach the Elders' motherhouse." Clayton paced the length of the drawing room, running a hand through his hair. "A reply would take about the same time. Yet, I believe in this circumstance, they will either send a representative to see to the matter or perhaps even come here themselves, which could take anywhere between a sennight and mere days."

William nodded in agreement, though his gaze was hazy with confusion again.

Clayton continued. "I think we should inform our people about the little countess's dangerous book before bringing the Elders into this matter."

Doubt filled the other vampire's features. "You want to begin the revolt so soon?"

"In political matters, sometimes it is best to act quickly, before your opponent has the chance to prepare," Clayton countered. "It is indeed time to set the wheels in motion. Tonight I want you to gather all our known allies, but first I need you to tend to my own prisoner."

William's expression of rapt interest dissolved into churlish reluctance. "What of my payment?"

Clayton rolled his eyes and withdrew a jeweled snuffbox from his breast pocket. The cloying stench of opium wafted out when he opened it. William licked his lips with longing. "Not until you feed Lenore."

"Why can't I have it now?" William whined.

"Because the effects of the drug will go straight from your blood to hers..." Clayton paused. "On second thought, perhaps that is not such a bad idea. It should make her more docile." He handed over the opium.

William seized his drug greedily and withdrew his pipe.

"Not in here, you fool. Go out to the rear garden. I cannot abide the stench."

The vampire scurried past him in a rush to feed his foolish addiction. When he returned, Clayton bade William to follow him down to the cellar.

Jovial laughter and the clatter of dice accompanied a moan of pain and clinking chains. The three rogue vampires looked up at Clayton and scrambled from their seats, their game forgotten.

Hamish, the leader, regarded him with feral intensity. "Have you another assignment for us, m'lord?"

A hot flood of pleasure rushed through Clayton at the title. Soon every blood drinker in London would address him so. "Not yet, though it seems I will be able to make my move sooner than anticipated."

"That's good to hear. Me and m'boys are growing bored."

Clayton raised a brow. "Tired of being on the run already?"

"No, m'lord. It is just that—"

"It appears you've found a way to occupy yourselves." He gestured toward Lenore's huddled form.

The captive female gazed at him with burning fury as she jerked her heavy iron chains. Her enraged screams were muffled by a thick, leather ball gag. Clayton watched her futile efforts with satisfaction.

An older vampire may have had the strength to break the shackles, but not Lenore. He had selected her because she was so young and weak. She was likely Changed by someone who hadn't waited at least a century.

From the sight of her torn dress and flecks of dried blood painting her thighs, it was apparent that the rogues had taken their pleasure of her. More blood caked her nose, which had been broken and healed crooked.

Clayton rounded on his new recruits. "You should take care not to handle her so roughly. This means I'll have to feed her more."

The three rogues looked at the floor in poorly shammed remorse. "Sorry, m'lord."

He sighed. "You may go hunt now. However, take care not to be seen again."

As the vampires departed, he motioned William forward and carefully removed Lenore's gag, which snagged on her fangs. Immediately, she growled at him.

"Tsk-tsk, show some respect, girl." Clayton wagged a scolding finger.

Lenore hissed, blood dripping down her fangs from her abraded gums. "You will not go unpunished for this, Clayton. Your mad scheme will fail and Lord Villar will destroy you."

"Oh, I don't think so. My plan is proceeding nicely."

"You call this nice?" Her voice dripped with scorn. "You're cracked!"

"I assure you, it is all for the greater good. You will see. When I am Lord of London—"

She shook her head. "I will never acknowledge you as Lord!"

Clayton leaned in close and spoke softly and dangerously. "I would think that over carefully, if I were you. If you have no intention of swearing fealty to me, then there is no sense in releasing you."

Lenore froze at his words. For a moment he thought she would still contradict him, but then she clamped her mouth shut and glared mutinously.

"William will feed you now, and if you behave, I may just bring you a human later this week."

Withdrawing his dagger, he sliced William's wrist. Though she must be starving, Lenore averted her face as the vampire drew near.

Clayton pressed the tip of the dagger to her chin. "Do not make me force you."

Just as the point of his blade drew a bead of crimson, Lenore complied, revulsion twisting her delicate features. The disgust quickly turned to reluctant pleasure as William's blood flowed into her mouth. Greedily, she drank, taking in the sustenance she needed to heal her wounds.

The moment she finished feeding, Lenore lifted her head to stare at them both with such hatred that William staggered back.

"What you are doing is wrong and unworthy of a lord." She pointed at Clayton, fingers twisted in the age-old gesture of a curse. "For this you will pay. Justice will be served and your bodiless head will roll in the dirt."

Unease prickled Clayton's body.

Thankfully, the opium in William's blood took effect and Lenore slumped into unconsciousness.

Rafe stomped up the stairs to Cassandra's laboratory. His arm continued to twitch, sending alternating needles of pain and numbness through his muscles. Clayton had noticed the spasms, and it was all Rafe could do not to send his healing fist crashing into his second-in-command's smirking face.

The only thing that held him back was the incontrovertible instinct to keep his healing secret until he was whole and strong again. Anthony agreed completely, especially in light of the suspicious circumstances of Lenore's disappearance.

When Rafe entered the laboratory, Cassandra's gaze seemed more welcoming than analytical. A twinge of surprise tugged his chest at how happy he was to see her.

"Did you find the missing vampire?" she asked with genuine concern.

He shook his head and slumped down in the chair opposite hers by the fire. He lit a cigar and felt an unfamiliar pang of gratitude when she did not complain. "We searched the entire city. Lenore was nowhere to be found."

He blew out a cloud of smoke with a sigh. The situation was much worse than that. The marks and gouges in the grass near Lenore's resting place, as well as the report from one of her neighbors that rogues had been spotted in the area, indicated that she had been taken. As it would be difficult for a rogue to hide in his city with all the patrols he assigned, Rafe had to face the near certainty that Lenore was no longer in London. Even worse was the likelihood of the bastards returning and abducting more of his people.

"I need my arm back. You must perform another surgery. Anthony is willing."

"No."

The cool defiance of her tone made him blink. "What did you say?"

Cassandra lifted her chin and placed her hands on her hips. "I said no." Looking like the goddess Athena about to deliver a divine edict, she continued. "Your muscle spasms are far too severe to risk surgery tonight. I do not want to take the chance of cutting the wrong tendon and hindering our progress. However, there are other treatments that I would like to try."

As much as he wanted to argue, her logic was infallible. At least she offered an alternative. "Very well. When may we begin?"

"R-right now, if you'd care to put out your cigar." Her hand shook as she held out a small silver tray she'd taken from his study.

Rafe raised a brow as he extinguished the cigar. "Do these new treatments involve you poking or prodding me?"

"Not at all." She held out her hands to show that she held no instruments. Instead she held out a pipe. "Would you please smoke this?"

He took the pipe and frowned at the pungent green substance stuffed into the bowl. "This isn't tobacco."

"It is cannabis. The herb is used for treating headaches, sore eyes, and most importantly, muscle spasms."

"And I am to smoke it?"

She nodded. "It could also be eaten or brewed into a tea, but with your unique digestion, I felt that this was the most efficient method of administration."

Rafe shrugged and lit a match. "Well, you are the doctor."

Praying that this "treatment" wouldn't make him ill, he lit the plant and sucked on the pipe. The taste was unfamiliar though not unpleasant. It was much harder than inhaling tobacco and made him cough when he exhaled. However, he felt an immediate sensation of being lighter, as if an invisible weight had been lifted from the top of his skull.

The second draw went easier as Rafe held the smoke in his lungs and exhaled slowly. The damned herb would not remain lit. He cursed as the match nearly burned his fingers before he lit another. By the time the cannabis was reduced to an oily lump of black ash, his muscles had become pleasantly heavy and relaxed.

"How do you feel?" Cassandra's voice came from far away, like a whisper from heaven.

"Quite good, actually." His voice sounded as surprised as he felt. His foul mood had completely abated. "I hope your next treatment is as pleasant."

"I hope you think so." Her cheeks turned crimson as she continued. "You will, ah, have to remove your shirt."

Her unexpected coyness delighted him. When he unfastened the buttons and shrugged out of his shirt, her quick intake of breath intrigued him further. Cassandra's gaze swept his bare chest with tangible intensity.

Rafe's mouth went dry as she slowly reached out to grasp his bad arm.

"I believe that if I work the muscles manually, the tension will loosen and they will begin to function as they should." Her tone remained clinical but held a shy tremor that he found endearing. "And I think this will ameliorate your pain."

Too bad she'd hidden her face behind her tumble of burnished curls. Rafe blinked, suddenly realizing that she'd never worn her hair down in her lab before. It was all he could do not to reach up and caress the tendrils. He observed her closer. Her gown was fancier as well, the blue taffeta revealing far more of her bosom than the peach muslin she'd worn earlier.

His musing ceased as her soft, warm hands wrapped around his bicep and applied the most delicious pressure. Rafe couldn't hold back a groan of pleasure.

"Am I hurting you?" she asked worriedly.

"*Dios*, no. Do not stop." Despite her innocent touch, he found himself hardening.

Cassandra resumed her heavenly ministrations, transporting him to a realm of bliss. As she kneaded the sore, stiff muscles, the agonizing tension loosened. Rafe threw back his head and closed his eyes.

"You are a miracle worker, *Querida*," he murmured.

"Nonsense, I merely gathered the knowledge from books and Wakley's teachings and successfully applied it."

Rafe chuckled and looked up at her. "It amuses me how you continue to shy away from the fantastical despite all you've been through recently."

"The existence of vampires does not negate science," she countered, blatantly avoiding his gaze.

He was about to counter that science wasn't everything, but then he paused as realization dawned. Cassandra's fixation on cold logic was likely because she lost her parents in such painful circumstances.

She'd never known a miracle, only tragedy. An ache bloomed in his heart.

"My mother also died when I was young," he said quietly.

She paused in her rubbing to place her warm hand on his, her voice soft with compassion. "What was she like?"

"Strong and beautiful. Or so my father told me. He was a conquistador, sent to subdue the 'savages' in the Americas and bring gold to the king of Spain. When he met my mother, it was *she* who conquered him." He smiled ruefully, surprised at how the story still affected him after all these centuries. "She died of smallpox shortly after I was born, along with the majority of her tribe. Grief stricken, my father brought me back to Spain."

Cassandra's eyes glittered with aching sympathy. "So you never knew her. How tragic."

He shrugged, trying to sound indifferent. "Perhaps it is best that way. I imagine I would have missed her more, had I knew her."

She remained silent for a long time, rubbing his shoulder with blissful, rhythmic pressure. "Well, I understand where you inherited your exotic coloring."

Rafe smiled at her attempt to cheer the mood. "Yes, my grandmother called me her 'little savage' due to my looks and my temper. *Eventually* the term became an endearment."

"Ah, so you've always been volatile?" Cassandra teased. "Somehow that does not surprise me." She removed her hands and stretched. Her knuckles cracked loudly in the peaceful quiet of the lab.

He frowned in concern. "I think you've done enough for the evening. I don't want you wearing yourself to the bone."

She nodded. "All right. How do you feel now?"

Rafe extended his arm and flexed his fingers. "The pain is much abated and the stiffness has all but vanished. My mouth feels very dry, but I think that is from the drug…" He eyed her delicious pulse on her throat. *Or my craving for you.*

"I am pleased to hear my treatment is effective." She grabbed a leather ball the size of a billiard ball and handed it to him. "Now I want you to squeeze this repeatedly every night to exercise and strengthen your fingers."

He frowned, resenting the return of her cool, practical demeanor. "Very well."

Cassandra wasn't finished with her orders. Facing him squarely, despite the sudden blush that returned to her cheeks, she demanded, "And you must stop sleeping on the floor. Such a hard surface can do nothing but ill for the healing process."

Rafe's brows rose in astonishment. *Surely she could not mean…* "But I must share your room to guard you, and I cannot very well have you sleeping on the floor."

She shrugged, though her blush deepened. "I know, though truly it shouldn't be too much of a hassle. The bed is, well…very large."

Her words made him harden further. "Too much of a hassle?" he repeated in disbelief, eyes raking her delectable form. "Surely you are not that innocent."

"Of course not," she whispered through temptingly parted lips.

Rafe frowned. Was she *trying* to seduce him? No, she couldn't be. No woman would want something as ugly as him. The herb he'd smoked must be altering his perception.

"Will you, ah, take your payment now?" she asked softly.

He shook his head. To kiss her now, after becoming so aroused from her touch, would surely make him lose control. "The pleasure you gave me with this treatment is more than adequate."

Her long lashes swept her cheeks as she closed her eyes. "Very well."

Rafe blinked. Could she possibly be disappointed? Surely that was wishful thinking. Wishful thinking compounded by the effects of the drug.

He stood and donned his shirt. He needed to get away from her before he changed his mind about their bargain. "I have some business to attend to. Thank you again for treating my arm, *Querida*."

"You are most welcome. Now, do not forget to squeeze that ball." Her eyes narrowed as she took a deep, shaking breath. "And I still must insist you sleep in the bed from now on."

Rafe fought back a surge of lust at the thought. "I told you—"

Unbelievably, she held up a hand and silenced him. "If you are that concerned with my proximity, then I shall sleep on the floor."

Rafe scowled. "I am not about to have a lady sleep on the floor like a dog."

"Oh?" she countered sweetly. "Yet it is perfectly acceptable for you to do so?" Her chin lifted in mute challenge. "Very well, then if you insist on sleeping on the floor, *I* shall do so as well, no matter what you say."

He gaped at her, stunned that she had cornered him. There was no way in hell that he would allow her to suffer such discomfort. "Fine. We'll share the bed."

Frustrated and confused at the direction of the conversation, he strode out of the room. *Stubborn, foolish woman.* How in the hell could she not understand the danger she'd just placed herself in? It would almost serve her right if he succumbed to the temptation she threw in his face and ravaged her the moment they were alone in the bedchamber.

Rafe shook his head and relit his cigar. No, he couldn't do that to her. He wasn't an animal. He could control his impulses, no matter how much she seemed to be taunting him. He frowned. *Was she?* Either way, he would resist her for both their sakes. He had enough guilt on his conscience for all he was putting her through. He didn't need to add to it.

His stomach roiled in hunger. He licked his fangs, realizing that his hunger was much stronger than it should be. Another effect of the cannabis? Rafe shrugged. Either way, he had better feed once more before rejoining his countess. Best to take all precautions to ensure her safety.

❧

Cassandra's pulse accelerated as Rafe entered the bedchamber. She glanced at him over her shoulder, hoping she appeared coy and seductive. "Will you assist me with my gown?"

As his fingers deftly unbuttoned the blue taffeta, she shivered at his touch.

"Does your foolish ultimatum still stand?" he asked levelly.

She fought not to stammer. "It does indeed."

He sighed. "I hope your stubbornness does not reap unpleasant consequences."

Triumph curved her lips in a smile as she removed her gown. Rafe was going to sleep in the bed with her. A thrill of anticipation made her knees weak. Would her strategy prove effective? Would he be tempted to take her?

Rafe loosened her stays, yet her chest still felt tight. She did not go behind the privacy screen. Summoning her courage, Cassandra removed her stays and stockings in front of the vampire. His harsh breath stole her own.

Once down to only her chemise, she climbed into the large bed. As he removed his boots, she tried not to stare. Would he undress completely? Rafe stalked closer, then stopped to look at her, his burning gaze searing her for an eternity.

Then he got on the bed...and lay down on top of the covers.

"Good night, *Querida*," he whispered and extinguished the lantern.

Cassandra bit back a sigh of disappointment.

Could it be that he didn't want her? No, if that were the case, then he would not have been so vehemently against sharing a bed...and she'd felt his hard length pressing against her body when he kissed her. His body desired her, at least. Likely he was trying to play the gentleman. His words the night he first brought her here swept through her memory: *I won't ravage you. I may be a monster, but not a reprehensible one.*

She sighed. If he was simply being stubborn out of a misplaced sense of chivalry, she would have to work harder to disabuse him of that notion.

Twelve

16 October 1823

HUNGRY, SO HUNGRY. LENORE'S THROAT WAS ARID from blood thirst as sharp pangs relentlessly assaulted her empty belly.

Three days had passed since Clayton had fed her. He was starving her, keeping her weak. Her head lolled on her shoulders as gray spots danced in her vision. His strategy was working. Another day or two and she would be unable to move.

The cellar door opened with a painful screech. Lenore tensed as loud footsteps plodded down the stairs. *Hamish.* Her lip curled up in scorn. One would think a vampire sometime beyond his first decade would have learned to walk more quietly.

"'Ello, luv," he said jovially, leering down at her with swinish eyes. "Did ye miss me?"

Lenore's flesh crawled in revulsion as he reached out to squeeze her bruised breasts. Another rape… She didn't know if she could bear it, but somehow she would. Just as she had survived all the others.

Clayton was a mad fiend to allow this. If he succeeded in usurping Rafael Villar and taking over London, his reign would be one of blood and terror. No vampire would be safe.

As Hamish drew nearer, her predatory hunger roared to life. Despite her disgust, she licked her fangs. She needed blood. Desperately.

The rogue vampire hiked up her torn skirts, smacking his fat lips in anticipation of the assault. The scent of his blood nearly overpowered her dread. Once he came close enough, she might be able to bite him… and he might let her.

Lenore gasped—not at his intrusion—but at an idea. The plan was tenuous, gossamer in fact. No matter, she would rather die trying to succeed than endure this degradation any longer without a fight.

❧

Rafe stalked in front of the gathered assembly of London vampires, barely suppressing his fury. Nearly half eyed him petulantly, as if he'd terribly inconvenienced them by calling this meeting. His fists clenched at his sides. How could they be so selfish when one of their own was likely dead or in danger? He sighed. At least all had obeyed his summons.

He held up a hand to silence their chatter. "Although I am certain many of you already know, I must announce it officially: Lenore has gone missing. Furthermore, I have reason to believe that rogues are in the city."

"Rogues?" Clayton's derisive snort echoed through the chamber. "How do we know your pet vampire hunter is not responsible? Or the surgeon paying her calls?"

Gasps and murmurs of agreement broke out among the congregation. Rafe rubbed his temples, eyes burning with exhaustion. Clayton had been resentful when Ian made Rafe his second-in-command instead of him. When Rafe became Lord of London, he'd hoped that making Clayton his second would mollify him. He had been catastrophically wrong.

Resisting the urge to bare his fangs, Rafe spoke patiently as if to a small child. "First, Lady Rosslyn is not a vampire hunter. She is a physician, as I informed you before. Second, she has been in my custody and under guard this entire time, as is the surgeon who is giving her lessons in the healing arts."

Clayton glared in obvious anger at Rafe's patronizing tone. "I still maintain that she is dangerous. And I do not understand why you haven't yet decided whether to kill her or Change her. The longer she remains alive and human, the more we are at risk."

"We have bigger concerns than a mere mortal prisoner," Rafe snarled. "One of our people is missing, and rogue vampires may be invading our land. We must address these issues immediately. *All* of us. Lady Rosslyn is *my* responsibility and mine alone."

Clayton lifted his chin. "I disagree, Villar. I believe—"

"Silence!" Rafe snarled.

The other vampires watched the exchange with perverse fascination. The situation was quickly getting out of control…which was likely what Clayton intended. It seemed his second needed to be reminded who was in charge.

"Clayton," he said softly, though he wanted to roar. "I have had quite enough of your insolence. I command you to leave this meeting and begin searching for the rogues."

His second-in-command bristled before giving him an insultingly slight bow. "Yes, my lord."

"Oh, and Clayton?" Rafe said to the vampire's retreating back.

"Yes?" he replied through clenched teeth.

"Contradict me again and I shall appoint a new second-in-command. Do it a third time and you will suffer the most painful consequences." Rafe wanted to strip him of his title right now, but to do it so suddenly in front of so many who admired Clayton would be perceived as nothing short of callous.

Clayton nodded and slunk out of the meeting chamber like the cur he was.

Rafe turned back to the other vampires, gratified to see more respect and humility in their gazes. Now they knew he meant business. "Back to the matter at hand. We all must work together to find Lenore. And we must see our city safe from intruders."

He walked over to the large map of London on the far wall. "You will be assigned in groups of four. Each group will be responsible for patrolling a section of the city for signs of Lenore or rogue vampires. The smallest clues or anything that is slightly suspicious must be reported to me immediately."

Pointing at the map with his jeweled walking stick, Rafe parceled out territories. "I want you all to travel in pairs at all times, and not only when you are patrolling. Until London is safe, no vampire should be out alone."

There were some pained grumbles at that last edict, but Rafe remained firm. "I know many of you are perfectly capable of handling a rogue on your own, but some of you are not. I insist that we err on the side of caution."

They bowed in assent. He surveyed the gathering for a long moment, assessing who appeared to be taking his command seriously and who was not. He was not surprised to see William leaning indolently against the back wall, whispering to another vampire. Rafe would deal with him next.

"You are all dismissed." He lit a cigar and watched them file out of the chamber, waiting until the last was out before he cursed under his breath. He'd done all he could for now, but he couldn't help but feel like everything was slipping from his control.

Rafe slowly blew out a cloud of smoke as he made his way up the stone stairs. Unfortunately, Clayton was right. In the eyes of his people, he was taking an unreasonable amount of time to decide Cassandra's fate.

Yet it would be far worse for them to learn the truth: that he couldn't Change her because he'd illegally done so with another. How they would scorn him if they knew about that hypocritical deed, especially since the one he Changed was a prominent figure in the mortal world—one of the main reasons why the Elders forbade Changing anyone without their approval. No matter that he'd been paying a debt of honor.

Rafe sighed. He'd been willing to Change the duchess's friend, John Polidori, because he hadn't anticipated ever having the desire to Change anyone else. Now he regretted the action even more than when he'd crippled himself by running out into the sun.

He'd give anything to take it back, to be able to make Cassandra truly his and see her safe from harm.

He slammed the door of the abandoned church. His shoulders slumped in defeat. No matter how badly he wished it, he couldn't Change her...and there was no way in hell that he could bring himself to kill her.

Not after she'd worked her magic and made him whole again, not after learning her hopes and dreams, not after feeling her soft heat in his arms or tasting the sweetness of her kiss. Not after he'd spent the day beside her in bed, waiting until she fell asleep so he could touch her silken, burnished curls.

He crushed out his cigar. When had he become such a sentimental fool? One of his people had gone missing and he was quickly losing his authority over the rest, and all he could think about was that soon he would be in the company of the most intelligent, beautiful, and engaging woman he'd ever met. Soon her miracle-working hands would be upon his flesh, healing him and giving him pleasure of which he'd never dreamed.

Rafe hunted quickly and headed home the moment his hunger was sated. The sight of the Elizabethan mansion against the backdrop of moonlit fog often filled him with admiration...yet now he realized that Burnrath House would never feel like home. His hacienda in Spain and even his modest flat in the East End had provided more comfort.

Maybe he was not fit to be Lord of London. He'd certainly botched things badly enough. Unfortunately, this was his duty until Ian returned in fifty years. He'd sworn an oath to do everything in his power to protect the vampires of this city as well as to keep them in line.

William opened the door, not bothering to hide his utter lack of respect. "My lord," he said sullenly.

Rafe bared his fangs. Speaking of keeping people in line... "William, you are relieved of your duties here. Pack your belongings and vacate the premises immediately."

"B–but why, my lord?" William pleaded, immediately contrite.

"Your insolence proves you unsuitable for a position in my retinue." *And I suspect you and Clayton are up to something*, he added silently.

William's face reddened and his fists clenched. He opened his mouth to protest, then thought better of it. Instead, he spun on his heel and stomped up the stairs. Rafe removed his coat and rang for Cassandra's housekeeper. When Mrs. Smythe arrived, he ordered brandy.

"I want you to retire for the evening. I have dismissed William and I fear he is in quite the temper. I do not want him taking it out on an innocent bystander."

Mrs. Smythe bobbed a curtsy. "Yes, *Don* Villar." The naked gratitude in her eyes made him regret not sending William away sooner.

He took his brandy and settled into a plush chair by the fire. Moments later, the front door slammed and Rafe sighed in relief. William was gone.

"What was that all about?" Anthony poked his head in from the doorway to the drawing room.

Rafe raised his glass and poured another for his third-in-command. "I've dismissed William."

Anthony grinned. "It's about time you got rid of him, my lord, if you don't mind me saying so."

"Yes, I had wanted to maintain a sense of stability by keeping on the duke's hierarchy. Alas, that appears to have yielded the opposite result…present company excluded, of course."

The vampire inclined his head. "Naturally."

"At any rate, it seems I would do best to establish my own reign." A great weight seemed to lift from his shoulders as he spoke the words.

"I've wanted to tell you that for some time," Anthony replied quietly.

Rafe raised a brow. "Why didn't you?"

"Well, for one thing, I thought it wise to wait until you got your bearings and evaluated the circumstances for yourself. For another, you strike me as the sort who pays little heed to the opinions of others."

"An apt assessment." Rafe couldn't hide his respect. "Perhaps you should have been interim Lord of London all along. Lord knows, I never wanted to rule." The irony weighed heavily on his mind. He'd accepted his *tío*'s offer to be an immortal guardian over his family because he didn't feel suited to the responsibilities as hidalgo of his village.

Anthony shook his head. "I don't know about that. It takes more than a talent for assessing the characters of others to rule a people."

"And what is your assessment of Lady Rosslyn?" Rafe blurted out without thinking.

The vampire remained silent as he took the seat opposite Rafe. Finally, he looked up, eyes intent. "You can't kill her. She would be too much of an asset to our people. Imagine having our own doctor for our kind. She might be able to fix Mary's leg." He smiled. "And I think she's completely smitten with you."

Rafe doubted that, as much as the thought still made his chest tight. "Does your offer still stand to Change her?"

Anthony's smile dimmed. "It would, if I had not grown so weakened donating blood for your surgeries. By the time I regain my strength, the deadline for the Elders' decree will have passed."

Rafe slammed his fist on the table. "Damn it! I should have had William open a vein before I dismissed him. At least then he could have been useful for once."

"He wouldn't have done it. He would have quit before lifting a finger to help anyone but himself." Anthony shrugged. "Anyhow, Lady Rosslyn is preparing for your next surgery as we speak, so we had best get a move on."

Rafe shook his head, stomach knotting with guilt. "I can't allow you to give more blood and be weakened further."

"Nonsense, my lord. It is my duty to do what is best to ensure the safety of our people as much as it is yours. And I believe that *you* are the one who can keep us safe. You will need all the strength you can muster to establish control and deal with these current issues, and I will do all I can to give you that strength." Anthony shrugged. "Besides, the countess says there are only to be three more operations. I am certain that I shall not perish before that."

A lump formed in Rafe's throat at his third's

loyalty. "Very well. I will do all I can to see that you are fairly rewarded for your incredibly noble sacrifice."

As he followed Anthony up to the lab, Rafe concluded that he had to find a vampire willing to save Cassandra. And as he beheld her in the laboratory arranging her instruments, Rafe hoped he was worthy of all that Cassandra and Anthony had done for him.

Thirteen

17 October 1823

CLAYTON GROUND HIS TEETH IN FURY. HOW DARE Villar dismiss him like he was a mere underling? And how dare the cripple publicly insult and humiliate him as well? His face burned as he remembered the looks of shocked amusement on the vampires' faces when Rafael had threatened to strip him of his title. Villar would pay for his actions. Oh yes, he would pay.

He growled as someone knocked on his door. Would he have any peace this night? Cursing under his breath, he lumbered out of his comfortable chair, vowing to slaughter the interloper if the interruption was not worthwhile.

William stood shivering on the stoop.

Clayton sighed. "I thought I told you not to come here unless I summon you. It's dangerous for us to be seen together until my plans are set."

William looked up sullenly. "Villar threw me out."

For a moment, all Clayton could do was stare in dumbfounded rage. First Villar dismissed him and now William? It could not be a coincidence. When he found his voice, the questions came rapid-fire. "Why in the hell would he do that? What did you do? Does he know about my plan?"

"I didn't *do* anything," William protested. "And I daresay that if he knew of our plan, he would have arrested me. He may suspect something, but I think he was merely in a foul temper and unjustly took it out on me. Truly it is a relief to be out from under his thumb, no longer at the mercy of his foul moods."

Clayton lifted his gaze heavenward. "Good God, you are such a fool. If you didn't do anything, then he certainly must suspect something. You're lucky he must not have any conclusive proof."

William gave him a vapid smile. "May I stay with you then?"

"Of course not, you idiot! Villar's suspicions would definitely be confirmed if I took you in." He stopped as another thought came on panicked wings. "And he may have set spies on your trail. You weren't followed, were you?"

William shook his head emphatically. "No, I am certain of it. I always check when I come here, just as you told me. I wasn't Changed yesterday, you know."

"Well, you certainly behave as if you were at times."

The other vampire ignored his words and looked over his shoulder at the blazing hearth with naked longing. "Could I at least come in for a spot of brandy?"

Clayton sighed and looked over William's shoulder, opening his senses to detect other vampires. "Very well, but you must be on your way soon."

William followed him inside eagerly, rushing to the fireplace to warm his hands. "I am ever in your debt."

"I know," Clayton said plainly as he poured another glass of brandy.

The vampire took it gratefully, gulping down a large swallow. "It was rather unsporting of Villar to toss me out in the cold without enough blunt to pay for a decent room."

The hint was pathetic in its obtuseness. *More likely you squandered your wages on opium, like the weak-willed addict you are*, Clayton said silently. Aloud he said, "I could give you some money for a room."

William grinned in triumph that his hint had been taken. "You will?"

"Yes, but you will have to earn it." Clayton pulled a square of parchment from his pocket, unfolded it, and handed it to William. "This is a list of the London vampires who have pledged their loyalty for my cause. I need you to seek them all out and tell them to come to my meeting place three nights hence."

"Very well." Obviously the lazy son of a bitch was holding back a groan as he took the list.

Clayton reached into his other pocket and pulled out a few banknotes. "And this"—he pulled out one more—"is for you to stay away from me until our next meeting. Are we clear?"

William nodded. "Yes, Clayton."

His eyes narrowed. "I think it is past time you start addressing me as 'my lord.' After all, every vampire in London shall do so at the end of this fortnight. Don't you agree?"

The other vampire bowed subserviently. "Yes, my lord."

As William departed, Clayton finally allowed himself to smile. Soon London would be his and Rafael Villar would rue the day he insulted him.

❧

Cassandra's smile lit up like the dawn when Rafe and Anthony stepped into the laboratory. "Oh, good. You're here. Everything is ready, so please be seated."

As Rafe removed his shirt and complied, he was nearly struck dumb by the heat of her gaze on his bared flesh. Could she possibly want him as much as he desired her?

"Anthony tells me only three operations are left," he finally managed, throat dry.

"If everything goes as planned, yes." She nodded and fetched two bottles from her pharmacopeia. "However, they will all be far more extensive and painful so I want to attempt to render you unconscious."

Rafe frowned. "I am not certain I like that idea." Not only did he loathe the thought of being placed in such defenseless circumstances, but being unconscious would also mean that he wouldn't be able to look at Cassandra or feel her touch.

Anthony met his gaze and removed a pistol from his belt. "Her ladyship discussed this strategy with me. I agree that her plan is wise. However, I am prepared should there be any trickery and she tries to harm you."

Cassandra rolled her eyes and poured a measure of laudanum into a spoon. "Open wide, Villar."

He complied reluctantly, wrinkling his nose at the

cloying smell of the medicine. It tasted even worse. And before he could recover from that, Cassandra held out the cloth soaked with ether.

Rafe inhaled deeply and grimaced at the pungent fumes. "Ah, *Querida*, an angel of mercy you are not."

The wicked woman actually chuckled. Yet she had never looked more beautiful than at home in her lab in a way he had never been in this house, doing what she loved and was born to do. And somehow, despite wielding sharp, cruel instruments and drawing blood in the most gruesome fashion, Cassandra remained poised and elegant, every inch a countess.

He stared in mute wonder. He was unworthy to be in her presence, yet here she was, touching him, healing him.

As Cassandra leaned forward to dab at his arm with a hot cloth, Rafe reached up to touch her hair, but then the effects of the ether and laudanum sank in, drowning his senses in a sea of blackness.

When he awoke, he was lying on the bed on his stomach and Cassandra was kneeling beside him. Her hands were working the most exquisite magic on his shoulder.

He met her gaze in the mirror across from the bed and gave her a lazy smile. "Did you carry me up here yourself, *Querida*?"

She laughed, the sound low and throaty. "Anthony helped. I thought it best to massage you now, before the muscles stiffen up." She paused and brushed his hair away from his face with aching tenderness. "How are you feeling?"

Rafe hardened at the gentle, yet sensuous touch.

Did she know what she was doing? "Quite euphoric, actually. However, I believe the effects of the medicine have yet to wear off." The muscles in his hand spasmed suddenly, sending sharp bolts of pain up his forearm. He hissed. "I spoke too soon."

To his dismay, Cassandra removed her hands and rose from the bed. Rafe watched her take a pipe from the end table. The strong, green smell of cannabis filled the air. He took the pipe, lit the substance, and inhaled the smoke carefully.

"Where does it hurt?" she asked as he lay back down, already relaxing from the herb.

He shifted so he could raise his other arm to point. "Here."

She scooted up further on the bed and pressed the leather ball into his bad hand. "Squeeze," she commanded softly but sternly.

As he complied, she put firm pressure on the knotted muscle in his forearm, working at the tension with a rhythmic motion. Rafe didn't know what felt more wonderful, her ministrations on his arm or the light brush of her breast against his shoulder.

"Now, release."

His grip loosened on the ball and a measure of tension in his hand bled away. Cassandra then pressed harder on the knot, deepening the pressure…and the pleasure.

"Squeeze again."

I could think of something much better to squeeze, he told her silently. As if to torment him, her breast pressed more firmly against his shoulder. Rafe's fist clenched on the ball as he warred with the urge to roll over and pull her into his arms.

She had him repeat the action four more times. The tightness and pain had nearly vanished.

"Your magic has prevailed again, *Querida*," he whispered, eyeing her in the mirror.

"I told you before, it isn't magic," Cassandra retorted before she noticed the teasing glint in his eye. Softening her tone, she added, "Besides, even with the cannabis and massage, the pain will return, though I have a few ideas on how to combat it and speed your healing."

He raised a brow at her determined tone. "Oh, you do?"

"Yes. First off, you need rest. I know you have been busy looking after your people, but I think it would do you more good to allow yourself enough respite to heal." As if to fortify the temptation of her words, her hands trailed up and down his back in a decadently soothing caress. "Therefore, you will feed from me tonight so that you may stay home."

Rafe sucked in a breath at the thought of once more tasting her sweet blood. Her heady scent of rose petals and woman made his lust rise to a furious peak. "That sounds tempting… Are your other ideas so pleasant?"

"I'm afraid not," she said ruefully, continuing to rub his back and shoulders. "I've also brought up more laudanum."

He groaned. "I was afraid you would save the worst for last."

"Well, as I said, you need to rest," she said firmly. "The medicine will help you sleep."

Ah, but sleep was the last thing on his mind.

Unfortunately, her logic was more than inarguable. "These are the doctor's orders then?"

"They are."

Rafe sighed. "Very well, I suppose I have no choice."

"Which would you like first?"

You, Rafe said silently. The truth of that word rang loudly in his mind, body, heart, and whatever remained of his blackened soul. He wanted her. Wanted her more than he'd ever wanted anything in the world. And he was beginning to suspect and hope she wanted him too.

But taking her wouldn't be right, not when her future was so uncertain and not when he was still a cripple, unable to hold her completely and worship her body in the manner she deserved.

"Rafe?" Her sultry voice brought him back to the present.

"The laudanum," he rasped. With the magnitude of his arousal, there was no way he'd be able to resist her once his fangs were in her neck, pain or no pain. Being drugged was the only solution.

Cassandra's welcome warmth left the bed. Rafe rolled on his side and leaned up on his elbow to watch her. She froze as her hand closed over the brown bottle on the end table, green eyes darkening to molten jade as they swept across his bare chest. Her pulse rose along with the scent of feminine arousal. It was all Rafe could do not to lick his lips.

As she poured a spoonful of the vile liquid, he concentrated on the curve of her breasts above her velvet gown. With such a delightful distraction, the medicine was far more palatable than the previous occasion.

Still, Rafe could not conceal his grimace as he swallowed.

"I know it is bitter," she whispered sympathetically.

He reached up and brushed his knuckles across her cheek, savoring her softness. "Yes, but soon I shall wash it down with something sweet. Turn around so I may help you with your gown before the laudanum takes effect."

"Yes, that would be most practical." She complied and gave him a coy glance over her shoulder as he undid the buttons. "I see you are able to use both hands now."

Rafe's jaw clenched as his other hand gave off dull twinges of pain. The cannabis was already wearing off. Still he continued to use his long-neglected fingers. The night would come when that would not hurt at all. He was certain.

Her gown fell to the floor in a midnight-blue pool. Cassandra kicked off her slippers, giving him an enticing glimpse of her shapely legs under her shift. Rafe's mouth went dry as she climbed back onto the bed and knelt, tilting her head to the side.

"Drink, Lord of London," she whispered. "Drink and heal."

Throbbing with hunger, he reached up and pulled the pins from her hair, sending it tumbling down her back. Rafe plunged his hand into the mass, tangling his fingers in her curls. She gasped as he pulled her closer. For a moment he was content to merely hold her, to feel the hot pulse beneath her neck against his lips.

"Rafe..." Cassandra breathed, holding him tighter.

It was all the encouragement he needed. Rafe plunged his fangs into her throat, hardening further at her soft cry. Cassandra's hot, sweet blood rushed into his mouth, filling him, nourishing him, healing him. His bad arm seemed to vibrate with renewed strength.

Then the laudanum took effect, washing over him in a wave of dizziness. Rafe fell back on the bed, taking Cassandra with him. He couldn't manage to feel the slightest bit of remorse for that.

When he withdrew his fangs, her eyes fluttered open, yet she did not struggle to extricate herself from his embrace. "How do you feel now?"

"Better, though sleepy." Which was a good thing for her sake, for if he weren't drugged, Rafe would have torn off her remaining clothing and been ravaging her at this moment. As it was, he couldn't stop himself from kissing her, not when her ripe lips were inches from his own.

Cassandra yielded with a sigh, opening her mouth to deepen the kiss. As his tongue thrust against hers, he knew at last what heaven tasted like.

Reluctantly, he broke away. "I am sorry, *Querida*."

"Do not apologize." She caressed his scarred cheek as if it were beautiful. "I enjoy your kisses."

He stared in awed disbelief. "Do you?"

"Yes, very much." She moved closer, molding her body to his. "In fact, I want more. I want—"

As much as he wanted to hear the words, he placed a finger over her lips to silence her. "We will discuss that later." *When I am whole*.

As Rafe descended into unconsciousness he focused on Cassandra's face, which was quickly fading in his dimming vision. Sentimental or not, foolish or not, he couldn't let her die.

❧

Clayton slammed his fist on the sideboard with such force that the wood shattered, sending bottles and decanters flying out to clatter to the floor. Hamish cringed as his shoes were soaked with claret.

"What do you mean, she got away? The little bitch was so weak from starvation that she could hardly move!" His eyes narrowed on Hamish, who was nervously scratching at his collar. "Unless…were you feeding her?"

Hamish flushed. "She'd bitten me the last few times when we were, ah, having a tumble. I thought she'd taken a shine to me."

Clayton shook his head in dumbfounded awe. "*Having a tumble?* Is that what you call rape? And you actually were foolish enough to believe she'd come to welcome such treatment?" He stalked forward. "You didn't for a moment consider the fact that she was using you for sustenance and plotting her escape?"

The rogue spread his hands in a gesture of helplessness. "What can I say? Women are wicked, deceitful creatures."

"How did she get loose from her shackles?" Clayton inquired in a low, dangerous voice.

"She suggested she'd be better able to pleasure me if she had more liberty to move," Hamish muttered, staring at the pool of wine soaking into the carpet as if it were of vital importance. "And then she bashed me over the skull with the fire poker and ran off." Straightening his spine, he looked up at Clayton. "I would have caught her if I hadn't sensed another vampire nearby. Paul and Francis are hunting for her as we speak, and I am going to join them. We'll have the wench back in no time."

Fourteen

20 October 1823

RAFE'S ARM TWITCHED AS IF PRICKED BY A THOUSAND needles. Biting his lip to hold back a hiss of pain, he slowly climbed out of the bed to keep from waking Cassandra. For a moment he stood watching her sleep. Her inquisitive features were relaxed in slumber, the dying embers of the fire casting soft light on her cheeks and giving a muted glow to her hair.

Between surgeries, she'd spent the last three nights massaging him, conversing with him, and kissing him into a juxtaposition of bliss edged with torment that wrenched his conscience like a medieval rack every time she inquired if he'd decided to change her yet. He couldn't bear to tell her about the Elders' looming deadline, couldn't tell her that he couldn't Change her. Instead, like a coward, he kissed away her questions and held her tighter as if he could keep her safe in his embrace.

The wall clock ticked away, counting down the minutes until her fate had to be decided. Only fifteen nights remained. There had to be something he could do to save her. Closing his eyes, he weighed his meager options. Only two desperate measures remained and it was past time to attempt the first. But now he needed to feed.

Cassandra made a small distressed sound and curled up tighter under the quilt. She was having a nightmare. "Shhh, it's all right, *Querida*." Rafe neared the bed and slowly reached out to stroke her cheek with his left hand—an action he'd never have been able to do if not for her. The realization was humbling...and it would take humility to save her.

Reluctantly, he withdrew his newly healed hand and pulled the bedcovers up over her shoulders before placing a chaste kiss on her brow. "I'll return soon. There's something I must do first."

God help him, he didn't want to leave her, not even for an hour. Before he could succumb to the temptation to climb back into bed and hold her, Rafe turned away, threw another log on the fire, and left to feed.

He took his meal from a passing mortal at the end of the street and rushed back to Burnrath House, the death clock still ticking in his mind. "I won't let her die." He repeated the mantra under his breath as he squeezed the leather ball in his pocket to exercise his spasming muscles.

Once settled in his study with a cigar and a snifter of brandy, Rafe closed his eyes and mentally listed all vampires he could call "friend." Damnably few suited such a description. And even fewer were able to Change a mortal at this time. Ian had Changed his bride the same night Rafe had Changed the writer John Polidori, and his newest friend, Vincent Tremayne, Lord of Cornwall, had Changed his ward—illegally—only last year.

A surprised chuckle escaped his lips. Since when did he consider Tremayne to be a friend? The vampire had caused an inconceivable amount of trouble for Rafe and Ian—beginning with delaying Rafe from taking over London and ending with the lot of them having to testify to the Elders on Vincent's behalf.

Yet somehow, throughout the debacle, Rafe had grown fond of the Lord of Cornwall and his brave fledgling, Lydia. And it would serve Vincent right to be called for a favor. Unfortunately, he wouldn't be able to help with Rafe's predicament.

Rafe drew deeply on his cigar and swirled the brandy in his glass. He'd become amicable with a few other vampires over the centuries. He could only hope one would offer aid in his time of need. Setting down the glass, he picked up his quill and parchment and began to write.

After composing five letters, Rafe sealed them and took out another piece of parchment, dread and humiliation coiling throughout his being. Loath as he was to admit ineptitude, Ian had to know of the strife in London, as well as Rafe's catastrophic situation with Cassandra. At least he could take comfort in hoping the Duke of Burnrath might be able to provide a solution to at least one of his problems. Taking up the quill, he explained his predicament as succinctly as possible. A chord of discomfort rang along his nerves as he sealed the missive with the Lord of London's insignia.

Setting down the seal, Rafe stood and stretched,

marveling at the new strength in his left arm. Eyeing the letters, he prayed that they would provide salvation for the woman responsible for making him whole again. With renewed hope, he tucked the letters in his breast pocket and went upstairs to help Cassandra dress.

When he opened the door, he spied her shapely silhouette behind the privacy screen. It appeared that she had tried to dress herself.

"Thank goodness, you're here," she said. "Wakley will be here any minute for another lesson, and I cannot get these accursed laces tied!"

"My apologies, *Querida*." He quickly crossed the room and tied up the back of her dark blue wool gown, biting his lip against a hiss of pain as his arm spasmed.

Thankfully, she was too distracted to notice. "Tonight he's going to educate me on the muscles and ligaments in the hands so I am prepared for the fine work on yours."

Honestly, she seemed more nervous than he was about the upcoming operation.

Unable to resist, he kissed her ear. "I have full confidence in your abilities, Dr. Burton."

She beamed at his praise and hurried down the stairs just as Anthony escorted Wakley to the drawing room.

The surgeon's usual jovial face was ruddy with rage.

Cassandra's brows drew together in concern. "Are you quite all right, Mr. Wakley?"

He heaved a gargantuan sigh. "It's that blasted cur, James Johnson."

"The editor of the *Medico-Chirurgical Review*?"

Wakley nodded impatiently. "The scoundrel all but

accused me of burning down my own house to collect the insurance money!"

"That *bastardo*," Rafe growled. "The insurance company declared you innocent of fraud and compensated you two years ago."

Rafe knew because he and Ian had personally ensured that Wakley received rightful recompense for a tragedy for which they felt responsible. He wondered if the tightfisted insurance man still had nightmares.

Wakley didn't appear to have heard him and continued in high dudgeon. "As a journalist, he has all the morality without a scintilla of the intellect of Machiavelli. His bad faith as a controversialist is neutralized by his utter feebleness. In his method of arguing he resembles a clumsy card sharper who, with all imaginable disposition to slip a card, has not sufficient quickness to elude the vigilance of the spectators. He is disingenuous without plausibility; and dishonest without dexterity. He has the wriggling lubricity without the cunning of a serpent!"

Cassandra applauded the impassioned monologue as Wakley caught his breath. "You are as skilled an orator as you are a journalist."

Rafe nodded, biting back a grin at the volley of witty insults to Wakley's rival journalist. "Have you ever considered running for Parliament?"

The surgeon nodded gravely. "I plan to do so when my children are older." A measure of his temper seemed to have abated with his outburst, and he gave Cassandra a cordial smile. "I apologize for my raving. Shall we carry on with your lesson?"

Rafe left them to it, going to seek his meal and

fetch his fastest runner to deliver the letters. As he walked out the gates of Burnrath House, he nodded at a vampire who stood in the shadows.

He'd hired James to watch over Wakley ever since he began giving Cassandra lessons. The last thing he needed was for the surgeon to end up in danger from his kind once more.

❦

Rochester, England

Lenore's feet dragged in the mud as she shambled along. It had taken every vestige of her strength to climb out of the crypt where she'd taken refuge in Dartford.

"Just another step." She gasped the dull mantra. "Another step."

Her head ached and swam with dizziness. The blood of the beggar she'd fed on the night before was a distant memory. For the third time she questioned the wisdom of her decision to leave the city. But what choice did she have? There was no way she would have been able to reach Lord Villar's mansion at the heart of the city. Clayton's rogues would have caught her before she traveled three blocks. It was much easier to reach the edge of town, to leave London and press forward.

At least it was until her meager strength wore thin. God, she was so starved and weak. Lenore needed blood and rest before she collapsed. But she couldn't fall here on the cold ground, out in the open where the sun could claim her before she woke.

That is, unless one of the Rochester vampires

discovered her first. Who knew what her fate would be then? She was a rogue now, without written permission to leave her city, much less invitation to enter another.

As if in answer to that inner realization, the ground vibrated with the sound of an approaching horse. Aching hunger and terror shook Lenore's frail body.

"Please be a mortal," she prayed. "Please." She was far too weakened to open her preternatural senses.

".I am sorry to disappoint you, youngling," the vampire answered as he brought his black stallion to a stop before her. "What have we here?"

"M-my name is Lenore, sir. I've come from London."

"A Town vampire, eh?" His cold, black eyes swept her bedraggled form. "I daresay you look a little shabby for a London blood drinker. May I see the writ of passage from your lord?"

"I-I d-don't have one, sir," she stammered.

He raised a brow and gave her a terrifying, cheerless smile. "You are a rogue then?" He climbed off his horse with predatory grace and stalked toward her. His dark shadow engulfed her like death's cloak.

"No! Please, sir," she implored, "take me to the Lord of Rochester. I can explain everything!" *And please*, she prayed silently, *let him be kinder and more merciful than you are.*

His mocking laughter chilled her bones. "Well, that will certainly be an easy task for me. *I* am the Lord of Rochester."

Lenore's breath left her body in a rush. Of course, how could she not have known? His expensive horse and fine black clothing trumpeted wealth. His rich voice, straight shoulders, and stern countenance

explore other parts of his anatomy. Looking down at his prone form on the operating table, she stroked the rough scars on his cheek and marveled at his savage beauty.

Thank God she'd been able to get him unconscious with a blend of ether and laudanum that would doubtless be lethal on a human. As it was, he would be thoroughly muzzy-headed when he came to, which hopefully wouldn't happen until she was finished. *If he moved*… She bit her lip and lowered the scalpel. She couldn't afford to panic.

Anthony blotted her damp forehead with a handkerchief. "Do not worry, my lady. You will do fine."

She looked up at the vampire with concern. Beads of sweat gathered on his upper lip and he was frightfully pale. They had been operating every night for the past week, and it was clearly taking a toll on Anthony. He had a pistol at the ready in case she decided to harm Rafe in his vulnerable state, but Cassandra doubted Anthony would be able to aim the weapon properly. All the same, she had nothing but respect for his loyalty.

Guilt knotted her belly. Despite the cost for Anthony, she knew she wouldn't do anything to slow her progress on Rafe, not when his complete recovery was nearly within her grasp. "What about you? We really should have given you more time to recover, or at least found another donor."

Anthony shook his head. "We likely could not have found another donor, especially one we can trust. As for waiting, that is entirely out of the question. Rafe must be healed as soon as possible. He has a bad feeling about the current state of events…and so do I."

"Do you mean Lenore's disappearance?"

"Among other things…of which I am not at liberty to speak." He held up a large syringe full of his blood. "You had best get to work before our master rouses."

"You're right." She took a deep breath and made the incision, exposing the extensor tendons.

The moment the inner workings of Rafe's arm were revealed, the rest of the world fell away. Time ceased to exist as Cassandra put all of her concentration into her work, cutting, probing, and applying Anthony's blood.

When the last cut had knit together, she wiped the blood away and exhaled. As always, primal triumph surged through her body. It was done, and God willing, she had been successful.

Rafe stirred, dark lashes lifting to reveal his piercing amber gaze. "*Querida*," he whispered in a sultry, decadent voice. "*Quiero hacerte el amor.*"

Cassandra wobbled on weak knees. "I-I beg your pardon?"

He blinked and rubbed his eyes. "I apologize, Lady Rosslyn. I was dreaming. Are you finished now?"

"Yes." Unable to help herself, she ran a hand through his hair.

Rafe raised both arms and spread them wide. "Amazing. I can move them equally now." He gave her a lopsided grin. "Although…I can't yet feel either limb."

Cassandra's heart fluttered at his smile. "I suppose we had best get you upstairs now so that Anthony may seek his meal." *If he has the strength*, she added silently.

As if he sensed her worry, Anthony gave her a stern look before hauling Rafe up and out of his seat. Unwilling to leave the care of her patient solely to another, Cassandra carefully ducked under Rafe's shoulder and locked her arm around his waist. Together, she and Anthony led him down the hall and into the bedchamber.

"I've never been so coddled," Rafe murmured as they laid him on the bed.

Anthony chuckled, but Cassandra saw that he was paler than before and his breath came in pants of exertion.

She turned to face him. "I think you need to feed right away. You won't make it past the street in your state."

Anthony raised a brow. "Are you offering?"

"You had better not be," Rafe growled from the bed and struggled to sit up, wincing in pain as the drugs wore off.

She shook her head. "Of course not. I was merely suggesting he feed from Mrs. Smythe. I know you consider it to be bad manners, but this is an emergency and she should not be ill-affected."

Anthony nodded. "Very well, as I am already tupping her, a little bite shouldn't be too much more of a breach in propriety."

Cassandra's jaw dropped, but before she could respond, the vampire departed from the room, leaving her alone with Rafe...who was still staring at her intently.

"You care for the welfare of my people," he said softly.

Her mouth went dry at the silken caress of his voice. "Of course I do." Before she lost herself in his eyes, she changed the subject. "How are you feeling?"

"The medicine has made me quite dizzy, though

I'm afraid my muscles are already tightening up." His stare intensified. "Are you able to attend to my other treatment now?"

Was it her imagination, or was there heated interest in his gaze? Perhaps this was the time to venture further.

Before her courage could abandon her, she answered, "Yes, but first I need assistance with my gown. It was difficult to move and reach the proper angle the last time."

At the mere mention of the last time, her face heated and she turned her back to him. After the previous surgery she'd massaged him on the bed to better reach the muscles on his shoulder blades. His low sounds of pleasure had driven her mad with desire. Desire that remained unfulfilled when she put him to sleep with the laudanum.

Now she would see if she could tempt him further.

The bed creaked as Rafe sat up and unlaced her gown. She'd purposefully selected one that would be easy for him to unfasten in his soporific state. Once it was loosened, she allowed the thin muslin to pool at her feet. A wicked thrill ran up her spine as she bent over to remove her boots. Not daring to look back, she then reached back and unlaced her stays before slipping the garment off her shoulders and tossing it to the floor.

Standing only in her chemise, she turned to face him. The hunger in his gaze turned her legs to custard. It took the utmost effort to speak. "If you would, ah, lie down on your stomach, I will proceed."

Rafe gave her a strange smile and complied. Her lips parted at the sight of his bronzed, muscled back.

Cassandra sat on the edge of the bed and placed a hand on his smooth flesh. "Now where does it hurt most?"

He seized her hand and pressed it below his shoulder blade. "Here."

She dug her fingers into the taut flesh, gratified to hear him groan with pleasure. "Yes, right there."

Unfortunately, the angle made her arm protest. Cassandra shifted to find a more comfortable position. She needed to be able to put her weight directly on the muscle. But the only way to do so would be to sit on him. She sucked in a breath at the thought.

Rafe turned his head to look at her through a curtain of black hair. "Is there something wrong?"

"I can't seem to find a decent angle. Perhaps if I…" She trailed off, cheeks burning at the prospect of voicing such a brazen suggestion.

"If you straddle me?" he finished, as if reading her mind. "Yes, that would probably work best."

Cassandra froze as her loins flared in heat at the prospect of such naughty intimacy. "W-would I be too heavy?"

He laughed. "Not in the slightest. Well, climb on up then."

Legs quivering, she lifted the skirt of her chemise to sit on his lower back. The feel of him between her thighs made her core ache with longing. Only a thin layer of fabric separated their flesh. Cassandra bit her lip to keep from moaning and concentrated on applying firm, rotating pressure on the muscle.

"Ah," Rafe groaned, "that feels so good." He shifted beneath her and moved his arms back so his fingers brushed her thighs.

Cassandra bit her lip harder. *Is he intentionally touching me there, or is he still muzzy from the drugs?* Daring to experiment, she moved her hips forward, gasping at the improper friction.

Rafe lifted his head to meet her gaze in the mirror. "Are you trying to seduce me, Countess?" With idle purpose he began to stroke her thighs.

"Yes." The answer tore from her throat before she could deem it unwise.

He remained silent for a long time. His fingers continued their gentle caress. It took all of her willpower not to gyrate against him.

Please, she cried silently. If he kept this up much longer, she'd go insane from need.

Suddenly, he sighed. "Cassandra, I confess that the idea of making love to you is tempting beyond reason." He withdrew his hands. "However—"

A knock sounded on the door.

Cassandra gasped and scrambled off Rafe, yanking the bedclothes up to cover her state of undress.

"Yes?" Rafe growled dangerously, rising from the bed with his fangs bared.

The door opened a crack and Anthony poked his head in. "Carlisle is here, my lord. He says he's seen the rogues."

Rafe's eyes narrowed. "So there are more than one?"

"He said he saw three, which is why he did not give chase." Anthony's gaze took in the sight of Cassandra buried under the quilt and Rafe's state of partial undress. The corner of his mouth lifted as he observed Cassandra's blush.

Eyes still slightly glazed from the drugs, Rafe

nodded and pulled on his boots. "Wise of him. You look better, thank Christ. I suppose we should gather a hunting party and see if we can round up the bastards."

"Yes," Anthony replied in a cold, dangerous voice that Cassandra had never heard before. He cracked his knuckles. "And God help them if they don't return Lenore in one piece."

Rafe followed him out the door, not even bothering to say good-bye to Cassandra.

She took a deep, shuddering breath and whispered a silent prayer for Rafe and Anthony's safety as well as Lenore's return. Not knowing what else to do, she pulled a novel from the bureau drawer, deciding to read while she awaited Rafe's return.

An hour later she threw down the book with a sigh. All she'd been doing was staring blankly at the words on the page as Rafe's words echoed in her mind.

"I confess that the thought of making love to you is tempting beyond reason. However…"

"However *what*?" she said aloud. "What is wrong with me?"

❧

Rafe ground his teeth in irritation as he walked through the freezing late-October rain. The rogues had been here. He could smell the unwelcome reek their presence had left behind. Unfortunately, they were long gone.

He lit a cigar, cupping his hands over the match flame for a semblance of warmth. The plume of smoke he exhaled looked the same as his breath. He didn't want to be out here in the rain and frigid cold, chasing

vampires who had no business in his territory. He
wanted to be back in his bedchamber with a warm fire
blazing…and Cassandra in his arms.

At least the search was nearly finished. Anthony,
Carlisle, Elizabeth, and even Clayton had joined
the hunt, their altercation temporarily forgotten.
Hopefully one of them would turn up something, though Rafe doubted they'd have any luck
this night.

Clayton materialized from the shadows of an adja-
cent alley. "I found them, but they escaped me, my
lord. They fled like cowards into Rochester's territory."

"*Hijo de mil putas.*" Rafe tossed the remains of his
cigar into an ice-rimmed puddle. "You were wise not
to pursue them there. Rochester can be ruthless with
uninvited vampires, and God knows we have enough
troubles as it is." He thrust his healing hand into his
pocket and clenched the leather ball Cassandra had
given him. The exercise helped him focus. "Perhaps it
is fortunate that you chased them there. He may very
well catch the wretches and deal with them for us."

"Unless"—Clayton stroked his chin thoughtfully—
"the rogues are his people."

Rafe shook his head. "No. The Lord of Rochester
keeps a tight rein on his subjects. He wouldn't allow
them to leave his jurisdiction to make mischief on
mine." But maybe he would be willing to help. "I will
send him a message."

"I'll do it, my lord," Clayton said quickly. "You
have enough burdensome obligations on your hands,
what with your prisoner and finding a new fourth-in-
command. Besides, I remember your last encounter

with Rochester. Perhaps he would be more receptive to communications from me."

Rafe hid a frown at Clayton's overly solicitous tone and resumed squeezing the ball in his pocket. What was the scheming *bastardo* up to now? However, he feigned agreement. "That may be. He and I are not exactly *compadres*. Go on with it then."

Rafe fully intended to send a message of his own. He looked up and saw Anthony approaching and greeted him with a brisk wave.

Clayton glared at Rafe's third-in-command before he bowed stiffly and stalked off.

Rafe ran a hand through his hair and resisted the urge to roll his eyes. He didn't trust his second-in-command's overeager offer of help in the slightest. Yet for now it was enough to get rid of the perfidious wretch for the night. And soon, forever. A new fourth-in-command wasn't the only position he'd be seeking to fill tomorrow night. Unfortunately, Clayton was unlikely to go quietly. He'd served as Ian's second-in-command for nearly a century.

Rafe shrugged. Perhaps Rochester or another Lord would be willing to take him.

"I don't like it, my lord," Anthony muttered once Clayton was out of earshot. "Not a bit."

"Do you mean Clayton?"

Anthony chuckled. "Well, yes. I've never liked the sanctimonious prig. This time I'm referring to the whole situation. The rogues, Lenore's disappearance, and Clayton's worse-than-usual nettlesome behavior. I tell you, that blasted cur may be behind it all. I wouldn't put it past him."

"I don't argue that he is up to something, yet I cannot see a motive for him to abduct one of our people and allow rogues into the city." Rafe shook his head as they walked back to Burnrath House. "Either way, I intend to have someone keep an eye on him."

His third nodded. "That sounds like a capital plan, my lord. Who is up to such an odious task?"

He spread his hands in exasperation. "That's the bitter rub. I don't know. Clayton isn't the only one who has been behaving oddly of late."

"Lord knows that's the truth," Anthony replied emphatically. After a moment, he added quietly, "Yourself not excluded."

Rafe paused and narrowed his eyes. "Are you saying I've become odd as well?"

"There's no need to be wary." Anthony smiled. "It's only that I cannot help noticing that your charming physician has brought forth a side of you that I've never seen."

"Quit speaking in riddles, Anthony," Rafe growled impatiently. "What are you talking about? I hope you don't mean to say that I've gone soft."

"Of course not, my lord." Anthony laughed again and held up his hands in mock surrender. "Well, you had been far less cantankerous, though perhaps I spoke too soon." He sobered. "You really care for her, don't you?"

Rafe nodded stiffly. "To my everlasting regret and vexation, I do. I don't know what I am going to do with her."

"You have less than a fortnight left to decide her fate."

Rafe sighed in defeat. "Yes, and I wrote letters to

every vampire over a century old that I can call friend, asking them to Change her. Thus far, I have not received a reply."

"Thank God, you are taking some action," Anthony said. "But if no one volunteers—"

"It is not necessary to remind me," Rafe snarled. "I am perfectly aware that—"

Anthony held up a hand. "What I mean to say is that our kind so often thinks we have eternity. We do not. Just as the humans we once were, we must savor every moment of our existence, for the next could be our last."

"I had no idea you were so poetic," Rafe said gruffly. He folded his arms and looked down before Anthony could see how deeply his words had struck him. *Cristo*, maybe he *was* going soft. "So..." He trailed off.

"So savor her, while you still can." Anthony stopped to observe a pair of drunken louts stumbling out of a tavern. "Ah, how convenient. Supper."

After they fed and returned to Burnrath House, Mrs. Smythe handed him two letters.

Rafe's heart swelled with hope as he rushed to his study and opened them. His spirits plummeted as he read both refusals. The death clock ticked louder in his mind.

"I will save her. Somehow, I will save her," he whispered as he burned the letters.

The need to hold Cassandra became a relentless ache. Rafe went straight to the bedchamber. As he headed up the stairs, he willed all of his worries to abate and be replaced with anticipation. For now, it was enough that he would soon spend the day lying beside her.

He opened the door and paused a moment just to enjoy the sight of Cassandra in his bed.

The lamps were extinguished and the fire had burned down to embers. Yet with his preternatural sight, Rafe could see her sleeping form clearly, from the glorious tumble of auburn curls on the pillow to the adorable frown line between her russet brows. Her lush lips pouted enticingly.

He stepped closer…and nearly tripped over a book on the floor. Rafe picked up the novel and frowned. Had she thrown it? It wasn't like Cassandra to mistreat a book.

A slow smile spread across his lips. She'd been vexed at his departure from the bed. Perhaps she'd even taken it as a failure to seduce him. If only she knew how close she'd come to succeeding.

When Rafe lifted the covers and got into bed, Cassandra made a small, satisfied sound and scooted closer to him. It was all the invitation he needed. Carefully, so as not to wake her, he pulled her into his arms. Instead of killing her, he would take her up on her other invitation. The Elders be damned. As Anthony had advised, he would savor her…thoroughly.

Sixteen

24 October 1823

"No, thank you." Cassandra waved away the luncheon tray.

Anthony set down the tray anyway. "You must eat, my lady." Before she could argue again, he left her alone in the dining room.

Cassandra's stomach churned at the sight of the food. How could she consider eating after Rafe's apparent rejection last night?

Hot waves of humiliation washed over her like rancid rain. Now he was avoiding her. After brusquely helping her dress, he'd left to seek his evening meal with a curt good-bye. When he returned, he'd gone straight up to his study and spent hours there before leaving again.

She sighed and swirled her spoon in the steaming bowl of watercress soup. Truly, she had only herself to blame. Time and again she'd been counseled that men preferred virtuous ladies. She shouldn't be surprised that Rafe had been repelled by her wanton attempts to seduce him.

Although he admitted that my offer tempted him, a tiny inner voice whispered. Cassandra shook off the indulgent attempt to soothe her wounded pride. *Yes, but he also tacked on a "however," which renders the statement nothing more than an empty platitude.*

And why was she obsessing over unrequited, inconvenient desires when her situation so far had more dire aspects? She was on the precipice of so many unknowns. Surely facing the prospect of eternal life or early death should be more than enough to occupy her thoughts.

Despite such cataclysmic prospects, Rafe's striking visage, piercing eyes, and sensuous lips refused to leave her mind. Cassandra's fists clenched at her sides. She *had* to stop thinking about him. Doing so served no practical use whatsoever.

Lifting her chin with determination, she forced herself to eat a few bites of her meal before retiring to the library. She could not allow her foolish fascination with this vampire to cause her to neglect her studies.

With that in mind, she retired to the Duchess of Burnrath's old writing room and composed her article on pain remedies for *The Lancet*.

Once finished, she studied a book on burn treatments, but as she started wondering if certain balms would work on vampires, Rafe's scarred face once more invaded her mind. Did his burns still hurt? Or were the damaged areas without sensation? How would it feel to run her tongue across that roughened skin?

When he joined her in the library after midnight, it was all she could do to appear composed and indifferent.

Why didn't he want her? Why did it matter? She thanked God he couldn't read her mind.

"Would you like to retire upstairs for your treatment?" she ventured carefully, setting down her book. "I think it should continue for at least another few weeks, especially the work with your hands."

He remained silent for the longest time, a strange and unreadable expression playing across his exotic face. "Yes, I would like to go upstairs…very much indeed."

At least he hasn't developed an aversion to my touch, she consoled herself as she followed him up the stairs to the bedchamber. *And at least I will enjoy the feel of his glorious body for a little while longer.* The secret place between her thighs throbbed in remembrance of last night's erotic encounter.

The door closed behind them and the sound of the lock clicking into place made Cassandra freeze. Rafe hadn't locked the door since he'd begun sleeping next to her in the bed.

"Well, my lady, shall I assist you with your gown?" he asked softly.

Her pulse accelerated. Did he want her out of her clothing, or was he simply being helpful?

"Y-yes, thank you." She turned around before he could see her flaming cheeks.

With unbearable slowness, he worked the buttons free, lingering on each one like a caress. Gently, he pulled down the dress, his fingers trailing down her body. Heat pulsed between her thighs at his touch. Then he went to work on her stays. Cassandra bit back a gasp. By the time she was down to her chemise, she was trembling.

Biting her lip, she turned around to see Rafe removing his own shirt. As always, she stared in mute awe, captivated by his savage beauty.

Before her silence became disconcertingly apparent, she retrieved the leather ball from the bureau and held it out to him. "Shall we b-begin now?"

Rafe regarded her with a burning look that had made her knees turn to water. "I think that instead of squeezing that infernal ball, there is a much more suitable way for me to exercise my hands."

"And that would be?" Cassandra had to look at the floor, lest she once more fell under the spell of the rippling muscles of his bare chest.

"I believe I should return the favor." Rafe's silken, rumbling voice commanded her to meet his gaze.

Fresh heat flooded her core once more at the thought of him touching her so intimately. "Y-you mean you want to…" She trailed off dumbly.

Rafe's lips curved up, giving her *that* smile, the one that sent her abdomen fluttering. "I am certain you are sore from your ministrations to me, so lie down."

Overcome with awe at the dreamlike situation, Cassandra nearly collapsed on the bed as she complied. When Rafe sat beside her, she looked up and met her own reflection in the mirror. Quickly, she shifted her hair to hide the improper longing in her gaze.

The heat of his hands through the thin fabric of her chemise immediately brought a low moan from her throat. Cassandra bit her lip to prevent from crying out in sheer bliss as his fingers worked deeper magic on her aching shoulders.

Suddenly, Rafe paused. "This will not do."

No! Don't stop! A small whimper escaped her lips. Cassandra struggled to feign composure and prayed he hadn't noticed.

"This infernal thing is in the way." His hands returned to her shoulders, grasping the straps of her chemise and pulling the garment down.

Though a voice from her well-bred past shouted that she was behaving like a harlot, Cassandra squirmed and shifted to aid him in exposing her bare flesh to the heat of the fire and the touch of a vampire. In fact, she felt a pang of regret when he neglected to remove her chemise fully, instead leaving the cotton bunched up at her hips.

Then Rafe's fingers once more worked their magic, the pleasure so much more intense that her core throbbed with desire. His hands left her shoulders to massage her back. A low moan escaped her lips at the intensely blissful sensation. No one had ever touched her like this.

"This angle isn't working," he said, softly in a teasing voice.

He shifted on the bed and knelt, straddling her hips. As he resumed his exquisite ministrations, Cassandra arched her back. His long hair brushed the sides of her rib cage in a tempting whisper. His groin was so close to her aching center that she wanted to scream in frustration. Did he comprehend what he was doing?

Then his hands moved lower, massaging the taut muscles of her hips and easing tension she didn't know she possessed. She looked up at the mirror. The sight of Rafe kneeling behind her and the sheen of firelight on his muscled arms as he touched her took her breath away. His glittering amber gaze met hers in the reflection, and his lips curved up in a wicked smile. Cassandra's lips parted in awe. He was so beautiful that it was decadent.

With sensuous slowness, Rafe bent down and kissed the backs of her thighs. His hands slid down her hips to grasp her legs. Gently but firmly, he moved them apart slightly. Her eyes widened at the brush of his hair against her skin and the sinfully tempting heat of his mouth moving closer to her... *My God!*

She gasped as his tongue flicked across the center of her womanhood.

"My, Countess, you are wet." His deep voice rumbled against her core as his fingers continued to stroke her trembling thighs. "*Te deseo, Querida.* I want you."

"Rafe..." she murmured.

He turned her over with dizzying speed. Before she could draw another breath, his delicious weight was on top of her, his hardness pressing against her wet cleft. He slid her chemise all the way off. His lips devoured hers with intoxicating ferocity before moving down. Drugged with pleasure, she watched his large hands gently caressing her breasts as he licked and sucked her nipples as if they were a banquet from the gods. His eyes were closed in pure, unmistakable bliss. Cassandra tangled her hands in his hair and shifted her hips, mad with the need to ease the pulsing ache he'd invoked.

"Please," Cassandra panted, writhing beneath him like one possessed. "*Please!*"

Rafe stopped and raised himself on his elbows to look down at her. "Is this what you want, Countess?"

His eyes glowed amber fire, his scarred face and bared fangs the epitome of predatory hunger. A small part of her knew she should be afraid, but all she could feel was utter and complete exhilaration.

"Yes!" she whimpered, certain she would die if he didn't take her soon.

His weight left her body, and she heard the harsh sound of fabric tearing as he removed his trousers in a blur of speed. Then he was on top of her again, his hot flesh pressed to hers.

With a low growl, Rafe thrust deep inside her. Cassandra cried out at the intense sensation. It was like being overtaken by a storm. Wrapping her legs around him, she rocked her hips to match his thrusts, urging him deeper. The feel of him brought her closer and closer to the peak of soul-rending ecstasy. A small scream escaped her lips as she was sent over the edge.

While she was still gasping and shuddering beneath him, Rafe suddenly grasped her thighs and thrust into her harder, taking her with unchecked savagery. Her body rejoiced in overwhelming submission. The sound of his flesh striking hers brought her arousal to new, unfathomable heights.

"Oh my God," she gasped. This was not what she expected. This was far more...

The thought fled as his fangs plunged into her neck, triggering another orgasm. Unbelievably, his thrusts deepened, intensifying the climax and sending her into a new realm of consciousness in which the universe seemed to simultaneously explode and unite.

Rafe let out a primal growl and collapsed in her arms. Cassandra quivered beneath him, reveling in the feel of his heart pounding against hers. His mouth nuzzled her neck, inciting aftershocks of her climax.

When he rolled over, pulling her into his embrace,

Cassandra gasped. "Well, that was quite…vigorous and…well…overwhelming."

Rafe raised a brow. "I didn't hear you asking me to stop."

She blinked and curled her fingers around his hair. "I suppose I didn't."

She waited for him to say more, but he remained silent, running a soothing hand down her back. Blissful tingles ran down her body, and once more she was filled with wonder at his dynamic juxtaposition of roughness and gentleness.

I love you… She clamped her lips shut before she could voice such an illogical statement aloud. Surely it was an overreaction to his introducing her to physical passion.

Instantly, her heart protested, but Cassandra shunted its dangerous assertions aside. For now there was nothing she could do except savor the peace and comfort of being in his arms. Besides, surely things would be further resolved when he Changed her.

As if sensing her thoughts, Rafe pulled her closer. Cassandra laid her head on his chest with a sigh, contenting herself to play with his silken hair and caress the captivating angles of his face before sleep claimed her.

Seventeen

"The time has come to take this city from Rafael Villar's reckless clutches," Clayton declared to his audience.

The assembly of vampires cheered in accord. He fought to hide the bright surge of triumph that swelled within him. Nearly half of the London vampires were here tonight.

"How are we to accomplish such a substantial feat?" Elizabeth, one of the wealthier and more powerful vampires, inquired blandly. "We cannot exactly storm Burnrath House with torches and pikestaffs as if it were the Bastille. The mortals would take notice."

Clayton concealed an irritated frown. He'd never liked Elizabeth. As they were nearly the same age, she had been his biggest rival in the vampire hierarchy. However, she seemed to have soured on Rafe's reign as well. Why else would she be here? He scratched his chin and eyed her speculatively. If he could guarantee her loyalty, she would be his best choice to serve as his second-in-command.

"We will not be doing any such thing, Elizabeth,"

he said with an indulgent smile. "Aside from drawing unwanted attention from the humans, that type of action would not be honorable. We will issue an official challenge and meet Rafael Villar and his meager company of allies in a discreet location to demand his surrender and negotiate terms."

"And if he doesn't peacefully step down and allow you to take over?" she asked politely, though with an unmistakable note of challenge.

His eyes narrowed. "Then we fight."

"Are you certain that taking such drastic measures is a wise course of action?" Elizabeth continued to argue in a damnably reasonable tone. Had she been a man, she may have made an excellent lawyer. "You are speaking of civil war. Lives could be lost. Not only that, but the Elders would be angered. We could all be punished severely for this rebellion…perhaps even executed."

"*This* is not a rebellion. This is a revolution. And revolution is the only course of action," Clayton said firmly. He raised his voice, addressing every member of the congregation. "As I've since made clear, Rafael Villar has placed us all in danger with his *involvement* with that mortal female of his. I was reluctant to say this before, lest I cause a panic, but I see now that it is necessary to tell you all…"

"Tell us what?" many vampires echoed. "What has the Spaniard done now?"

Elizabeth remained blessedly silent and watched him with avid interest.

Clayton's fists clenched in righteous outrage as he faced them intently. "He is harboring a mortal who may be even more dangerous than a vampire hunter…

which I am still not convinced that she is not. You all saw that she carried a journal when Villar presented her to us, yes?"

"Yes!" another vampire called out. "She tried to write in it during the meeting, before the Spaniard stopped her."

Many others nodded in agreement, declaring that they saw her as well.

Just on cue, William raised his voice over the clamor. "What was she doing with that book, my lord?"

"She was writing down the secrets of our kind, almost certainly with the intent of sharing the information with her fellow mortals. I have already reported this to the Elders…" Clayton was gratified to hear pleased gasps and murmurs at this bit of news. "In the meantime, Villar must be stopped, and Lady Rosslyn must be destroyed"—he paused dramatically before adding—"as the Elders themselves already commanded. Our very safety depends on it!"

The vampires roared and bared their fangs in enthusiastic agreement. Elizabeth remained silent, all of her meddlesome arguments torn away. Clayton gave her a satisfied smile. He had shown her who was in the right.

Clayton paced in front of them, imagining himself a noble general rallying his troops. "On the fifth of November, Rafael Villar *will* surrender to us or fall to our fangs, swords, and might in battle."

Cheers and applause shook the rafters until dust rained down upon the masses. When his audience quieted, he bowed with a flourish and made his exit as a star performer should.

Adrenaline still pumping from his rally, Clayton

grinned in satisfaction as he made his way home. He would be a far better Lord Vampire than Villar. He knew how to hold a crowd under his sway.

"M'lord." William's footsteps and whining voice cut through Clayton's euphoria.

"What?" he snarled.

The vampire emerged through the thick fog coming off the Thames, regarding him with hunched shoulders. "C-could you spare a bit more blunt? I need... I need..."

From the sight of his bloodshot eyes and trembling hands, Clayton knew exactly what William thought he needed. He ground his teeth in fury. The vampire's petty opium addiction had made him more of a liability than an asset of late.

He sighed. "Come here."

William approached with a wide-fanged grin, resembling a happy bulldog.

Clayton glanced around and sniffed the air for any sign of witnesses before snaking his hand around the back of William's neck and slamming him face-first into a nearby brick wall.

"I told you to quit that vile drug," he snarled.

Over and over he pounded the vampire's face against the hard surface, a red haze of rage overlaying his vision thicker than brick dust. He pounded until William's skull shattered in his hands, leaving behind a mess of flesh, bone shards, and gobbets of brain matter where a head should be. Still, William's body twitched.

Reaching past his overcoat, Clayton withdrew a long knife from the sheath at his belt and plunged it into William's back, twisting until he reached the heart. When at last the vampire went still, Clayton threw the corpse into the Thames. He prayed it would sink before sunrise.

Yet another inconvenience to blame on Villar. A proper lord should never allow drug-addled cretins to live.

After washing his hands in the stinking river, he shoved his hands in his pockets and continued home.

Lenore moaned in bliss as the sweet blood flowed in her mouth. She could feel her body being rejuvenated, coming back to life like a hawthorn after winter's long chill. For the first time in weeks she was warm, cocooned in heavenly soft blankets.

"That is enough for now," a deep and somehow ominous voice declared.

The source of her sustenance was gently but firmly withdrawn from her mouth. Lenore whimpered in protest. She was still so very hungry.

"Come now, open your eyes. You've been unconscious for four nights. I know you're awake and I'm ready for some explanations," the voice commanded.

Though Lenore shivered in reluctance, her eyelids fluttered open. A small cry caught in her throat at the sight of the Lord Vampire of Rochester poised above her, healing a wound on his wrist where her mouth had been. No wonder the blood had been so potent.

Her tongue ran across her fangs, tasting the dark spice of his power. A hot tremor flashed though her body, pulsing deeply in the sore place between her thighs. The sensation triggered memories of her recent violations. Lenore bit her lip to hold back a scream and turned her focus to her surroundings before her traumatic recollections could overtake her sanity.

She was lying in the softest bed imaginable in the largest, most ornate bedchamber she'd ever seen.

Rochester leaned forward, lacing his long fingers together as he regarded her with cold, black eyes. "Now that we are alone, Lenore, would you care to tell me how you came to be wandering in my territory, starved and beaten like a mongrel dog?"

"I–I…" she stammered, overwhelmed and intimidated by his powerful presence. He could never know the shameful details of what had transpired in Clayton's cellar.

No one could.

His already dark features twisted into a harsh mask. "It wasn't Lord Villar, was it?"

"No!" She shook her head fervently, wishing she had the strength to rise. "It was Clayton Edmondson, his second-in-command."

"On Villar's command?" he inquired sardonically.

Frustrated with his insistence on twisting her words, Lenore slammed her fists on the mattress. "Certainly not! Clayton had rogues abduct me, and then he held me captive as part of his plan to discredit Lord Villar."

Rochester raised a brow, his gaze rife with scornful disbelief. "Why does he want to discredit him? And why bring rogues into the mix?"

Lenore fought to maintain composure under the intimidating force of his presence as she explained everything she'd overheard during her nightmarish imprisonment. "His ultimate plan is to overthrow the Lord of London and take his place."

"Ah, so there is to be a revolution in our esteemed capital," the vampire mused aloud, running a hand through his long, dark curly hair.

She nodded solemnly. At least he believed her. A small light of hope illuminated her consciousness. Perhaps he could help. Rochester was certainly a powerful vampire, and Lord Villar could use all the help he could muster.

"Clayton is like a deadly spider, spinning a web of deception around London's vampires. Nearly half the lot have fallen for his lies." Lenore shuddered in fear and disgust as vivid memories of her cruel treatment under his care haunted her like malicious phantoms. "He plans to challenge Lord Villar soon."

"I do not see why this should concern me," Rochester said coldly. "I have always been neutral. Aside from that, Villar and I have never been on agreeable terms. Frankly, it would surprise me if he was amicable with anyone. He's such a prickly fellow."

"I think it very well *should* concern you." Lenore used all of her strength and courage to sit up and face him boldly. It was time to stop cringing. "If London comes under Clayton's control, countless vampires will suffer as I have. That is something that should concern all of our kind. And if he can allow rogues into his territory and abduct vampires, what is to stop him from meddling with your people?" She softened her tone. "Please, my lord, help Lord Villar stop this insurrection."

"You plead a pretty case, my dear." Rochester's thin lips curved in a patronizingly indulgent smile.

"However, it has never been my policy to become involved with the struggles of others. Now, enough about me. There is something else that has me curious. Why is it that you came here instead of running to your own lord for protection?"

Lenore sighed. She'd anticipated this question, knowing that on the surface her actions didn't reflect well on her lord. "Clayton and the rogues he set to pursue me blocked all routes to Lord Villar's abode. If I had tried to go there, they would have caught me for certain." Chills ran over her flesh at the vivid memory of that harrowing chase. "Once I had left the city, a better plan came to mind."

"And what would that be, youngling?" His voice was tinged with mockery.

Refusing to be daunted, she told him.

For an endless moment, he stared in thunderstruck silence.

Finally, he threw back his head and laughed. Lenore shivered at the rich, decadent sound. When he recovered, he eyed her with the first genuine smile she'd seen on his cynical countenance. Something warm and unfamiliar fluttered in her belly.

"That is the most reckless and hazardous plan you could possibly conjure up. Also, the boldest. I toast your courage, little one." His black eyes glittered with amusement. "Yet I must ask: How did you expect to reach your destination on time in your weak and malnourished condition?"

Her shoulders slumped as the bleak logic in his words sank in. "I do not know."

With unbelievable gentleness, he ran a hand through

her tangled hair. "Very well, I shall tell you. You will stay here another day and recover your strength. Then I shall see about securing your passage on a ship."

"Thank you, Lord Rochester. I will never forget your kindness." Overwhelmed with gratitude, she placed her hand on his.

Rochester blinked as if surprised at her touch. Slowly, he took her hand and squeezed it gently before firmly moving it away. "Oh, I would not say I am helping you out of kindness. You will owe me a favor for this, Lenore, as will Lord Villar. And I always collect my debts."

Eighteen

25 October 1823

RAFE STUDIED CASSANDRA'S LIPS AS HE MOVED HIS rook across the chessboard. They were red and puffy from his kisses. He could not wait to kiss her again. He licked his fangs, eyeing the mark on her neck from his bite. He couldn't wait to taste her again as well.

Last night had been a revelation. It had been more than achieving long-denied physical gratification, more than reveling in the joy that he could once more elicit cries of pleasure from a beautiful woman. It had even been more than having the ability to use both of his arms for such a delightful experience.

Last night had been *everything* because it was with her.

"Check," she announced, not even bothering to hide her triumph.

Rafe smiled at her enthusiasm. He'd had centuries to perfect the game. Thus far no mortal had beaten him, and very few vampires for that matter. The Lord of Cornwall, however, trounced him regularly.

"It is only because I am distracted, *Querida*," he argued gently.

She blinked and that lovely mouth of hers gave the most delightful moue. "Distracted by what?"

"You," he said, blatantly staring at the curves of her breasts above her emerald brocade gown. How he longed to touch them again.

The way her cheeks pinkened and then turned crimson filled him with delight he'd never known. Tonight he would ensure that blushes covered every inch of her succulent flesh.

Rafe shook his head and sighed in exaggerated regret. "Alas, for now, I shall have to put forth the utmost effort to focus my attention on the game. Losing under such circumstances would be most humiliating for me."

Cassandra grinned and opened her mouth for a rejoinder, but then she fell silent as they heard approaching footsteps in the corridor outside. Rafe cursed the interruption to the seventh circle of hell.

Anthony entered the library, pale and gasping with exertion. "My lord, Elizabeth is here with urgent news."

Rafe looked up from the chessboard and sighed. "Bring her to me." Meeting Cassandra's concerned gaze, he attempted a glib smile. "I shall never have any peace here, it seems."

"Perhaps the news is good," she ventured. "Maybe the missing vampire has been found."

Her hopeful tone warmed him more than the cheery fire in the hearth. He coughed and looked down at the game lest anyone see how calf-eyed he must appear.

The door opened and Anthony ushered in Elizabeth. She was tall, regal, and feminine despite her shabby male attire. And she looked terrified.

"What is it, Elizabeth?" he asked in as gentle a tone as he could manage.

She took a deep, shuddering breath. "My lord, I've just come from a meeting that Clayton arranged."

"Clayton isn't supposed to hold meetings without clearing them with me first," Rafe growled. Then it dawned on him. He cursed himself for a fool. "He is plotting an insurrection."

Elizabeth nodded and Anthony cursed behind her.

Rafe sighed and lit a cigar. "How many stand with him?"

"Nearly half of London, my lord." She cringed as if expecting to be punished for bearing bad news.

"But you do not," he mused aloud, warmed at her loyalty. "That is why you've come to warn me."

A measure of anxiety left her features before she bowed. "Yes, my lord."

"When is he planning to make his move?" He tried to sound unconcerned as he tapped his cigar in his little tray.

Elizabeth's voice shook as she replied, "He will issue an official challenge on Guy Fawkes Night."

"How terribly gauche. 'Remember, remember the fifth of November...'" He shook his head. "At any rate, he's a quick bugger. And a conniving one as well, for the Elders' deadline would be up on the fourth and all his people would see Cassandra alive and still human."

"There is something else you should know,"

Elizabeth continued as if reading his mind. "William is with him."

A bitter chuckle escaped Rafe. "I should have known."

"What are you going to do, my lord?"

Rafe drew deeply on his cigar and considered the two vampires before him. It was far past time for him to have made this decision. "Well, since both my second- and fourth-in-command have betrayed me, I suppose I had better replace them before I can do anything else. Elizabeth, you have demonstrated sufficient loyalty. Are you willing to serve as my third?"

Elizabeth sank to one knee and bowed. "I would be honored."

Rafe turned to Anthony. "And would you be second?"

"Of course, my lord." He bowed as well, eyes sparkling with the smile he tried to conceal.

Cassandra frowned and shook her head.

"What is it, *Querida*?" Surely she would not see fault in his edict.

"The situation with William," she said slowly, toying with a chess piece. "I know it sounds strange, but he tried to help me once. Perhaps that was the beginning of his turning against you. I should have mentioned it sooner."

Rafe's eyes narrowed in suspicion. "Help you *how*?"

"He offered to help me escape." Cassandra's brows drew together in confusion. "It was very odd. I thought he didn't like me, but there he was, trying to be helpful."

"Oh, he wasn't trying to help you, *Querida*." Rafe's voice was low and dangerous, betraying his fury. "If you had left my custody, your life would have been forfeit. William wanted to see you dead and me discredited. Likely it was Clayton's idea. I wish you had told me sooner." His fists clenched until his knuckles turned white. "I would have throttled them both."

Elizabeth gasped. "My lord, your hand! When did it get better?"

Rafe gestured to Cassandra, unable to hide a tender smile as he gazed at her. "When I absconded with this magical healer."

The female vampire's eyes widened. "So she truly is a physician!" Elizabeth turned to face Cassandra. "My lady, you cannot know what this means for our kind. What you have done for our lord is nothing short of a miracle."

She turned back to Rafe. "We could have our own doctor! The first one of our kind. Lord vampires around the world and even the Elders themselves would benefit greatly."

"You mean vampires have never had their own physicians before?" Cassandra interjected, green eyes wide with fascination.

"We heal fast and do not suffer from any illness," Rafe explained, charmed with her inquisitiveness. "Also, not only has a practitioner of medicine never joined our ranks, but we never saw a great need to have one. Though considering that others have surely suffered injuries like mine, it is a great oversight."

Elizabeth leaned forward. "Don't you see, my lord? You must Change her at once! Not only to ensure her safety from Clayton and his allies, but because she could be one of the greatest assets our kind has ever seen!"

"I would if I could," Rafe replied almost too

softly to hear. His entire soul writhed in miserable self-loathing.

Cassandra gasped and whirled to face him, eyes wide with fear and accusation. "I beg your pardon?"

Elizabeth's jaw dropped. "What do you mean?"

"I mean"—he choked out the words, full of burning regret—"that I Changed another only two years ago...and illegally at that."

Why had he wasted the strength he'd gathered for centuries just to repay a debt of honor? It seemed so pitiful now.

The female vampire blinked in outraged disbelief. "Who?"

"It is best you do not know," Rafe told her tiredly. "The Elders may get wind of my actions, and I don't need anyone else implicated in my folly."

❧

A lump of ice formed in Cassandra's chest, the chill spreading to pool in her stomach.

She opened her mouth to say something, she didn't know what, and all that came out was a feeble squeak.

"*Querida*?" Rafe's voice sounded tinny and far away, as if he were speaking through a long, dark tunnel.

She averted her face. If she looked at him now, she would cry, and there was no way she would allow such an indignity. The other vampires' faces blurred in her vision.

"Anthony," Rafe said softly. "Take Lady Rosslyn upstairs."

The other vampire bowed stiffly, sherry eyes glimmering with pity. "Yes, my lord."

Gently, as if assisting an elderly woman, he took Cassandra's hands and carefully pulled her up from the chair. She wanted to tear away from his grasp, to demand explanations, to rant and rail, but the shock of Rafe's confession refused to relinquish its paralyzing hold.

Numb and as empty of will as a discarded toy, she allowed herself to be led away. Only when she was alone in the bedchamber did the tears begin to fall down her face. Cassandra dashed them away with an angry fist, but still they came.

How could he have led her to believe that he would Change her? How could he have made love to her in this very bed when he'd known he would eventually have to kill her? She hadn't believed him capable of such monstrous deception. She'd been a fool.

Cassandra glared down at the massive bed as if the elegant piece of furniture had also betrayed her. Though the bed was now immaculately made with fresh sheets, her traitorous mind called up images of Rafe's hands and mouth working their dark magic on her naked body. Even worse, the place between her legs pulsed with acute arousal at the memory.

"I have to escape this place," she whispered, dread choking her words. "I can't let him kill me."

Despite that dreadful truth, her heart ached so severely that she almost wanted to die. Cassandra frowned as she shook off the macabre thought and clenched her fists. *I will not give him that satisfaction!*

Forcing her mind to cut itself from her tumultuous emotions, she focused instead on how to escape.

She would have to leave London; that much was

for certain. She didn't think William had lied about everything when he'd offered to aid her escape. Rafe probably could sense her Mark. It would be best to get out of his territory as soon as possible.

Besides, there was nothing for her in this city anymore. She'd always been an outcast, and now aside from Sir Patrick, she was completely ostracized. Sir Patrick would be willing to take her in, but there was no way she'd put him in danger. Rafe had said if she left this house, her life would be forfeit, along with any who offered her aid. Her fists clenched. Her life was also forfeit if she stayed.

So, where *would* she go? Unfortunately, her usually agile mind was drawing a blank—except for haunting images of Rafe's rare tender smile and memories of his decadent kiss. *No! That way lies madness.* Closing her eyes, she tried to conjure up a prospective destination.

Regrettably, none came.

To her frustration, tears once more threatened. *Maybe I'll just catch any dratted ship and go wherever it takes me.* The more she thought about it, the more attractive the idea became. Perhaps it was best that she didn't have a destination planned. Theoretically, that should make her more difficult to track.

Cassandra threw open the wardrobe and began seizing gowns and throwing them on the bed. By the time she'd stripped the mahogany relic bare, she was panting in exhaustion.

Too late she realized that there was no way she'd be able to pack and haul a trunk without the vampires taking notice. Groaning in vexation, she fetched her valise and stuffed it with as many articles of clothing as would fit, along with a few novels.

Taking a deep breath, she hefted the stuffed valise over her shoulder and tried the door. It was unlocked. Rafe still seemed to trust her, even though he'd betrayed *her* trust. *I must not think of him anymore.*

Squaring her shoulders, Cassandra tiptoed down the corridor as quietly as possible. As she passed her laboratory, her mind and spirit screamed at her not to abandon her precious texts and equipment. Things she'd painstakingly worked for years to acquire. But they would be of no use to her if she was dead.

Swallowing a lump in her throat, she carefully made her way down the servants' staircase and out the back door.

As she left the rear gate reserved for servants and delivery men, Cassandra turned and looked back at the ancient Elizabethan mansion, yet she did not see it. All she could see was the glowing amber of Rafe's eyes and all she could hear was the warmth in his voice as he called her "*Querida*."

Go back! the lunatic inside her heart called.

Cassandra ignored its tempting plea and allowed logic to carry her away.

Nineteen

"My lord?" Elizabeth's voice came from far away, as if obscured by thick fog.

Rafe focused his attention back on his new third-in-command. It was difficult, for the Mark between him and Cassandra was pulsing with searing pain. She was hurting. He longed to go to her, but he did not know what he could say.

"I'm sorry. What did you say?"

"I said, you do not intend to kill her, do you?" Elizabeth repeated, eyeing him warily.

He slammed his fist on the table, sending the chess pieces airborne before they clattered to the floor. "No, of course not! I have written letters to every vampire I call friend, asking them to Change her." Crushing defeat wrenched his soul at his next admission. "Thus far, every reply has been a refusal. But I can't kill her. I don't know what to do."

Rafe buried his face in his hands. The confession was crippling. He was supposed to be a leader, keeping order among his people, punishing the wicked, and protecting the innocents from harm. Now everything was slipping from his control.

"Have you told her this?" the vampire prodded. "Does she know that instead of preparing to kill her, you are doing everything in your power to see her live?"

Rafe's head jerked up and he stared at her with dawning horror. No, he hadn't told Cassandra anything of the sort. His pride had restrained him from revealing his legion of failures. What if she believed that he would truly——? He couldn't finish the thought.

Elizabeth mistook his expression for one of outrage. "I apologize if I was insolent, my lord. I only say this because she appeared to be awfully distraught by your confession…and so terribly pale, as if she were facing the specter of Death himself."

"No, Elizabeth. You are not at all insolent. You are wise." Laboriously, as if the weight of all of his problems threatened to crush him, Rafe rose from his seat. "I, however, am a fool. Excuse me while I look in on her."

As he slowly made his way up the stairs, Rafe racked his mind about how to assure Cassandra. He must make it clear to her that he had no intention of killing her; that much was certain. But other than that, what could he say? What if no vampire agreed to Change her? What then? If he refused to kill her, the Elders would likely send an enforcer to do the deed, then arrest him and possibly execute him.

Perhaps they could run away together… Rafe dashed away that tiny seed of hope before it could take root. He would be declared rogue then. He may even be hunted down, with a price on his head for disobeying an edict from the Elders. And with his scars and foreign looks, he would be easy to find.

Rafe's shoulders slumped in defeat. If Cassandra could not be Changed, he would have to send her away for her own safety. Somewhere far away where she would be less likely to be noticed by other vampires...somewhere on the other side of the world, safe from the Elders' immediate influence. He'd likely be punished for allowing her escape, but it would be worth it to know she lived.

The Americas would likely be the best option. He had not been to that vast and untamed land since he was an infant five centuries ago. The vampires there would sense his Mark on Cassandra, but they wouldn't recognize his identity. Plenty of vampires Marked their mortal descendants out of sentimentality, so they would leave her alone and not think anything of it.

The thought of never seeing her again made Rafe's heart contort in agony. He loved her; he knew that now. He loved her intelligence, her boundless inquisitiveness, and her formidable determination in the pursuit of miracles. He loved how she never saw him as a crippled aberration or an object of pity. He loved the way she came into his arms like someone arriving home.

Because he loved her, he would have to let her go if it became necessary. For her to die would be more than he could bear.

Still, Rafe clung to a faint wisp of hope that she could be Changed, that the Elders would give him more time...that they could be together...that she could somehow love him too.

His lips twisted in self-mockery. Doubtless she would laugh if she knew how he felt. No woman in her right mind could love a monster that had cruelly abducted her and put her life in danger. But she didn't loathe him, and for that incredible gift, he would move heaven and earth to see her safe.

Rafe paused with his hand on the doorknob. The hand Cassandra had restored to him with her medical magic. *Dios*, his debt to her was insurmountable.

He opened the door. "*Querida*, we must talk."

There was no answer.

"*Querida?*" He stepped into the room. His gaze lit on the rainbow mess of gowns strewn across the bed and darted to the gaping empty wardrobe.

Though her Mark still screamed with pain, it was drawing farther and farther away.

She was gone.

Rafe's heart clenched in agony as icy terror coursed through his veins.

She truly had believed he would kill her. Bitter regret flooded his mind, thick enough to choke on. Why hadn't he told her the truth? Because of his foolish pride, she was out in the cold London night, placing herself in danger from Clayton and his allies or even a human cutthroat.

Biting back a roar of impotent fury, he rang for Cassandra's housekeeper.

"Yes, my lord?" Mrs. Smythe inquired timidly.

"Lady Rosslyn had a fit of pique, I'm afraid," he said as civilly as possible. "Please see that these gowns are put back properly…and see that someone dusts her laboratory."

Mrs. Smythe bowed, not bothering to hide her perplexed frown. "Yes, *Don* Villar."

Refusing to indulge her curiosity, Rafe left the

room and strode down the stairs to inform Anthony and Elizabeth of Cassandra's flight. His fists clenched at his sides as he cursed this disaster and silently vowed that he would see her safely returned home tonight.

⁓

Cassandra hefted her valise over her other shoulder. Her arms and back muscles continued to scream in protest from lugging its pendulous weight for seven blocks. She stared down the expanse of Marlborough Street, the light of the gas lamps obscured by the thick night fog. There was still no sign of a hackney or any other mode of transportation.

Too late, she realized that this would not be the best location to find a ride. The little season had not yet begun and Marlborough Street was all but deserted, most of its aristocratic residents still tucked away in their country estates.

Go back, that meddlesome, unreasonable inner voice pleaded yet again.

But she couldn't. Rafe would kill her! But her words held even less conviction than her previous utterance.

What if he didn't intend to kill her? What if he had another plan in mind? Cassandra shook her head, refusing to indulge in such whimsical thinking. He had made the rules governing her situation quite clear.

Yet some wayward part of her continued to cry out for Rafe with every step that took her away from him. It cried out to see his tender smile, to hear him call her "*Querida*" in that gentle tone, to feel his sensuous kiss, to experience the furious storm of his lovemaking once more.

With an aching sigh, she plodded forward.

Suddenly, the clatter of horseshoes on cobblestone reached her ears. *A carriage at last!* The sound came from one street over. Cassandra gripped her valise and ran with every vestige of strength she could muster.

But it wasn't enough. She rounded the corner just in time to see the carriage's rear wheels disappear into the fog.

Cassandra threw down her heavy baggage and sank to her knees, panting in exhaustion. Had this night anything but misfortune to bestow upon her?

It was then that she realized she hadn't any money with which to pay for a ride. A harsh, bitter laugh like the sound of a crow escaped her lips.

"My, my," a soft, male voice remarked amiably. "You *are* a queer one."

Cassandra's face flushed in humiliation at being caught so out of sorts. She scrambled to her feet and frantically dusted off her gown. Perhaps this gentleman would offer her aid if she could convince him she wasn't cracked.

Just as she was about to curtsy, she glanced up at the stranger. Mortification turned to terror as he stepped out into the meager light of the gas lamp.

Clayton bared his fangs.

He laughed at her cry of dismay. "Well, Lady Rosslyn, how fortuitous to encounter you here. Is Villar nearby?" Before she could open her mouth, Clayton shook his head and grinned. "Do not bother with a pretty fabrication. I can sense that he is not."

She turned to run, but another vampire materialized before her, blocking her escape.

"Ooh, she's a pretty one, by Jove." He reached for her with thick, sausage-like fingers.

Clayton pulled her back. "She's not for you, Hamish."

"Aw, but I could have a bit o' fun with her," Hamish grumbled petulantly.

Clayton sighed in exaggerated weariness. "What makes you think I'd give you another plaything after you allowed the last one to slip away?"

Cassandra's horror escalated at the exchange. *Good Lord, what sorts of monsters are they? Do they make a habit of kidnapping women regularly?*

"But this one's nothing but a frail human female! What can *she* do?"

She gasped at the implication. Had these vampires been responsible for Lenore's disappearance? If they were, the vampire had escaped...so where was she now?

The thought broke as another vampire slunk out of the fog with such a sickening leer that Cassandra unconsciously shrank back against Clayton.

There was something off about those two vampires. Something alien and unfamiliar.

Cassandra blinked as she realized why. These vampires had not been in attendance when Rafe had presented her to his people. She was certain of that. Her exceptional memory had never failed her.

That meeting had been mandatory for *all* of his people to attend. Which meant that these two hulking blood-drinkers were *not* Rafe's people. They must be the rogues that he and Anthony had been hunting. Rogues who were working with Clayton and doubtless had been responsible for Lenore's disappearance. Was the poor vampire even alive?

"Tell me, Lady Rosslyn." Clayton trailed his fingers down her arm. "How did you come to be out here alone in the perilous night? Did you escape Villar?"

Cringing at his loathsome touch, she nodded, unable to see a benefit in lying. "He intended to kill me."

"Well, at least he is at last doing something right," her captor remarked agreeably. Then his voice darkened. "Unfortunately, I cannot have that at this point."

The oafish one called Hamish strode forward, his porcine nose practically wriggling. "What are you going to do with her, my lord?"

The other one remained still and continued to stare, as if he were striving to perceive how she would appear without skin.

Clayton gripped her shoulders with bruising force. "We will take her to the warehouse and call a meeting. I must make an example of her. As the new Lord of London, I will show my subjects what happens to those who endanger my people."

"I have not endangered anyone!" Cassandra protested. *Where in God's name did this accursed lout get such a ludicrous idea?*

The vampire paid her no heed and tugged her forward. The rogues followed behind. Dread filled her every pore. She never should have left Rafe. With him, death would have been far more merciful.

Her heart cried out for him as she was dragged along. Did he even know she was gone? Or was he still in the library with Anthony and Elizabeth, discussing battle plans? Somehow, she doubted that very much…not if he truly had put some manner of preternatural Mark on her.

The thought brought on an idea. Feeling somewhat foolish, Cassandra closed her eyes and focused on Rafe, calling his name silently. Immediately a faint, warm buzz crept into her head. She could almost smell his cigars.

Shocked, Cassandra gasped and stumbled at the force of her connection with Rafael.

Clayton jerked her up before she fell.

"Damn clumsy human," he snarled and lightly cuffed her on the side of her face.

She flinched but did not cry out. The stinging pain was completely obliterated by a blooming rose of hope.

Rafe! she screamed in her mind, focusing her entire being on him.

Once they reached the wharves, the stink of the Thames grew thick enough to choke on. A third vampire joined them, muttering quietly to the silent, leering one. Fresh dismay sank deeper into her bones, yet she refused to give up.

As they hauled her into a dilapidated warehouse and Clayton ordered Hamish to fetch the chains, Cassandra's silent cry grew louder.

Twenty

RAFE CHARGED THROUGH THE COLD, WET LONDON streets with Anthony and Elizabeth at his heels. He willed his preternatural senses to locate Cassandra's Mark. The overwhelming anguish had slightly abated, only to be cut through with abject terror.

A low growl rumbled from his throat. She was in danger. Madre de Dios, *please do not let it be Clayton*.

Though he already knew it was unlikely he'd be that fortunate.

As if in answer to his prayers, the Mark suddenly opened between them, flooding his senses in a rush of warmth. Rafe felt her calling to him, the words unfocused and indecipherable, yet enough to pinpoint her location. Hope and triumph welled within.

"This way!" he called to Anthony and Elizabeth. "Toward the river. *Apúrese! Corra!* Hurry! Run!"

He continued on, having no time to look back. He would free Cassandra with or without their aid.

Rafe! Cassandra's voice screamed in his mind as he felt a sharp burst of pain as if it were his own.

All of his protective instincts roared through him

with savage intensity. How dare anyone try to hurt his woman! They would pay. His fists clenched as he ran faster, heedless of the drenching rain.

I am coming, Querida! he shouted silently, praying Cassandra could hear him.

As he reached the wharves, he nearly slipped in the putrid slime that perpetually coated the cobblestones. Anthony and Elizabeth slid to a stop behind him.

"Can you sense her exact location yet?" Anthony panted, still pale and weak from his blood donations.

Rafe held up a hand to silence his second and closed his eyes, concentrating. Almost immediately, he heard her voice and detected a faint aroma of rose petals. *Rafe! Please, hurry!*

"There!" he shouted, pointing at a ramshackle warehouse a hundred meters away.

The vampires wasted no time, arriving at the building in a rush of preternatural speed. Rafe kicked open the door with such force that the rotted wood shattered like glass. Fury boiled through every vestige of his being at the sight before him.

Clayton stood on a raised platform, holding a struggling Cassandra. The raised red weal of a handprint marred her cheek. A rogue vampire approached with an armful of chains with which to lock her up, while a second rogue looked on with a grotesque expression of rapt interest.

A low growl trickled from Rafe's mouth. He could taste Cassandra's rapid pulse.

Clayton looked up and smirked, eyes blazing with insolence as he snaked his arm under Cassandra's chin. "Not another step, Villar, or I will snap your pretty countess's neck like a matchstick."

Rafe inclined his head in mild acceptance of Clayton's threat. Of course the traitor would attempt to shield himself with an innocent.

Cassandra's sea-green eyes met his, wide with fear.

"I'm sorry," she whispered brokenly.

His former second-in-command flashed a triumphant smile, oblivious as Rafe reached behind his back and withdrew Anthony's pistol.

Before Clayton could react, Rafe lifted the gun, aimed, and pulled the trigger.

The rafters shook at the deafening sound. Clayton roared in pain, releasing Cassandra as bright red blood bloomed from the bullet hole in his shoulder.

Rafe shot forward and reclaimed his woman just as Anthony and Elizabeth launched themselves at the two rogues.

Cassandra hugged him tightly, looking up at him with such joyous relief that his heart clenched.

He stroked her hair. "Are you all right, *Querida*?"

"As well as one could be under such circumstances, I suppose," she said calmly, though he could feel the tremors racking her body.

Rafe's eyes narrowed on the welt on her cheek. "He hurt you."

"Nonsense, it was a feeble blow." She shook her head, then flinched as a wet lock of hair slapped her injured flesh.

A hiss escaped his clenched teeth. As much as he was loath to admit it, she was correct. If Clayton had put any force into the slap, the side of her face would have been shattered beyond recognition. That didn't stop him from wanting to pound the son of a bitch into the ground like a rail spike. If Rafe weren't so reluctant to release Cassandra, he would be doing just that. Thankfully, Clayton thus far was in no condition to fight.

However, Rafe's new second- and third-in-command were making short work of the remaining rogues. In moments they could arrest Clayton and this whole infuriating business would end. He could have the traitor in chains and exact his wrathful punishment at leisure. The bastard would suffer. Of that Rafe was most certain.

"Paul, go fetch reinforcements!" Clayton commanded, blood spurting between his fingers from where he grasped his wound. "Now!"

A third rogue scuttled out from the shadows and out the rear exit before anyone could react. Rafe cursed under his breath. He should have anticipated that.

The sound of nearing footsteps reached his ears. Rafe and Clayton simultaneously sniffed the air like wolves and locked gazes. Humans were approaching, doubtless to investigate the source of the gunshot.

"It may be a constable," Clayton whispered.

His wound was healing, but he was pale and weak from blood loss. Easy to vanquish...

Rafe shook his head. Unfortunately, the *hijo de puta* was most likely correct. Cursing inwardly, he silently commanded Anthony and Elizabeth to withdraw. Clayton did the same with his rogues.

Rafe gathered Cassandra in his arms and Clayton's henchmen rushed to their master, holding him up before he could fall.

As Rafe and his would-be usurper drew apart,

they both paused and eyed one another like opposing monarchs across a narrow sea.

The sound of the approaching humans drew nearer.

"This is not finished," Rafe snarled.

Clayton nodded. "Enjoy the last days of your reign, Villar. Soon there will be a revolution the likes of which our kind has never seen. London shall be mine, and you and your pet countess will pay for your crimes against our people."

Rafe laughed humorlessly. "I think you have that reversed, Edmondson."

He inclined his head in a mocking half bow and carried Cassandra away without a backward glance as Clayton shrieked insults and mad vows of retribution. Damn the interfering mortals. If not for them, he could have had that traitor's head on a spike.

Yet somehow it didn't matter much, not when Cassandra was once more in his arms. He would deal with Clayton later. After all, he had other matters to address right now.

How could Cassandra have put herself in danger like this? How could someone with a brilliant mind such as hers be so goddamned foolish? Rafe looked down at the bruise on her cheek.

A fresh torrent of rage roared through him like an inferno.

                                ❧

Cassandra's pulse lodged in her throat at the fury in Rafe's eyes as he carried her out of the warehouse. When he'd rescued her from Clayton, he'd seemed so relieved and concerned for her well-being. Now he looked cold and cruel. Had she imagined his earlier warmth? Was he angry that Clayton had abducted her because he wanted to kill her himself?

The moral of an old tale came to mind: *De piscibus e sartigine in prunas desilentibus*. She was just like the fish that leaped from the boiling fat into the burning coals.

Despite her doomed situation, her traitorous body reveled in the feel of his arms around her and his compelling scent of dark spices and tobacco. She bit back a moan as a frisson of heat pulsed between her thighs.

No! I will not succumb to this madness again. Before she melted against him, Cassandra made a valiant effort to struggle out of his grip. People had entered the warehouse now; she could hear them. If she made it to them—

Immediately, Rafe's arms clamped down like iron. "Don't even think about it, *Querida*."

Her brows drew together and she emitted an unladylike snort. How could he continue to use that endearment?

Rafe scowled down at her as Anthony and Elizabeth approached.

"Damn those nosy humans!" Anthony growled. "In another moment, I would have had that bloody rogue—"

Rafe cut him off. "Leave, both of you!"

"Where, my lord?" Elizabeth asked timidly.

"I do not care, as long as you do not return until tomorrow night."

A hollow chord of dread echoed through Cassandra's soul at his words. The last whisper of hope vanished like fog from a windowpane. He truly was going to kill her. Why else would he have ordered them away?

Anthony took Elizabeth's elbow and led her off, glancing back over his shoulder at Cassandra. The sympathy in his warm eyes brought a lump to her throat.

A hackney rolled near and Rafe flagged it down. Cassandra bit her lip, holding back a bitter chuckle. *Of course one would come for him when it was convenient.* Briefly she contemplated calling to the driver for help, but she dismissed the thought immediately. Rafe would tear him apart.

After dictating the destination to the driver, Rafe lifted Cassandra into the rickety carriage and sat down, keeping a firm grip on her hand. She shivered. It was all so similar to when he'd first taken her prisoner.

"*Cristo*," he growled. "Your hands are like ice." He proceeded to rub them roughly, bringing forth more than one kind of warmth.

"Why should you care about my hands when you are going to kill me soon?" she whispered, trying to pull away.

Rafe's hands clamped down on hers. "I am *not* going to kill you, *Querida*. The deadline is in nine nights, but I refuse to do it. Not after everything you've done for me. Not after…" He shook his head and leaned forward and stared into her eyes as if he were trying to capture her soul. "How could you be so foolish?"

Her pulse stopped for a moment. She was barely able to utter, "There was a deadline? Then why—"

"We will discuss that later." His tone was so harsh, so final that all arguments died in her throat.

Cassandra slumped back against the bench so hard that her back cried out in protest. She would have a bruise tomorrow. The side of her face where Clayton had hit her emitted a twinge in agreement. Her arms chimed in as well, aching from where both he and Rafe had grabbed her. All right, then she would have several bruises tomorrow.

Tomorrow. The magnitude of the word struck her full force, for there would be one for her. Rafe was *not* going to kill her. Aside from the immediate relief of knowing that simple fact, a multitude of contradictory emotions swept through her with dizzying intensity. Joy at the prospect of returning to her laboratory and being with Rafe warred with her trepidation about countless unknowns.

If he did not intend to kill her, then what *was* he going to do?

Twenty-one

RAFE PAID THE DRIVER AND LIFTED CASSANDRA FROM the carriage, his countenance still blazing with fury. As he set her down and led her into the house, a heavy weight of foreboding settled in her belly.

Mrs. Smythe glanced up from dusting a gas lamp, eyes wide with concern as she took in the sight of Cassandra shivering in her sodden clothes.

"Is there a fire built in our bedchamber?" Rafe all but growled.

The housekeeper nodded, still eyeing Cassandra. "Yes, *Don* Villar. Do you require anything else?"

Rafe shook his head. "You may retire for the night. Remind me tomorrow to double your wages."

Mrs. Smythe froze and blinked at him for a moment before curtsying and bustling away.

Placing a firm hand at the small of her back, Rafe guided Cassandra upstairs. Her knees quaked.

They entered the bedchamber and she sighed in appreciation at the welcoming warmth of the fire.

Rafe slammed the door and jerked her into his arms, claiming her lips in a devouring kiss. Her body melted into his embrace of its own volition, as if *this* was the home she'd been seeking. Cassandra's legs turned to jelly and she nearly collapsed before he dragged his mouth from hers.

Eyes still burning with unholy wrath, he drew back and lightly stroked her bruised cheek. "*Jesucristo, mujer tonta*! Foolish woman! How could you have put yourself in such danger?"

Before she could answer, he once again pulled her into a fierce embrace and covered her face with kisses. Her breath fled as Rafe clung to her so tightly that she could feel the strong beat of his heart.

A stream of Spanish words poured from his lips between kisses. They sounded like curses. The dichotomy between his words and actions made what little remained of her common sense reel in confusion. The rest of her reveled in his touch and yearned for more.

Still muttering angrily in his beautiful language, Rafe tore off her soaked velvet cloak and shrugged out of his coat. "Turn around, *Querida*."

"What are you doing?" She felt foolish the moment she asked.

She knew *what* he was doing, but it was the precise *why* that she wished to discern. Was he undressing her to ready her for bed or in preparation for ravaging her? The woman inside her hoped it was the latter.

His tone was turbulent and indecipherable. "I must get you out of these wet clothes before you fall ill and render worthless my efforts to save you."

Cassandra turned around and had to place her hands on the wall for balance as he attacked the buttons on the back of her gown, resuming his torrent of exotic expletives.

Once he'd removed her damp gown and gone to work on her stays, his ministrations gentled and the words he spoke sounded less like oaths and more like endearments.

Rafe tossed her stays on the carpet and proceeded to rub her arms briskly, bringing comforting warmth to her chilled limbs. In spite of such a practical touch, Cassandra's loins quivered as if he were doing something far more intimate.

Unable to help herself, she uttered a small cry of protest when he stopped and sank down on his knees to remove her boots.

A wicked smile curved his lips as he reached up under her shift and unfastened her garters. His fingers stroked her bare thighs just above the tops of her stockings. As he slid each stocking down, his mouth brushed across every new inch of exposed leg. Electric sensations raced up her spine.

"You are feeling warmer, *Querida*," he whispered as he cast the stockings aside.

All she could do was tremble and murmur, "Mmm-hmm…"

"However, you are still shivering. I will have to increase my efforts." Rafe slowly lifted her chemise, kissing the backs of her thighs, her hips, and even her back and shoulders.

Once she was completely naked, he began to caress her with soft motions. As his strong hands slid up her legs, his fingers just barely grazed the tender flesh of her labia. Cassandra moaned and parted her thighs farther in invitation, but he moved on to her rib cage, his knuckles brushing the undersides of her breasts.

Rafe withdrew one hand and Cassandra glanced over her shoulder to watch him unbutton his shirt. Her mouth went dry as each tantalizing inch of his muscled bronze flesh was revealed.

Then his hot, bare chest pressed against her back, his lips trailing kisses up and down her neck and shoulders. One hand reached around to stroke her breasts, while the other crept down to tease and fondle her throbbing core.

A harsh gasp escaped her lips and she arched forward against his hand. Her sensitive flesh grew slick and hot with need.

Yes, this was what she longed for. As his fingers lightly circled and pinched her nipples, Rafe's hips moved forward, his hardness pressed against her soft, yielding center. She quivered against him, biting her lip to keep from begging for more.

As if sensing her primal craving, his hand left her breasts to unfasten his trousers, while his other hand continued to work its sweet magic.

Then his hard, hot length touched her core, its tip circling the folds of her sensitive flesh with intoxicating torment. Cassandra moaned and writhed against him until the tip just barely slid inside her entrance. *More. God, please, more.* Her nails scratched the fine mauve wallpaper in her frenzy.

As if reading her thoughts, Rafe's fingers crept up the back of her neck to tangle in her hair…and he slid inside her a tantalizing inch farther.

His lips grazed her earlobe, sending tingling pleasure

through her body as he whispered, "Do you want more of this, Countess?"

"Yes!" she cried, trembling with mindless yearning.

Unable to hide her desperation, she arched her hips to guide him deeper. Every semblance of shame and modesty was abandoned, transposed by all-consuming desire.

Rafe's hand squeezed her labia, his middle finger flicking wickedly over her clitoris. As he firmly gripped her hair, his rigid shaft slowly penetrated her deeper, inch by tantalizing inch, until he was completely inside her. Cassandra sucked in a breath, awed by the new sensations, the more intense fullness, that this position evoked.

With excruciating slowness, he withdrew, then roughly thrust deeper into her. She cried out and spread her legs farther in unconscious encouragement. He repeated the action, drawing cries and moans she didn't know she possessed.

"Please," she gasped, still craving more.

With a fierce growl, he slammed into her with animalistic brutality. The heady scent of his exotic male spice, coupled with the sound of flesh striking flesh, engulfed her consciousness. Never before had she been so utterly and completely taken.

Rafe's fist clenched tighter on her hair. His fingers danced more rapidly on her clitoris as his turgid cock thrust even faster and harder. The barrier between pain and pleasure blurred into an ethereal translucence, sending her into a frenzied climax that defied the parameters of her awareness.

When her cognition seeped back into the physical

realm, Rafe wrapped his arms around her and lifted her, carrying her to the bed. "I am not finished with you."

Her eyes widened in shock. *Dear God, can I even handle more?* Before she had time to answer that inner question, Rafe pulled her on top of him, claiming her lips in a savage kiss. Cassandra moaned and nibbled his lip, shifting her hips to guide him inside her.

He shifted so they were both sitting up, which made him go even deeper, touching new places, invoking new sensations. Rafe broke the kiss and bent down to worship her breasts with his mouth. The provocative sight made her even wetter.

She gyrated against him as if in a forbidden dance, panting in excitement as the base of his cock slid across her center. The pleasure built and spread through her body like a raging inferno. Rafe held her tighter, whispering Spanish love words into her ear before scraping his fangs across her neck. Cassandra cried out as the second climax roared through her.

The intense orgasm became overpowering until she could do nothing but cling to him and tremble. Rafe was merciless.

He seized her hips and rocked her faster, sending her even further over the edge of ecstasy. "That's it, *Querida. Madre de Dios*, you feel so good."

Without warning, his fangs plunged into her neck, sending her pleasure into a sharp crescendo. He climaxed with a low growl that vibrated through her being as she felt him pulse within her core.

At last, he withdrew and collapsed on the bed, gathering her into his arms. Panting and boneless, Cassandra rested her head on his chest, listening to his pounding heart. She closed her eyes in awestruck silence at the experience they had just shared.

The things he had made her body feel defied all reason and logic. He had given her pleasure worth dying over. Was it some sort of preternatural ability due to him being a vampire? Or was it a natural phenomenon between certain men and women? Had her late husband shared this with his lover?

As odd as it was, she hoped they had.

Rafe placed a gentle kiss on her forehead, bringing her back to the present. Slowly her muddled thoughts cleared and awareness of her situation returned.

"Rafe," she began cautiously, "if you're not going to kill me, and you can't Change me, then what—"

He cut off her words, pressing a gentle finger to her lips. "Please, *Querida*, let this wait until tomorrow. For now all I want to think about is the pleasure of holding you."

Warmth flooded her at his words. Cassandra sighed and rested her head on his chest. He did care for her after all…but how much?

As sleep claimed her, his earlier words flitted through her mind. *"I am not going to kill you. Not after what you've done for me…"* But he did not say that he loved her.

Twenty-two

26 October 1823

RAFE HID A SMILE AS HE RETURNED FROM HIS EVENING hunt. He could see Cassandra through the window, pacing the drawing room while waiting for him. She'd still been asleep when he rose for the night, tired and sated from his lovemaking.

He should have known that was not to last.

Anthony chuckled behind him as they headed to the front door. "She looks ready to do battle. I cannot believe you haven't talked to her yet about her situation. Whatever did you do last night to put it off?" He winked. "And was it worth banishing me for the night?"

"I will not dignify that with an answer." Rafe shook his head, fighting off seductive recollections of her naked body entwined with his. He sighed and paused with his hand on the door handle. "I still do not know what to tell her."

His new second-in-command pulled an envelope from his breast pocket. "Perhaps you will have good news for her."

"One can only hope."

Rafe glanced at the letter adorned with the seal of the Lord of Blackpool. At nearly three centuries of age, he would be a good, powerful candidate to Change Cassandra. However, Rafe hadn't spoken with Blackpool in over a decade, so he was also likely to refuse.

Unwilling to relinquish hope just yet, he tucked the envelope in his waistcoat and entered the house.

Cassandra immediately rushed over to him, hands shaking with apparent nervousness. "Are you ready to talk now?"

He laughed softly, though on the inside he was seething in fury at the sight of the bruise on her cheek. "Aren't you the impatient one? Have you even eaten?"

"Mrs. Smythe brought me a tray." She gave him a pointed look. "And yes, I am impatient, which I feel is quite justified under the circumstances."

Rafe inclined his head in mock surrender. "You have a valid point. Very well, let's adjourn to the study."

She managed a shaky smile before lifting her skirts and following him.

Once settled in the overstuffed chairs by the desk, Rafe lit a cigar and exhaled slowly. "For a vampire to Change a mortal, the vampire must be at least a century old. It takes a great amount of power and strength. And once a vampire Changes someone, that vampire will not be able to repeat the action for another century."

Cassandra leaned forward, lush lips parted in rapt fascination. "What happens if they try to Change someone too soon?"

"The mortal will almost certainly die, and the vampire attempting the transformation will be greatly weakened." Rafe tapped his cigar in the ashtray. "This is why I won't risk it with you."

She nodded and frowned. "What *are* you going to do then?"

"I have been writing letters to every vampire that I can call friend." He held up a hand before the hope in her eyes could undo him. "So far all have refused." He pulled out the letter and inhaled deeply from his cigar. "We will see what the Lord of Blackpool has to say on the matter."

Carefully blowing out smoke away from her, Rafe broke the wax seal on the envelope, pulled out the letter, and whispered a silent prayer before he read.

My dear friend Rafael Villar,

It is with my most sincere apologies that I must decline your request. I pray that you will understand.

However, I have heard word of your other problem and am currently departing for London to provide assistance with that matter.

I look forward to renewing our acquaintance, and I have nothing but the best wishes for both issues to be resolved in the best and most efficient manner.

Regards,
Aldric Cadell,
Viscount Thornton

Rafe crushed out the cigar and tore up the letter before tossing it into the fireplace. "Damn it."

"Another refusal?" Cassandra inquired softly.

He nodded. *Dios*, she was so brave, facing the possibility of her impending death with such serenity. His heart clenched painfully. God help him, he would see that she lived, no matter what the cost.

Another detail from the letter had him frowning in confusion. "It seems the Lord of Blackpool is on his way to help me stand against Clayton and his horde."

Rafe's frown deepened. How had Blackpool heard about Clayton's rebellion? Who had told him and how had *they* found out? Were there spies among his people? If so, who were they working for?

"At least that is good news," Cassandra ventured. She fell silent a moment before asking tremulously, "What if no vampire will Change me?"

Reluctantly, the words tore from his throat. "Then I will put you on a ship for the Americas where you will be safe."

She shook her head. "Absolutely not."

"I beg your pardon?" Would this woman never cease to stun him?

"For one, I will not leave you." Her eyes blazed in challenge. "And for another, what will happen to you if you disobey your rulers' edict?"

"I'll be punished," he said plainly. "But you will be safe." That was all that mattered.

"I won't go." She lifted her chin in determination.

He scowled at her stubbornness. How could she cling to such flagrant disregard for her life? "We will discuss this later."

"Very well." She folded her arms and leaned back in her seat, refusing to budge. "Then let us discuss the upcoming battle with Clayton. It is good that the Lord of Blackpool has volunteered his aid, yes?"

Rafe nodded. No matter how puzzling Blackpool's offer was, Rafe couldn't ignore the fact it was a godsend. "Yes, I will need all the allies I can muster for this confrontation to ensure that there is little bloodshed. Despite half of my people now against me and siding with Clayton, I do not want to hurt them any more than necessary."

Cassandra placed a warm hand on his. "You are a good leader, Rafe."

Her sincere words touched him, even though he doubted they were true. If he were a good leader, he never would have allowed Clayton to get so completely out of control…and so many of his people would never have lost faith in him.

He owed his people recompense for these failures. Furthermore, he needed to do everything in his power to see that his people were not hurt. To accomplish that, he would need more than Blackpool at his side.

Rafe opened his desk drawer and withdrew parchment, quill, and ink.

Who could he trust enough to tell them that his territory was facing civil war? Many vampires would see his tenuous grip on his territory as a weakness and interfere in hope of snatching power for themselves.

Only one vampire came to mind. The Lord of Cornwall was definitely one of the most intelligent and honorable vampires Rafe had ever met. Unfortunately, he and Vincent Tremayne had never been on the most amiable terms. Rafe chuckled bitterly. That had been his own fault. When Vincent had come to London seeking aid from Ian and Angelica, Rafe had been nothing but hostile.

Ironically, Rafe had gotten on well with Tremayne's new bride after Vincent had been forced to illegally Change her and Ian had been forced to place Vincent under arrest until he could face an inquest from the Elders. Rafe had needed to supervise Lydia while Angelica taught her to hunt. He'd been greatly impressed with how well she adjusted to the Change. She possessed almost enough courage and intelligence to match Cassandra's.

After hearing testimony from Ian, Angelica, and Rafe, Vincent had been exonerated, to everyone's relief, including Rafe's. Though he and Vincent hadn't gotten along, he respected the Lord of Cornwall...and he genuinely liked Lydia.

Perhaps it would be best to contact Lydia first. Rafe shook his head, immediately rejecting the idea. Vincent was unlikely to take kindly to another vampire consorting with his wife. Rafe couldn't blame him. Glancing over at Cassandra, he lit on an idea.

"*Querida*, do you remember Angelica's friend Lydia?"

She raised a brow at the change in subject. "Are you speaking of the American who was the Earl of Deveril's ward before becoming his wife?"

Rafe nodded. That had been a debacle he would not soon forget.

Cassandra eyed him curiously. "Yes, I remember Lydia. A brilliant girl, not the usual featherheaded ninny one expects of a debutante…and her match with Lord Deveril was so romantic." She paused and frowned. "They are vampires also, *aren't* they?"

He smiled at her astute conclusion. "Yes, though Lydia wasn't one of us until Lord Deveril, who is also the Lord of Cornwall, Changed her without permission from the Elders. She'd been attacked by a cutthroat and would have died if he hadn't."

"Ah, so that was why Deveril married her." A note of disappointment tinged her voice.

Rafe answered firmly. "He married her because he loves her." Shame pricked his soul at how he had at first scorned Vincent for it. He sighed and handed her a piece of parchment. "Anyhow, I would like you to write to Lydia…and I will include a message for Lord Deveril."

She took the paper and reached for a quill, looking perplexed. "I am happy to do so, but what would you like me to say?"

"Tell her that you are under my care at Burnrath House. That should make it clear that you are privy to our world." He thought carefully. "And say that you hope she and her husband accept my invitation to stay here for the little season."

Cassandra dipped the quill. "Are you asking the Lord of Cornwall to help you fight Clayton?" At Rafe's nod, she continued, "Why are you initiating this request through me?"

He closed his eyes and rubbed his temples. "I wasn't exactly the model of kindness during Vincent's situation with Lydia. If I sent him a letter directly, I would not be surprised if he tore it up unread."

The corner of her mouth curved in a half smile. "I see. Would you care to elaborate?"

"No."

Her smile spread as she began to write. Rafe retrieved his own quill, racking his mind about what exactly to say.

Cassandra finished long before he'd penned an opening salutation.

She rose from her chair and walked over to his side of the desk. "Perhaps the words will come better if I leave you in peace." She kissed him on the cheek and left the study.

After what felt like an eternity, Rafe finally scratched out a few curt sentences. With a sigh, he folded the letter along with Cassandra's. He had never been known for eloquence.

He sealed the envelope and brought it downstairs for Anthony to deliver.

"What did Blackpool have to say?" Anthony asked as soon as Rafe found him in the library.

He shook his head. "He won't Change Cassandra, but he said he is on his way here to assist me with Clayton."

Anthony blinked in surprise. "How did he know?"

"Someone told him, but I haven't the faintest idea who." Rafe handed him the envelope. "Could you see that this is delivered to the Lord of Cornwall immediately?"

"Certainly. Do you think he will fight for you? I hear his new bride is a crack shot with a pistol."

"I do not know."

Mrs. Smythe entered the room, giving Anthony a

curious glance before curtsying to Rafe and presenting a tray holding another letter. "This just came for you, *Don* Villar."

"Thank you, Mrs. Smythe." After she left, he glanced at the seal with surprise. "It's from the Lord of Rochester."

Anthony stroked his chin. "Interesting."

"Indeed." Rafe read the letter and smiled. "Well, now I know how Blackpool heard of Clayton's defection. Rochester must have told him. It doesn't surprise me that *he* knew. That blood drinker has an uncanny way of getting wind of everything."

Anthony chuckled. "Which is ironic given his immovable stance of neutrality any time a conflict erupts. So what does he want?"

"He says that he will stand with me but that he will demand a price, later to be named." He sighed, unsurprised by such a condition.

His second bared his fangs. "Tricky bastard. What will you tell him?"

Rafe shrugged and lit a cigar. "As much as I'd love to tell him to go to hell, I have no choice but to accept. I have plenty of money, and other than my territory and Cassandra, there is little I would be unwilling to relinquish."

Twenty-three

Castle Deveril, Cornwall

"Vincent?"

The Earl of Deveril and Lord Vampire of Cornwall looked up from his account ledgers at the sound of his wife's beloved voice. "Yes, love?"

"I've received the most perplexing letter from the Dowager Countess of Rosslyn." Lydia's honeyed southern American drawl distracted him from the meaning of her words.

He tore his gaze from her succulent mouth. "Who?"

"Cassandra is a friend of Angelica's. She assisted with her phantasmagoria and"—her golden eyes narrowed in reproach—"she was a witness at *our* wedding."

Vincent gave her an apologetic smile and lifted his snifter of smuggled French brandy. "Ah yes, the eccentric one who aspired to be a doctor. What does she have to say?"

"She is staying at Burnrath House as a *guest* of Rafael Villar." Lydia frowned. "The word 'guest' is underlined."

He choked on his brandy. "*What?*"

"I said she is staying with Rafael Villar." Confusion and worry tinged her voice.

Still coughing, he sputtered, "Good *God*!"

Lydia leaned forward and spoke more quietly. "That means she *knows* about what we are, doesn't it? Why else would he have her there?"

Vincent nodded. "I can't think of any other reason why Rafe would have a mortal under his roof. She's most likely his prisoner. They must have had an encounter after which he wasn't able to vanquish her memory." His eyes narrowed as a horrifying thought came to him. "She isn't asking you to free her, is she?"

"I don't think so." She pulled another envelope from the pocket of her painter's apron. "Lady Rosslyn said she hopes we will accept Rafael's invitation to come and stay with him at Burnrath House for the little season."

Vincent took the missive and shook his head. "An invitation for the social season from someone who is less socially inclined than I am. This cannot bode well."

He slit open the envelope with a fang and unfolded the letter. His eyes widened in incredulous wonder as he read.

Lord Deveril,

I hope you and your new countess are well. I am not so fortunate. My business has become fractured since Clayton and I have renounced our friendship. In spite of that unfortunate situation, it is my fondest wish that you and Lady Deveril come to London for the little season and visit me at Burnrath House.

There is to be an interesting celebration of Guy Fawkes
Night. I'd be eternally grateful for your attendance.

Sincerely,
Rafael Villar

As if the news that the Lord of London was facing
an insurrection were not shocking enough, a hastily
scrawled postscript was added.

As you've by now heard from your wife, Lady
Rosslyn is my guest and I would greatly appreciate
any advice or assistance in providing company
suitable for a lady of her rank.

Vincent set down the letter with a laugh and
took a large swallow of brandy. Rafael was facing
certain betrayal and possible war—and was asking
for *his* help.

After all of his objections, scorn, and general lack
of helpfulness during Vincent's ordeal with Lydia, the
surly Spaniard not only needed his help to maintain
control over his territory, but also was asking for
assistance with a situation involving a mortal woman.
The irony was too rich.

"Oh, *hell*." His laughter increased into full-blown
hilarity.

❦

Clayton threw down the letter from the Lord of
Farnborough with a curse. "Lily-livered jackanapes,"
he growled.

"Hmm?" Hamish blinked at him over the rim of his glass of whisky.

Clayton answered, though he was mostly talking to himself. "Farnborough agrees to stand with us, but just like Grimsby and Liverpool, he refuses to enter London until the day of the battle." He shifted on the sofa, hissing in pain as his bullet wound protested. Burn wounds took so much longer to heal. "Cowardly sods."

To add further salt to the wound, the Lord of Blackpool, one of Villar's allies, had entered London and was now settled in a town house far more luxurious than Clayton's.

One consolation, however, was that thus far Blackpool seemed to be the only ally that Villar was able to muster. Clayton smiled, not surprised that he wasn't the only vampire who despised the pernicious, disfigured Spaniard.

"I still cannot believe he appointed Elizabeth as his new third-in-command. She's an uppity wench." Clayton shook his head. "The real farce is Villar promoting Anthony to be his second. I've never met a more foolish vampire. That buffoon cannot take anything seriously." Despite the pain of his wound, a slow smile spread across Clayton's lips. "However, his greatest folly is in allowing his little countess to live."

It was time to notify the Elders of what Villar had been up to behind their backs. "Hamish, fetch me parchment and quill."

The vampire heaved a melodramatic sigh. "Can't Paul or Francis do it? I only now became comfortable."

In a flash, Clayton launched from his seat and seized Hamish by the throat. Lifting him off the settee,

Clayton leaned in and growled. "Never refute my orders in such an insolent manner!"

Hamish's skin went chalk white. "Y-yes, my lord," he choked out.

"The next time you do so will be your last." Clayton threw Hamish to the floor. "Now do as I bid and then fetch me a harlot. You've aggravated my wound."

The vampire scurried away and Clayton sighed, rubbing his temples. He must take a firmer hand with his people. He could not be as lax in his reign as Rafael had been. All would obey him without question or suffer the consequences.

When Hamish returned with the writing implements and departed with a much more subservient demeanor, Clayton managed a smile. The smile broadened as he dipped his quill and composed a scathing report, cataloging all of Rafael Villar's transgressions.

Folding the letter, he absently rubbed his healing bullet wound. He still couldn't believe the bastard had *shot* him. Trust a cripple to use such cowardly methods. Villar would pay for that insult as well as all the others.

After sealing the envelope, Clayton ordered Hamish to place it in the hands of a trusted messenger. He congratulated himself on his ingenious timing. The Elders should arrive in London just when he would need them.

Twenty-four

30 October 1823

CASSANDRA WATCHED RAFE STARING OUT THE LIBRARY window with concern. The night was so foggy that it was doubtful he could see anything, even with superior sight.

"Are you all right, Rafe?" she dared to ask.

He sighed and pulled a cigar from his breast pocket. "I don't think he's coming."

"Who? Rochester or Deveril?" She tried to keep her voice casual, though inside she was aching for him. She had a fairly good guess of whom he was referring to. How could they abandon him in his time of need?

Rafe lit his cigar and turned to face her. "I was referring to Deveril…though I suppose it very well could be both, since one never knows with Rochester."

"Well, at least the Lord of Blackpool is here," she ventured with a cautious note of optimism, though her stomach churned with worry. What if Rafe lost the battle with Clayton?

He saw right through her feigned hope. "Things are

not as bleak as they seem, *Querida*. Half of London's vampires still remain loyal to me, and my meeting this evening went well. Blackpool and I—"

A knock sounded at the door before Anthony poked his head in. "The Lord of Cornwall is here, my lord, and—"

"Send him in," Rafe said with barely disguised urgency.

Anthony obeyed with a quick bow and Cassandra breathed a silent prayer of thanks.

Moments later, Vincent Tremayne, Earl of Deveril and Lord Vampire of Cornwall, entered the library, towering over Anthony and, well, everyone. His disheveled silver-gold hair hung in his face. Lydia, his former ward turned vampire bride, walked in at his side. The top of her head only reached just below his chest.

Cassandra blinked in surprise, not recalling that the earl was so tall. *How did they…?* Her cheeks flamed and she cut short the thought.

As if reading her mind, Lady Deveril flashed a mischievous smile, her golden eyes glowing like a blacksmith's forge. Her wavy black hair gleamed like spun obsidian, and her pale skin resembled alabaster. How had she ever thought them to be human?

Lord Deveril strode over to Rafe, brushing aside a lock of moonlit hair. "I apologize for the delay. Lydia had to pack her guns. They should arrive along with the rest of our trunks the night after tomorrow."

Rafe closed his eyes a moment and mouthed something indecipherable before meeting the earl's gaze. "So you will both stand with me? I cannot begin to—"

"Save your thanks for later," the earl said levelly and sank to one knee, his tone suddenly turning formal. "Lord of London, I humbly beg your indulgence to allow my bride and me to hunt in your territory." His stormy eyes glittered as he glanced at Cassandra. "We are quite depleted from our long run, and I'm afraid Lydia's restraint will not last long around your, ah... Lady Rosslyn."

Lydia glared at him and put her hands on her hips. "I am perfectly all right!"

Despite her vehement declaration, Cassandra couldn't help stepping closer to Rafe. The fresh-faced Lady Deveril was eyeing her as if she were a side of roast beef.

Rafe pulled her closer against him and inclined his head respectfully. "As Lord of London, I grant you and Lydia permission to seek sustenance in my lands for the duration of your stay so long as you adhere to the Elders' laws."

Lord Deveril began to bow, then jerked back abruptly. "Your arm! It's... But how?"

"Healed?" Rafe supplied with a wry grin. At Deveril's nod, he continued, "As for the *how*, I thought you knew Lady Rosslyn was a physician."

Deveril rounded on Cassandra, mouth agape. "*You* repaired his arm?"

She nodded slowly, overwhelmed by his intent scrutiny. "I performed a long series of operations."

"Yes, she filleted me like a trout several times." Rafe took Cassandra's arm and turned toward the door. "But we can speak more on that later. For now, let us hunt."

Deveril held up a hand. "You're not bringing her along, are you?"

"I am."

Lydia frowned and looked at her feet. "Are you certain that is the wisest idea, my lord?"

Rafe gripped her tighter. "I am not letting her out of my sight. Besides, she has witnessed me feeding before."

Deveril nodded in agreement. "Even if she hadn't, it would still be expedient to educate her in our way of life."

"I suppose..." Lydia trailed off, still looking embarrassed.

Cassandra felt a pang of sympathy. "Don't worry, Lady Deveril. I won't watch you."

Lydia flashed Cassandra a grateful smile, which was slightly unnerving with the glimpse of sharp fangs.

Once they were out of the house and away from the view of passersby, Rafe pulled Cassandra into his arms. "Wrap your legs around me, *Querida*," he whispered in his rich, decadent voice.

Giving the earl and countess a blushing glance, she complied, melting into his warmth as he lifted her up.

"To Cheapside?" Rafe asked Deveril.

The earl took his wife's hand and nodded. "Prepare to choke on my dust, Villar."

The two vampires vanished from the spot. Rafe grumbled a Spanish curse and tightened his grip on Cassandra before taking off with such a burst of speed that she had to close her eyes or lose her breakfast.

In seconds, they were in the poor section of town. Cassandra glimpsed the earl and countess following a pair of street drabs into an alley. Rafael set her down and sighted his own prey, a drunkard stumbling out of a ramshackle pub.

Grasping her hand, he strode over to the human and mesmerized him. Like a placid lamb, the mortal allowed himself to be led behind the building. As Rafe released her and plunged his fangs into his victim's throat, Cassandra felt a wayward pulse between her legs, remembering the pleasure of his bite.

Afterward, they rejoined the earl and countess.

"I feel so much better," Lydia said, dabbing her mouth prettily with a handkerchief. "Thank you, Lord Villar."

As the four made their way out of the poor district, Rafe explained the situation with Clayton to Lord Deveril. He didn't yet elaborate on the reasons for Cassandra's presence under his roof. She pushed down a nervous tremor.

The earl shook his head. "I am not shocked in the least. I knew that foppish idiot would make mischief eventually. I'm only surprised that Ian never guessed his duplicity."

Rafe sighed. "Ian had other business distracting him over the last few years... The folly was truly mine. I should have kept a sharper eye on him."

"Hindsight is ever a demon," Deveril said dryly. "Where is the confrontation to take place?"

"The Wilderness region in Vauxhall Gardens. That area is shut down this time of year, and the humans will be occupied in the main section with the fireworks display."

Deveril nodded in satisfaction. "That seems to be the most reasonable choice, though it is a shame that it will be a setting for such a dismal event. Lydia and I quite enjoyed our last tour of Vauxhall." He gave his wife a salacious smile. "Didn't we, my love?"

Cassandra blinked in surprise at the realization that they were already approaching Burnrath House. She had been so engrossed in the vampires' conversation that she hadn't noticed how far they'd walked.

Anthony greeted them at the door to take their coats and shawls. "Thomas Wakley is waiting in the drawing room for Cassandra." He reached in his pocket and withdrew two embossed envelopes. "And these arrived for you and Lord Deveril from the Duke of Wentworth."

"Wentworth?" Rafe frowned as he took his envelope. "What the hell does he want?"

Vincent shrugged. "Let us see what Lady Rosslyn's visitor wants first."

Cassandra needed no further urging as she rushed to the drawing room.

Wakley rose from his seat and held out the newest issue of *The Lancet* with a smile. "I thought you'd want it fresh and warm from the press."

Cassandra took the paper, mouth moving in wordless astonishment.

"It's on the third page, under Anonymous." He gave her a rueful look. "I wish I could have put your name down as the author, but you know what would have happened."

She nodded, her disappointment diminished by the fact that she was now published in a medical journal. Her only regret was that she couldn't shove the paper in the faces of those who'd mocked her.

Rafe placed his arm around her shoulders and pulled her tight against him. "I'm so proud of you, *Querida*."

Wakley gasped as he observed Rafe embracing her with his left arm. "You did it! By God, your operation worked!"

He strode over to the vampire, reaching out. "May I?"

Rafe raised his eyes heavenward but extended his arm slowly and with a pronounced tremor that only Cassandra and the other vampires knew was fabricated. There was no way Wakley could be allowed to know the supernatural extent of Rafe's healing process.

The surgeon ran his hands up and down Rafe's arm, murmuring in astonishment. "How far can you raise it? Can you make a fist?"

"I can lift it nearly to my shoulder." Feigning weakness, he fumbled in his pocket for the leather ball Cassandra gave him. "And my hands are starting to work."

Wakley rounded on Cassandra, still staring. "How did you do it?"

"I repaired the *extensor carpi ulnaris*. The rest of the issue appears to be atrophy, so I've been implementing a combination of exercise and massage."

"Speaking of exercise…" Rafe addressed the doctor. "I believe you can help me in that."

Wakley peered at him curiously. "How?"

"I understand you are a respected pugilist. I wonder if you could spar with me so I may learn how to use my left arm in a match."

The doctor gaped. "Do you mean you learned to box after the injury?"

Rafe nodded. "I did not want to be seen as a weak cripple."

"And you're among the most renowned pugilists in the city," Wakley said softly. "However, as much as I'm tempted by the opportunity to face off with such an infamous fighter, I fear that boxing so soon after your operation may damage your arm. The stitches can hardly even be healed yet." He turned back to Cassandra. "And you still haven't described the exact details of the surgery."

Rafe tapped him on the shoulder and captured Wakley's gaze with his amber eyes. "You do not need to know the details of the operation. You will box with me tomorrow evening."

"Yes, tomorrow." Wakley blinked suddenly as if awakened from a dream. "I would be delighted, Villar. How about tomorrow evening, say at six o'clock?"

"That is most agreeable, thank you."

Cassandra fought back a gasp at Rafe's power to hypnotize the surgeon. This was what he'd tried to do to her when he caught her in the cemetery. Why didn't it work on her? Before she could wonder more, Wakley bade her good-bye.

"I want an article on atrophy next." He squeezed her shoulder in a fatherly fashion before heading out the door.

"All right," she murmured to his retreating form. If she lived to write it.

Lydia and Vincent peered at her curiously. Lydia recovered herself first. "What was that about?"

Rafe shook his head. "It is a long story. Now I want to see what Wentworth wants before we turn to important matters." He withdrew his envelope and looked to Vincent to open his.

Cassandra's eyes widened as the vampires opened cards that looked like invitations.

Rafe came to the same conclusion as he scanned the contents. "We're invited to a ball."

Vincent nodded with a slight smile. "I think we should accept."

Rafe rounded on Deveril with a fierce scowl. "Why in God's name do you think we should do *that* when everything is going to hell?" He shook his head, eyes blazing. "*Especially* when you despise mingling with people almost as much as I do?"

Cassandra nodded. He had snatched the words from her mouth.

Vincent smiled slowly, indifferent to the angry outburst. "Because I think this will be the perfect opportunity to prepare to announce your engagement to Lady Rosslyn."

❦

The earth seemed to plummet beneath Rafe's feet. Was Deveril in fact as mad as he was reputed to be?

Cassandra's jaw dropped. "Whaaaat?"

Rafe shrugged helplessly, having no idea what he could say to reassure her, not until after he'd wrangled a number of explanations from Vincent.

"Lady Rosslyn, perhaps you could show Lady Deveril your laboratory," Rafe commanded, eyeing Vincent.

Cassandra visibly bristled, but either she grasped his sense of urgency or was won over by Lydia's enthusiastic grin. She nodded slowly and led Lydia up the stairs.

Vincent followed Rafe up to the study, declining a cigar and accepting a glass of Madeira.

Rafe clamped his teeth around his cigar. "What is the meaning of this?"

Curling his long fingers over the glass, Vincent regarded Rafe solemnly. "First, tell me everything about your situation with Lady Rosslyn."

Drawing deeply on his cigar, Rafe exhaled with a sigh and explained, beginning with their encounter in the cemetery and ending with her healing his arm and the Elders dictating a deadline for him to kill or Change her…which would end the night before Guy Fawkes Night. He omitted mention of the development of their intimate relationship, though he had the feeling that Vincent already suspected as much.

Vincent leaned back in his chair, eyes gleaming with sympathetic understanding. "So you cannot Change her, but you care for her too much to bring yourself to kill her, despite the fact that it is the law."

Rafe nodded slowly. "Yes, I'm certain you are laughing at me after how I treated you during your trials with Lydia."

"I had a brief chuckle at the irony, though to be honest, my heart aches for you." Vincent shook his head. "I would not wish your dilemma on my most hated enemy."

The sincerity of his words made Rafe's chest tighten. Humbled, he replied slowly and hoarsely. "I cannot thank you enough for coming to my aid. I have never done well with making friends, and I—"

Vincent held up a hand. "Do not thank me yet. My efforts to aid you may very well come to naught."

"Then I suppose we should move to the next concerning subject at hand." A measure of tension left him as he turned his scrutiny on Deveril. "Now tell me why I should become engaged to Lady Rosslyn." He fought back a tendril of pleasure at the idea.

The Lord of Cornwall leaned back in his chair. "I had thought the answer would be obvious."

Comprehension struck like a bolt of lightning. "You think doing so may deter the Elders from ordering her death." Rafe cursed himself for not grasping the obvious. "Just as when you wed Lydia."

"I would have wed her anyway. I simply could not wait any longer for…" Vincent broke off his words with a salacious wink.

Rafe laughed. He now knew such anticipation. Then the gravity of the situation settled upon his soul, crushing all levity. "It may not work. I made Cassandra a pariah the moment I brought her into this house. Her peers cross to the other side of the street when they see her."

"And many will continue to do so," Vincent agreed calmly. "However, these people thrive on gossip and intrigue to season their dull, insipid lives. Many will welcome the engagement simply because it will give them the opportunity to keep your scandalous adventures as a subject of titillation."

Rafe's agonized sigh echoed through the room. "As much as I am loath to say so, you are likely correct. Now how do you propose I make my debut in Society and resurrect Cassandra's reputation?"

Vincent took a deep drink. "First, you will both require new wardrobes, which would cost the earth at such short notice. Thankfully, I have two vampire seamstresses."

"The Siddons sisters?" Rafe nearly choked on his brandy. "Do you think it's a wise idea to bring them back to London after all the trouble they caused last year?"

Vincent sighed. "Not in the slightest. Unfortunately, they're the only ones who can prepare you for the ball in time…and I'll have a guard with them at all times."

As the Lord Vampire of Cornwall continued to rattle off an inexhaustible list of requirements, Rafe resisted the urge to bury his face in his hands. This would be impossible.

Twenty-five

"AND THIS IS A GENUINE VAN LEEUWENHOEK MICRO-scope." Cassandra's hands trembled as she held the precious device out to the vampire countess. "It can magnify up to five hundred times."

Lydia glanced at the microscope distantly before her gaze once more narrowed on Cassandra's face. "Lady Rosslyn, as fascinating as this is, I cannot help noticing that you seem flustered."

"I am perfectly all right," Cassandra protested weakly. "I confess I was taken by surprise at your husband's idea of a feigned engagement, though I am certain a logical explanation exists for such a ruse."

Lady Deveril placed her hands on her hips, golden eyes intent, as if trying to peer into her soul. "*Cassandra*, I realize that you are trying to handle this complicated situation with your usual aplomb. However, I do think it would be easier for you if you talked about it."

Cassandra heaved a sigh. "Everything in my life has become so complicated, so confusing, and so far out of my control. I cannot believe that Rafe's people are waging a war against him because of me and—"

"You mustn't think any such thing," Lydia admonished. "From what I have discovered, Clayton is an utter and complete rapscallion and has been planning this foolish rebellion for quite some time. If you hadn't ended up with Rafe, Clayton would have concocted another excuse for his treason."

Despite the comforting reason of the countess's explanation, it did little to ameliorate Cassandra's other worries.

As if reading her mind, Lydia folded her arms and fixed her with an intent stare. "Now, tell me exactly how you came to be here."

Cassandra opened her mouth to protest, but the countess's will was irrefutable. With a sigh, she complied. The words came slowly at first, then rushed out like floodwaters held too long in restraint.

She began with her fateful jaunt to the cemetery to gather a specimen for her studies and her subsequent encounter with Rafe. She told the countess about how he'd been forced to take her prisoner when he'd been unable to erase her memory. She described his surgeries and the accelerating trouble with Clayton. Yet she did not speak of his passionate, drugging kisses or his intoxicating mastery over her body. Her own mind was still struggling to process and analyze that unprecedented phenomenon.

Lydia took a deep breath and exhaled in a rush. "I cannot believe he Changed someone without sanction from the Elders! He has always been so staunch about following the rules. I would laugh if it hadn't resulted in such dire circumstances. And he was supposed to have killed you a few nights ago?"

Cassandra nodded. "Yes. He told me that he couldn't bring himself to do so, and now he is trying to find another vampire to Change me."

Lydia smiled warmly. "I knew he was interested in you since I witnessed your first encounter. He used to watch you so intently when he thought no one was looking. I was afraid he planned to carry you off and devour you."

"Frankly, he seemed more annoyed with me than interested." Cassandra laughed bitterly. "Now I fear he is suffering from a juxtaposition of guilt for imprisoning me and gratitude for my healing his arm."

Lady Deveril shook her head adamantly. "No, Rafe is ruthless as well as a tiresome stickler for the rules. If he didn't care for you, he would have killed you without a whisper of remorse."

"He's never said a word to indicate that he feels anything aside from the aforementioned remorse and thankfulness." Her heart ached at the admission.

"He is a man of action, not words." Lydia's voice remained implacable. Suddenly, her brow rose and a ghost of a mischievous smile hovered on her lips. "Has he kissed you?"

Cassandra's face flamed, remembering the original bargain Rafe had made with her and its sinful, sensuous culmination. Images of his torrid lovemaking flashed through her mind, momentarily suspending her capability of speech and rational thought.

Lydia gave her a knowing grin. "Ah, I see he has done more than that. Has he made love to you?"

"I don't know if he *has* exactly," she blurted out without thinking, overcome with frustrated confusion.

"'Made love' seems to be such a placid term for what he…"

The countess's eyes widened in concern as she placed a hand on Cassandra's sleeve and whispered, "Did he *hurt* you?"

"No, not at all…" Cassandra was so embarrassed by the subject that even her ears felt hot. Were all Americans this candid about such intimate subjects? "Though he was quite, ah, vigorous."

After Lydia made a small relieved sound, her devilish smile returned. "Yes, they can be that way at times. However, vampires are much stronger than humans, so it speaks volumes that he made an effort to not cause you pain."

Unbidden, a tendril of warmth curled through Cassandra's belly at the words. She managed a light, awkward laugh. "This is a rather unseemly conversation."

Lydia nodded, undaunted. "Yes, it is. Very well, I shall change the subject." Cocking her head to the side, she asked, "Do you love him?"

Cassandra sucked in a breath. Forcing composure, she said in a monotone, "Love is an affliction without any logical basis."

"Hence its grand mystery, power, and endless capacity for wonder," Lydia answered levelly. "Now answer my question. Do you love him?"

Cassandra dropped her gaze to the floor, unable to face the woman's sympathetic gaze. "*Yes.*" The word choked out against her will. "But there is no sense in it. I cannot understand how—"

"Not everything in this world is comprehensible. Nor is it meant to be, in my opinion." Lydia's smooth drawl washed over Cassandra like a soothing balm. "You should permit some mystery in your life."

"I am not sure that I can." Cassandra shrugged helplessly. "Such a concept deviates from my nature." Even now, her capacity for common sense was in turmoil with the idea of conversing with a vampire about romance like a debutante at her first ball.

Lydia seemed to understand Cassandra's inner struggle. "We can talk more another time." She closed her eyes and turned her head toward the door, like a doe scenting the air for predators. "Our gentlemen are finishing up in the study."

The moment Lydia finished speaking, Cassandra heard a door open with a creak and hushed, solemn male voices echoing softly in the corridor outside. Taking a deep breath, she straightened her spine and willed herself to present a serene countenance before they entered the room.

Lord Deveril came in first, blue-gray eyes wide with fascination as they perused her laboratory. When those stormy eyes settled on his wife, they warmed, taking on a hint of turquoise. "And how are you ladies getting on?"

Lydia's features softened, transforming her into the very image of rapturous adoration. Cassandra wondered if her own face gave away her feelings so readily—and fervently prayed that was not the case.

As Rafe approached her, she turned to the earl. "We are quite well, thank you, Lord Deveril. Would you care to tell me why Rafe and I are pretending to be engaged for the sake of the *ton*'s approval? And why are we bothering with this nonsense over a ball when war is imminent?"

"I already discussed my scheme with Rafe," Vincent told her levelly.

Cassandra gave Rafe a stern frown. "Don't even consider giving me the brush-off as well."

Rafe chuckled. "I had no intention of doing so, *Countess*. Vincent believes that if we have a more prominent place in the mortal world, the Elders may be more reluctant to kill me...or you. It may not work, but there is little harm in trying." For a moment he looked like he would say more; then instead he lit a cigar.

"Well, I can see the reason in such a scheme," Cassandra said with forced brightness. Her stomach continued to churn in discomfort at certain aspects of the deception.

"It was all I could think of on such short notice," Lord Deveril said apologetically. "The pair of you will need any scrap of mercy you can garner."

She managed a wan smile. "Thank you, my lord."

"Please, call me Vincent." The vampire bowed with a friendly smile and gestured around her laboratory. "You have a very impressive working space here. Would you care to show me around and perhaps tell me the tale of Rafe's miraculous recovery?"

Cassandra smiled gratefully at the change of subject and gave him a tour of her laboratory, showing him her surgical instruments and explaining how she had used them for Rafe's operation. Indeed, it was a relief to talk openly of her procedures rather than evading the truth as when she spoke with Wakley.

Lydia chimed in with avid, perceptive questions. Rafe leaned against the door frame and supplied answers when required, smiling more than she had ever seen him. A rare comforting air filled the room as the vampires looked at her with respect and admiration, rather than the pity and concern they had first displayed.

By the time they left the laboratory and Rafe showed Vincent and Lydia to the guest chamber he'd had prepared for them, Cassandra truly felt as if she had allies in this frightening, confusing situation.

❧

Once Vincent and Lydia were settled for the day rest and Rafe and Cassandra had returned to their bedchamber, Rafe couldn't wait a moment longer to pull her into his arms. *Dios*, she had been so brave. So astoundingly practical and so damned beautiful. For a while, he was content to merely hold her, savoring the much-craved heat of her body against his.

But when he helped her out of her brocade gown, a surge of undeniable lust roared through him as his eyes took in her naked perfection. Rafe gritted his teeth and resisted the primal urge to ravage her. Tonight he would be gentle.

"Would you like me to rub your back, *Querida*?" he asked softly, unbuttoning his shirt.

She turned to face him, and he sucked in a breath at the sight of her perfect breasts. "That would be lovely, thank you."

As she lay on her stomach, Rafe sat on the edge of the bed, pretending not to notice her admiring the reflection of his bare chest in the mirror. His pleasure in that observation, however, was impossible to conceal. He hid his face in a curtain of hair and concentrated on massaging her neck and shoulders.

Her low moan of pleasure made his cock harden. Rafe struggled to tamp down his lust. Her muscles were alarmingly tense and knotted, physical testimony of the strain she'd suffered the last few nights.

His gaze narrowed on the fading bruise on her cheek, and a fresh well of rage roared through him. Clayton would pay for hurting her...for merely *touching* her.

Rafe bit down on his anger, instead focusing on the feel of her silken skin beneath his fingertips as he applied gentle pressure and the heady mixture of triumph and arousal as the tightness eased and she made exquisite, blissful sounds.

He worked his way down to the middle of her back, biting his lip as she let out a small cry and wriggled her hips in silent invitation. It was torture to remain true to his task, but since the sexual torment seemed to be double edged, it was all the more sweet.

The scent of her arousal perfumed the air, driving him mad with desire, but still he restrained himself from delving his fingers lower into the succulent heat between her thighs.

Suddenly, she struggled beneath him, as if wanting to get away. Rafe froze. What had he done wrong? Had he hurt her?

Cassandra twisted around to face him. The hunger in her eyes made his mouth go dry. "I want you, Rafe."

She rose up and seized his shoulders as her long legs encircled his hips. Her fingers tangled in his hair, pulling him down to meet her kiss. As her mouth devoured his, she ground herself against the hardness in his trousers.

"*Querida*," he gasped when she broke the kiss.

He didn't know what he was going to say next, for his thoughts dissolved into pleasure as her lips trailed over the scars on his cheek, lavishing the rough flesh with tender little kisses.

Then she gently brushed his hair to the side and took his earlobe in her mouth. Electric sensations riveted him at the feel of her teeth scraping the skin as she licked and sucked the sensitive area.

Rafe sucked in a breath and thrust against her, cursing the barrier between them. Cassandra's hands caressed his chest, kisses gliding down his neck in a torrent of moist heat. She moved lower and he nearly came out of his skin as her tongue flicked across his nipple and her fingers stroked his hard length, straining through the fabric of his trousers.

With a small, unladylike growl, Cassandra fumbled with the fastenings, panting in desire and frustration. Rafe chuckled and removed the offending article, enjoying the way she licked her lips at the sight of his naked body. It seemed his countess had a naughty side. Rafe found he quite liked that.

As she straddled him and the tip of his cock slid into her tight, wet heat, he closed his eyes in bliss. She sank down, drawing him in with tantalizing slowness. Rafe felt like he'd gone to heaven. Cupping her breasts, he worshipped them with his mouth, his tongue circling her nipples and teasing the tiny firm peaks.

Cassandra gasped, clinging to him as she gyrated upon his stiff length. His mouth met hers, hands sliding down to grasp her hips, urging her to continue riding him with that delirious rhythm.

When he felt the tight spasms signaling the beginning of her climax, Rafe gripped her, thrusting even deeper. She cried out and rode him harder. Her tight sheath clenched tighter and faster as her pleasure peaked even higher.

His own climax began, roaring over him with such intensity that spots of light danced before his eyes. Unable to stop himself, Rafe pulled her down atop his chest and plunged his fangs into her neck, her essence filling his mouth as he came inside her.

Cassandra screamed his name. Her nails raked across his back. He could feel her orgasm crest a higher wave, feeding his own like potent fuel to form a resplendent conflagration. For a while, time ceased to exist. Only this moment mattered, this transcendental fusing of their bodies and souls.

Cassandra's cries died down to low whimpers and she collapsed in his arms, quivering as the aftershocks continued to rack her body. Rafe withdrew his fangs and held her until her tremors subsided, and still he did not want to let her go.

"*Te amo, Querida,*" he whispered, stroking her hair. "*Tu eres mi luz en la oscuridad.*" *I love you. You are my light in the darkness.*

"Hmmm?" she murmured sleepily.

He didn't dare repeat himself in English. With her brilliant, scholarly mind, she might laugh at such fanciful words. "Never mind, *Querida.* Go to sleep. We both need rest for that blasted dinner with the Wentworths tomorrow."

With a gentleness he didn't know he possessed, Rafe carefully shifted her and pulled the bedclothes over them, still unwilling to relinquish the joy of holding her.

Dark forebodings fluttered through his mind on sinister wings, threatening to engulf him. Between reentering Society and having half of London's vampires standing against him, so much could go wrong.

Twenty-six

1 November 1823

RAFE PACED THE LENGTH AND BREADTH OF THE DRAWING room, casting frequent glances at the grandfather clock. Wakley was due to arrive in less than five minutes.

Cassandra leaned in the doorway, a playful smile playing across her lips. "Don't be so nervous."

He ran a hand through his hair. "I am not nervous. I am impatient to try my skills against such a renowned pugilist."

"I cannot imagine why. I've seen you box. Even with one arm, no human is a match for your speed and strength. Now with two…"

"When and where did you see me box?" Rafe interrupted, already suspecting the dreaded answer.

"I snuck into Scallywag John's last year. You were magnificent."

He growled at the thought of her in the presence of the ruffians who frequented that squalid place. "Do you have any notion how dangerous that was? You could have been—"

Before he could continue his tirade, Anthony announced Wakley's arrival.

Cassandra greeted the surgeon warmly and began asking questions about an article in the latest issue of *The Lancet*. Rafe cleared his throat when it became apparent that they'd prattle all night if he didn't intervene.

"Are you ready, Mr. Wakley?"

The surgeon nodded, though he frowned doubtfully. "Are you certain you wish to do this, *Don* Villar? I do not want you to damage your newly healed ligaments."

Rafe smirked. "I wager I could defeat you with one arm."

Wakley cracked his knuckles and grinned. "We shall see about that."

"I have gloves in the ballroom. I lack a ring, unfortunately, but I'm sure we can manage."

They went into the vacant ballroom, their footsteps echoing in the vast, empty chamber. Rafe lit the gas lanterns and unbuttoned his shirt.

As the surgeon stripped to the waist, Rafe regarded him with a touch of envy at his athletic, unblemished physique. The man looked like an Adonis, the sort of man Cassandra should be with.

His thoughts broke as Lydia entered the ballroom. "I see we're on time—" She froze in the doorway, eyes wide and openly assessing the shirtless men. "Oh my."

Vincent came in behind her and frowned. "I think we should leave them to it."

"No, we won't. You and Ian thwarted my last attempt to see Rafe box." Lydia crossed her arms stubbornly. "I will not be denied this time."

As the Lord of Cornwall continued to look disapproving, his bride laughed and locked her arms about his waist. "Perhaps you should remove your shirt as well, my lord?"

His countenance softened. "Later."

Rafe couldn't resist teasing him. "Thank you for sparing me the sight of your pallid, gangly form."

"Oh hush, you brute." Lydia nuzzled her cheek against her husband's chest. "I like my gentlemen long and lean."

"Gentle*men*?" Vincent growled.

"Only you. Forever."

Cassandra cleared her throat and held up the boxing gloves. "Shall the match begin?"

Wakley nodded and took one of the proffered pairs. Rafe took the other pair and donned the gloves easily, no longer having to struggle with his left hand. But could he box with it? He gritted his teeth. Soon he would find out.

They circled each other, taking measure. Raising their gloves, they counted to three. Wakley threw the first punch, which Rafe deflected with his right glove. He attempted to counter with an uppercut with his left, but it was clumsy and Wakley easily dodged out of the way.

The entire match continued that way. Rafe landed several good blows with his right fist, but his left refused to obey his intent and always flew too slowly and at the wrong angle.

Wakley was a formidable opponent, landing plenty of blows to Rafe's face and head, blows that stung despite the cushion of the gloves. The man was impressively quick for a mortal, making it difficult for

Rafe to balance his own pace and not reveal his inhuman speed. Wakley dodged every blow from Rafe's left and even a few from his right.

After they had sparred for a while, Wakley dropped to one knee, bowing out. "I cede the match to you. I confess that I do not feel inclined to take a tumble without ropes to catch me, which is inevitable with your prowess. And we must not overtax your healed limb."

Rafe inclined his head. "It was a very good match. You are a worthy opponent."

"I was the bare-knuckle champion during my school days at St. Thomas and Guy's." Wakley declared proudly. "How is your left arm feeling?"

"Quite well, actually." Rafe was surprised to notice that there was no pain or tingling. "I think the exercise was beneficial. However, it still remains inept."

"Yes, I'd noticed. You do have a remarkable style. And I wondered at your blocking with the shoulder rather than the glove."

"Habit. It was the only way I could block until recently."

"Remarkable," the surgeon replied. "I would enjoy another match. I believe with practice we can get your left hand trained as well as your right."

"I would like that as well." Though between the upcoming battle and his inevitable confrontation with the Elders, he doubted he'd have another opportunity. Still, it had felt so good to box again—and to use both fists, even if one remained clumsy. He removed his gloves and extended his hand. "I will call on you at the earliest opportunity."

Wakley removed his own gloves and shook Rafe's

hand before donning his shirt. "And now I must be going. I promised my wife I would not tarry too long."

He bowed to Cassandra and Lydia and shook Vincent's hand on his way out.

"That was incredible!" Lydia exclaimed. "Like a primal dance!"

"Yes, he is indeed magnificent," Cassandra said, eyes raking over Rafe's bare chest in a way that made him straighten his shoulders with pride.

"Speaking of dancing," Vincent said, "the Siddons sisters have arrived to prepare us for the ball."

"*Cristo,*" Rafe grumbled. Immediately his good mood dissipated.

∽

2 November 1823

Rafe felt like a game bird being prepared for a banquet. For two nights straight he'd been measured, poked, and dressed. Trifling details about dancing, title addresses, and seating arrangements had been drilled into his head ad nauseam.

Preparing for war suddenly held far more appeal than readying for this goddamned ball.

At least he'd received a note from the Lord of Blackpool that he would also be in attendance. The vampire was a bit of a knave, but at least his alliance was firm and his oath to ally with Rafe in London was solemn and fervent.

The Lord of Rochester still had yet to arrive in London. Who knew if he even would? Perhaps his offer of aid had been a jest.

Rafe glared as Vincent shook his head, reached forward, and removed Rafe's poorly tied neckcloth. "No, that will not do. Try it again." The Lord of Cornwall tossed him another length of snowy linen.

"What sort of madman devised this ridiculous contraption?" Rafe growled. "I have half a mind to take all these cravats, fashion a noose, and string up the *hijo de puta*."

Vincent laughed. "I completely share your sentiment. Alas, that does not change the fact that you shall require a cravat. After all, you do not want to shame your countess."

"No, I suppose not." Reluctantly Rafe took the fabric and once more attempted the intricate knot that Deveril had demonstrated. "What?" he demanded as Vincent stared oddly.

Vincent blinked and shook his head as if waking from a dream. "I apologize. I am still unaccustomed to the sight of you using both hands. I've never seen such a miracle."

Again that new, poignant warmth curled through Rafe's heart at the thought of all Cassandra had done for him. "She has my undying gratitude," he said awkwardly.

"I should assume so," Vincent agreed fervently. As if sensing Rafe's embarrassment, he changed the subject. "Shall we move on to selecting your waistcoat?" He held out a collection of garments with a sardonic grin.

Rafe's eyes narrowed. "You're enjoying this, aren't you?"

"After all the curmudgeonly treatment you favored me with during Lydia's debut? Yes, I suppose I am," Vincent replied proudly as he clapped Rafe on the shoulder. "Buck up, man. You only have to contend with this silliness for a short time, while I had to suffer through it most of the official Season."

"I suppose I deserve that."

Vincent nodded. "Indeed."

"And I am certain Cassandra is suffering worse than I am." The women were downstairs with the Siddons sisters, being fitted for ball gowns. "The mad sisters have more pins and needles in their hands than she has in her laboratory. I hope she isn't being pricked to death."

"Lydia is enduring the same fate, I may remind you," Vincent remarked. "And she is doubtless freezing, being forced to stand there in only her chemise." A rakish smile spread across his features. "Perhaps we could go down and have a peek."

Rafe scowled. "I don't want you looking at my woman."

Vincent folded his arms and glared. "Well, I don't want you looking at *my* woman!"

For a moment, they stared in mute challenge before both burst out laughing.

"Good God, what has become of us?" Vincent shook his head.

Rafe shrugged. "I do not know, but I hope they are worth the trouble."

Deveril spread his hands in surrender. "Very well, we shall leave them be for now."

"What is your next scheme?" Rafe asked, lighting a cigar. "As much as I've enjoyed playing the dandy, we *do* have a war to prepare for."

Vincent nodded. "Yes, and I have plans for that as

well. Tonight we are going to Hyde Park. Lydia will teach Cassandra how to shoot."

Rafe stiffened. "I was under the impression that she was to remain under guard and as far away from the fighting as possible."

He and Cassandra had had a terrible row about it last night. She'd insisted on coming with him to the battle to treat the wounded. He'd refused, and she'd pointed out that she would follow him anyway, and besides, he could not spare a single vampire to leave behind to guard her.

He'd then said he'd lock her in the room. Then Anthony, Elizabeth, and Vincent had joined the argument, agreeing with Cassandra's logic that they needed a healer on the field.

And then they'd all, including the Siddons sisters and their guards, donated vials of blood for her to use. And now they wanted her to have a pistol.

Rafe remained reluctant. "Are you certain that is wise? What if a constable comes to investigate the noise? What if she is hurt?"

"Don't be a ninnyhammer. She needs to have some way to defend herself." Vincent leaned back and steepled his long fingers. "And as for her safety, for one thing, we will be there and if any mortals intrude, we shall have ourselves a meal. For another, Lady Rosslyn is a competent woman and strong. If she can wield the monstrous instruments in her laboratory without nicking herself, a simple firearm should prove to be no difficulty for her."

Incredulous, Rafe leaned forward, eyes narrowed. "Did you just call me a *ninnyhammer*?"

"I did," Vincent replied cheerfully. "Or would you prefer goosecap, chicken heart, or perhaps lily-livered?"

"All right, you have made your point," Rafe snarled, rising from his seat. "You should be grateful I do not call you out."

"You wouldn't. You need me too much."

Rafe stalked out of the room, grumbling curses in his own language.

Vincent's laughter echoed behind him.

❧

Cassandra's arms ached as she lifted the heavy flintlock pistol. Her eyes strained to see the target: a rusty pail hung on a tree limb about ten yards away. Taking a deep breath, she aimed and fired.

The sharp report made her ears ring. The dratted bucket did not move.

"Are you certain we cannot bring it closer?" she pleaded.

Lydia shook her head. "Though the fighting will likely be at close range, Rafe will want to keep you as far away as possible."

"Why *did* he agree to bring me with him?"

The countess smiled and lifted her finger. "Well, first, you determinedly refused to remain behind and your inarguable logic about the need for a healer was difficult to deny. Second, he doesn't trust anyone but himself to protect you. Third, if things do not go well, he wants to be sure he can get you out of the city as quickly as possible."

"I do *not* want to leave him."

"You may not have a choice," Lydia said firmly and

handed her the leather pouch containing the powder horn, lead balls, and wadding. "Reload and try again. You almost nicked it that time."

Cassandra gripped the ramrod with a frown. She knew Rafe was nearby, patrolling the park with Vincent to make certain no one disturbed her lessons. She couldn't see him, but she could feel him watching her from somewhere in the shadows.

Apparently, Lydia could as well, for she called out, "Get on with you! She can't concentrate with you hanging about and making her nervous!"

"You seemed to handle my supervision well enough." Rafe's voice whispered through the trees like warm wind. "Very well, I shall grant you ladies your privacy."

Cassandra rounded on Lydia. "What did he mean by that?"

"Oh, he supervised Angelica while she mentored me when I was first Changed." The countess shrugged. "Be careful with that powder, remember?"

Curiosity burned hotter than the gun's barrel. "What was that like?"

"He was very surly at first. And he made me dreadfully nervous with the way he loomed over us in ominous silence as Angelica taught me how to hunt and move through the night." Lydia chuckled and loaded her own pistol with deft fingers. "For the first few evenings he wouldn't say a word. Only when the night's lesson was finished would he offer cutting words of criticism...or a rare morsel of reluctant praise."

Cassandra shook her head in sympathy. "That must have been a miserable experience."

"It was beyond disheartening," Lydia agreed, lifting her pistol, taking aim, and firing. The ball pierced the center of the pail clean through. "Despite that, I believe Rafe's supervision truly helped me excel…though for the most part he only stood there scowling and radiating disapproval rivaling that of my former chaperone."

A wave of sympathy infused Cassandra at the young vampire's words. Rafe said Lydia had been Changed suddenly and without consent. She could not imagine such a drastic introduction to the preternatural world. "It must have been very difficult for you, being human one moment and waking up a vampire the next."

"It was, though not nearly as miserable as sailing across the ocean after being orphaned only to be repudiated by my own kin." Lydia sighed. "Vincent is my family now, and I have been more welcomed and respected in the vampire world than in my mortal life."

Cassandra's heart ached for her. Then a sudden thought made her frown in confusion. "Why didn't Vincent mentor you? He was the one who Changed you."

"Because he believed that I hated him for doing so," Lydia said quietly. "His guilt was so pervasive that I had a devil of a time convincing him otherwise."

"Oh my!" Cassandra breathed. Now the awkwardness between the couple before their sudden marriage made sense. Her heart clenched in sympathy. "I couldn't imagine such a terrible misunderstanding."

Lydia nodded. "Rafe was the one who cleared up that agonizing matter, which proves that he is not nearly as cold and heartless as he wishes to appear."

A small smile played across Cassandra's lips. "He never fooled me for an instant."

"Who?" Rafe called from the distance before emerging from a copse of trees.

She didn't bother to shout. Obviously he could hear her from where he was. "Never mind." In an effort to hide her heated cheeks, she finished loading her gun.

He stalked closer, scowling at Lydia. "If that gun misfires…"

Before he could finish his warning, Cassandra aimed at the target and pulled the trigger. This time, she hit the pail, leaving a hole a few inches from the one Lydia made. A surge of primal triumph surged up from her toes.

"Huzzah!" Lydia shouted.

Cassandra grinned. "You may just make a marksman out of me yet."

"It was a good shot," Rafe said grudgingly. "All the same, don't become overconfident and careless."

Lydia raised her gaze heavenward. "Now you see what I had to endure."

Cassandra attempted to laugh, but the pistol suddenly grew heavier in her grip. Rafe had a point. She was being taught to shoot vampires, not milk pails. To be careless could mean her death.

Twenty-seven

4 November, 1823

RAFE TAPPED HIS FOOT IN IMPATIENCE AND RESISTED the urge to tug at his suffocating cravat. "*Cristo*, what is taking them so long? I want to get this damned ball over with."

Vincent gave him a sympathetic smile. "As do I. You'd better remove that scowl from your face before we arrive at the Wentworths' town house. We must do our best to pretend to enjoy ourselves or our suffering will be for naught."

"Suffering is certainly the appropriate term for this. I only pray it is worth enduring."

He stopped speaking as Cassandra made her way down the stairs.

Garbed in a Grecian gown of blue-green satin that matched her eyes perfectly, she looked like a goddess descending from Olympus to bestow a rare blessing. Her upswept auburn hair gleamed like burnished copper with silken tendrils framing the sculpted perfection of her face and brushing her smooth bared shoulders.

The breath fled from his body. Surely he was unworthy of touching such a miraculous creature.

"Rafe?" She frowned.

He dragged his gaze from the curves of her breasts. "Yes?"

Her frown deepened and she gave him a strange look. He realized she must have asked him a question.

"I am sorry. What was that, *Querida*?"

Vincent guffawed behind him, but fell silent as Lydia appeared in a matching gown of gold-spangled ivory. "*God*, Lydia…" He breathed.

"You look quite smart as well, my lord," she drawled sweetly. "Albeit a trifle overdressed for my taste."

The Lord of Cornwall eyed his wife. "I could say the same of you."

Rafe looked down at his feet and sighed. The sight of those two mooning over each other used to make his stomach roil. Now a twinge of envy gnawed at his heart. If only Cassandra would look at him with such adoration. If only they could share such suggestive, silly banter.

"The carriage awaits." Vincent interrupted Rafe's thoughts, bending down comically low to kiss his wife's hand.

Cassandra's eyes widened with a curious blend of excitement and trepidation. Rafe bowed before her and held out his arm as her escort, not daring to place his lips on her gloved hand.

As he led her to the carriage, he cursed himself for such ridiculous cowardice. He'd savored and tasted every inch of her naked body. Why was he now so reluctant to touch her through a thin barrier of shimmering fabric?

She looked up at him and gave him a tremulous smile that made the world seem lighter. Rafe decided to put his worries aside for the time being. Paradoxes and mysteries were more her area of expertise anyway.

Cassandra was quiet throughout the ride. Signs of strain were showing around her eyes. Had she not slept well? Seeing that she was preoccupied, Rafe felt a twinge of concern. Was she ashamed to be seen in Society with him? Was she repulsed at the prospect of becoming his bride? Though she obviously enjoyed their sojourns between the sheets, matrimony could be a far different matter. Especially for his kind, when it could mean eternity.

His scars burned as he remembered her offhand rejection of his mocking proposal after her former mother-in-law had accused her of becoming Rafe's mistress. Perhaps she still felt the same.

But when they stepped down from the carriage, Cassandra seized his hand and moved closer to him. Her face paled and she began to tremble. When the butler took their cards and announced their names to the glittering throng, her grip tightened so fiercely that it would have hurt a mortal man.

She's afraid of crowds, he realized with humbling astonishment. That is why she was so indifferent to being scorned by the *ton* and, in fact, appeared to welcome them shunning her. Rafe had at first thought she'd possessed the same spirit of blind rebellion that characterized the Duchess of Burnrath.

Now he realized he'd been a fool. Every time her kind had rejected her, Cassandra had felt a sense of blissful reprieve at not having to endure another large gathering, rather than the impish glee that would have been typical of Angelica.

A brief wave of joyous relief warmed his heart. Her rigid tension wasn't because of him. She wasn't embarrassed to be seen with him. Now as she shivered at his side, Rafe was immediately overwhelmed by an all-encompassing need to protect her.

He opened his mouth to tell her they could turn back, could order his carriage to return and take them back home. A fleeting vision teased his will…of carrying Cassandra upstairs and then locking her in their bedchamber with him, of holding her and shielding them both from the worries of their worlds.

Vincent gave Rafe a sharp look, as if reading his thoughts. Either way, it didn't matter. Rafe gritted his teeth. Deveril's plan was their best hope of ensuring Cassandra's safety when the Elders found out that he'd failed to kill her. They could not go back now.

Thankfully, the gathering was half the size of a typical fete. How, Rafe wondered, had Cassandra handled grand-scale balls during the official Season?

As they took their place in the receiving line, several people raked Cassandra with contemptuous gazes, while many of the men openly leered at her lush curves and exquisite beauty.

Rafe didn't know who he wanted to pummel first. Many stares were directed toward him as well. He ignored the familiar morbid curiosity and whispers laced with mockery and disgust. His usual annoyance paled in the face of their snobbish scrutiny of Cassandra.

His only consolation was that Vincent and Lydia were drawing a significant amount of attention of their own. Their scandalous marriage and subsequent disappearance had set tongues wagging for more than a year. From the *ton*'s reaction, the Deverils' return was seen as a treat to dine on with relish.

Rafe lifted his gaze heavenward. The four of them seemed to be a banquet of scandal, packaged and delivered for the *ton*'s enjoyment.

The Duchess of Wentworth greeted them with a cheerful smile and genuine warmth. The scorn on many of the faces in the room changed to surprise and curiosity at such amiability from their hostess. As Rafe kissed her gloved hand, he wondered *why* she was so welcoming. He knew she had a tendency to associate with eccentrics as well as those who were less than paragons. That was why she and the Duchess of Burnrath had become such fast friends. Still, welcoming a disfigured foreigner and his mistress would be seen by many as far beyond the pale.

As she kissed Cassandra's cheek, the duchess looked at a group of disapproving matrons and gave them a triumphant grin. Ah, so she enjoyed flouting custom and causing a stir.

Rafe froze suddenly. His preternatural senses vibrated at the presence of others of his kind. Muscles tensed and poised to fight, he scanned the drawing room and relaxed as he caught sight of the Lord of Blackpool entering the ballroom. That was right, Blackpool was a viscount and the Wentworths had mentioned inviting him. The others he sensed must be his retinue.

He nodded and bowed before Cassandra. "Shall we dance, my lady?"

More shocked glances and speculative whispers echoed in his ears at that. He hadn't danced since his injury. But Cassandra's astonished gaze made him determined to show everyone—especially her—that he was no lout.

❧

Cassandra fought the urge to flee as Rafe led her into the grandly lit, mirrored ballroom. He was supposed to have killed her tonight, but this was nearly as frightening. She'd always despised being among large groups, but after her years of isolation and mourning, her discomfort with these situations seemed to have intensified.

A few of her former acquaintances gave her the cut direct, and all she could feel was relief. However, many also eyed her curiously and appeared to be on the verge of approaching her for the typical delicate dance of questions. Dread rose at the sight of them. As if sensing her disquiet, Rafe squeezed her hand.

Just as Lady Pemberly smiled and lifted her skirts to approach, he gently pulled Cassandra toward the dance floor. The musicians struck up a waltz, and Rafe took her in his arms. She couldn't keep from raising a brow.

Did he even know how to dance? The only time she'd seen him at a ball was at Burnrath House, and throughout the dancing, he'd leaned against a pillar and cast a pall on the festivities by scowling at everyone.

Rafe gave her a roguish smile and led her in the steps with such practiced grace that it was as if he danced every night.

"You seem astonished by something, *Querida*." His

voice was low and teasing. "Did you assume that I could not dance?"

She nodded sheepishly. "I had never seen you do so before…and with your arm…"

"What about it?" He deftly whirled her and she nearly missed the right step.

Her face flamed in embarrassment. "It seems I am the one who is unaccomplished." She looked down at her feet, encased in fragile satin slippers, and laughed awkwardly. "Truly, I never was good at this sort of thing."

"Neither was I." His hand gripped her a little more firmly and moved closer, reaching the verge of impropriety. "But if you try to relax and simply concentrate on the music, perhaps this ordeal will be less distasteful."

Her heart gave a little twinge. *He thinks I do not want to dance with him.* Lifting her gaze to meet his, she gave him a shy smile. "It is the fact that I am dancing with *you* that makes this enjoyable."

He blinked in surprise, and the sudden tenderness in his amber eyes made her belly flutter. For a moment he seemed about to say something, but then his hand squeezed hers and he merely smiled.

So Cassandra did exactly as he advised, concentrating solely on the music and the fluid beauty of the dance. Everything else vanished from her consciousness, and for a while, she and Rafe were the only two beings in the universe. Never had she felt such sublime tranquility. Now the breathless manner in which other ladies spoke of the waltz made sense. Though it went beyond impropriety, she rested her head on his shoulder. People stared. She paid no mind.

"Rafe?" she murmured.

His deep voice rumbled against her ear. "Yes?"

"Do you ever wish that it could just be this?"

"What do you mean?"

"That we were here not to save our reputations or in a likely fruitless attempt to ensure our survival." To her dismay, a lump formed in her throat, threatening to rob her of speech. "That we were here to dance and laugh like everyone else, instead of facing a war."… *And that our engagement was real*, she added silently.

Rafe's knuckles brushed her cheek in a soft whisper. "I wish it above all things."

As if to mock such an impossible dream, the music stopped and the waltz ended. She could have cried in frustration.

A fresh wave of trepidation swept through her insides as she took her place beside the other ladies for the contra dance. Cassandra focused on Rafe, drawing strength from his presence.

It's only a silly dance, she scolded herself as the musicians struck up a merry tune. *I've done this at least a hundred times*.

Yet dizzying dread threatened to topple her where she stood. Closing her eyes, she breathed deeply, willing herself to feel composed. If she fainted, fresh scandal would abound. The last thing she and Rafe needed was for people to assume she was pregnant. Lydia had vehemently advised her and the dressmaker to fashion this ball gown to emphasize the flatness of her belly. She couldn't render those efforts useless.

Just in time, she joined hands with Rafe and made

the proper steps. His smile and steadying grip secured her world once more. Unfortunately, their time together for this dance was all too brief and she was spun to her next partner.

Sir Patrick grinned at her as they whirled in time to the music. "Lady Rosslyn, it is such a pleasure to see you again!"

She returned the smile, cheered at the presence of an old friend. Perhaps this night wouldn't be so unbearable after all. "And you as well, Sir Patrick."

"I hope you do not think me too forward, but I noticed that you've danced with *Don* Villar twice in a row." His normally ruddy face turned crimson. "People are already talking…and unless an engagement is to be announced—"

"One will be." She cut off his words and whispered, "Tonight." She winked. "Please do not spoil the surprise."

His eyes widened and he tripped slightly on the next step. "Brilliant! That gives me great relief for your sake. And, I confess, a measure of dismay on my account." His smile dimmed as his lips formed a rueful frown. "I had hoped to court you one day. I suppose I waited too long to work up the courage."

"Oh, Patrick." She placed a hand on his sleeve. "I had no idea…"

He shook his head. "Nor did I give you reason to. I have always been a bumbling fool at this sort of thing. Either way, I suppose it is for the best. I will always value our friendship, no matter what. And to the devil with what others say. I believe you would have made a damned fine physician. Mr. Wakley told me that you treated Villar's arm, and I do not know a sawbones who could have performed such a miracle."

His praise lifted her spirits. Irrational though it might be, she dared to hope that everything would turn out all right—that Rafe would win his war, and that she would be allowed to live and be Changed and maybe even practice medicine.

Rejuvenated with optimism, she spun to her next partner, and then her stomach plummeted to her feet.

"Hello again, Lady Rosslyn." Clayton leered down at her.

Twenty-eight

CASSANDRA BIT BACK A SCREAM AND INSTEAD REGARDED Rafe's rival with icy contempt. "I'm surprised you merited an invitation. Or did you skulk in unbeknownst to our gracious hosts?"

Clayton's brows drew together in a combination of surprise and irritation. Clearly he'd expected her to be frightened and was flustered that she failed to behave in accordance. "All here know I was the Duke of Burnrath's solicitor and *dearest* friend. It was a simple matter to reacquaint myself with Her Grace and be welcomed here tonight."

"How nice," Cassandra replied through clenched teeth, searching for Rafe. Her heart sank when she spotted him. He was struggling to keep up with fidgety Lady Pemberly and had yet to notice Clayton.

Leading her through the dance like a well-versed courtier, Clayton smiled sweetly. "Tell me, my lady, why are you all here tonight? Don't you realize that Villar and Deveril cannot save you? Neither can Change you, and when the Elders read my report on Villar's negligence in dealing with you properly, you will be killed and he will be executed."

A pit of ice formed in her belly at his words, but she refused to allow him to see her fear. As she turned in his arms, she slammed her heel on his foot. "Oh, how clumsy of me."

His eyes flared with feral heat. "You cannot hurt me, frail human. However, I could return the favor and shatter every bone in your petite foot."

Thankfully, it was time to switch once more. Her new partner was a sullen stranger, but a blessed relief from Clayton's odious company. Imaginary worms crawled on her flesh where he had touched her.

"You are overheated, my lady," her new partner said severely. "It will be a pleasure to escort you outside for fresh air."

She opened her mouth to protest such forwardness, but then the man opened his mouth slightly so that she could glimpse his fangs. "Clayton cannot touch you here, no matter how much he may pretend otherwise."

Blinking in astonishment, she nodded and allowed him to lead her off the dance floor. Clayton glared at the vampire with such malice that she was reassured this was an ally. Her fear reduced, she followed him out the French doors.

Once outside, the vampire frowned at her and shook his head. "Honestly, for a countess, you are shockingly inept at duplicity."

"And who are you?" she asked faintly.

The vampire bowed. "I am Aldric Cadell, Viscount Thornton and Lord of Blackpool. I have come to assist with the war."

Cassandra curtsied. "Rafael and I are grateful for your assistance."

Rafe burst out the French doors, eyeing Blackpool suspiciously. "I would greatly appreciate it if you would inform me before absconding with my fiancée."

"I was not absconding with her," Blackpool replied calmly. "I was rescuing her from Edmondson. Did you not notice his odious presence?"

Rafe snarled. "I did. But *I* should have gotten her away from him. It is my duty to protect her."

"You couldn't have left the dance without shaming yourself and her as well," Blackpool retorted. "As your ally, it is *my* duty to provide aid when it is required."

Rafe rubbed his temples. "You are right. I apologize, and thank you for taking her away from our enemy." He held out a hand and Blackpool shook it.

Turning to Cassandra, Rafe's amber gaze narrowed. "You look shaken, *Querida*. What did the *hijo de puta* say to you?"

"He said the Elders will kill us both, and then he threatened to break my foot after I trod upon his."

His lips twitched. "You stepped on his foot?"

She nodded. "Stomped on it, more like."

"I am reluctant to interrupt, but we are drawing an audience." Blackpool inclined his head toward the door where several people were unabashedly peering at them through the glass.

Rafe sighed and held out his arm to Cassandra. "I suppose we had better return to the crush. Shall we fetch you some punch?"

The moment they returned to the party, Clayton intercepted them. "Do you honestly think hiding among these humans will keep you safe from me, Villar?"

"To think myself safe from you, I would have to consider you to be a threat," Rafe said mildly.

Clayton's eyes flared, but he closed his mouth as Lord Deveril arrived with the Duke of Wentworth. With a curt nod, Rafe dismissed Clayton to exchange pleasantries with their host.

Two other strangers emerged to flank Clayton. The Lord of Blackpool glared at them and bent to whisper in her ear. "Clayton's minions. At least three others wait outside."

"Will Anthony be all right?" A pang of worry gnawed at her heart. He was out there with the carriage.

Blackpool nodded serenely. "He will be fine. They can't do anything to jeopardize our secrecy among mortals. Besides, I'm certain Rafe has more of his own people stationed around this house."

The music stopped and footmen made their way through the ballroom carrying trays laden with glasses of champagne. When everyone had been served, the Duchess of Wentworth stepped forward and gestured for silence.

Cassandra sucked in a breath, freezing where she stood. It was time.

"As much as I regret interrupting the evening's festivities, it gives me the utmost pleasure to be the first to announce an engagement!" Jane declared with a grin.

Immediately, pleased gasps and speculative whispers echoed through the cavernous room. Clayton and his minions leaned against the wall, eyes heavy-lidded with boredom. Cassandra's lips twitched. They wouldn't be bored much longer.

"Lady Cassandra Burton, Dowager Countess of Rosslyn, has accepted an offer from *Don* Rafael Villar!"

Her blood turned to ice as all eyes swiveled in her direction, staring at her as if she were a new laboratory specimen. Rafe took her hand and she gripped it like a lifeline, forcing a bright smile. All she wanted was to tug him away from here and flee to the safety of Burnrath House.

Applause broke out all around and many people who'd given her the cut before were now regarding her with friendly smiles, as though their previous hostility had never occurred. Plenty continued to give her sour glares, while others held expressions of profound relief. All looked positively rabid with curiosity, and within a matter of moments, an army of ladies would descend upon her for the inevitable interrogation.

However, Clayton's thunderstruck expression was so comical that her spirits lifted enough for her to gather her thoughts and recall the story Vincent and Rafe had worked out.

As she was congratulated by the ladies of the *ton*, Vincent, Lydia, and Blackpool glared at Clayton and his companions with thinly veiled hostility. Cassandra's senses reeled and she wondered once more how her life had taken such a turn to the incomprehensible.

⌘

Rafe couldn't hold back a smile in the face of Clayton's fury. The expression on his face nearly made the ordeal of this evening worthwhile.

He watched as a group of matrons swept Cassandra away, clucking congratulations and questions like a brood of overanxious hens. She cast him a desperate look over the mass of jewels and furs. Rafe moved forward to rescue her, but Clayton blocked his path.

"Do you believe that this ridiculous farce will save you and your pet countess?" his former second hissed through clenched teeth.

"Why shouldn't he?" Vincent stepped forward, looming over the other vampire with such a menacing air that he stepped back. "It saved me and mine."

Clayton bristled. "That was different. She was Changed." His eyes narrowed on Rafe. "A feat that neither of you are capable of performing again for at least another century."

"That may well be." Rafe shrugged. "Though at least I've repaired the damage I did to her reputation."

His rival stared in confusion. "Why in the hell would you care about that?"

"It's a matter of honor. Something a traitor like you wouldn't understand."

"Honor won't keep her alive," Clayton sneered.

"No, but *I* will." Rafe turned on his heel and waded through the crush of females to take Cassandra's arm for one last dance.

Clayton's mocking laughter echoed softly behind him. "Tomorrow when I am Lord of this city, she will be the first to taste my wrath."

Rafe slowly glanced back at him over Cassandra's shoulder. "I'll see you dead before I see you as Lord of any city."

Twenty-nine

WHEN THEY LEFT THE BALL, RAFE FELT CASSANDRA'S
relief strongly indicated by her audible sigh. Despite
her courage in facing Clayton, he could see that her
hands continued to tremble. That made his words even
more difficult when they reached Burnrath House.

"We need to feed," he told her when he assisted
her from the carriage. "I think it best you stay here
under guard. Anthony, Elizabeth, and Carlisle will
remain with you since the Lord of Blackpool is to
meet us here soon."

Cassandra's eyes were wide with trepidation, yet
she managed a tight smile. "I understand."

Anthony hopped down from his driver's perch to
unfasten the horses from the carriage. Elizabeth and
Carlisle emerged from the shadows.

"Do not worry, my lady." Elizabeth drew a rapier from
the sheath strapped to her hip. "We will protect you."

Cassandra nodded and allowed them to lead her
into the house. Rafe rang for tea and coffee before
pulling her into his arms and claiming her lips in a
hungry, gentle kiss. "I will return quickly."

Once outside, Vincent eyed him with a smirk. "It is strange to see you play the gallant."

Lydia slapped her husband on the arm with her fan. "Oh, leave off. We have a meal to seek." She frowned and looked down at her elaborate ball gown. "It will be difficult enough in this attire."

"Perhaps we may pay a call to your grandmother," Rafe suggested.

Lydia laughed. "Oh, that is tempting. However, I am hungry for blood, not vinegar."

In the end they feasted on a group of richly garbed aristocrats leaving another ball. Rafe was pleased that his meal was one of the two females who'd snubbed Cassandra on the street a month earlier.

Rafe, Vincent, and Lydia returned from their hunt to find Blackpool's retinue stationed outside Burnrath House with Anthony and Carlisle. Cassandra was talking with the Lord Vampire in the blue salon.

Rafe's fists clenched at his sides, and a surge of territorial protectiveness speared through him at the sight of her alone with the other vampire. Then he glimpsed Elizabeth sitting unobtrusively in a chair by the fireplace, watching over his woman. His hands relaxed.

Blackpool looked up and met Rafe's gaze, brown eyes solemn. "I gather you have not apprised the Elders of the situation with Lady Rosslyn yet?"

Rafe shook his head. "I do not know what to tell them, and with the situation with Clayton—"

"*Precisely!*" Blackpool drummed his fingers on the oak table. "Your first explanation of the delay should be the truth. That you have been handling a mutiny… unless you've already reported such."

Stomach writhing in discomfort, Rafe looked down to withdraw his cigar case, avoiding the vampire's gaze. "I have not just yet. I wrote to Ian first, as is protocol since he is the true Lord of London. The Elders frown on being pestered about every little territorial squabble. A good Lord should be able to handle the matter on his own."

"Yes, they have been known to replace Lords who cannot manage their people without intervention." Vincent poured a cup of coffee. "Has Ian replied?"

Rafe lit his cigar. "No, and I hadn't expected him to. He and his wife are traveling. It will take an eternity for my letter to catch up to him."

"What will you tell these Elders about my situation?" Cassandra spoke up suddenly.

Rafe's heart froze in terror at the inevitable. "I—"

"For the time being, you must find a way to stall them." Blackpool waved off a cloud of smoke. "Give them some pithy explanation for now, until Clayton is subdued."

"Agreed." Vincent blew on his coffee to cool it. "Lady Rosslyn should not be put to death. It is no fault of hers that you were unable to vanquish her memory."

Elizabeth stood from her seat in the corner. "Furthermore, she healed Lord Villar. Such a vital talent should not go to waste!"

"Indeed." Blackpool folded his arms. "What she did with your arm was nothing short of a miracle."

Vincent nodded. "Which is why I shall write a petition outlining Lady Rosslyn's skills and virtues and recommend that she be permitted to live until arrangements can be made to Change her." He paused. "As I was under censure with the Elders the previous year, I believe more signatures would bring further weight to the testimony."

"I will sign!" Elizabeth declared vehemently.

Lydia nodded and placed her hand on Cassandra's. "You may rely upon my support."

"And I as well." Blackpool leaned forward. "After all, who knows when I may need you to heal one of *my* people?"

"Thank you, all of you." Rafe watched Cassandra's eyes fill with grateful tears at this fervent display of support. A lump formed in his throat at the sincere and much-needed aid from these vampires. "Elizabeth, please fetch a quill and parchment."

"What are we signing?" A deep, cheerful voice intruded.

Gavin Drake, Baron of Darkwood and Lord Vampire of Rochester, sauntered into the room, trailed by a shamefaced Anthony.

Vincent growled and moved closer to Lydia, while Blackpool smirked and Cassandra gave the newcomer a wary smile.

Rafe's new second spread his arms helplessly, still pale from giving blood for the surgeries. "I told him to wait, but he wouldn't listen. Forgive me, my lord."

"That is quite all right, Anthony." Rafe's gaze remained fixed on the grinning Rochester. Despite the vampire's belligerence, Rafe was relieved he had come. "Lord Darkwood, I am grateful for your presence."

Rochester bowed. "Thank me when you've won." Turning to the other lord vampires, he inclined his head to each in turn. "Thornton, Deveril, it is a pleasure.

Now, if you would care to enlighten me about the current situation, perhaps I may be of assistance."

Crushing out his cigar, Rafe outlined Clayton's betrayal and gave Rochester a brief account of Cassandra's imprisonment and the letter from the Elders.

Rochester smiled at Cassandra, pretending he hadn't yet noticed her. "Ah, so this is the little grave robber who started so much of the trouble." Cassandra bristled at the appellation as he turned back to the others. "Tell me, is she worth the hassle?"

Rafe raised his healed arm, flexing his fingers. "*You* tell me."

The Lord Vampire's jaw dropped in comical astonishment. "*She* did that?"

"I did," Cassandra answered with a stern frown, making it clear that she resented being spoken of as if she were not present. Primly, she rose from her seat and moved to the settee.

Rochester inclined his head respectfully before taking the seat she'd vacated. "I withdraw my doubts. I shall sign this petition as well. Now, as for the fact that you cannot Change her, yet you have not provided an explanation, I assume the reason must be something that will not aid your cause…"

Rafe frowned and nodded, refusing to elaborate.

"Do not look as if you want to chew my liver. I don't see any reason for me to be privy to the details. Unfortunately, the Elders will feel otherwise. Now I am not suggesting you lie…" He paused, shook his head, and smiled. "On second thought, yes, I am."

Blackpool scoffed. "Such counsel from you does not surprise me in the slightest."

Vincent gave Rafe a level stare. "He has a point. Perhaps you could tell them you gave a great amount of your blood to heal an injured vampire."

"Actually, that was me," Anthony remarked.

Rafe nodded. "And you have my eternal gratitude for that." He took the quill from Elizabeth. "I will do it, though if I am caught in the lie…" He didn't finish the thought.

After finishing his letter, Vincent took the quill and wrote out the petition for Cassandra's life. Every vampire in the room signed. Once the envelopes were sealed, Rafe handed them to Anthony. "Tell Carlisle that he is to go to Amsterdam and place these directly in the Elders' hands. With all of Clayton's meddling, I can't trust this with a runner."

"Yes, my lord." Anthony took the envelopes and hurried out.

Rochester leaned back in his seat. "Tell me, Villar, how many London vampires remain on your side?"

"Fifty-three," Rafe answered, appreciating the fact that this vampire didn't waste time.

"And how many did you bring?" Rochester asked the Lord of Blackpool.

"Thirteen."

"Deveril?"

"Fifteen." Vincent smiled, looking pleased at having outnumbered the other vampire.

Rochester nodded. "I have twelve at the ready, so we shall have quite the force." He folded his arms. "How many does Clayton command?"

Rafe looked to Elizabeth.

She regarded the other Lord Vampires with cool

confidence. "From what I've gathered, Clayton will have nearly as many London vampires behind him. He has also formed alliances with Grimsby, Farnborough, and Liverpool. Unfortunately, I've been unable to find out how many vampires each will bring."

Vincent shrugged. "Those are all small boroughs, thankfully. It seems as though we are fairly evenly matched."

Rafe lit another cigar as they launched into their battle plans. The discussion continued until nearly dawn.

As Blackpool and Rochester took their leave and vowed to return at the arranged meeting place, Rafe couldn't hold back his feeling of dread. They had done all they could, yet it didn't seem like enough.

Lydia seemed to sense his unrest. Before Vincent led her up the stairs, she placed her hand on Rafe's. "It will be all right. You are much stronger than Clayton, and so are your friends."

Throat too tight to speak, he nodded.

Once alone, Rafe stood and stretched, rubbing his aching neck. Cassandra dozed on the settee, looking like a wilted flower only far more ravishing. Reverently, he approached the slumbering healing goddess, marveling at how much she'd come to mean to him. He would give up his reign, even his life, for her.

Rafe bent down and kissed her lush lips, overcome with the inescapable need to have her. As her eyelids fluttered open, he stared into her sea-green eyes and whispered a silent prayer. *Please don't let this be the last time.*

Thirty

THE THREE ROGUE VAMPIRES WATCHED THE MESSENGER leave Burnrath House while glancing fitfully in all directions. Hamish bared his fangs in a savage grin. Clayton had been right. Villar was sending a letter to the Elders. Though they had failed to intercept Villar's communications with his allies, they would succeed in seeing that this one would not reach its destination.

Hamish looked to his comrades and placed a finger to his lips. The Lord of Blackpool's retinue flanked the grounds of Villar's manor, talking among themselves in low voices. The first messenger, an envoy from the Elders, had come and gone with her escort. The rogues had been powerless to stop that.

But they must detain this vampire. It was vital that the Spaniard be made to look a fool in the eyes of their supreme rulers.

Not to mention that if they failed in another task, Clayton may very well renege on his offer to make them legitimate citizens…or worse. Hamish frowned, foreboding gnawing at his gut.

He verified once more that they were downwind

from Blackpool's vampires before motioning Paul and Francis forward. They pursued the slender messenger with predatory stealth and preternatural speed.

They trailed the vampire until he neared the border of the city, where nothing stood but a few ramshackle cottages and stunted trees. Hamish signaled the other rogues, and they were on Villar's messenger in a flash. Paul pinned the vampire's arms behind his back while Francis held a knife to his throat.

"Be still or Francis will give ye a red smile and let ye bleed out on the ground," Hamish growled. "What is yer name?"

The messenger gasped and strained against the blade. "C-Carlisle. Now release me, you filthy rogues!"

"There's no need to be rude, Carlisle." Hamish smiled humorlessly. "When Clayton wins the battle and becomes Lord of London, we won't be rogues any longer, and we will be sure to remind him who was on the wrong side."

Carlisle hissed as the knife pierced his flesh.

Hamish stepped closer. "Give us the message you carry and we'll let you run back to your master, though he won't be able to protect you long."

Carlisle glared and remained still.

"Do ye want yer throat slit? Paul has a box of matches as well to dispose of your worthless corpse. And yon trees will make excellent kindling."

Baring his fangs, Carlisle hissed, "All *right*!"

Paul released his arms and Francis withdrew the knife.

Carlisle thrust the papers into Hamish's hand. "Intercepting this message will not keep the Elders from learning of Clayton's treachery for much longer.

Furthermore, when Lord Villar hears what you've done, the Elders will be the least of your worries." His haughty gaze raked over them in distaste before he spun on his heel, ready to take off in a blur of speed.

Hamish withdrew a sickle from a strap at his back and plunged it into Carlisle's spine before he could leave, jerking the blade upward to pierce the vampire's heart. Paul and Francis seized Carlisle's wrists and plunged their fangs into his flesh, forcing him down on his knees. Hamish seized a fistful of the vampire's finely groomed hair before rearing back and striking like a cobra.

When Carlisle was drained dry, Hamish wiped his mouth and turned to Paul. "Do ye still have yer matches?"

❧

Cassandra awoke on the settee to the sensuous feeling of Rafe's lips brushing across hers.

"It is time to go upstairs, *Querida*."

Her drowsiness fled, replaced by heated anticipation. Taking his hand, she rose from the settee, gasping when Rafe lifted her in his arms. His lips trailed a hot path up her neck and along her earlobe as he carried her to their bedchamber.

When the door closed behind them, he set her down and removed his jacket and cravat before kneeling in front of her.

"I *do* like this dress." Rafe reached under her skirts. "But I prefer what lies beneath."

Slowly, he slid his fingers up her calves and along her legs, caressing her beneath her silk stockings. Cassandra couldn't help gasping at the teasing sensation.

Toying with her garters, he glanced up at her face, giving her a wicked smile before moving up farther. One hand gripped her hip while the other crept between her thighs.

As always, he gave her enough time to pull away before touching her most intimate place. She sucked in a breath as his fingers danced along her tender flesh, stroking her sensitive folds with sinful intricacy. Cassandra's gasps turned into rapid little pants.

Rafe met her gaze, that wicked smile deepening as he ducked his head under her gown. Knees weakening at the feel of his breath on her thighs, she placed her hand on the bureau for support.

A cry escaped her lips as his tongue flicked across her clitoris, eliciting electrifying sensations that rocked her core. She nearly stumbled when Rafe's hands tightened on her thighs until she could do nothing but squirm. Her cries broke off into low, helpless moans when his lips closed over her sex and his tongue darted into her hot center.

His grip was relentless as she tried to jump away, the pleasure intensifying until it was unbearable. He continued to lick and suck as Cassandra whimpered, then screamed as the ecstasy peaked. The orgasm slammed through her body, her hips bucking under its force.

Shuddering from the climax, she nearly collapsed before Rafe rose from his knees and tore off her gown.

"I'll buy you another…if…" His expression sobered.

Cassandra would have none of that. Kicking off her slippers, she pulled him into her arms, tangling her hand in his hair to draw him down for a kiss. The taste of herself on his mouth only intensified her arousal.

Her other hand reached up to tug at the buttons on his shirt. With a low laugh, he obliged her. She stared hungrily at the golden expanse of his chest, sliding her hands all over his bare skin.

He made a rough, pleased sound at her touch. Emboldened, she leaned forward and flicked her tongue across his nipple, smiling at his harsh intake of breath. Languorously, she lavished her attention on every inch of his exposed flesh with her hands and mouth, licking, kissing, and touching him until his eyes glowed with hunger.

As her lips grazed Rafe's body, his fingers unlaced her stays. Inspired, she unfastened his trousers just as he slid her chemise down past her shoulders. Meeting his gaze once more, she pulled down his trousers, releasing his erection before sinking to her knees.

"*Querida...*" he whispered. "You are driving me mad. I—"

Cassandra took him in her mouth, silencing his words. Her tongue explored the ridges and curves of the rigid head of his cock as her fingers idly slid up and down the base of his shaft. She'd never before done anything as carnal.

From the fascinating revelations of the shape and texture of his manhood to the primal sense of power that surged within at his gasps of pleasure, the experience surpassed her wildest imaginings.

Rafe tangled his hands in her hair almost forcefully enough to hurt. Her sex pulsed with a fresh flood of moisture. She licked and sucked harder, gratified at his deep groan.

Suddenly, he seized her shoulders and pulled her up. "I must have you now, *Querida.*"

He claimed her lips in a devouring kiss. By the time he broke off, she was light-headed with desire. Before she could recover her senses, he bent her over the bed and thrust deep inside her.

A low, throaty cry escaped her at the intense full-ness within…a fullness she craved. Cassandra arched her back and shifted her hips to guide him even deeper. Rafe growled and seized her hips, quickening his thrusts. She gasped at the delicious assault, clawing at the bedspread.

Just when she thought she'd perish from the plea-sure of it all, his hand slid up her back and his hands once more tangled in her hair with a roughness that made her moan in excitement. Mad with lust, she ground against him, matching his thrusts. The move-ment caused him to touch a place deep within, a place that ached with need.

"Harder," she begged.

He immediately complied, slamming into her with such savagery that she screamed. Her core seemed to erupt with hot spasms of ecstasy. The climax fed on itself, building and cascading over her in a torrent of heat-crested waves until she could do nothing but whimper and writhe against him.

Slowly he withdrew, leaving her gasping for breath as she reeled with dizziness. Rafe lifted her in his arms and laid her on the bed, kissing her once more as he joined her.

He trailed his lips along her cheek and jaw, flicking his tongue across her earlobe before he whispered, "I am not finished with you yet."

His mouth clamped down on her neck, fangs

grazing her flesh as he licked and sucked, sending electric frissons of newly kindled pleasure coursing through her veins. His hands cupped her breasts, stroking and teasing.

Cassandra moaned and tangled her hand in his hair, pulling him closer, her body aching for more. Rafe covered her with kisses, from her neck to her shoulders, even down her arms and across each fingertip. He then returned to her breasts, stroking and nibbling until she was panting with renewed desire.

Rafe paused and rose on his elbows to look at her. "*Dios*, you are a treasure."

She shivered under his gaze.

He proceeded to prove his words, lavishing his attentions upon her body as if she were cherished and priceless. Tears formed at the corners of her eyes as he kissed her belly, her hips, her thighs, her knees. He lifted each leg and worshipped every inch with his hands and mouth.

"Please," she gasped.

That wicked smile returned as he knelt between her thighs, teasing her entrance with the head of his cock. Cassandra gasped and shifted to guide him in deeper, but he held her still, stroking her clit with his thumb as he entered her inch by inch with agonizing slowness.

When he'd fully penetrated her, he settled his powerful weight on top of her, motionless except for the rapid pounding of his heart. For a moment she was happy to hold him and savor the feeling of him inside her. Until her body took on a mind of its own and began to shift against him, creating the most delicious friction.

Rafe's hands slid down her arms until his hands met

hers and their fingers linked as his hips moved in slow, tantalizing thrusts. Her pleasure built slowly, ascending a towering peak. Small electric jolts punctuated the throbbing heat in her core. Once her climax reached its crest, she became incandescent.

Her hands clenched his as she threw back her head and cried out his name. Rafe's eyes glowed like an amber flame as he bared his fangs in an unspoken question.

"Yes," she gasped.

When he struck, her orgasm crested a higher wave. Rafe growled and pulsed within her as he reached his own climax. Cassandra shuddered beneath him, feeling as if she would die from the blinding pleasure.

At last he withdrew and collapsed, leaving her feeling boneless and sated. After she recovered her breath, she curled up in the haven of his arms, resting her head on his chest.

"*Te amo, Querida*," he whispered suddenly, stroking her hair. "*Tu eres mi luz en la oscuridad.*"

"This is the second time you've said that," Cassandra murmured. "What does it mean?"

"I love you." His voice was as rough as his hand on her cheek was gentle. "You are my light in the darkness."

Her breath halted. Her heart surged. "I never imagined anyone could love me. The concept seemed so irrational. I never believed in love."

"*I* can never imagine *not* loving you." He lightly kissed her shoulder. "To me, *that* is irrational."

He tensed, and her heart clenched as she realized what he was waiting for.

"I love you too, Rafe." Joy welled up in her at the words. "Thank you for teaching me to believe."

He tightened his embrace, caressing her back in long, tender strokes. "I think you are the far superior teacher. Now we must get our rest before—"

"Hush. You love me, I love you. I finally believe in miracles. Let that be all for now." She twirled a lock of his hair around her finger, determined to enjoy every last moment with him until nightfall.

❧

Despite her assurances, Rafe couldn't let it be. Her talk of miracles had kindled hope that warmed his heart. Even though the matter paled in comparison to all the trouble they faced, he had to ask.

Before she dozed off, he brushed his knuckles across her cheek. "Cassandra?"

"Hmmm?" she murmured drowsily.

"If we make it through this debacle alive, do you suppose you could…" He trailed off, chest tight.

She leaned up on her elbow, eyes becoming alert. "Could what?"

"Fix my face," he whispered, hating how weak and broken he sounded.

Her lush lips pouted as she regarded him with such intensity that he wanted to take his words back. "Considering the fact that my operations on your arm diminished the scars there, I see no reason why it shouldn't be possible." He held his breath as she paused and frowned. "However, I would not wish to."

He blinked. "Why not? You deserve a whole man who will not shame you in public. You deserve—"

"Stop that," she said, cutting him off firmly. "Allow me to explain. My secondary reason is that I would not want to risk damaging your face." She studied his horrid scars with such scrutiny that he fought not to flinch. "It may be scarred, but the muscles are functional. I couldn't bear it if I cut the wrong tissue and hurt you."

Somewhat mollified, he dared to ask, "And your primary reason?"

She reached out and caressed his scarred cheek, her eyes moist and luminous. "I love you just the way you are. To me, your scars represent strength. They mark you as a survivor."

"You truly believe so?" He seized her hand, speaking past a lump in his throat.

"I do." Proving her words, she covered every inch of his scars with light kisses.

His eyes burned with unshed tears. "*Dios, Querida,* you are a treasure."

As he pulled her into his arms, he prayed to every god he'd ever heard of that she'd survive to see tomorrow's dawn.

Thirty-one

5 November 1823, Guy Fawkes Night

CASSANDRA'S HEART POUNDED IN ANXIETY THE moment she awoke. Nightfall had come far too soon, and with it, a war between more than a hundred vampires for control of London.

Rafe pulled her into his arms for a devouring kiss, as if he wished to brand her memory with his touch. "I must prepare my people for battle, *Querida*. Elizabeth will be in soon to attend you."

The moment Rafe left the bedchamber, Elizabeth marched in with a man's shirt and trousers.

"You cannot run in a lady's finery," she explained in a tone that brooked no argument.

After Cassandra dressed, they met Lydia downstairs. Also garbed in trousers, Lady Deveril gave them a cheerful wave while perusing an array of pistols, swords, and rapiers spread out on the dining room table as she sorted through a case of holsters.

At the sight of the weapons Cassandra's stomach churned with fresh anxiety. What if she fumbled in loading her gun and it misfired? What if she accidentally shot someone on their side? She gnawed her lower lip.

If she could even hit one of the enemy vampires she'd be lucky. She'd seen how fast vampires could move. A pistol was a pitiful weapon compared to their sharp fangs, lightning speed, and brute strength. Added to the futility was the fact that if she didn't shoot a vampire in the heart, little damage would be done.

"Here." Lydia held out a belt and holstered pistol. "This one should fit you."

After they were armed, Cassandra barely had time to force down a quick breakfast and pack her supplies while the vampires took turns leaving the house to feed.

The journey to the meeting place passed in a blur of mounting panic. Cassandra could do nothing except huddle in Rafe's arms and pray for his safety.

When they met with his people and allies, she was tucked safely on the sidelines as Rafe roared out commands in rapid fire. Battle cries reverberated through the stone chamber.

Before they filed outside, Rafe pulled her in his arms and addressed his people. "This woman is not only the most miraculous healer to walk the earth, but also the love of my life. Do everything in your power to see that she remains unharmed."

Cassandra held her chin high, refusing to show fear as she walked between the four vampires Rafe had chosen to be her honor guard.

Lydia stalked quietly at her right, pistol held securely at her hip. Anthony strode at her left, equally armed and ready to fire. The vampires leading and flanking her were unfamiliar, though trusted by Rafe. They certainly appeared formidable.

Biting her lip, she grasped the butt of her own pistol strapped to her hip, her palms sweating despite the chilly November air. She wasn't made for killing, much less wounding.

Her other hand patted the satchel containing her medical supplies. The bandages, lancets, syringes, and scalpel were light enough. The ice-packed vials of vampire blood, donated by every vampire who stood with Rafe, contributed to most of the heaviness. However, the satchel was a comforting weight, far lighter on her conscience than the heft of the gun. She prayed she wouldn't need to use it.

Her purpose was to heal, not to harm.

No matter how this battle ended, the wounded would need tending. Rafe had told her that very few would die…at least during the fighting, yet many would be injured. Already, her physician's mind railed at the waste of it all.

Her gaze moved up the line to take in Rafe, marching in the vanguard with Vincent and Elizabeth. All three carried swords as well as pistols. The Lord of Blackpool joined them, along with the Lord of Rochester and their respective retinues.

Gradually, other vampires swelled their ranks as they neared the Wilderness region of Vauxhall Pleasure Gardens. Two vampires pulled a wagon clanking with the weight of iron chains intended for the inevitable prisoners.

However, Cassandra knew that if Rafe's side won, Clayton would not be taken alive.

Fireworks lit the night far to the east, echoed by faint jubilant shouts as the mortal populace celebrated Guy Fawkes Night, oblivious to the battle that would occur within a stone's throw of their revels.

By the time Rafe's army reached the edge of the designated battleground—a large clearing surrounded by walnut trees—their force was nearly a hundred strong. Lydia and Anthony pressed closer to Cassandra, holding their weapons at the ready.

For a long time, everyone stood as still as a pride of hunting lions, scenting the air for the approaching enemy.

"They're coming," Lydia whispered.

Cassandra fought back a shiver. Moments later, she could hear the enemy as well.

Like sinister locusts, Clayton and his vampires emerged from the fog several yards away, steadily approaching like an ominous tide. Rafe's people moved forward to meet them.

As if by some unheard signal, both factions halted, about thirty meters apart. Clayton and Rafe faced each other with blazing eyes and shining fangs.

The host surrounding Clayton was equally armed with rapiers and pistols. Two of the rogues flanked him, each bearing wicked scythes.

Clayton surveyed Rafe's forces with an insolent smirk. "Are you ready to find out if there is a hell for our kind? I have always been curious."

Rafe yawned. "Get on with it, Edmondson. We do not want to be standing here until dawn."

The vampire stiffened, eyes narrowing with malice. "Very well. I, Clayton Edmondson, hereby accuse

Rafael Villar of treason. Before all blood drinkers present, I declare myself the new Lord of London and challenge Villar and his followers to battle." Eyeing Rafe's people, he addressed them with a sickly sweet smile. "Any of you who wishes to renounce this traitor is welcome to cross the lines and fight at my side. Those who do not will forfeit their immunity at battle's end and suffer my punishment."

"I, Rafael Villar, deny your accusation of treason. In fact, I accuse *you* of being the traitor. Therefore, I accept your challenge." Rafe's voice reverberated with power and authority. "All vampires who return to my side shall be pardoned."

Four vampires immediately left Clayton's lines and crossed to Rafe's. The first gave Elizabeth a broad smile, which she returned. Cassandra nodded at the exchange.

So *that* had been how Elizabeth had been receiving her information on the enemy's doings.

"Bloody turncoats!" Clayton roared at them. "I'll have your heads when this is over!"

Rafe cut off his tirade with a bored shrug. "Is this current location and time acceptable to resolve the conflict?"

Clayton's lips twisted as if tasting something sour. "It is indeed."

"Then let us see our battlefield secure from mortal eyes."

Rafe and Clayton turned from each other and signaled their vampires at the rear. Like points on a compass, ten vampires from each side fanned out to guard the perimeter of trees from prying humans.

Cassandra fought the urge to shake her head in bemusement. The irony was almost too much to bear. To fight against each other, they first had to work together.

Another heart-stopping silence ensued as the two armies stared at each other with unchecked hostility.

The vampire in front of her curled his fingers over the hilt of his sword, armed and ready to draw blood.

Belatedly, she realized her gun was still in its holster. With shaking hands, she drew the deadly weapon, praying once more she would not have to pull the trigger.

Rafe let out a roar that shook the earth like thunder.

The other vampires echoed his cry with such force that Cassandra nearly dropped her pistol. Everyone except her guard charged forward. Her heart lodged in her throat as the two armies met with a clash of steel, fangs, fists, and gunfire.

For an interminable time, she could only stand there frozen as a startled doe while chaos erupted all around her.

The vampires moved so quickly that her vision swam in a blur of black and crimson. Her senses numbed at the noise and carnage, her mind at first unable to make sense of it all. Gunshots echoed all around, indiscernible from the sound of the fireworks.

One of Clayton's vampires charged at them with a snarl. Lydia lifted her pistol and fired, dropping him like a stone.

Cassandra swallowed and shakily raised her own gun to fire at another. She clipped him on the shoulder. The vampire grasped his arm and hissed in pain, but did not slow until Anthony put a bullet in his head.

Vincent was locked in sword combat with another vampire, their blades clashing in graceful, deadly arcs. With a flick of his wrist, the Lord Vampire of Cornwall disarmed his opponent and lifted the tip of his sword to the center of her chest.

"Yield or die," he told her.

She sank to her knees. "I yield."

Vincent nodded to the Cornish vampires behind his back. They retrieved chains from the wagon and shackled her to a tree. Two remained to guard her at sword point.

The vampires engaging Blackpool and Rochester were not so fortunate. Rochester beheaded his enemy with a merciless stroke, while Blackpool pierced his opponent in the heart with an indifferent shrug at his refusal to surrender. Cassandra shook her head sadly at the waste of life even as she wondered what would become of the prisoners.

A hand suddenly grasped her ankle. The vampire Lydia had shot hissed up at her with bloody fangs.

With a startled shriek, Cassandra took aim at his face and pulled the trigger.

The loud bang temporarily deafened her. Blood and brains splattered all over her trousers. She stumbled, ears ringing as the stench of gunpowder and burned flesh filled her lungs.

Stomach roiling, Cassandra moved back from the mangled vampire only to sink to her knees and vomit. Breakfast had been a terrible idea.

Elizabeth helped her to her feet before kneeling by the downed enemy and plunging her dagger in his chest.

"What are you doing?" Cassandra gasped in horror at such irrational savagery. "He's dead!"

"No, he isn't," Rafe's third-in-command growled. "I must end his suffering."

Elizabeth was right. The vampire's chest continued to move, and a wet, wheezing noise came from the holes in his ravaged face. As Elizabeth began to carve out his heart, Cassandra gagged and averted her gaze.

That was when she noticed that most of the other fallen vampires on both sides remained alive.

Some had broken limbs, twisted at painful angles. Others were missing arms or legs, blood gushing from ruined stumps as they crawled away from the field, their forms illuminated by the fireworks.

Too late she saw one of Clayton's rogues charging toward her with impossible swiftness. His lips curled back in a hateful snarl as he swung his scythe in a terrifying arc.

As the blade whistled through the air, a gray blur stepped between her and the rogue, shielding her from the strike.

Anthony's headless body fell to its knees. Blood rained in a torrent, splattering her face and hair. Anthony's hand grasped at Cassandra shoulder, as if to offer a comforting pat, before sliding away.

He collapsed at her knees. His chest rose once and went still.

The rogue resumed his charge on Cassandra. "Now you die, pretty mortal."

His triumphant grin dissolved into a gape of surprise when Lydia buried a stake in his heart.

With a wailing cry, Cassandra scrambled to

Anthony's body. Heart contorting in agony, she grasped the hand of the vampire who'd given his life for her and Rafe.

The colorful illuminations in the sky and cheers of the human revelers in the distance provided a sickening contrast to this tragedy.

"I'm so sorry," she whispered, hot tears streaming down her face. "I am so sorry."

Thirty-two

Elizabeth pulled Cassandra away from Anthony's body. "There is no time to grieve," she choked, eyes brimming with moisture. "We must get out of the way!"

The fear in her voice made Cassandra glance up. Her heart leaped in her throat at the sight of Rafe and Clayton locked in combat, ringed by snarling vampires on all sides.

More than a third of each vampire's forces lay on the grass, dead or wounded. Another third had been shunted to the side in chains.

Cassandra's breath fled at the sight of the combatants.

Every time Clayton swung his sword at Rafe, her heart refused to beat until her lover blocked the blow with a ringing clash of steel. Their booted feet slipped on the bloody grass, adding to their growls of frustration.

This was the final skirmish. Countless lives, including hers, depended on the outcome of the fight.

Her fist clenched at her side, the fingers on her other hand tightening on the gun. If she could shoot Clayton…

A hand clamped down on her shoulder. Cassandra

squeaked and turned to face one of the vampires assigned to her guard. He shook his head.

"No interference is allowed at this point. It would be best to avert your eyes until it is over."

She slumped in despair. She could do nothing to aid Rafe.

Eyeing the agonized faces of the fallen, her soul ached with sympathy. The weight of her satchel suddenly filled her awareness.

There was *plenty* she could do.

Cassandra touched the vampire's sleeve. "What is your name?"

"Eric, my lady."

She curtsied awkwardly in her trousers. "Eric, could you cover me while I tend to the wounded?"

At first he looked as if he were about to object. Then his eyes scanned the writhing, wounded vampires and his mouth compressed in a grim line. "Can you help them?"

"Some, though unfortunately not all," she answered honestly.

He nodded and gestured for the remainder of her guard to come forth and flank her.

Cassandra knelt before the nearest wounded vampire, a young male with an ugly gash in his chest above his heart. With vampires' rapid healing abilities, it must have been much worse before she'd gotten to him. He bared his fangs and snarled.

Swallowing her trepidation, she placed a gentle hand on his. "I am going to help you, but you will have to lie still."

She opened a vial of vampire blood and poured it

into the wound. The vampire's eyes widened as his wound knitted shut.

"I am in your debt, my lady," he whispered.

Rafe's yell of pain made her flinch. *I must not look, I mustn't. I'll lose my senses.*

As Rafe's battle raged on, Cassandra waged one of her own with the injured vampires. She administered blood, bandaged, and stitched wounds for what seemed an eternity. Some were cooperative patients, while others needed to be drugged and held down. Eric assigned a pair of vampires to aid with that.

The worst were the ones who had to be killed. Thankfully, Eric took care of that heartrending chore for her. Despite that, many looked on her with tear-filled eyes and thanked her profusely.

Giving a dying vampire's hand a final squeeze, she rose and squared her aching shoulders to move on to the next patient. There were too many wounded for her to manage alone. She needed another doctor or three.

Immediately an idea crept to her mind. A dangerous idea. She surveyed the multitude of injured vampires with determination in her mind and an ache in her soul. *I must.*

She approached the first vampire she'd healed. "I need you to fetch the surgeon Thomas Wakley. I've seen you guarding him, so I know you know where he lives." Holding up a hand to ward off his protest, she rattled off his address. "Please, the lives of your people depend on it!"

The vampire nodded shakily. "Only because I owe you my life will I do this. I pray you know what you are about, my lady."

With that, he was gone and Cassandra was left to face the bleeding masses and pray that Rafe won the battle—and that her decision to involve Wakley hadn't cost another life.

⁓

Rafe swung his sword at Clayton with a roar. Again, his enemy blocked the blow. Steel clashed so hard that sparks flew to rival the fireworks in the sky.

They had been fighting for hours. His people had held strong against Clayton's, though with heavy losses on both sides. Vincent had taken many prisoners, while Rochester mercilessly cut down turncoat London vampires and Clayton's allies alike. He and his retinue had driven the Lord of Derbyshire's vampires off shortly after the melee commenced.

Blackpool and his people fought Farnborough's forces with such savagery that Rafe wondered if some previous personal hostility existed between the two lord vampires.

The most agonizing part of the fighting was the effort it took not to look for Cassandra. The last time he'd turned to check on her, he'd nearly been stabbed in the back by one of Clayton's people.

A bullet had whizzed past Rafe's ear and dropped the cowardly sod like a sack of rubbish. He'd turned to see Lydia raising her pistol in a salute. He nodded in thanks and plunged his sword into the craven's black heart.

By the time he and Clayton faced off, fewer than half of the fighters remained on their feet. Rafe's lip curled up in disgust while his chest ached with grief and rage.

Such senseless waste of innocent lives…all because of a foolish vampire's mindless greed for power.

As the opposing fighters circled them, Rafe met the traitor's gaze and vowed to make him pay for all of it.

"This ends now," he hissed, not bothering to salute Clayton with his sword.

Clayton's maniacal grin matched the fevered madness in his eyes. "Quite so."

His foe was a much stronger swordsman than Rafe had anticipated, matching him strike for strike.

Rafe took bitter enjoyment in the battle, relishing every cut he made on Clayton's traitorous body. As he blocked another blow with his sword, Rafe ducked low and slammed the flat of his blade into Clayton's kneecap.

The vampire went down with a howl of pain, and Rafe would have ended it there with a thrust to the heart, but someone threw a rock with obscene force and deflected his blade.

Vincent roared and drove his blade into the miscreant's throat. No mercy would be shown to those who interfered with this fight. Rafe gave him a nod and met Clayton's parry.

The Mark between him and Cassandra suddenly pulsed with throbbing grief. Rafe glanced over to see her kneeling beside Anthony's headless corpse.

His own heart ached at the sight. Anthony had sacrificed his own life force for Rafe only to die because of Clayton's madness and greed. A howl of fury erupted from Rafe's throat. The bastard would pay.

Viciously, he struck at his enemy, taking pleasure at the growing lines of exhaustion forming at the corners of Clayton's eyes and mouth. Soon he would have him.

Rafe slipped in the blood-sodden grass, clenching his teeth as Clayton nicked his shoulder. Hopefully he wouldn't have to switch to his left hand. He had plans for that later.

"Yield, Villar," his former second growled, "and I may consider allowing you to leave this field alive."

Rafe laughed, not only at the ludicrous concept of surrendering to this cur, but at such a ludicrous lie. He laughed so hard that he nearly dropped his sword to clutch his stomach.

"What is so goddamned amusing?" Clayton snarled, eyeing Rafe warily as he attempted to jab him in the neck.

Rafe deflected the blow and answered with all the scorn in his being. "Your limitless capacity for delusion and ridiculous lies. You should have remained on the stage, Edmondson. You're a bloody mummer, not a leader."

Gasps and snickers erupted from the vampires on both sides at the announcement of Clayton's secret past.

Clayton froze, gaping and spluttering in outrage at the mention of his past. "How—"

"Did you think I didn't know?" Rafe affected a bored tone as he flicked his wrist and knocked the sword from his enemy's grasp.

As Clayton's sword skidded across the slick grass, the vampires opposing Rafe stepped back, bowing their heads submissively.

Flinching at their defection, Clayton sighed. "Make it quick."

Rafe shook his head and tossed his blade to Vincent. "I think not. I've been waiting for this for too long."

Unbelievably, the traitor's face split into a wide grin. "You think to take me on, cripple?"

"I am no cripple." He lunged out with his left hand and seized Clayton by the throat, lifting him in the air.

The vampire's eyes bulged like a toad's as he struggled and wheezed, "Your arm! But how——"

"I *told* you that Lady Rosslyn is a doctor." Rafe clenched his wholly healed fingers tighter on the vampire's windpipe. "You should have listened to me."

Just as Clayton's lips began to turn blue, Rafe slammed him on the ground.

Before Clayton could escape, Rafe leaped on him, pinning his legs with his own. Raising his left fist first, he punched the vampire so hard his lip split open. Another blow with his right smashed Clayton's nose to a bloody pulp.

Unlike in his boxing matches with mortals, he did not hold back his speed or strength.

On and on, Rafe rained down blows, mentally assigning each punch as punishment for one of Clayton's vile deeds.

This one was for being disrespectful as his second, this one for recruiting William as a spy. This one for turning against him. One for each rogue he allowed in the city, one for Cassandra. Another for Cassandra... and more for all the deaths he caused.

Only when his knuckles began to ache did he stop and remove his weight from the vampire. "Vincent, my sword."

Clayton sluggishly sat up and spat out a mess of blood and teeth before turning to the side and vomiting. As Rafe raised his sword, the vampire almost looked grateful.

Aching fingers tensing on the sword hilt, Rafe met the traitor's gaze. "I am sorry it had come to this."

Just as he drew back to plunge the blade into Clayton's heart, a wave of terrifying power rumbled through his awareness like thunder.

A bone-crushing, commanding voice roared, "Stop!"

Six of the Elders strode into the clearing, radiating ancient power so potent it stole his breath. One by one, all of the vampires fell to their knees.

Rafe's sword fell from numb fingers as he too knelt.

Clayton's swollen eyes gleamed with triumph. Blood bubbled from his torn lips along with a high, strained cackle. "It theemth London ith mine athter all!"

Thirty-three

RAFE'S HEART PLUMMETED AS HE BOWED BEFORE THE Elders. Despair curdled in his gut. Why couldn't they have waited until he'd killed Clayton? Now all was lost.

Cassandra. Terror gripped his throat at the thought of his love in the presence of the most powerful vampires in the world. She needed to get away from here.

He searched everywhere for her, but he didn't see her. Unless she was behind the towering figures of the Elders, she could be one of the bodies littering the ground.

The thought cut him like razors. Even worse was the realization that she might be better off that way.

The Lord of Rome strode forward, interrupting Rafe's macabre speculations.

He surveyed them both with cold gray eyes before turning to Clayton. "Are you Clayton Edmondson?"

"I am." Clayton's remaining teeth glistened red as he smiled. "I cannot thank you enuthh thor coming to my aid. You thee what—"

A bronze blur obscured Rafe's vision before blood splattered the side of his face as Clayton's still grinning head flew from his shoulders.

The Lord of Rome withdrew a cloth from his waistcoat and wiped the blood from his ancient blade. Rafe breathed a small sigh of relief though he remained on his knees. The hair on his arms and the back of his neck stood on end. He was far from out of trouble.

The other five Elders stepped closer. The Lord of Edo lifted the hem of her kimono and kicked Clayton's head out of her way with a dainty slipper-clad foot.

Her exotic black eyes coldly surveyed the litter of bodies on the field. "I see we have come too late."

Rafe blinked. Had they come to aid him? "I presume you received my message?"

"We received no messages from *you*." The Lord of New York glanced over her shoulder and gestured.

A small female vampire stepped out from behind them and slowly approached Rafe. Her shoulders were hunched and a curtain of long brown hair obscured her face. When her trembling hand brushed aside her hair, Rafe's jaw dropped.

It was Lenore.

The frail vampire gave him a tremulous smile. "I am so happy to see you safe, my lord."

"*Dios mío*, you're alive!" Rafe gasped. "Where were you?"

Before she could answer, the Lord of Edinburgh placed a hand on her shoulder. "Miss Graves was sent to us by the Lord of Rochester after she escaped Mr. Edmondson's captivity. According to her testimony, Edmondson had employed three rogue vampires to imprison her with the intention of discrediting your rule."

"That *hijo de puta*," Rafe growled.

Yet he was not surprised that his former second had resorted to such a dastardly action.

What was surprising was Rochester's involvement. He glanced over at his ally. The vampire gave him a smug smile before turning back to the Elders. So that was how the vampire had learned of Clayton's betrayal. Though Rafe greatly appreciated his aid, the scoundrel could have had the courtesy to inform him about Lenore.

Turning to his newly returned vampire, he met her gaze and asked as gently as possible, "Why didn't you come to me?"

"Because Clayton's rogues were chasing me." The pleading terror in her eyes made his chest tight. "They would have caught me if I hadn't left the city."

He nodded. "I understand, Lenore. That was very brave of you." It was beyond brave. Lenore had taken an incredible risk in entering Rochester's territory without a writ of passage. He could have imprisoned or executed her. He should have returned her to Rafe.

"What happened when Clayton held you captive?" He slowly stepped closer, pity clenching his heart as she stepped back.

The Lord of Berlin held up a hand. "She may report the full details to you later. Where are the rogues who took you?"

Lenore pointed a shaky finger at two chained vampires guarded by Vincent's people. "There are Hamish and Paul. I do not see Francis, the third one."

Hamish spat and jerked his head to the left. "He's dead."

Lenore cringed at his voice. Yet when she looked

down at the corpse of the third rogue, her lips peeled back in a vicious smile that was more of a grimace. *What had they done to her?*

The Lords of Berlin and New York approached the chained rogues. "What did Edmondson offer you in exchange for imprisoning one of Lord Villar's people?"

The one called Paul cowered before the might of the ancients. "H-he said he'd make us legitimate citizens of London."

The Lord of New York rubbed her temples before replying in a voice laced with exasperation. "Aside from the fact that it is illegal for any but a Lord Vampire to hold another captive, Edmondson did not have the power to do such a thing without our approval, which we never would have given for known rapists."

Outraged gasps echoed from the surrounding vampires. Lenore bowed her head in humiliation.

A growl of fury trickled from Rafe's throat. Not only had they kidnapped and imprisoned one of his people, but they had *violated* her as well? They must die.

The Lord of Rome restrained him as he lunged forward. "I am sorry, Lord Villar. These rogues had warrants for their capture before they came to London, and they are ours to judge and punish. But first we must deal with you."

"Keep them under guard," the Lord of New York commanded Vincent before turning back to face Rafe. "Now tell us exactly what occurred to lead up to this battle."

Taking a deep breath, Rafe told them of Clayton's secret meetings with half of London's vampires and

his declaration of war. He described how the Lords of
Cornwall, Blackpool, and Rochester came to his aid.
He avoided mention of Cassandra, though he knew
that subject would soon be broached.

Holding his breath, he surreptitiously scanned the
area for a glimpse of her.

There she was. His heart stopped as he saw her in
the shadows of a distant copse of trees kneeling beside
one of his injured people, oblivious to the dangerous
presence of the Elders. Instead, she was in the process
of unwrapping a bandage and handing it to… His
brows rose in disbelief. Was that Thomas Wakley?

To Rafe's horror, the Lords of Edo and Stockholm
had taken notice, watching her and Wakley tend the
wounded with indecipherable expressions.

The other four Elders commanded the Lords of
Farnborough and Grimsby to come forward and give
testimony as to why they had allied with Clayton.

Rafe didn't pay attention to their answers. He was
too busy trying to get Cassandra's attention to signal
her to flee.

"You are dismissed for now," the Lord of Berlin
said coldly to Farnborough and Grimsby. "Return to
your territories and we shall send notice of when you
are to stand trial."

"What about Derbyshire?" Grimsby protested.
"The yellow-bellied cur fled the field!"

The Lord of Edinburgh silenced him with a glare.
"That is our concern, not yours."

After Clayton's allies slunk away, all six Elders
surrounded Rafe.

"Now, Lord Villar, it is time to address one last

matter. Why haven't you done as commanded with your human prisoner?" the Lord of Rome queried in an ominous, silken tone. "You were supposed to have killed or Changed her last night, yet here she is, still alive and still mortal."

As he pointed at Cassandra, she glanced up for a moment, then looked away and returned to stitching a wound. Though she did her best to appear indifferent, Rafe could feel her terror.

Rafe took a deep breath and confessed. "I am unable to Change her."

"And why not?" The Lord of Edinburg cocked his head to the side. "We do not have record of you Changing another in the last three centuries."

Lie, Rochester's voice whispered in his mind. Rafe faced them with a level stare. "I used too much of my blood healing another vampire a few months ago."

"Oh? *Which* vampire was that?" The Lord of Berlin's voice was laced with skepticism.

Rafe hesitated, feeling the noose tighten around his neck.

"It was me, my lords," Lenore declared firmly. "I'd attempted to leap a tall fence and impaled myself in the effort." She looked down at her toes in feigned embarrassment. "I would have died if Lord Villar hadn't saved me."

The Elders remained still for a heart-stopping moment.

At last they nodded and the Lord of Rome surveyed Rafe with a raised brow. "Then why have you not killed the woman?"

"I do not believe that she should die," Rafe

answered with more conviction than anything he'd ever said. "This woman may be the greatest healer to have ever walked the earth. She healed my arm"—he extended his left arm, flexing his fingers—"and she is now healing my people."

All five Elders gaped in astonishment, staring at his arm as if they hadn't seen one before.

"*Mein Gott*," the Lord of Berlin breathed. "You are no longer crippled. I hadn't noticed."

Rafe fought back a disparaging sigh. No one ever noticed when things were right, only when they were wrong.

Before the urge to make a cutting remark became too strong, he continued to plead his case. "I believe Cassandra could be a priceless asset to our kind. I sent letters to my allies requesting them to Change her. Unfortunately, none were able to oblige me. However, Lord Deveril wrote a petition for you to allow her to live until arrangements can be made to Change her—"

"Is this true, Lord Tremayne?" The Lord of New York addressed Vincent by his surname. The Elders cared nothing for mortal titles.

Vincent nodded and stepped forward. "Yes, and the Lords of Blackpool and Rochester signed the document along with my wife and Rafael's second- and third-in-command. Each also added their own testimonies to Lady Rosslyn's merits."

"How very touching," the Lord of Rome purred. "Unfortunately, we received no such petition."

One of Clayton's rogues cleared his throat and rattled his chains. "I know where the letter is. If I tell you, will you have mercy?"

"If the information is useful, then yes, Paul." The Lord of New York stepped over to him.

Paul returned her smile. "We killed the vampire that Lord Villar sent to deliver the message. Hamish still has it in his pocket."

In a blur of speed, the Elder reached into Hamish's coat and withdrew the envelope. She tore it open with a fang and read the contents.

"Yes, this is useful indeed." She nodded at Vincent. "Your sword, Lord Tremayne?"

Vincent handed her his blade. She smiled and plunged the sword through Paul's heart.

"I thought ye said ye'd have mercy!" Hamish whined, face pale as clotted cream.

The ancient vampire smiled. "We did. Intercepting communications to the Elders is punishable by death. I gave him a quick one. You, however, will *not* receive the same courtesy." She turned her back on him and handed the letter to the other Elders.

When all had read Rafe's letter and Vincent's petition, they pressed together in a circle, talking too quietly to hear. Often they broke off to watch Cassandra tending the wounded.

Please, Rafe prayed, *please let her live.*

After an eternity, the Elders separated from their huddle and approached him. "This mortal's talent for healing is indeed impressive. However, we cannot allow this to continue."

Rafe's fists clenched until his nails made bloody crescents in his palms. He couldn't let them kill her. They would have to kill him as well, and he would take as many as he could down with him.

As if sensing his dissent, the Lord of Rome poised his sword at Rafe's throat.

"Bring her here," the Lord of Edo commanded. She inclined her head in Thomas Wakley's direction. "*And* the other mortal as well."

Thirty-four

AN ICY STONE SETTLED IN CASSANDRA'S BELLY AS Rafe's voice boomed out in strained command. "*Doctor* Burton, Mr. Wakley, come to me now."

Quickly, she finished stitching her patient's wound and patted his hand absently before rising and hefting her satchel over her shoulder.

Thomas joined her, his blue eyes bulging with fear. "What do they want, my lady?"

Probably to kill me. She gave him a tremulous smile. "They likely believe it is time to erase your memory, as I warned you."

He nodded, only the tightness of his jaw and the whitened corners of his mouth betraying his trepidation. Admiration filled her at his courage and acceptance during this ordeal.

When the vampire had delivered Thomas to the battlefield, he'd raised a brow and then calmly asked her to tell him what was going on. Once Cassandra had explained the basics about vampires and how to heal them, he'd opened his own medical bag and gotten to work.

Before long, they had the wounded lined up in an orderly fashion with uninjured vampires standing by to donate blood.

The surgeon had worked beside her with cool efficiency despite the fact that many of his patients eyed him hungrily, as if he were a juicy steak. When one lunged to bite him, Thomas stuffed a cloth soaked with ether in the vampire's mouth and continued working.

Now nearly all of the wounded had been treated. Cassandra could not have managed without him. She prayed she hadn't cost Thomas his life.

The hairs on the back of her neck stood on end as she neared the oldest and most powerful vampires in the world, who held her fate and Rafe's in the palms of their ancient hands.

A petite Japanese female met her stare. Her burning black gaze seemed to delve into Cassandra's soul. "Dr. Burton, tell us about how you healed Lord Villar's arm and how you treated these fallen vampires."

She took a shaky breath and recited her methods exactly as she'd explained them to Thomas Wakley.

Rafe took her hand and squeezed it, giving her strength to not stammer and curl into a shivering ball before her formidable judges.

"And who taught you these things?" a large male vampire with a thick German accent inquired, stroking his chin.

Cassandra met his gaze, refusing to cower. "I had studied medicine on my own for over ten years. Thomas Wakley then gave me the Oxford examination and offered me a few lessons."

"The Oxford examination?" The Scottish Elder laughed. "Women aren't allowed!"

Thomas glared at him. "I am well aware of that. It was a courtesy gesture so that she had some assurance that she is worthy."

The Elders stared at the surgeon until he flushed and looked at his feet. Their piercing attention returned to Cassandra. "We have been discussing what to do with you, human."

Rafe pulled her into his arms. She rested her cheek against his chest, seeking the haven of his embrace.

The other female Elder laughed. "Oh, *that's* how it is."

The male Elders chuckled and leered, though Cassandra hardly heard them over the pounding of Rafe's heart and the fine tremor in his body. His fear intensified hers.

The Japanese Elder silenced them with a glare. "Your skills in healing are impressive and could be an invaluable asset to our people." She smoothed her kimono and breathed a regretful sigh. "It is a shame that Lord Villar is unable to Change you. Yet we cannot allow you to go on as you are."

Cassandra clung tighter to Rafe, her heart sinking. This was it. She buried her face in his chest, breathing in his beloved spicy scent for the last time.

"Therefore *I* shall do so."

Rafe gasped. Cassandra slowly lifted her head, uncertain she'd heard the vampire correctly.

"Y-you will?" she whispered faintly.

"Yes, and I will also permit you to remain in London under Lord Villar's rule." Her liquid almond-shaped eyes narrowed. "However, you shall both owe me a favor."

Rafe squeezed Cassandra's hands as he drew them both down to their knees. "Thank you, my lord. I will gratefully pay any debt in return for her life."

"And I as well, for allowing me to remain with Rafe," Cassandra told her. "Will you Change me now?"

The vampire shook her head. "No, I will do it tomorrow evening. I advise you to savor your last sunrise."

One of the male Elders cleared his throat. "We must deal with the other one now."

Cassandra tore herself from Rafe and approached the Elders. "Please, don't kill him! It is my fault that he is here. There were too many wounded vampires and I needed his help."

"And what did you think would happen to him after being exposed to our secrets?" the German Elder demanded.

"I had intended to ask Rafe to vanquish his memory."

The Elder nodded and stroked his chin. "Clever woman. Unfortunately, after spending so much time in the presence of our kind, it may be impossible for one vampire to banish so many memories."

Her stomach roiled with guilt as Thomas's face paled further. She opened her mouth to apologize, but one of the Elders grumbled a curse.

"Oh bloody hell, quit frightening the poor mortals!" the Scottish Elder burst out. "Between the five of us, we can easily manage the task." He turned to Thomas Wakley. "However, Edinburgh's vampires could use a skilled sawbones as well. How would you feel about possessing eternal life and strength and power beyond imagining?"

Thomas took a deep breath and shook his head. "I

am honored by your offer and it tempts me greatly. However, I have a wife and children whom I cannot bear to leave. I also have a great number of responsibilities that prohibit a nocturnal lifestyle. I want to continue my work on *The Lancet*, run for a seat in the House of Commons, continue my pursuit of reforming the policies of the College of Surgeons, improve conditions for the working poor, and..."

The American Elder held up a hand. "We have gathered your point." She turned to Cassandra. "Did you purposefully choose such a prominent human to be here tonight?"

Cassandra smiled. "He was my only option, I'm afraid. No other practitioner in Town takes me seriously due to my sex."

The vampire gave her a sympathetic chuckle. "I do hope that will change." She grinned at Thomas. "Well, it is a pity. We could use more of your sort."

"You honor me, madam." Thomas bowed. "Are you certain I won't remember a thing?"

The Elders nodded in unison before the Scottish one answered. "If you'd like to return home now, we shall take you there and you will wake up believing this was a dream. If you'd like to remain with your colleague, then we will make you believe one of them found you drunk at a tavern and invited you to join yon festivities." He gestured toward the fireworks.

Thomas sighed. "I don't drink, sir. Besides, after such a madcap evening, all I want is to go home." He turned to Cassandra and bowed. "Despite the harrowing experience, it was an honor to work beside you this night, my lady. You are a fine doctor."

"Thank you, Thomas, for all you've done for me." Cassandra rubbed a bit of stray moisture from her eye and took his hand. "It is probably best that we do not see each other anymore. However, I shall always remain a faithful reader of *The Lancet*."

The surgeon smiled. "I hope the publication continues long enough to have faithful readers." He turned to leave with the Elders.

"Wait." Rafe stepped forward. "Which vampire brought you here, Wakley?"

Thomas gave Cassandra a panicked glance. "He said his name was Eric."

"Eric, come here."

Eric reluctantly shuffled over and knelt. "Yes, my lord?"

"You made a very dangerous decision, bringing a mortal in our midst, especially during a battle."

"I know, my lord, but Lady Rosslyn—"

Rafe waved off his words. "Yes, I know. It was, however, a very wise decision that saved many lives. I am promoting you to serve as my third-in-command. Elizabeth is now my second due to losing Anthony."

Eric blinked in pleased surprise. "My lord, I am honored to accept."

"Good. Now round up all the vampires who remain standing so we can sort out the prisoners and see to the dead. A pyre needs to be built."

Seeing that Rafe had everything under control, the Scottish and German Elder vampires escorted Thomas home. The American, Swedish, and Roman Elders followed, taking a squalling Hamish with them.

The Lord of Rochester bade Rafe and Cassandra farewell afterward.

"I am in your debt," Rafe told him.

Rochester grinned. "I know."

The prisoners were hauled onto carts or carried off by Rafe's people to be judged and sentenced later. Cassandra forced herself not to dwell on the matter.

Next came the building of the pyre and the gathering and identification of the dead. The gruesome task took hours. Unfortunately she could not hide from the sight and smell of the multitude of dead vampires burning on the pyre.

Sensing her distress, Rafe stroked her back in soothing motions. "Twice as many would have perished if it weren't for you, *Querida*."

The Lord of Blackpool kissed her hand before leaving with his retinue. "It was a pleasure to meet a woman worth fighting for."

The remaining London vampires left the battlefield, all bowing and paying homage to her on the way out. Despite her face burning from the attention, she held her chin high and gracefully acknowledged their praise.

Only Vincent, Lydia, Rafe, Cassandra, and Neko, the Lord Vampire of Edo, remained.

As they watched the flames burn away all evidence of the carnage, Rafe pulled Cassandra into his arms. "At first I wanted my arm back to feel whole again and to not appear weak before my enemies. Now I only want it to hold you."

Epilogue

Three months later

CASSANDRA WIPED HER BROW AS SHE BENT OVER HER patient, wrapping her hands around the vampire's forearm.

She met the studious gazes of her three students. "To heal this arm properly, it must be broken again. We must work quickly before he wakes up. Now hold him down."

Akio and Hiroshi seized the patient's shoulders, watching closely as Cassandra used her new preternatural strength to snap the bone that had healed the wrong way.

"Kaito, hand me the splint."

Quickly she splinted and bound the arm, just in time, before the patient woke up, hissing in pain. Akio gave him a small dram of laudanum.

"You did very well," she told her students.

Neko, the Lord Vampire of Edo, had called in her favor from Cassandra the week before. She'd sent three of her vampires to London as soon as Rafe established a hospital where Cassandra could treat their people. Cassandra was teaching the vampires of Edo medicine so they could have their own healing establishment.

Thankfully, they spoke English, were extremely competent, and had no hostility in taking orders from a female. Such a refreshing change from her experiences in the mortal world.

The only drawback to the experience was watching the Japanese vampires endure English ignorance. Several times they had to be restrained when they were laughingly called "Chinaman."

"Remember, you can bite them all you like. Just do not kill them," Rafe had admonished.

Cassandra sympathized. She herself had preyed on nearly every man who'd mocked her for her sex. And with the blood of an ancient running through her veins, she had to take care to control her strength.

"Someday, you may be more powerful than me," Rafe had teased, though his eyes were serious.

Just thinking of Rafe made her pulse quicken with anticipation.

She bade her students to clean up the operating area and packed away her supplies before putting her gold-and-emerald wedding ring back on her finger. They had been married on Christmas Eve.

Hiroshi remained behind with the patient while Kaito and Akio walked out with her.

"Thank you for your lesson, Dr. Villar." Kaito bowed before he and Akio turned in the opposite direction to return to their flat.

Once she returned to Burnrath House, it was all she could do not to throw herself into her husband's arms.

As if sensing her need, he pulled her into his embrace. "*Querida*, I've missed you. How was your evening?"

"Quite well. My students helped me reset James's arm. I think it shall heal correctly. Their training is progressing well. Honestly, I am happy to pay the Lord of Edo this favor."

"Thank God she hasn't called hers in from me yet." Something in his tone made her look up at him with concern.

"What is it?"

"I've received letters from Blackpool and Rochester, calling in their debts. Blackpool wants me to keep an eye on his great-niece when she makes her debut this Season. That's easy enough, though quite a nuisance. However Rochester…" He sighed and rubbed the bridge of his nose. "He wants Lenore."

"Lenore?" Cassandra's chest tightened at the thought of the frail vampire who had been kidnapped and tortured by Clayton's rogues. "What does he want with her?"

"He didn't specify except to say that he needed more vampires with her loyalty and courage." Rafe gave a rueful shrug. "I don't think he means her ill, but she is still terrified of being in the company of males. I do not know if she can handle the strain of changing territories."

After all Lenore had been through, Cassandra could not blame her. She wished she could heal wounds to the mind and soul, but that was beyond her power. "Is there any way you could refuse?"

"No. I promised I would give him anything he

asked, except for my territory." Rafe shook his head. "The blackguard actually jested by asking for you first."

Before Cassandra could respond to that irreverence, Eric entered the study. "The Duke and Duchess of Burnrath are here to see you, my lord."

Rafe's eyes widened as Ian and Angelica strode into the room. "I apologize for the delay, Rafe. Due to my wife's desire to run pell-mell across the Continent, your message reached me only last week." Ian rubbed the back of his neck. "I am relieved to see that you came through your ordeal successfully."

Angelica gave Rafe an apologetic look before her eyes widened at the sight of Cassandra. "Lady Rosslyn! What are you doing here?"

Cassandra grinned, showing her fangs. "It is *Doctor* Villar now."

Ian chuckled. "Ah, so that situation was also resolved."

"Yes, my wife is the first vampire physician. I've opened a hospital so she can treat our people." He raised his left arm and wiggled his fingers. "*I* was her first patient."

The ducal vampires gaped like landed fish. Ian recovered himself first. "I see you have a long story to tell me."

Rafe nodded and rang for port. "*Very* long."

Author's Note

Thomas Wakley (1795–1862) was an English surgeon, pugilist, political activist, and the founder of the prestigious medical journal *The Lancet*.

He became a surgeon at the age of twenty-two after taking anatomy classes and becoming a member of the Royal College of Surgeons. In 1820 he set up his own practice and started a family. Shortly after Wakley was comfortably established, he was attacked by a mysterious mob in his own home, and his house was set aflame. Many suspected it was the Thistlewood gang, who wrongly blamed Wakley for decapitating the bodies of their cohorts after they were executed for treason. The insurance company suspected that Wakley had set fire to his own house.

Despite such tragedy, Wakley persevered. He won his case with the insurance company, purchased another house, and reinstated his practice. In 1823, he and his associates began publishing *The Lancet*, a weekly medical journal that is still in circulation today.

In 1831 he attempted to launch the London College of Medicine, a rival institution to the Royal College of Surgeons claiming, "The Council of the College of Surgeons remains an irresponsible, unreformed monstrosity in the midst of English institutions—an antediluvian relic of all…that is most despotic and revolting, iniquitous and insulting, on the face of the earth." The London College of Medicine would have been a democratic institution with no biases based on religion or social standing. The project failed, but the call for reform was made.

In 1835, Wakley became a radical member of Parliament in the House of Commons and spoke out for medical reform as well as improved laws and conditions for the working poor.

With Wakley's apparent passion for social equality, I believe he would have supported a woman's quest to pursue a career in medicine and thus he became the perfect mentor for Cassandra.

Speaking of Cassandra, unfortunately medicine was still primitive in her time, though she arrived on the cusp of advances. Pain medication and anesthetics were in their infancy. Common treatments available were laudanum, morphine, and cannabis—the latter of which is perfect for a vampire's limited metabolic capability.

Ether and nitrous oxide were experimental measures soon to become commonplace in the late nineteenth century. However, in Cassandra's time, most people were using those substances for their euphoric side effects without realizing their medical capabilities. Fortunately for Rafe, his doctor possessed a broader mind.

Acknowledgments

Thank you to everyone who helped me bring Rafe and Cassandra to life on the page. Thanks to Megan Records and Skye Agnew for the awesome edits. Thanks to my critique buddies, Shona Husk, Terry Spear, Shelly Martin, Bonnie R. Paulson, and Millie McClaine.

Thanks to those who helped me with the medical research, Wendy Masten, Bonnie Paulson, and, my college biology teacher, David Foster.

Thank you to Kent Butler who gave me a quiet place to write during a hectic college year and kept cheering on my word count.

Thanks to my buddies at Gus's Pub and all of my friends and family for the encouragement and support.

Bite Me, Your Grace

by Brooklyn Ann

London's Lord Vampire has problems

Dr. John Polidori's tale "The Vampyre" burst upon the Regency scene along with Mary Shelley's *Frankenstein* after that notorious weekend spent writing ghost stories with Lord Byron.

A vampire craze broke out instantly in the *haut ton*.

Now Ian Ashton, the Lord Vampire of London, has to attend tedious balls, linger in front of mirrors, and eat lots of garlic in an attempt to quell the gossip.

If that weren't annoying enough, his neighbor Angelica Winthrop has literary aspirations of her own and is sneaking into his house at night just to see what she can find.

Hungry, tired, and fed up, Ian is in no mood to humor his beautiful intruder…

What readers are saying:

"It was romantic and quirky and a lot of fun. The author writes with such heart. I can't wait for her next one!"

"I loved this book! Absolutely amazing!"

For more Brooklyn Ann, visit:

www.sourcebooks.com

One Bite Per Night

by Brooklyn Ann

He wanted her off his hands...

Vincent Tremayne, the reclusive "Devil Earl," has been manipulated into taking rambunctious Lydia Price as his ward. As Lord Vampire of Cornwall, Vincent has better things to do than bring out an unruly debutante.

Now he'll do anything to hold on...forever

American-born Lydia Price doesn't care for the stuffy strictures of the *ton*, and is unimpressed with her foppish suitors. She dreams of studying with the talented but scandalous British portrait painter, Sir Thomas Lawrence. But just when it seems her dreams will come true, Lydia is plunged into Vincent's dark world and finds herself caught between the life she's known and a future she never could have imagined.

"Solid writing, a tasty dash of originality, and realistic relationships that zing with sexual energy. A strong sense of fun mixed with a little feminism keeps things lively and light, while the well-developed story keeps eyes on the page." —*Publishers Weekly*

For more Brooklyn Ann, visit:

www.sourcebooks.com

Kiss the Earl

by Gina Lamm

❦

A modern girl's guide to seducing Mr. Darcy

When Ella Briley asked her lucky-in-love friends to set her up for an office party, she was expecting a blind date. Instead, she's pulled through a magic mirror and into the past...straight into the arms of her very own Mr. Darcy.

Patrick Meadowfair, Earl of Fairhaven, is too noble for his own good. To save a female friend from what is sure to be a loveless marriage, he's agreed to whisk her off to wed the man she truly wants. But all goes awry when Patrick mistakes Ella for the would-be bride and kidnaps her instead.

Centuries away from everything she knows, Ella's finally found a man who heats her blood and leaves her breathless. Too bad he's such a perfect gentleman. Yet the reluctant rake may just find this modern girl far too tempting for even the noblest of men to resist...

❦

Praise for Gina Lamm:

"Gina Lamm writes excellent [time-travel romance] with humor and great storytelling." —*Books Like Breathing*

"Snappy writing and characters who share a surprising, spicy chemistry." —*RT Book Reviews*

For more Gina Lamm, visit:

www.sourcebooks.com

Of Silk and Steam

by Bec McMaster

---— ❧ —---

Enemies. Allies. Lovers. How far will they go to protect their hearts?

When her father was assassinated, Lady Aramina swore revenge against the Duke of Caine. Leo Barrons, the duke's heir, has long been her nemesis, and when she discovers he's illegitimate, she finally has leverage against the one man who troubles her heart and tempts her body.

Sentenced to death for his duplicity, Leo escapes by holding Lady Aramina captive. A woman of mystery, she's long driven him crazy with glimpses of a fiery passion that lurks beneath her icy veneer. He knows she's hiding something; he doesn't know it's the key to saving his life.

---— ❧ —---

Praise for Bec McMaster:

"McMaster continues to demonstrate a flair for wildly imaginative, richly textured world-building." —*Booklist*

"Bec McMaster brilliantly weaves a world that engulfs your senses and takes you on a fantastical journey." —*Tome Tender*

For more Bec McMaster, visit:

www.sourcebooks.com

Vampires Never Cry Wolf

A Dead in the City Novel
by Sara Humphreys

❧

Vampires are nothing but trouble…

As far as beautiful vampire Sadie Pemberton is concerned, werewolves shouldn't be sticking their noses into New York's supernatural politics. They don't know jack about running a city—not even that hot-as-sin new vampire-werewolf liaison who's just arrived in town.

Werewolves are too sexy for their own good…

The last thing Killian Bane wanted was to end up in New York City playing nice with vampires. Unfortunately, he's on a mission, and when he encounters the sexiest, most stubborn female vamp he's ever met, he's going to have to turn on a little of that wolfish charm…and Sadie's going to learn a thing or two about what it means to have a wild side…

❧

Praise for the Dead in the City Series:

"Humphreys is undoubtedly a rising star in the genre… The tension that unfolds between the vampires and the werewolves will have readers on the edge of their seats!" —*RT Book Reviews*

"A fascinating and complex paranormal world with captivating and intriguing characters that draw the reader deeper into the stories." —*Paranormal Haven*

For more Sara Humphreys, visit:

www.sourcebooks.com

Just in Time for a Highlander

by Gwyn Cready

❧

For Duncan MacHarg, things just got real

Battle reenactor and financier Duncan MacHarg thinks he has it made—until he lands in the middle of a real Clan Kerr battle and comes face-to-face with their beautiful, spirited leader. Out of time and out of place, Duncan must use every skill he can muster to earn his position among the clansmen and in the heart of the devastatingly intriguing woman to whom he must pledge his oath.

Abby needs a hero, and she needs him now

When Abigail Ailich Kerr sees a handsome, mysterious stranger materialize in the midst of her clan's skirmish with the English, she's stunned to discover he's the strong arm she's been praying for. Instead of a tested fighter, the fierce young chieftess has been given a man with no measurable battle skills and a damnably distracting smile. And the only way to get rid of him is to turn him into a Scots warrior herself—one demanding and intimate lesson at a time.

❧

"Cready's highly satisfying creation is filled with humor, witty dialogue, double entendres, and clever schemes, and a wonderful cast of imaginative characters keeps this twisty story lively to the end." —*Publishers Weekly* Starred Review

For more Gwyn Cready, visit:

www.sourcebooks.com

The Highland Dragon's Lady

by Isabel Cooper

He's out of the Highlands and on the prowl…

Regina Talbot-Jones has always known her family home was haunted. She also knows her brother has invited a friend for an ill-conceived séance. But she didn't count on that friend being so handsome…and she certainly didn't expect him to be a dragon.

Scottish Highlander Colin MacAlasdair has hidden his true nature for his entire life. But in his hundreds of years, he's never met a woman who could understand him so thoroughly…or touch him so deeply. Drawn by the fire awakening inside of them, Colin and Regina must work together to defeat a vengeful spirit—and discover whether their love is powerful enough to defy convention.

Praise for Isabel Cooper:

"Cooper's world-building is solid and believable." —*RT Book Reviews*

"Isabel Cooper is an author to watch!" —*All About Romance*

For more Isabel Cooper, visit:

www.sourcebooks.com

About the Author

A lover of witty Regencies and dark paranormal romance, Brooklyn Ann combines the two in her new vampire series, about which *RT Book Reviews* says: "It's a dark world, but with Ann's propensity for subtle humor and eccentric characters, it's an enchanting world as well." The former mechanic turned author lives with her family in Coeur d'Alene, Idaho. She can be found online at www.brooklynann.blogspot.com.